# Family
# Interrupted

Linda Barrett

Cover art by Melyssa Naujoks

www.purplegirldesign.blogspot.com


Copy Editing by Amy Knupp

www.blueotterediting.com


E-book and print formatting by Web Crafters

www.webcraftersdesign.com

Dedicated to my Houston Writing Buddies, Pat Kay and Pat O'Dea Rosen. Thanks for the tough critiques.

# PART I

"Thou are thy mother's glass and she in thee

Calls back the lovely April of her prime."

-Wm. Shakespeare, *Sonnet Three*

# CHAPTER ONE

*CLAIRE BARNES*

*Houston, Texas*
*September*

"*Bellisima! Brava!* Your best work yet, Signora Barnes. Maybe you give Leonardo some competition?"

I rolled my eyes and grinned at my instructor. "Leonardo can rest easy."

Dr. Colombo teased, exhorted, or flirted with his students on a regular basis, especially the talented ones, but comparing my work to the *Mona Lisa* was going too far, even for this powerhouse.

I stepped away from my easel and focused on a portrait of a young girl peeking sideways under half-closed lids. I'd called it *Girl with Secrets*. The child held secrets I wanted to know.

"Your daughter, yes?" Colombo asked, his voice a deep rumble.

DNA didn't lie. I nodded and said, "On the outside, Kayla's mine, brown eyes and blonde hair, but inside, she's her dad, an unquenchable extrovert. Sometimes my daughter's surrounded by more friends than my house can hold." My pride in Kayla overrode the mock complaint. "She's twelve-and-a-half, almost a teenager—almost grown up, as she likes to remind me."

"Ahh." He sighed as if he understood. "I have two daughters, Signora, and I know how they too much wanted to be women but were not ready, *never* ready in the eyes of their mama."

The man had nailed it, nailed my heart. I wasn't ready for Kayla to grow up and fly away, especially with her brother applying for college this year. I wasn't ready to let either of my children go.

"This portrait of your daughter.... It is...is..." Colombo waved his arm this way and that as he searched his English vocabulary. "Exceptional!" His voice rang out, eyes shone. The young student at the next easel walked over and stared.

"Holy Toledo, Claire," she whispered. "Your kid could step right into the room. How'd you do that?"

Surprised and uncomfortable—I was just a student like the others—I wondered how to respond. Capturing Kayla's image had come easily. I knew every smile, nuance, and angle of her face. I knew how she looked when she was happy or sad or puzzled. The work hadn't been *that* difficult to execute.

"I'm her mom," I finally said as if that explained everything. To me, it did. A few of the students nodded. Others seemed to be waiting for more, which I guess was not surprising. I was old enough to be their moms!

"I know all Kayla's moods and expressions," I said. "I can picture her rolling her eyes at her dad's bad jokes. And I've seen those dark eyes shine when he walks through the door each night."

My classmates seemed glued to my words, so on I went. "And her hair...it's so thick and long, she still needs my help combing it after a shampoo." I thought about how I could never resist kissing her neck and laughing when she groaned, "Ooh, Mom."

Pointing to Kayla's hair in the painting, I said, "See the rich auburn color here? In the summer sun, it glows like a banked fire. Maybe next time, I'll paint her outdoors."

I finally shut up, and in the quiet room, I felt the other students' eyes on me and forced myself not to squirm. Being the center of attention was Jack's specialty, not mine.

"Don't be too impressed," I quickly added. "I've sketched her hundreds of times. Maybe thousands." I was trying to be modest for the sake of my classmates, but dang, I found it hard not to celebrate. *See, Jack? I told you I had talent! And the validation feels damn good.*

My endless drawings through the years had meant less to him than the bottom line of our construction company. But when I turned forty-five last year, I knew I couldn't keep waiting for Jack's promise of "one day." I'd seized my own moment and enrolled in the University of Houston's MFA program.

I was a second-year student now, and whatever artistic gifts I possessed were being revealed under the guidance of a marvelous staff. No instructor, however, could match the gusto and intuition of Professor Colombo. Like the original explorer, this Colombo also led his crew on a voyage of discovery. *Create like Michelangelo! Find the heart, the soul of the stone, and chip away the rest. Fall in love with your subject, and it will show.*

The teacher had a point. I certainly loved *my* subject.

"So, Signora, we will spotlight *Girl with Secrets* in the *galleria* next month, at the exhibition."

I pivoted toward the man so sharply I almost tripped. "Exhibit? But I'm not ready." Was I? Sure I was living my dream, learning and improving, but didn't I need more experience and confidence before showing my work in public? If I'd spent the past twenty years painting instead of decorating model homes for Barnes Construction, I would have been more than willing to exhibit.

"With respect, Signora Barnes, you do not decide who is ready." Colombo swept away my protest with no hesitation. "I, myself, handpicked the twelve artists in this class. I studied the portfolios from last year. You are more than good enough. Art is to be shared and enjoyed. To touch the soul. Claire—or Clara, I may call you Clara? Good. Let me tell you something else, a secret between us."

He glanced around the room while I stood alert, heart racing at being the focus of his pointed attention. Handpicked for his class? I'd had no idea. When he turned to me again, his gaze holding mine, a frisson of electricity danced down my back. His index finger covered his mouth for a moment, reminding me that this was a private conversation.

"You are my most promising student in a long time," he began. "Your hands transform what your heart feels and your eyes see." He tapped his chest. "The emotions here, inside, are on the canvas too! Do you think everyone can do that?"

I took the question seriously. "Well, not the man on the street, but the other students...?"

"You are not listening, Clara! Am I speaking with the 'other students'?"

As his words began to sink in, my excitement soared. My attention focused exclusively on Colombo, and my classmates seemed to disappear, leaving the professor and me in our own private world. The man was implying I was extra special, wasn't he? Oh, Lordy, I hoped so. And then I'd tell Jack. And maybe we could hire a decorator, someone to replace me at work. If that happened, I could finally devote more of my time to art and less to business. Could the day get any better?

"Thank you. Thank you." I'd finally found my voice. "I appreciate everything you've said and done. I know I've improved as an artist because of you." *Take a breath. Calm down.* I turned my attention back to my painting of Kayla. Despite all the compliments, evaluating my own stuff was difficult, especially at this professional level. Sometimes I was too critical, sometimes too soft.

"All right, Professor. I'll agree with you. It's pretty good."

"Very good, Clara. Excellent."

During the past month, I'd started trusting Colombo's judgment despite him being a showman. His own work had impressed me—his use of light and shadow in particular—and the Art Department had been delighted to attract this visiting professor. Now I felt lucky to be studying with him. Even privileged. I knew my talented classmates felt the same. But to be called his best student in a long time?

I scanned the room for glimpses of the others' work and realized my fellow students had already put away their easels and were leaving the studio.

Quickly checking the wall clock, I felt my stomach tighten. "Oh, God, I'll be late. And Kayla has a dental appointment." Forgetting about my schedule and kids was unlike me. Had I encouraged the professor's compliments? Our lingering after class?

Pushing those thoughts aside, I quickly became a focused mom again. I carried Kayla's portrait to my private studio space, threw my smock on a chair, and shouted a goodbye to the professor while running toward the staircase. Down, down, down, until I exited the building to the parking lot, digging for my car keys at the same time. Finally, I thrust myself into the driver's seat and revved the engine. Back to reality. Back to Jack, the kids, my domestic life, and my working life. Tomorrow was soon enough to face Colombo and his compliments. A handsome Colombo with his dark mane of hair touched by wings of silver. I wondered how many art students, both in Italy and America, had produced his portrait while studying with him. My fingers reached for a phantom pencil.

#

I followed the restrained campus speed limit but hit the gas as soon as I reached the interstate. Twenty-four miles stood between the University of Houston and home. I gave myself fifteen minutes. The miles disappeared until sirens blared and lights flashed in my rearview mirror. Damn, damn, damn. I slowed down, pulled over, and prepared to smile my widest. Jack always said my smile was my secret weapon. I didn't necessarily agree but was prepared to give it a try if it meant getting Kayla to her appointment on time.

I rolled down my window and beamed.

"License and registration, ma'am." No twinkle, no smile, no sense of humor. Pure cop face.

I handed over the documents and used my cell as I waited for Houston's Finest to check out my identity. I had to leave a message at the house but wasn't really surprised. If Ian had to watch his sister, he'd be sure they shot hoops in the driveway or kicked a soccer ball on the lawn. God forbid he'd set a good example by doing homework right away. So irresponsible. I sighed a frustrated sigh. A mother's sigh.

"Ma'am, you were clocked doing eighty in a sixty. That's twenty miles over the limit."

I could do the math. "Any chance of turning this into a warning? I'm usually excellent at following the rules." *Smile.* No answer except for the scratching of his pen. Five minutes later, I was on my way with a ticket nearing two hundred dollars and an invitation to driving school. For the rest of the trip, I crept at posted speeds until, with a sigh of relief, I finally entered my subdivision and turned left around the lake toward Bluebonnet Drive.

As I approached, I saw a small crowd milling on the corner, blocking my street. In the mid-distance was a revolving red glow. My body tensed, every muscle taut with strain at the possibilities. I lowered my window when I saw my friend Anne Conroy waving at me.

"She's here," Anne called over her shoulder while rushing toward my vehicle. "Pull over. You need to park right now."

I didn't like how she looked. My hands began to tingle, but I followed her directions.

"There's been an accident, Claire."

"What? Who?"

Instead of answering, Anne opened my door and pulled me out. "It's Kayla. She was hit by a car. The EMTs are lifting her into the ambulance right now."

*My worst fear....* I took off like a track star. A path opened as I headed for the gurney. Around me were familiar faces I could barely recognize because I saw only one face. Kayla. My beautiful Kayla, lying on that narrow bed, her complexion snow-white, forehead swollen, head enlarged, and blood oozing from her ears. Her stillness frightened me most.

"I'm here, baby-girl. Mama's right here." I leaned over her and kissed her cool cheek. No response.

"Ma'am, we've got to get her in the truck."

One medic spoke to me while the other was arranging stuff—tubes, IVs, and God-knows-what. They hoisted the gurney, and I jumped in beside it while scanning the crowd for Ian. Where was that boy? Then I saw him, right in front of me, sobbing aloud with tears running thick down his face.

"I'm sorry, I'm sorry, but we were only throwing a football," he cried, his voice cracking. "That's all...."

"You should have been doing homework," I snapped.

He ignored me and pointed at a young woman sitting on the ground, a stranger. "She was driving and...and..."

Glancing at her, I took a mental snapshot, certain I'd recall the details later. I didn't care about the driver then. Instead, anger, fear, and dread filled me, and I lashed out. "How could you have let this happen? You were in charge."

"But it wasn't my fault! I've told you a million times I'm not a babysitter. Maybe if you were home more, Kayla would be okay. It wasn't my...fault."

*Because it's my fault. My fault for being late.* That was the bottom line. My son and I were at odds again, and remorse filled me. "I'm so sorry, Ian," I whispered. "It's all right. You'll be okay. Kayla will too." *She had to be.* "Hang out with Anne and Maddy for awhile, and I'll see you tonight."

"Gotta close these doors, ma'am," said the EMT, suiting action to his words.

For a moment, I worried about leaving Ian but later was glad I did. My son didn't need to witness or hear the conversations that followed.

#

Kayla lingered for five days. Jack and I slept at the hospital, neither of us wanting to leave. We drank strong tea, wrapped ourselves in warm blankets, and had quiet conversations with the staff.

When I mentioned to Jack how kind the nurses were, he shrugged and stepped closer to Kayla's bed. "It's part of their job." His words were abrupt, curt, and cold, a rarity for my husband.

"But only kind hearts become nurses in the first place," I argued, as if making my point would make everything better. It made nothing better.

Six weeks had passed since Kayla died, but I still remembered the name of every medic on the unit. I still pictured the IV bags with their liquids dripping into Kayla's arm one drop at a time, the orange chairs Jack and I dozed on, and the plantings between the parking lot and Kayla's hospital wing. Most of all, I remembered holding Kayla's hand, stroking her cheek, and talking, talking, talking, praying she'd hear my voice and smile. I remembered that insulated hospital world in detail.

But I couldn't remember my daughter's funeral.

Vague recollections of friends and family surrounding us at the service were all that stayed with me. I'd watched their mouths move but heard nothing. I'd seen nothing. Usually, I'd notice particulars—the cut of a blouse, a change of hairstyle, a newly framed picture— but my powers of observation disappeared that day. All gone. Just like Kayla.

Friends said that Jack and I had been amazing. What nonsense! We were numb. Paralyzed by the unthinkable. They described Jack catching me as I fainted at the cemetery. I didn't remember falling, but they said I'd collapsed the moment our daughter's casket was lowered into the ground. I believed them. I'd become a zombie, one of the walking dead.

At home, meals arrived, coffee brewed, and the refrigerator and house remained equally full. Our loved ones surrounded us, stayed with us, supported us. My parents. Jack's parents. Their lips trembled and pain etched their faces.

But no one managed to answer the one question that mattered: how could a vibrant twelve-year-old kick a soccer ball one day and lie in a coma the next? The question haunted me still. I knew there were reasons.

Cause-and-effect type reasons. But I hadn't been able to accept them. How would I ever cope with this nightmare? The memories...the memories...

When Kayla was five years old, she'd said, "Mama, if you turn the number eight on its side, you know what you get?"

"What?"

"Infinity!"

A grown-up word. She'd giggled, eyes beaming, so proud of herself for surprising me. I hadn't known how she'd come up with the word, but I'd been pretty sure her brother had some influence there. *Infinity*. An appropriate description for the days that now came and went, unremarkable one from the other, simply periods of light and dark I sometimes noticed through the windows of my diminished home.

So, six weeks later, I was still a mess. Jack too. Not sure about Ian. He'd been hanging out with his friends almost twenty-four/seven. Maybe if I started cooking—really cooking—again every day, he'd find his way home for dinner. He loved meatballs and spaghetti. Heck, he used to love anything I'd put on the table. A growing boy needed nourishment, and we all used to laugh about our skinny boy devouring more than his dad. He'd filled out some this year.

Jack finally returned to work yesterday because he'd been afraid to leave me alone sooner. He'd taken calls at the house after the first two weeks and depended on his staff to keep Barnes Construction going. He had great employees, but we all knew that my Cracker Jack was the engine driving the company. It was his baby, his creation, and certainly his success. I sensed he was anxious to get back to work full-time while I, on the other hand, had no heart for anything, not even painting.

Thirty minutes after Jack left, the doorbell rang. I sure didn't want any company, so I peeped through the sidelight curtain, ready to ignore any social caller. But I couldn't ignore a FedEx delivery. Occasionally, items for Barnes Construction were shipped to the house. This item was a pretty large box, which the driver pushed over the threshold for me.

Return address: University of Houston, Art Department. I hadn't stepped onto the campus since that horrible day. I hadn't contacted the department or the registrar to officially drop out of school. Maybe they wanted clarification. I opened the outside envelope and extracted a note:

*Whenever you are ready, Clara, come back. I am keeping your last painting here. You have much art still to make, and I am saving your place. CC.*

The man would have a long wait. None of it mattered anymore. Only Kayla mattered. I didn't open the box, didn't look at any of my portfolio items. Instead, I dragged the carton into the guest room and closed the door. I brushed my hands together and walked to the kitchen. My college adventure was over. Maybe someday, I'd have the courage to retrieve *Girl with Secrets*.

I spent the rest of the morning alone, looking through photo albums, torturing myself. Jack called me every hour.

"How're you doing?" he asked.

How did he think I was doing? "Fine."

But of course, I'd never be fine again.

After four phone calls, I threatened to ignore his number on the Caller ID. We finally compromised. He'd stop phoning if I promised to take a walk. He said I hadn't gone out of the house since the funeral. Somehow, I also promised to track Ian down, cook a real dinner, and then make love to Jack that night. I promised a lot of things because when you lived in a time warp, nothing mattered. Not even promises made.

As it turned out, however, I did take a walk in the afternoon. Maybe the milder temperatures and gentler sun lured me, or maybe it was the general quiet with everyone else at work or school. I thought a solitary walk would be a perfect first venture outside. Unfortunately, one of my neighbors spotted me, a neighbor I didn't know well, and I wanted to retreat but couldn't.

"I'm so sorry, Mrs. Barnes...Claire," she said, full of sympathy.

I just nodded. A tiny nod. I pressed my lips together and began to stride past her.

"Sometimes," she continued, "it's hard to accept God's will."

I jerked to a full stop. My heart pounded, my vision blurred. God's will? God's will? I screamed silently. What had my innocent child done to deserve this fate? I whirled and stared at the woman for what seemed hours. Her self-righteousness oozed like the slow-running sap of a sugar maple tree. My palm itched. My fingers curled. Her cheek would make a good target. *Don't do it, Claire! Don't do it....* But I was in my time warp, watching myself from afar as I lifted my arm and smacked her across the face.

"That was God's will too," I said and walked off, confirming I was a long way from acceptance. If there was such a thing.

#

When Jack arrived from work, a home-cooked meal waited for him. Ian sat at the table too, thanks to my meatball bribe. The men ate with gusto. I managed one bite to ten of theirs and hoped Jack wouldn't notice. When their first hunger pangs had been satisfied, I announced, "I might go to jail."

Ian's mouth made a perfect O.

"You might what?" asked Jack. But when he heard the story of my walk, his blue eyes glowed, and his grin stretched across his face. Then he swung me around, laughed, and cried. "I couldn't survive without *both* my girls, and you're coming to life again. I love you so much, Claire. We'll get through this. Somehow, we'll get through." Then he looked at me with his I-have-a-great-idea expression.

"It's been more than a month, Claire. How about coming back to work? The company needs you. More importantly, *I* need you. You know how the economy sucks, and I might have overreached, but we've contracted to build in the Eagle Ranch subdivision. We've got four brand-new models for you to work your magic on."

I felt myself shrivel. Jack depended on me to dress up our models to their best advantage. I supposed I could manage the decorating part, but interacting with all the people involved in the business? Making intelligent conversation with Realtors, decorators, home buyers, vendors, and municipal departments was beyond me. I couldn't focus for more than ten seconds on anything but the family photo albums I'd browsed through that day. I couldn't fathom how Jack managed to handle his responsibilities.

"Sorry," I said, shaking my head. "I'm not ready." When I saw his disappointment, I added, "But I am ready to keep my promise about this." I snaked my arms around his neck, tugged him toward me, and tilted my head back. His eyes brightened again, and our kiss sizzled at first contact.

"Yuck. I am so outta here." Ian grabbed his backpack and left the room, calling, "I'll be at Danny's."

"The kid has great instincts," mumbled Jack, his lips on mine again.

I wanted this raw encounter with Jack. I'd been thinking about it on and off all day, knowing I needed it more now than when I was twenty-one. I didn't know why. Didn't care about the reason. Not then, anyway. I just wanted the numbness to go away, if only for a few minutes.

Interlocked, we headed toward our bedroom, automatically kicking the door shut before pulling at our clothes. I was desperate to be skin-to-skin, touching, rubbing, stroking. Feeling! Feeling Jack's muscles move under my fingers. Borrowing his warmth, his strength. He knew my hot spots...just where, just how.... I knew his, too...just where, just how....

We twined closely around each other on the bed, our limbs weaving like yarn on a loom enveloping each other, so in synch, so frantic that soon there was no rhythm at all. And then, and then...oh, God...approaching that point of no return...vibrating through shimmering reds, scarlet and crimson, heading toward the neons, gold and hot orange...until the sun shattered, and we shattered. Together.

Our first communion since Kayla died.

I burst into tears.

Jack was still trying to catch his breath, but he reached out and coaxed me against him, across his chest. A very familiar position. "Aww, Claire. Don't cry. You're all right. You're all right."

No, I wasn't. "I shouldn't feel this good. Kayla—" But I hadn't thought about my daughter for the past ten minutes. Had it taken the most basic of human instincts to break through my grief? As though in punishment, a new wave of grief surged through me. *I'm sorry, sweetheart.*

"We can't bring her back," Jack whispered. "But it seems that you and I are still alive." He spoke slowly, emphasizing each word. "In fact, we're very much alive.

That was good, Claire. And healthy for us. So keep it on your to-do list, will ya?"

I couldn't blame him for wanting to reclaim as much normalcy as possible in our abnormal world, and intimacy had always been a healthy part of our marriage. However, my tears kept dribbling onto Jack's chest.

"If you keep on crying, my love, then I will too. And we'll both go back to being zombies like in the beginning."

"I still feel like one," I said between sobs. "I think I always will."

"No, no. I don't think it works like that. It's not forever. But in the meantime, I like having a naked zombie in my arms."

Jabbing him, I said, "No jokes."

"I'm just trying to—"

"I know, Jack. I know. You're trying to pretend we're okay."

"What's wrong with pretending for awhile if it works? I have to believe we'll get there someday, that we'll be strong again someday."

Granted, my numbness had disappeared during our sexual encounter as I'd suspected it would. But I didn't believe Jack and I would ever be strong again. I didn't care about "someday," a nebulous time in a hazy future. My heart was breaking now.

# CHAPTER TWO

*CLAIRE*

Ian left at his usual time the next morning, and Jack lingered over his coffee. I could sense his concern before he spoke.

"What will you do today, Claire? I don't want you spending it alone."

"I'll be fine." I forced a smile and said, "My sister's working, but maybe Mom will come by. Who knows? Or maybe I'll clean the bathrooms. Or cook. What would you like for dinner?"

"You."

"Go to work, Jack!"

He stood, headed to the kitchen door but then turned toward me. "If you can't come with me, then go back to the university. You were happy there."

I stood frozen. Couldn't breathe. A heat wave preceded a hard shiver, and perspiration covered me. I almost puked. "No. No. That's over. I'm dropping out."

"What are you talking about? You wanted it so much."

"Things are different now." That was all I could manage. Could I confess that Kayla died because I flirted with my professor? Jack figured I was simply running late and ran into bad luck getting the speeding ticket. According to him, no one escapes traffic cops indefinitely, and my ticket was no big deal.

"Yeah. Life is different," said Jack, "but you need to return to work or school. Part-time, full-time. I don't care which. I just don't want you hiding in the house!"

Why didn't he leave already before...before...?

"But that's where Kayla knows she can find me!" The crazed words burst from my soul. Jack stared, eyes wide, mouth open, his disbelief apparent before pain kicked in, before tears formed and a sob emerged. A big sob from a big man.

He collapsed back onto the chair he'd been using. "I may seem strong to you, Claire, going back to work and doing the usual chores, but you've seen me cry. You know the truth. I miss our little girl. I miss her so much I'm barely hanging on myself." His whispered confession floated in the air between us. "I love you, Claire, and I'm worried about you and simply want to help. But I guess I don't know how."

Of course he loved me. After twenty-three years together, I'd know if he didn't. I also knew that Jack couldn't help me harness my grief.

"You're off the hook," I said. "Dealing and healing are up to me, not you." No fairy godmothers, no magic wands. That job would be mine, and I didn't have a clue.

#

Jack finally left, but not before thrusting one of my drawing pads and pencils at me and demanding, "Draw something."

Mr. Psychologist. To accommodate him and get him out of the house faster, I drew a circle.

"Oh, c'mon, Claire. You can do better."

I added the simple features of the iconic smiley face. "Done," I said.

"Anyone can draw that," he mumbled as he finally headed out the back door toward the garage.

That was my point. I didn't want to be pushed and prodded. I didn't know how I felt about my "talent" now. I'd give it all up in a heartbeat to get my daughter back. Not even worth a discussion. I'd already learned at the hospital that bargaining with God and doctors didn't work. Begging didn't either. Maybe they were too used to desperate parents.

I opened the freezer and took out a whole chicken, thinking about a honey-mustard recipe the guys loved. *See Jack? No need to worry. I'm functioning.* After checking for the other ingredients—the spices and frozen orange juice—I sat down at the table again. Now what?

The simple sketch stared back at me. "Stop being so damn happy," I ordered before sticking out my tongue. I grabbed my pencil and changed the icon's smile to a frown. "That's better. Let's keep it real, my friend."

I pushed the drawing aside in favor of a fresh page in my art tablet. "And reality would be a police report calling Kayla's death an accident. According to them, the sun blinded the driver as she turned the corner—like this." I was talking to a cartoon and didn't care.

My pencil flew back and forth, quickly filling in the scene as I imagined it. I sketched the woman with her eyes closed. We'd been told she'd blinked and sneezed several times, like an allergic reaction.

I turned to another clean page. "And there's Kayla," I explained, depicting my daughter running for the football Ian had thrown, her long hair bouncing on her shoulders. I drew another scene where she grinned triumphantly at her brother as she caught the ball. But then, in my mind's eye, she continued backward into the street...and I...I...

"No, no. Stop!" I threw the pencil across the room, clutched my stomach, my insides on fire. For the first time in forty-five years, imagination had become my enemy, torturing me with Kayla's last happy moments.

Was it wrong to have daydreams about choking the driver? Of grabbing her shoulders and shaking her to the ground? I imagined myself screaming at her. *Do you understand what you've done? Do you understand that Kayla wasn't simply a twelve-and-a-half-year-old girl going on thirteen? She was my beautiful, loving, delightful child, filled with dreams and laughter and secrets. And a soccer star! Passionate about the game and her team. Can you understand how precious she was— and is—to her father and me?*

In a daze, I saw my hands fisted on outstretched arms.

Except for her name, I didn't know the driver, and she didn't know me. I guess it was better that way.

#

I crept to the family room, curled up on the couch, and fell asleep. Making art had never been so exhausting. Neither had getting through each day. Napping had become a regular activity since the funeral, but I hadn't mentioned that to Jack either. When I awoke, my stomach growled, reminding me to eat or at least try. I studied the contents of the fridge. Maybe I could manage some cottage cheese with a few grapes. After mixing the items, I took my bowl to the patio and plopped into a chair.

The heat of summer had started to wane, but the sun was as bright as ever. I moved into the shade. From this vantage point, I could see the entire length of the garage and my art studio behind it. Jack had built this workroom for me several years ago, when my dreams of becoming a studio artist could no longer wait, and my efforts had cluttered up half our bedroom. He'd done a wonderful job, providing the place with full electricity and plumbing. The studio was air-conditioned and had a slop sink. My husband hadn't stinted on anything. The poor guy wanted a happy wife but also wanted me to view art as a hobby. I guess he figured drawing at home would reinforce that idea. The more I'd painted, however, the more I wanted classes.

I hadn't been inside the studio since Kayla died, but I could picture it clearly, especially the area reserved for the kids, an unexpected but beautiful bonus. Right from the beginning, Kayla and her friends wanted to know what I was doing in there. Ian made some solo appearances too. So, instead of cautioning, "don't touch, don't touch," I bought a couple of child-sized easels, a table, chairs, and all kinds of arts and craft supplies. And I invited the children in. They called it "making art."

Sweet memories could kill, especially when unexpected. I rubbed the tears from my face, surprised to find them there. A headache threatened too. How had a simple lunch become an emotional crisis? I took a deep breath, then another, until I regained a sense of calm. No more fainting, no more sleeping all day. I needed to tell Jack I'd accomplished *something* when he came home that night.

I headed to the studio determined to "make art" in some way. Just one item. Even starting one project would do. And no more crying. I would not cry for at least an hour, a worthy goal.

But as soon as I opened the door, memories sucked me in. Memories tinged with the aroma of paints and turpentine. Clay and chalk. Turning on the light, I saw a dozen kids' work samples on the cork walls. My glance zoomed to Kayla's offering, and I forced my tears back.

Kayla had imagination and loved bold colors. But the artistic gene I'd gotten from my own mom had passed her by. No matter. She'd had a fun time with her projects, especially when her friends joined her. Jack insisted that Kayla simply loved being with me. The studio had become an extension of her little-girl years when we'd done "arts and crats" together at the kitchen table.

It was Ian who'd inherited the talent. But of course, he never pursued it. He never followed through on anything. How many times had I nagged him to clean his room or take out the garbage? Did he ever take responsibility? No, not even with his sister. A young girl like Kayla shouldn't be left alone. Sometimes she had to be picked up after soccer practice. Reluctantly, he'd do it. In reality, he only wanted to hang out with his friends. If he weren't an A student on an academic fast track, he'd have a lot more to answer for.

My head started to throb, and I cautioned myself not to think too much.

I opened a tin of clay and extracted a large handful. At the very least, I'd enjoy kneading it or rolling it. Punching it sounded fine too. After wetting the mound, my fingers pressed hard again and again, and soon I was back in the zone, pushing and pulling, letting my hands lead the way. Sometimes my hands saw more clearly than my eyes; without my sense of touch, I'd be half-blind. My thoughts started to wander. Had I imagined my days at the university? If wishing could make it so, Kayla would be alive.

Kayla...she seemed to be coming alive right in front of me, on the table. I became more focused as the statue took shape. Her head—chin up, eyes wide open, a playful grin. With a stylus, I etched in her long hair. I added clay to mold her body, clothed with the suggestion of her soccer uniform, her number in front. Time lost all meaning until my neck and back stiffened up, and I had to stretch.

I stepped away from the table and studied my work. My daughter smiled back at me, and I grinned at her...before the tears rolled. Why had I lingered with Colombo that day? Why hadn't I paid attention to the clock? If only I'd gotten home on time. If only that driver had been thirty seconds sooner or thirty seconds later. Was that too much to ask? *Please, God, I want my baby back, oh, how I want my baby back with me.*

I kissed the statue and covered it with a damp cloth. A day's work. For better or worse, I didn't know. I didn't know anything.

#

The rise and fall of children's voices floated on the air as I stepped outside the studio. I glanced at my watch and automatically headed toward the driveway where I could see the kids clamber from the school bus. Walking between the studio and the driveway had been a familiar route; waving at the children and looking for Kayla, a familiar afternoon routine. But I hadn't done either in two months. My feet were rooted as I stared at each child, whispering each name as the group filed by.

A couple of the kids waved to me. I pasted a smile on my face and lifted my arm in return. One girl called, "Hey, Miss Claire." Petite Madison Conroy, Anne's daughter and Kayla's best friend, bounded over, offering a hug so tight I'd be bruised by morning.

"Hey, Maddy." I tried to keep my faux smile bright.

The girl stepped back. Her mouth quivered, and I knew she sensed the truth. "Were you making art today?" She pointed toward the studio, a place she knew well.

I couldn't tell her about the clay. Too painful for us both. "Oh, I just played around, a little of this and that," I said. "It's actually my first day in there."

Her head bobbed. "I bet that was hard, like my first day back at school. Mama said I had to try. So at least now, when I write to her, I can tell Kayla you're trying too. She'll want to know."

Her information had come so fast, I could barely keep up, but the last part—about the writing—that was the moment my heart ka-boomed. Evidently Jack and I weren't the only ones on the street trying to grapple with reality.

"Madison...?" I drew out her name, my hand resting on her shoulder. "Are you writing to Kayla?"

"Every night before bed." She looked at me and took a step back. "Isn't that okay? Mama said I could. In a notebook."

My breath came shallow and short; another waterfall threatened. I wanted to run inside and curl up on the couch, but this loving, beautiful girl needed me to be strong. Surely, I could fake it for another minute. I leaned down until we were on eye level.

"I think it's more than okay. It's wonderful. You know what? I talk to Kayla all the time myself. So keep on writing. And if you want to make some art...?" I waved my arm toward the backyard. "You know where the studio is."

"With you?"

*Me? Oh, sweetheart. You don't know what you're asking.* The kid had blindsided me. Maddy and I making art without Kayla? I couldn't do it.

"Bring your mom," I said. "Wouldn't that be great?"

"Way cool!" She high-fived me, and I watched her stride away. I ran up the driveway, opened the back door, and fell onto a kitchen chair. Then I wept.

#

Afterwards, totally exhausted, I threw a frozen lasagna into the oven. No time for the honey-mustard chicken that took several hours to roast. I set three places at the table. If Ian had come directly home from school, he was probably in his room doing homework mixed with a few computer games. On the other hand, if he'd decided to go to his friend Danny's, then I'd get a call telling me he'd be having dinner there. I couldn't blame him for trying to escape.

"Hey, Mom?"

I whirled toward the sound of Ian's voice. "Oh! You scared me. I guess I was lost in thought." He stood in the entryway from the hall, and I was glad to see him. I'd sensed something wasn't right between us but kept hoping my imagination was working overtime. Maybe we'd have a quiet conversation now and iron it out.

"I saw the light on in the studio when I came home," he said. "So, are you getting back to normal again?"

In an instant, my good intentions took flight. Was my son that immature? Staring at him in disbelief, I said, "Normal? Don't you understand? Your sister's never coming back. This family is never going to be 'normal' again."

His mouth compressed to a slit across his face, and he took off toward his room.

*Oh, why had I snapped at him so quickly? He's just a kid. My child too.*

I was right behind him, but he'd had a head start and his door was locked by the time I arrived. Music began to blare. I could hear the lyrics through the walls.

"Open up, open up," I yelled while banging on the door.

No response.

"I'm sorry, Ian. Come on. Let's talk." Not that I seemed to say the right thing. Maybe the truth hurt too much to put into words. Maybe a hug would have been better. What the hell did I know except Kayla was gone. Gone forever.

So why had I expected to see her charge into the house, full of chatter about her friends and school, chatter about her *very important life*. I would never forgive myself for lingering with the professor. I wondered how my heart still beat.

I glared at Ian's doorknob, knowing I could jimmy the lock with a tiny tool used for fixing eyeglasses. Jack would know where it was, and thankfully, he'd be home soon.

Making my way to the family room, I sat on the couch to wait. Funny how drained I was for someone who hadn't put in a hard day at work or school.

#

Jack's voice woke me up. "Something's burning in the oven, and where's that god-awful music coming from?"

I jumped from the sofa, caught my balance, and ran to the kitchen, Jack at my heels.

"Oh, everything's a mess, including this lasagna!" I pulled the casserole out of the oven, relieved to find it still edible. "Ian's in his room, not talking to me. And Maddy's writing letters to Kayla, so I have to call Anne. And then, in the studio today, I felt Kayla everywhere, like she was wrapped around me, and I was wrapped around her.

"More importantly, I want to know how the cops could call our daughter's death an accident. Dropping a bag of groceries is an accident. Tripping on a garden hose is an accident. But killing someone...? How do you compare them? That woman—Sarah something—should be arrested. And then I almost burned supper."

He held me tight and rocked me like I was a baby, my face hidden in his chest. I felt him shudder a couple of times. "Are you all right?" I asked. "Or have I scared you too?"

"Holding you is right. But everything else?" He shook his head. "I'm not sure what to think. If Maddy's letters help her cope, then it's good. Just like I keep busy at work." A smile flickered. "Juggling projects distracts me. Lots of planning and details to oversee. And," he sighed, "one more day passes. I think we need to keep busy."

At that moment, I could have told him about my sculpting today, about the hours I spent creating the clay statue of Kayla. Instead, I held back. Perhaps I wanted the close mother-daughter relationship to remain private, just between Kayla and me. Or maybe I didn't want Jack to think I was obsessed with her. Not that he wasn't! Or maybe my artistic self wanted its usual privacy until the project was complete. Whatever the reason, I kept silent while Jack trotted down the hall to Ian's room.

# CHAPTER THREE

*IAN BARNES*

I heard Dad calling my name. Then came the pounding on the door. The good cop was cleaning up after the bad cop. That was the way they'd been working lately.

Mom blamed me for the accident. No matter how she tried to hide her feelings or apologize, I could tell she blamed me because she never looked me in the eye. Everyone knows that looking someone in the eye meant they were telling the truth—unless the person was a sociopath. So Mom was lying.

I opened the door and let my dad in. He scanned the room and turned to me. "Geezus, Ian. Your mother's not wrong about this. It's a mess."

"So what? It's my mess. I know where everything is. She doesn't have to come in here."

"Nice attitude. You're acting more like seven, not seventeen and off to college next year."

I'd been wrong. They were now bad cop on bad cop, both ganging up on me. Just as I was about to shoot my mouth off, Dad did his dad thing as only he could.

"Come here." He grabbed me and hugged me like he'd never let go. "I love you, son. No matter what. And your mother does too."

I had to think about that for a minute. These kinds of discussions made my brain hurt. Math, science, grammar...they were so much easier to understand. Master the basics and run with them. Everything made sense. But psychology had no rules. Behavior had no rules, only emotions. People just did whatever they felt like doing.

"Mom wishes I'd never been born," I said.

"What! That's ridiculous, Ian. Not your mother. She loved you even before you were born." He went to the doorway and called her name. "Where did you get that stupid idea?"

I shrugged. He'd have to see for himself. We'd always been close, Dad and I. Those first days after the funeral, we'd cried on each other's shoulders. Two guys hugging and crying. Then all the visitors stopped coming, and we were alone. Mom, Dad, and me. The three of us at that kitchen table. Three, not four. And Mom barely looking at me, thinking it was my fault.

"Hi, guys." Mom turned from me to Dad. "Supper's ready. The lasagna's okay, and I made a big salad too."

"That can wait a minute, Claire. We need to straighten out something first with Ian, and I'm not talking about this bedroom."

Her brow narrowed. "Good. Because I'm not touching it."

*Promise?* But I kept my mouth shut.

"Let's sit down," said Dad, glancing pointedly at me.

I moved my clothes, baseball and glove, earphones, and books from my bed to my desk and offered the desk chair to my mom. Dad and I sat on the bed.

"Ian thinks you blame him for the accident, Claire. He needs to hear that you don't. It's time to clear the air about this and begin again."

Mom's forehead wrinkled before she shifted toward me. "Think about this, Ian. Were you driving the car that hit your sister? The answer is no. Did you push her in front of the moving vehicle? Again, the answer is no. Therefore, you're not guilty." She paused and gave me a quick smile. "You seem confused, honey. I thought you liked logic."

I did, but she was hiding behind it. Using it to distract.

"Forget the accident," she added, jumping from the chair. "Want to know what really ticks me off, what you're really guilty of? Let's start with not taking responsibility. Like with this messy room. Like playing video games all the time and hanging out with your friends instead of coming home. Like arguing with me about looking after Kayla when I asked. All you want to do is fool around. All you think about is yourself. How are you going to go off to college when you can't get organized? You're spoiled rotten." Her eyes flashed at my dad. "That's what he's guilty of, and it's our fault."

Mom was on a roll. It must have made her feel better. "None of my friends have to—"

"Our son's a good kid," said Dad, breaking in. "His report card proves it with all those As. And now I'm confused. We were talking about the accident. How did we ever get onto this topic?"

"I think they call it being passive-aggressive," I said, mentally flipping through the psych chapters I'd had to read for school. "She's pretending to be calm about the important question, the one about blaming me for Kayla, which, by the way, she never directly answered. And then she switched everything around and yelled at me for other, less important things."

My folks were silent. They stared at me with wide eyes and open mouths, stunned, especially Mom. I hadn't been looking for a "gotcha" moment. Just wanted the truth. And I got it. Mom saw me as a spoiled brat. She'd like to blame me—or someone—for Kayla's death. She needed a scapegoat, but she wasn't sure who it should be.

I guess psychology came in handy after all.

# CHAPTER FOUR


*JACK BARNES*

*January, four months after accident*

I dreaded going home today. Dreaded my upcoming talk with Claire. As if the recent holidays weren't bad enough for the family, my business concerns had become worse. With the lousy economy, home buyers were drying up. Potential buyers thought two and three times before investing in a house, and when they did, they wanted everything for free! Did they think we were HGTV or something?

After meeting with my accountant that afternoon, I headed home and hoped for the best. Claire would have to pull herself together and come back to work. At this point, she had no choice.

"Something smells good," I said, walking through the back door into the kitchen. My wife was bending over the oven. "But I like the view better."

Claire straightened, a tinge of pink in her cheeks. "Just in time. Turkey breast with sweet potatoes on the side."

"In the middle of the week? That's quite a meal." I hoped she'd eat a lot of it.

Shrugging, she said, "It's easy, and the turkey will last a couple of days, ready to pop into the microwave."

I put my attaché case down and washed my hands. "Where's Ian?"

"At Danny's. He called to check in with me. But I knew he'd rather be at the Goldbergs' than here. So I said okay." She bit her lip, shook her head. "I yell at him too much. I'm too impatient. Why am I picking on him?"

"Claire...?"

"What?"

"You're really not blaming him, are you?"

"No," she replied quickly, turning away from me. "If only I'd gotten home on time..."

Her back was to me. I stepped closer and wrapped my arms around her. "Don't talk that way. You couldn't know." I kissed her temple and nuzzled her neck. "It's just as well Ian's not home this evening. We need to talk privately."

"We do? About what?" She jerked away, then grabbed my arm. "Don't tell me! Has someone else died? At work, maybe? Oh, my God." Her complexion paled to an alabaster white, and before more horrible thoughts tripped from her tongue, I cupped her face and kissed her. "Rein it in, babe. No one's died. Stop it. Stop thinking the worst."

"Then don't scare me."

"For crying out loud, Claire, you're going to have to toughen up. What did you do today? I sure hope you left the house."

She began setting the table while I brought the turkey platter over. "Anne and I ran around the lake a few times this afternoon," she said. "We did two miles. So how's that for keeping busy, bigshot?"

I examined her closely, up and down. Too slender, almost skinny. Her clothes hung, shapeless. "Did you manage a two-mile run? I'm really impressed."

"Well...I kinda walked toward the end. I won't lie about that, but at least I completed the circle." She spoke over her shoulder as she brought a salad and the sweet potatoes to the table.

"Good for you. And if you eat your dinner every night, soon you'll be able to run the entire distance."

She glared at me, eyes smoldering, chin high. "I'm doing the best I can."

"But now you're going to have to do better," I said quietly. "Barnes Construction is hurting."

I'd gotten her attention, so I began my spiel. "You know that with any business, if you don't grow, you die. And home building is tough right now with the down economy. I need you back with me, Claire. The temp I hired while you took this 'leave of absence' has got to go. She's an expense we don't need."

With her posture alert, she seemed to be listening hard, but I couldn't detect whether she was onboard or not. I plunged ahead.

"What we need to do is bring in as many dollars as possible. We need to maximize every sale. One area where we can accomplish this is in the design center. If we expand it and offer more customized services and selections, we can increase profit margins. Customized color schemes, upgrading backsplashes, tile, fixtures, and window treatments.... Are you listening?"

"I hear you, Jack. But I don't think I like where you're going."

Damn! "Well, like it or not, I need you in that new design center. Instead of just taking on the model homes and helping buyers with basic selections, I'd like you to run the expansion. This is your bailiwick, Claire, a natural fit. I have full confidence in you."

But she was already shaking her head. "It's too much. I can't concentrate on all those people. It's not what I want to do. I'm working in the studio every day now, a-and I'm happy there. At least...happier. It's tolerable."

"Happy? Who said anything about being happy? That's a luxury for people like us." As I spoke, I realized how true my words were, and I wondered if we'd ever laugh again.

"I know you're grieving, Claire. We both are. But you're wallowing in it. Don't you think I miss Kayla every minute of every day?" I tapped the left side of my chest. "She's here with me, in my heart, all the time. Or do you think I've forgotten?"

She was crying by this time, but so was I, and I wasn't ashamed. Grief had a way of sneaking up on a person. It lay in wait and pounced when your back was turned. Or it clung with sticky fingers twenty-four/seven, giving no reprieve. Claire and I had been bungling along day by day, just trying to get through each one without drowning.

"I know the timing's awful, sweetheart. But if we don't change our business model and try to increase sales, we could go under. We're lucky that Houston's not been hit as badly as some other parts of the country, but we haven't escaped either. I might have to lay off people, people you've known for a long time. And if I have to hire someone to handle the new design center, that's money out of the family budget, because you'd be paid instead."

Claire rubbed her face with a tissue. "I understand. But you're scaring me about everything."

"I need you, Claire. I want you with me just like we used to be."

And with those last words, I knew I'd lost her. She was shaking her head, holding up her hand in a stop motion. Bringing up what "used to be" was a hot button.

"I don't want to go backwards and work the business full-time," she began. "When we first started the company, that was okay. Putting in sixteen-hour days was no problem. But, Jack, it took me twenty years to return to college, and the truth is that, after the accident, I didn't want to go back there either. Wouldn't consider it. Maybe I just need a break. Maybe someday I'll finish up. Someday, I'll have a showing. I don't know when that might be, but I can't give up."

Disappointment surged through me. I'd been prepared to be flexible, maybe a part-time schedule at first until she regained her confidence. She'd reduced her hours the past two years anyway. Of course, for the expansion, I'd need her full-time. She normally would dig into a project like this. But going up against her dreams? Her art? I could never win those rounds.

"Too bad Ian's not ready to join me."

"Maybe I could work from home...?" Claire offered.

"And turn the house into a design center? I think not. Besides, our subdivision isn't zoned for business." Pushing my chair back, I stood, my appetite for dinner gone but not my need for an antacid pill. I popped one in my mouth. "I do my best thinking while walking, so I'll see you later. Maybe I'll figure out if I can save Barnes Construction without you. I can't believe you won't give it a try. Maybe you should figure out if you need counseling."

Claire's jaw dropped, her eyes bulged. She looked horrified. So maybe I'd been too hard on her.

"Do you think I'm crazy?" she asked. "It's only been four months, Jack. Are there rules I'm supposed to follow for this kind of grief? Rules I don't know about but you do?"

She stood facing me now, no longer aghast but ready to argue. She almost seemed like the Claire I used to know. I wanted to cheer, but I also wanted to make my point.

"I don't know about any rules. All I know is that we've lost our daughter. But does that mean we should lose the business too?"

"The business! The business!" she shouted. "How can you compare Kayla to a business?"

"I'm not comparing, Claire. I'd give the company away in a New York minute if it would bring Kayla back. But it won't, and I don't know what else to do except work and...love you."

I took her in my arms. She resisted for a moment and then sagged against me. We held each other, a quiet time for catching our breaths, collecting our thoughts. I sincerely hoped this intermission wasn't a prelude to another round of arguments.

#

*CLAIRE*

I sent for the posse, and at nine o'clock the next morning, Judy and my mom rapped at the door. My sister is a petite brunette, just a bit over five feet, but somehow she always seems a lot taller. Jack said it was all about attitude, about being fearless. I said she had a Napoleon complex. We'd laugh and agree it was the same thing.

"Good girl. I smell the coffee," Judy said after kissing me on the cheek. "It's the least you can do after I rearranged my morning for you."

Judy managed the Human Resources Department at the local Macy's department store, no small task. The company had a myriad of full-time and part-time employees. Judy supervised everything staff related—the hiring, firing, training, benefits, scheduling, and a host of incidentals.

"How can we help you, Claire?" asked Mom, giving me a mama-bear hug.

I filled our three cups, took out the milk and sugar substitute, and sat down with them. "Don't you love a kitchen table?" I asked. "It's the best place to talk."

Mom's eyebrow arched so high I thought it would hit the ceiling. "What are we discussing, Claire? Is it about Kayla?"

"Not exactly," I replied slowly. "It's just that last night, Jack and I were talking a-and I just want a second opinion. So, here's the question: do you think I need counseling?"

The room became so quiet the proverbial pin could have dropped to the floor with a bang. I first sought my mother, but tears had already started to flow down her cheeks. God, I'm so selfish. Why hadn't I thought she'd get upset?

"Okay. Forget about this conversation. I'll be fine," I said. "Judy, go to the store. Mom, did you bring your crocheting? I'll work on something with you."

"Oh, no," said my feisty sister. "You asked a serious question. You deserve a serious answer." She dug out a tissue from her purse and threw it at our mother. "Wipe up. Claire needs us."

She focused her dark eyes on me. "I'm certainly not a shrink. But it seems to me, because you've asked us to come here, that the topic is bothering you. What about counseling? Do you think you need it?"

"I think you're turning the question around."

"Then let's back up," Judy said, raising her forefinger. "I wasn't trying to play a game, sweetie. I was trying to help. So, maybe we should start at the beginning. What brought this on?"

I told them about Jack's fears for the business. In our family, everyone knew everything, so I never considered I was telling tales. "And when I couldn't commit to working with him, he said I should get counseling. As if he's so perfect and has all the answers."

"Aw, Claire. He's just being Jack," said my sister. "Trying to fix things. He always does that."

*While I break things. I killed Kayla. I destroyed this family because of dallying with Colombo. And we can never be fixed.*

"Claire! What's wrong? You look like you're going to faint." Mom's voice. "Maybe she needs a medical doctor, not a psychologist."

"Maybe she needs both." Judy leaned over and stroked my hair. "Or maybe a visit to the hairdresser might help. You're very gray, Claire. There's no shine. You need to make an appointment. And look how thin you are. You definitely need to eat. Has Jack mentioned these things?"

I shook my head. "I don't think he's noticed. Everything is secondary to Barnes Construction."

"Oh, come on. I know my brother-in-law. The man notices details. That's why he's got a stellar reputation in the home-building industry."

"And we've got to help him save the company and keep that reputation," said Mom as she clasped my hands. "I have an idea, Claire, and I think it's a good one. Why don't you and I work together for Jack? Who knows fabrics better than me after all my years in retail? I helped customers make selections all the time and then taught them to quilt or sew. You and I could be a design team. Furniture, fabric, wallpaper, paint colors. You know I love doing all that. And as for the customers, I'll meet and greet and ease you in with each client so you won't get buried." Her hands tightened on mine. "I'm seventy years young, my dear, and have more energy than some women half my age. I can help you with this, Claire. And maybe help you with other things too."

Barbara Anderson had always been a dynamo, and she knew her daughter well. She knew I was shyer and would rather work behind the scenes. I had to force myself into a sales persona while she'd never met a stranger.

Judy got on the bandwagon, proffering insane ideas. Mom and I could each decorate half a house. Or Mom could work with the husband, and I'd work with the wife. The artistic gene had definitely skipped her. Between the two of them, I didn't know what to think or what to do. I walked to the back door and looked through the glass panes, seeing the studio just beyond the garage. I'd accomplished quite a bit since I'd first entered it again, but of course, everything there centered on Kayla. I'd had calm hours there, productive hours, and I didn't want to leave.

But Jack needed me. I knew the business. But my life at Barnes Construction wouldn't be calm. Did I owe him a try?

I turned to my two loving ladies. "Mom, you've worked your entire life and finally have a chance to play. I can't ask you to give that up. You've earned a fun time."

"Claire, my dear Claire, you'd do the same for your daughter if she needed you because that's what mothers do. They help out whenever they can."

She was right, of course, but I told her I'd think about her generous offer. I couldn't make snap decisions, no matter how tempting. And I needed to take baby steps. Jumping into a critically important expansion, even with Mom, scared me. It was too huge a commitment.

Judy had the last word before leaving for her job. "So, you've got some choices to think about, Clarabelle. Four months is a short time. Of course the grieving is still fresh; in fact, it's fresh for all of us. If you think you need counseling, there are support groups right here in the city for parents who've lost a child. On the other hand, maybe Jack's right, and you should get back out into the world and interact with people. You can even do both. Your call. However, the bottom line is that you cannot continue to hide in the house or in the studio."

"I'll think about it." But they didn't understand. I wasn't hiding from the world. I simply enjoyed working in the studio, which wasn't anything new. They were right about a couple of other items, however. Like my hair. Like my weight. It didn't matter what I looked like, did it? I sure didn't deserve to look good or feel pretty, but I picked up the phone and made an appointment with Juanita. One baby step that would make everyone else feel good.

# CHAPTER FIVE

*CLAIRE*

"I'll drive," said Jack a week later as we stood at the kitchen counter, drinking coffee. He pocketed his keys.

"No, let's take both vehicles." We were heading for the office. It was my first day back, and I wanted the ability to come and go in my own reliable sedan. He drove a long-bed pickup. I rinsed my cup and reached for my purse.

"Planning an early escape?"

Only if I had to. "It's a baby step, Jack. Just like I told you. I'll do my best, but my brain is jumpy. I don't know how long I'll be able to focus."

"And you're afraid I won't drive you home?"

Guilty as charged. "You might be too busy."

He placed his hand over his heart. "I promise to take you if you want to leave early."

Man, he was pushing it. Sighing, I followed him to the garage and got into his passenger seat. As we put the ten miles behind us and I studied our surroundings, the trip seemed like a shadowy memory from long ago. The passing scenery was almost that of a strange land and I, a tourist. So, my family had been right. I hadn't ventured away from home and the immediate neighborhood since the funeral. Everyone had noticed except me.

My tension mounted the closer we got to Barnes Construction. The unknown scared me, and yet I knew every corner of the building. By the time Jack parked in his reserved spot, I was talking out loud to myself. "Stay calm. Stay calm."

Jack turned the key, and quiet surrounded us. "You'll be fine," he said, squeezing my hand. "I'll be nearby."

The design center occupied its own wing in the main building. Jack was around the corner and down the hall.

"There'd better not be a welcoming committee," I said. "No more condolences. I couldn't handle that. I just want to creep into my office."

A quick kiss. "I took care of it." Another kiss. "I'm planning to stay put today. No site visits."

"Oh...I'm sorry..." I'd made it a point never to interfere on the construction side of the business. My husband was truly the Jack-of-all-trades.

"Don't worry about it," he said. "Today, I'm investing in you."

I bit my lip. He'd probably lose on this investment. We both knew I didn't want to be there, but I owed him a try. *Suck it up, girl. You can do it. You used to love the work, and you're good at it.* In the beginning, when Jack started the venture, I was as excited as he and at his side with a million ideas beyond decorating. I altered blueprints and changed layouts too, as long as the construction cost didn't change.

Now, I just wanted to hide away.

Walking into the lobby, I stared straight ahead, pretending not to notice Mary Toomy, the front-office face of the company, as she set up for the day. Instead, I shadowed Jack and headed down the familiar hallway and around the corner. He stepped aside as I walked through the door of the design center. I passed the countertop and carpet sample displays. Passed the tile and cabinet choices, as well as the racks of bathroom and kitchen fixtures. Choices, choices. A million choices. How would I handle this again?

As soon as I entered my own office, I smelled the lemony furniture polish and had to admit the place sparkled. On the large oak desk stood a vase of fresh-cut daisies, the perfect choice. Jack had heard me call them a happy flower at least a thousand times. Inch by inch, my gaze traveled around the familiar room, the room I used to call my home away from home. Sample books of wallpaper and fabrics lined the shelves; some were piled on the floor. Lifting them was akin to lifting weights—great for keeping muscles taut.

A set of blueprints stretched across the desk with pads, pencils, and a calculator alongside. I absorbed everything, taking my time, studying the walls where framed pictures of decorated rooms were showcased. I usually updated the displays regularly, but these pictures had hung for a long time.

Finally, I nodded, pulled out my chair, and sat down. Automatically opening the bottom right drawer, I threw my purse inside. The instinctive routine overrode my five-month absence.

I plunged ahead. "So, tell me about this new model," I said, pointing at the blueprint.

"I think I'll stick to the old one. She suits me just fine." Jack's eyes gleamed in a shade of blue I'd tried to reproduce a hundred times but couldn't.

I smiled at his joke, but a mass of doubts tumbled inside me, doubts Jack didn't want to acknowledge. The man knew darn well what it took to provide the individualized decorating services our buyers deserved. I needed to be friendly, to listen, concentrate, and come up with selections and ideas. I hadn't had an original idea in...a very long time. The challenges ahead made me nervous, and I almost asked for one of his antacids.

Within an hour, I knew Jack should have believed me. I'd promised a dozen callbacks by day's end. I wasn't familiar with the new construction sites, the locations, the buyers' names. I wasn't familiar with our four new models and hadn't memorized the room measurements. These buyers wanted the decorating consultation they'd been promised.

Jack wasn't in his office, so I called Mary at the reception desk. "I'm drowning here. And I just remembered about the temp. Has Jack let her go already? And if he has, who's been fielding these calls?"

The woman paused. "Well, either Jack or the site managers. Sometimes me. And...and that local decorator was more of a kitchen designer. She wasn't very good with anything else. We're so happy you're back, Claire. In fact, there's a couple here right now who need help. They're very excited. They've already bought a home in the Grand Lakes subdivision. Get it?" she whispered into the phone.

Oh, I got it. Mary was cluing me in. Make this couple happy. She hung up, and within seconds, Mr. and Mrs. Hoffman were in my office.

I listened. I took notes. They'd forgotten the name of the model. I'd never been to Grand Lakes. It was a three-bedroom, two-bath, one-story, they explained. Could I decorate theirs like the showcase house? I had no idea. The temp must have done a good job beyond the kitchen on this one.

The Hoffmans watched me search through the blueprints. Where the hell was a three-bedroom, two-bathroom? Where the hell was Grand Lakes?

Frantic, I pulled open one desk drawer after another until I reached the bottom left and found myself staring into Kayla's beaming face. Her happy, sweet face. I picked up the framed photo and burst into tears. Reaching blindly into the drawer, I pulled out Ian's picture and barely noticed the couple leave my office.

Jack showed up a moment later. And I pointed at our kids. "You put the daisies where the pictures used to be, didn't you?"

"Sure, I did. You would have run like hell if they'd been on top of the desk."

The flowers had been a distraction. A postponement of the inevitable. He knew I'd ask about the pictures sooner or later, but not right away if he could help it.

"Take me home. Now," I said, grabbing my bag. "I'm done."

He glanced at his watch. "You've been here only an hour or so. Give it more time. Mary will take messages."

I gestured to the walls, the blueprints. "I barely know the number of square feet in a square yard anymore. Grand Lakes? People coming in and out. I don't know the new stuff, Jack, and can't remember the old. I'll scare everyone away. If you want Barnes Construction to keep succeeding, get me out of here."

"Stay until noon, sweetheart. We'll have lunch and talk."

But I was out the door, racing down the hall, keys in hand. I could drive his truck. "I'll pick you up later."

"Coward!"

His voice carried through the halls where half the employees could hear, and I winced. Trouble at the top trickled down to the bottom. Gossip and rumors could start. Jack didn't deserve more problems.

My fault again. Always doing the wrong thing. I knew it but couldn't turn back. I charged toward the truck and collapsed behind the wheel. With shaking hands, I turned on the ignition then glanced into the rearview mirror and laughed. My hair looked great—blonde, bouncy, shaped. So what? It didn't matter at all. Jack had been almost right. I was not only a coward but a guilty one at that. *Kayla, Kayla...I love you so much, and I'm so sorry. I can't bring you back to us, but what can I do? How can I make it up to you?*

#

I turned into my driveway just after the school bus pulled away. Maddy waited for me with a big smile across her face.

"Mama's coming over," she said, hugging me. "She said she'd meet me here after school because we want to make art with you. For Kayla."

I forced myself not to cry as I held her, inhaled her. "You want to draw? You won't be bored?" Maddy had a better eye than Kayla, but she wasn't an undiscovered genius. More to the point, she didn't have Kayla to gab with. I wondered how her kind little heart could bear it.

"Nope. I won't be bored. I need pictures for my stories. Mom says I write great stories."

"I sure do think so. Hey, Claire. I hope it's okay for us to take advantage of all the goodies you've got in there." Anne joined arms with me, and we trekked up the driveway.

"Of course. In fact, there's not much being used now. Help yourself." I sighed a deep, quavering breath and felt Anne's grip tighten.

"Easy does it," she murmured.

"I've had a bad day," I said. "Just give me a second." I entered the studio and flipped on the light. I made sure my finished works and work-in-progress were covered with cloths. "All's clear. Come on in."

Maddy headed directly to the kids' table, dropping her books on the bench and searching out the supply of colored paper. "I need to make a collage for art class," she began. "And I already know what I'm going to do. Our soccer team. On the field. So I need a big background sheet, and a scissor..."

She chatted on about her plans for the project, gathering materials—glue, colored paper, popsicle sticks...

Maddy knew what she wanted to accomplish, and I didn't make suggestions. I tried never to interfere with the creative process, especially with children.

"And Kayla will be on the team too," she said. "Do you have crepe paper? I need yellow for the halo."

My stomach tightened, and I glanced at Anne. She shrugged back at me. "It's healing for her," she said. "She's sad when she begins her 'Kayla projects,' but she's smiling when she's finished. Her efforts seem to be doing some good."

"Therapy?"

"Well, yes. I think you could say that."

Anne led me outside. "I know your grief—yours and Jack's—is unimaginable. And God knows five months is not long. But I have to help my daughter through this too. It'll take time, so thanks for letting us use your studio. Maddy very much wanted to come here today."

Well, if I couldn't help Kayla, at least I could help her best friend. "Would you like a key? I might not be home each time Maddy wants in. Today was a disaster at the office, but I'm probably going to work for Jack again."

"Is that such a bad idea?"

"I'd rather be in there," I replied, nodding at my retreat. Anne glanced away then, as though taking courage, held my gaze. "I noticed quite a few items under wraps. You've been busy. Do you smile, like Maddy does, when you've finished a piece? Does working here make you feel better?"

She sounded concerned, not snarky, a dear friend wanting to help. But I didn't have an answer. "I don't know," I whispered. "I'm just driven to making another one."

"I wish I were I psychiatrist," she said, "instead of a book seller. Hey! Shall I bring home some books about grieving?"

"No, thanks," I replied. "I'll figure it out on my own."

She turned down my offer of the key but left me with a hug and the promise of another walk around the lake very soon.

Now all I wanted to do was take a nap. I'd boil hotdogs for dinner. Dinner! Jack! Dang. I'd almost forgotten about picking him up at the office.

# CHAPTER SIX

*IAN*

*March-six months after accident*

"Have you told your dad yet?"

I slammed my locker door, hoisted my backpack, and pushed my arms through the straps. "Yeah. Last night." And I didn't want to think about that conversation.

"How loud did he yell?"

Danny Goldberg had been my closest friend since Kindergarten. Now we were both in our high school honors program. He knew me better than my parents did, knew how to score a direct hit. Somehow he had a way of asking questions that made me want to bawl louder than a calf getting branded. I had to turn away.

"He didn't," I finally replied. "He didn't raise his voice at all." But maybe he should have. Maybe he should have shouted: *Not go to college? What are you talking about? Now get those applications in. I don't care about late fees.*

"So you got off easy, huh?"

"As easy as riding a bull. He hauled my mom into it."

"Oh boy." That's all he said, all he had to say.

*Let him alone, Jack. Let him do what he wants. He's miserable here.* Then she stared at me for a long time. What will make you happy, Ian? No, never mind. That's a stupid question. Better is, what can make you *hopeful again?*

"Hopeful? What world is she in?" I muttered as Danny and I headed to the exit, to the lot where his third-hand vehicle was parked. "She doesn't say it, but she still thinks it's my fault about Kayla and that I'm the most juvenile, irresponsible person she knows. I can't do anything right. How could I know the damn car would turn the corner just then?"

"You couldn't! No way."

"And Dad thinks I just need a break from school. He should know school's the easy part. I need a break from my family. I had to give him all kinds of other reasons for job searching instead of working with him."

"Your dad's a good guy. That must've been tough."

"Yup. And tricky 'cause...because..." I almost couldn't tell him. "You're my best friend, Danny, and my own thoughts are getting me nowhere. I've got to share this. Can you keep your mouth shut?"

"C'mon, Ian. Don't we always?"

Yeah, we did. "I think there's trouble with the company. Dad's worried. If I were a good son, I'd drop out of school and work with him like I do in the summer. Maybe I'd save him some money. Whaddyathink?"

Danny's brow furrowed, and he stared off into space—his usual expression while figuring stuff out. I knew to give him time. A shrink would probably say I'm "too close" to the situation to evaluate clearly. All I knew was that I needed Danny's help, and I'd get it.

Nothing had been right at home since Kayla died. My mom was in her own world, I guess cleaning the house all day, or working in her studio. She didn't talk much to me except to complain. But I wasn't arguing with her anymore about anything. It wasn't worth it. I kept remembering how she keeled over at Kayla's funeral, and I thought she'd died too. So I was keeping my mouth shut before something else bad happened.

As for Dad, well, he claimed to hear me, but he didn't really listen. He couldn't believe I wanted to turn down college and go out on my own. Before Kayla died, he assumed I'd join him in the business after I got my degree. But I'd never said so.

"You couldn't save your dad enough money to make a difference." Danny's dark eyes held my gaze, his usual easy going demeanor absent. "Compared to his real expenses, at your level of work, your salary's nothing. What's happening between you and your dad is not about the money. It's about leaving home, leaving him and your mom."

"That's what I was afraid of." In my gut, I'd known it. Just needed affirmation.

We got into Danny's car, but I didn't feel like going to a silent house. "How about a little one-on-one?"

"Your driveway or mine?"

Ten minutes later, we were dribbling, driving, and shooting for the rim. Sweat ran down my face. I was quick, but Danny was taller. I took one shot after another, pivoting left, then right. Soon, my vision blurred. I became two people, like in a dream, one of me making baskets and one speeding toward the street, toward my sister. Pointing at the car. Shouting at her and running, but I was too late. Always too late.

Kayla was into sports like me. She had a better arm than most girls and even some guys, and she was always ready for a catch. I drove the football; she ran backwards, jumped, caught it, but Newton's Second Law kept her going right into the road. And that's when I saw the car coming. Kayla was there, and I wasn't. I couldn't stop her, and I couldn't stop the car. I saw her go down, and I'll never forget it. Never ever.

The police asked a million questions, but I was shaking so hard I could barely talk. I pointed at the driver.

"She's the one. Ask her. She called you. She told me to get a blanket for Kayla."

That was true. The woman—her name was Sarah something-or-other—had to take charge. I wasn't too proud of myself but glad she knew what to do. I thought she'd really kept her cool until I saw her vomit after the cops showed up. Then she fell to the curb, her arms and legs shaking as hard as mine. Maybe she was the one in shock. In the end, it was all about angles and velocity and coincidence.

"Not your fault, man." My friends gathered round all through the following weeks, their presence needed, their loyalty matching the Marine Corps code. Without Danny and the guys to lean on, I would have gone nuts. Sometimes, they couldn't hide their pity; sometimes they still couldn't, but I'd rather hang out with them than be at home. My senior year of high school had gone down the sewer.

"Hey, Ian. Give it a break, will ya?"

"Huh? What?" I looked around. Danny was on the sidelines, watching me play alone, watching me take all the shots, catch all the rebounds, dribbling and driving.... I was soaked with sweat. I looked over at him then down at myself. My legs began to shake just like on that day, and I slowly folded to the ground.

*Stay with her, Ian. I don't want her alone in the house.*

*But, Mom, I've got my own life. Danny's waiting. We've got practice and projects. C'mon. I'm not a friggin' babysitter!*

"Oh, shit, Ian! Don't die on me." Danny was hauling me to my feet. "Come on inside. You need some Gatorade. And we'll have something to eat."

"You sound like your mother. *Have something to eat*," I mimicked, trying to regain my composure.

Danny roared. That's exactly what I liked about him. He could laugh at everything, especially at himself. "So, maybe she has the right idea," he countered. "Food's always good."

I began laughing too. And for a moment, it was like old times at Danny's house or mine.

We washed up and dug into leftovers that could pass for a meal anyplace else. Chicken drumsticks, meatballs, and Italian bread. I filled up. Now I wouldn't have to eat with my folks.

"So, if you're not going to work with your dad in the business, where are you going to work?" asked Danny, continuing the conversation we'd started in the locker room.

"I've got some ideas floating in my brain. I went to the career office today, and the staff is helping me get organized for that job search."

"I didn't even know we had a career office. So, you gonna work on the Geek Squad at Best Buy?"

"Nope. At least I don't think so. The counselors are lining up an interview for me at Gulf Coast Oil Refinery."

Danny's eyes almost popped out of his head. "An oil refinery? Hell, Ian. That's crazy! What do you know about oil plant operations?"

"Not much, but we figured out in the career office that I'm hot with a computer, great in math and science, know something about the construction trades, and I'm used to tackling projects and organizing information."

That last one definitely came from the counselor. My mom would appreciate it too. *Yeah, Mom, I can organize some things.*

I had Danny's full attention now and gave him the clincher. "The most important part is that the job's fifty miles away from here, and that's absolutely perfect."

I didn't care about being an apprentice, about the low pay. All I cared about was leaving the dark days behind me and escaping my mother's gaze.

# CHAPTER SEVEN



*CLAIRE*

Ian's decision to "postpone" college and move out had shaken us up. His mature demeanor when explaining himself revealed a young man we'd not seen before, and that jarred us too. Jack and I told ourselves that our son was simply putting off his college education. Ian suggested he wanted to build a career elsewhere. He planned to accept a job right after graduation in June, only three months from now.

Of course, Jack was crushed, but Ian had an answer for everything. "Does a doctor's son have to become a doctor? Construction is all I know. I need to try other things."

He sounded almost reasonable until he turned on me and snapped, "That's what will make me happy. Okay? I need to be independent, earn my own way."

*Since when?* But I'd nodded and hoped he'd change his mind before high school ended.

As though Ian's decisions hadn't upset us enough, I'd finally agreed, once more, to return to Barnes Construction. I agreed, because a few nights ago, I'd lost track of time again. Jack found me in the studio and went ballistic.

"You're done here, Claire! Done." He waved his arms to encompass the entire room. "If you can concentrate on this...this *stuff*, you can come to the office. I worry about you being alone all day, moping in the house. You need to get out, and I need your help. Barnes Construction is a *family* business." His eyes blazed, his nostrils flared. He stepped outside, twirled on his heel, and shouted at the clear night sky, "Why doesn't anyone understand that? Doesn't anybody care?"

His wife. His son. That's who he meant. The ones he loved the most. My man was in pain, and only a harder heart than mine could have refused his request. I couldn't. So, once more, I tried to brace myself for the onslaught of customers, staff, blueprints, site visits, and decisions. Jack laughed at me but didn't sound too joyful.

"If we had an 'onslaught' of customers, I wouldn't be worried about our company. You can't have it both ways."

My husband is such a people-person—a term I've grown to hate—he can't conceive of how hard I find making myself smile and acting friendly *all day long*. It's exhausting. And I've had no energy since we lost Kayla.

My second *Day One* would begin tomorrow. Jack had tried to be encouraging. He knew I was nervous again and after dinner led me into the family room, turned on the radio, and opened his arms. I'd always loved dancing with him. Fast. Slow. The beat didn't matter. Tonight we heard the sounds of soul.

"Pretend you've been a stay-at-home mom," he said as Gladys Knight sent us on the *Midnight Train to Georgia.* "And pretend you're re-entering the job market after fifteen or twenty years. Lots of women face that sooner or later."

"Pretend? But that's exactly the way I do feel, and it's damn scary," I replied. "How about continuing my two days a week at the office like I did before...before Kayla died, and I'll work from home as well? I really think that would be better." I wasn't finished bargaining yet and flashed him the smile he adored.

I received a big kiss and a chuckle in return.

"I love you so much, Claire, and I need you. The business needs you. You can do the work. We'll take it slower this time."

"We certainly will," I said, "because I have a plan."

His blue eyes twinkled. "Let's hear it," he said immediately.

Gladys was still singing about her man leaving L.A., and I kept dancing with mine.

"Baby steps," I said. "Little by little, I'll get it done. I'll go to the new subdivisions and walk the houses by myself. I want time alone in the office to study the blueprints. And if we're upgrading our options, I need to call our suppliers and visit their showrooms. But I need to do it at my own pace, or...or..." I tilted my head back. "Or I'll get overwhelmed, and it just won't work at all. And I also might take on a helper—your favorite mother-in-law."

His sigh of relief should have been audible to our neighbors.

"But there's one thing I cannot promise, Jack." He leaned back in order to see me clearly.

"I can't promise not to cry."

His arms tightened around me, and I felt him kiss the top of my head. "Neither can I. Does that surprise you? And I also can't stop my stomach from burning. At the rate I'm going, I'll be popping these pills for the rest of my life."

"I'm so sorry about...everything." *I'll be sorry forever.*

"Me too. I miss her so much."

Choking up, I couldn't speak so just nodded.

"But Claire?"

"Hmm?"

"You've got nothing to blame yourself for. Being late is not a crime. Please...please, honey, don't do it anymore."

Oh, I wished it were as straightforward as that. I deserved Jack's hatred, not his understanding. Except Jack didn't know the whole truth, and I could never tell him how I flirted with Colombo, how I basked in his praise and responded to the gleam in his eye with one of my own. Now *my* stomach started to burn.

#

I took a deep breath when we pulled up to Barnes Construction in the morning. I also took a moment to appreciate my former second home. It was a stone and glass building, which now struck me as darn impressive. Ignoring it for almost a year prompted me to view it with new eyes.

"People might think we're awfully wealthy when they see all this," I murmured, gesturing at the building, pointing out the professional landscaping. "I guess looks can be deceiving."

"If you're suggesting we relocate the company to some small shack..."

"No, no, nothing like that," I replied quickly. "That would be a public announcement and run off our vendors and potential buyers alike." Shivering, I patted Jack's hand. "If anyone can turn the numbers around, you can."

With my smile firmly in place, I waved at everyone I saw. No more hysterics. No more outbursts. I was determined to stick to my plan. By the end of the first week, the design center had become my new daytime refuge, a comfortable hidey-hole. Maybe I was simply trading my studio at home for my assigned space at the company. Maybe the old nesting instinct had kicked in. Or maybe my basic survival instinct had taken over. I smiled, I made calls, I began putting together some lovely rooms. At least, that's what Jack told me after he viewed them online, complements of the amazing software program I used.

Despite the positive feedback, however, my heart wasn't in it. I didn't care about the designs, furniture, or home buyers. My brain was functioning on automatic pilot, and I had no idea how I was pulling off being pleasant and upbeat. But my husband was cracking jokes and whistling as he walked the halls—my reward for all the effort. I owed him that much.

But I still couldn't control my sadness or tears. They flowed without warning while I added figures, examined fabric, or chatted with an employee. A release of tension, perhaps, or a reminder of the guilt hiding deep within me, in that place where truth resided. If anyone had suggested removing Kayla's photo from my desktop, however, I would have shot them. The way I figured it, had I still been at home or in the studio during the day instead of at night, I would have cried too.

On the second Monday, my mom joined me on a part-time basis. I heard her intake of breath when she saw her granddaughter's beautiful face. She said nothing, however, just squeezed my hand.

"We're some pair," she said, "but we'll get through this."

Whether she meant the workload or Kayla's death, I didn't know. But I had no choice about soldiering on. Living was my penance.

# CHAPTER EIGHT


*JACK*

*June, nine months after accident*

Proud parents crammed the high school auditorium by the time Claire and I arrived to watch Ian graduate. Some mothers dabbed their eyes, but Claire's tears ran like Houston's bayous after a storm.

Squeezing her hand, I said, "We raised a winner. A great kid. Good looks, good heart, good brain...he's got it all. That science award proves it."

"Yes. Yes, I'm proud of him...it's just..." Fresh tears began to stream down her cheeks, and my chest tightened. I understood what she didn't say. Kayla wasn't here. Kayla would never graduate from high school. My wife's mind was on her daughter, not her son, and I felt myself begin to teeter on that edge too. Claire thought I was stronger than steel, but I had to swallow hard a couple of times before I could speak.

"For God's sake, Claire, please focus on Ian today. This graduation is a milestone for him." I was lecturing myself as much as her.

"I know. I know. But—"

"But he should be going to college instead of to a dead-end job. Is that what's bothering you?" I knew that was only part of it, but sometimes I had to tap dance in place trying to distract her. "A *college* degree is the one we'd have celebrated with gusto. He's taking a little detour. That's all."

A detour. That's what I told myself. That's how I rationalized. First, we lost Kayla, and now we were failing Ian. Claire didn't seem to understand or care; if she did, she was hiding it well. If Ian wanted to postpone college right now, I could live with it. But this...this...job he'd landed at a refinery? It didn't sit right with me. I wanted my boy at home. I wanted him in the construction business, our *family* business.

I'd been trying to change his mind ever since he told me about this new job. A refinery! Those people in the career office should be fired. Couldn't they see Ian was college material? I'd talked myself hoarse and gotten nowhere with my son, so I'd put his two grandfathers on the case. In the end, however, they'd both sighed deeply, offering their own insights.

"His heart's as heavy as yours and Claire's," my dad said. "I guess our boy needs to do what he needs to do. At least for now."

"But he'll be back," added Claire's father. "He's a good boy."

I don't know when my "good boy" became so stubborn. Ian may have won this battle, but neither of us was winning this tug-of-war.

#

At home after the graduation ceremony, I stood in the backyard, grilling steak and burgers for a host of relatives. Despite the downturn in business, I could have treated everyone to a restaurant celebration, but I was trying to keep Claire busy and happy doing something she liked. Home entertaining used to be on the top of the list, especially with our combined families. Everyone always clamored for her summer salads, especially the five-bean and potato salads, and Claire always came through. Today was no different.

I watched her smile, circulate, and visit with everyone before she went indoors, and I felt myself grin. That was my wife! The real Claire. A glimpse of her laughing face through the window gave me hope. Sooner or later, we'd get back to normal.

I left my brother-in-law, Charlie, in charge of cooking, waltzed into the air-conditioned house, and made a beeline to my wife. "Love you, sweetheart."

She chuckled. Her eyes brightened. "I know."

"It's a great party." I glanced around. "You've done it again. The salads are disappearing. The hors d'oeuvres too...I just wish you'd eat more of them yourself." She'd used a safety pin in the waistband of her slacks today, and in a sleeveless blouse, her arms looked like sticks. Maybe a gym...

"I'll attack Judy's desserts later," she said, "but my specialties? I can prepare them in my sleep."

Claire's sister had been a rock, calling Claire every day. As for her mom...well, Barbara had become invaluable to both Claire and me. "How about another specialty?" I asked.

Her cheeks became rosy. "I thought we had our evenings worked out to perfection."

I almost blushed myself. Most folks would envy our love life; they'd think it was unbelievable. I'd thought so too—in the beginning, until doubts began to shadow me.

Claire continued to be so intense, so frantic about it. I don't remember her being this gung-ho during our first years together. Our nighttime pursuits, however, weren't top priority at the moment.

"I wanted to thank you, Claire, not only for making Ian's party so terrific but for coming back to work. I know it hasn't been easy, even with your mother to help. But your presence is making me hopeful about our bottom line next quarter. So thank you very much." And if I were sugarcoating her importance or the swift turnaround, so what?

And dang if tears didn't well again. She put her finger over my mouth and shook her head. "You're the brains behind the operation, so don't thank me. It's the least I can do for you."

The least she could...? Like she owed me something? Good Lord, my wife was still blaming herself about Kayla. Trying to expunge her guilt. At this point, I had no answers for her. How many times could I tell her she wasn't to blame? I supposed there was no easy fix, and I was certainly no shrink, but maybe she needed one.

Scanning the room, I saw Ian chatting with Claire's folks, Maddy Conroy standing right next to him. Seemed my son had picked up a little sidekick. According to Claire, the child still came around to make art almost every week. The spare key now had a permanent home under the studio's doormat. But my attention reverted to Ian.

"Look how our son hits the right notes with our folks."

"Why are you so surprised? He's their first grandchild, and they adore him." But now another shadow appeared on my wife's face. "I'm glad he's enjoying himself. But...Jack?" Her voice became a whisper.

"Yes?"

"What's the real reason he's moving out? I mean, why isn't he working with us at Barnes Construction?"

She'd touched an already frazzled nerve, but more worrisome were her bizarre questions. "Honey, you were with me when he told us about his new job. You heard me ask him about it since then. Don't you remember?"

"I think...I really think it's my fault he's leaving. I'm a bad mother...such a bad mother." She began walking toward the bedroom wing, away from our guests, and I grabbed her arm.

"Buck up, Claire. No running. You've got people here, a party going on. And by the way, you're normally a great mother."

A kaleidoscope of scenes ran through my mind. Claire pushing a baby carriage, Claire playing catch with Ian and then with Kayla, Claire and the kids working in her studio—a fun project we worked on together. Claire loved being a mom.

And I thought I was a pretty good dad. Always imagined Ian and I had a special relationship, that he trusted me. Now I wasn't sure. He had a home. No one was pushing him out the door.

"I want him to be happy," Claire said. "I told him so. You know I told him." She paced two steps back and forth, her hands fluttering. "But his bags are packed to the brim. He's ready to head out, maybe even tonight."

Too many memories accosted me, too many emotions. Ian was leaving us. He was really doing it. And my wife? I couldn't understand her strange questions and thoughts. A heavy ache lay in my heart, almost as heavy and familiar as the one from last September. I was the one who wanted to be alone now. I popped an antacid instead, left Claire, and approached my son.

#

"Hey, champ," I said, putting my arm around him but facing Maddy. "Can I steal him for a minute?"

She grinned and disappeared. But Ian's brow lifted; suspicion darkened his chip-off-the-block blue eyes. He glanced at his doting grandparents, and instantly his natural smile and accompanying dimple were in place. "No more homework lectures, Dad. School is definitely over."

Everyone chuckled, including me. Ian had never needed lectures about schoolwork. His report cards had reflected his fine abilities...at least until this year. Other than saying "do the best you can" a few months ago, I avoided berating him on his falling grades. However, I wouldn't avoid another attempt to change his mind about leaving.

"Take a walk with me, Ian. Let's have a man-to-man conversation."

He paused then continued with me down the hall, away from the crowd. "I don't want to talk, Dad. Please, just leave me alone. You and I? We're good. But I've got to be on my own now. I've got to get out of here."

"That's what I don't understand. We're all sad, we're all grieving. Each of us in our own way. There are no rules about it. You're free to cry, yell, curse." I took a breath. "Ian, Ian...don't you think families should stick together in a crisis?"

He stared at me but remained silent. At least he was listening.

"Work with me at the company until you're ready to go to school again. It'll be like the last three summers, but better. Better pay for you," I joked, "and more responsibility. The refinery can survive without you. Barnes Construction can't—not in the long run. It's your future too, a future I thought you wanted."

Tears glistened in my son's eyes. "I-I do. Someday. But not now. I-I need my own space. I'm sorry, Dad, but I have to work this out for myself."

I pictured him driving away in the morning, and my gut twisted in the kind of pain an antacid couldn't touch.

# CHAPTER NINE

*CLAIRE*

I heard Ian stirring early Sunday morning, the day after his graduation party, anxious to be on his way. Anxious to be rid of us.

Sure enough, when I reached the kitchen, he was wheeling one of his bags through the door. I stepped outside and watched as he hoisted it into his new truck. New to him, that is. A six-year-old genuine beater with almost a hundred thousand miles and two previous owners. He hadn't asked our advice; in fact, he drove it home after making the purchase. Jack immediately brought it to our mechanic for an in-depth engine check. Of course, it needed fixing with a new water pump, a new alternator, and God knows what else. And of course, it would have been smarter and less expensive to buy a better vehicle in the first place. Ian paid for the repairs, wouldn't take a penny from us. I guessed he used up almost all his savings between the car and his new apartment. I let Jack handle the situation and kept mum.

My son was avoiding me, couldn't even look at me. I'd apologized for lashing out at him, so now he was free to blame me for Kayla's death. And he did. He never said the words, but I understood. Because of me, he had to live with the memory of watching his sister get mowed down by an SUV. He hated me. I hated me too.

None of it mattered now. Kayla was gone. Ian was leaving. He and Jack just hauled two more cartons to the truck and returned inside.

"Hey, Mom. I'm heading out. Thanks for the kitchen stuff. Oh, I also left something for Maddy in my room. Could you give it to her?"

"Sure." Anything. I wasn't even curious.

He leaned over, air-kissed my cheek, and I grabbed him.

Fear's metallic flavor edged my tongue, slowly consuming me. My breaths became shallow. I squeezed Ian as tightly as I could, and he froze in place, his limbs and muscles quiet except for his heart, which pounded under my ear. *My son, my son!* Pain joined fear, stabbing and pulsing in my head to a salsa beat. I released Ian and pressed my temples, trying to stave it off.

"Don't go, Ian. Don't leave. You're our child too. We love you."

He turned toward his father. "I gotta get outta here."

"Wait, wait," I said, latching onto a different tack. "Did the landlord clean your place? Shampoo the carpets? Exterminate?" Jack had seen the apartment. He'd come home shaking his head. "It can't be ready yet."

"I'm doing most of the work myself and getting a month's free rent."

Jack said, "By the time he's finished, the place will be in better shape than when it was new. He's replacing windowsills."

Which probably meant termite damage. Roaches. A wave of nausea had me running to the sink. "Please, Ian...."

"Sorry, Mom. Feel better. I have to go. Talk to you soon."

The door closed behind him. Silence filled the kitchen, and my husband popped another antacid. I wanted to crawl into bed and hide under the covers, but Jack looked so sad, so lost, I needed to do something nice for him, something he'd appreciate. Inhaling deeply a few times, I got the nausea under control then said, "Come on. Let's go to bed. A little hands-on therapy should help."

But he didn't answer. No laugh. No happy face.

"Jack, did you hear me?"

"I just lost my son!" he shouted, and I lost my breath. "I don't care about bedroom antics right now!" His fists hit the table; his face took on a purple hue. "How the hell did this happen? How the hell did we go from a noisy, kid-filled house to a tomb? How did we go from two children to zero? I talked myself hoarse with Ian, don't know what else I could have said or offered. What else could I have done?"

I stroked his shoulder. "You did everything right. His leaving home is not about you. It's about me...and Kayla."

"Oh, please. That's such bull. You weren't even home at the time."

And that was the crux of the matter between us. My husband didn't give credence to the horrible jokes life could play. It was Sarah Levine, not Claire Barnes, who drove the car that hit Kayla. End of story. He totally ignored my lateness getting home.

"Do you think Ian might be happier if we moved?" The words formed slowly as the idea came to me. "Maybe he relives the accident every time he turns down our street."

Jack rolled back on his heels, his complexion returning to normal, his forehead creased in thought. "What has that got to do with him 'having to earn his own way?' But...do you think that's a possibility?"

I shrugged. "You can ask him." But dear God, what if it were true? Or even partly true? What if our home really did haunt Ian? My off-the-cuff distraction for Jack might boomerang on me. I didn't want to uproot. I didn't want to leave my memories of Kayla in this house, helping me in the kitchen, running through the halls, bent over her desk doing homework.

In her bedroom, I could still inhale her fragrance as I placed her stuffed teddy bear on the pillow. Grandma Pearl had crocheted the doll, and Kayla had cuddled with it every night even at the great age of twelve-and-a-half. In my mind's eye, I could see her applying nail polish to her toes and fingers in the bathroom. Part jock with her soccer team, part woman-in-training. Discovering the differences between girls and boys. Trusting me! Trusting me to share the secrets, a woman's secrets.

Jack stood close now, but his shoulders slumped, and his mouth was bracketed with familiar lines of pain. "I think we're driving ourselves crazy with guessing games. We've got to stop it. We've got to put it behind us."

*Like forget we had a daughter?* I thought about my recent visits to the cemetery where I chatted with Kayla. Oh, no. I'd never forget. My head started its salsa dance again, and I rummaged for some aspirin as Jack continued to speak.

"Folks who know about these things say the first year is the toughest. I think they're right."

"Maybe." But in my heart, I didn't believe it. I couldn't imagine our lives any other way—first year, second year, third year. Would I love Kayla any less as time passed? God forbid. I could put up a good front with other people for awhile. I'd already done that a few times.

Heck, I'd been doing it every day at work in between crying jags. But genuine laughter was for others. As for me, I wanted my daughter...I *yearned* for my daughter and always would. I felt tears form but managed to thwart them. I had to try—for Jack's sake.

"Hmm... Are you finished lecturing and yelling?" Forcing a smile wasn't easy, but he needed to see one.

"I guess...for now." His brow rose and he grinned. "Scared ya, huh?"

"I'm shaking." At that moment, our glances locked, and I started to laugh. Almost giggled. The sound shocked me.

Jack stared, eyes wide open. Seemed I'd shocked him too. "Wow! What was that strange music?"

"Don't know what you're talking about." I looked aside.

"Sure you do." He caressed my cheek and added, "I'd call it the sound of...of hope."

Naturally, he would, the optimist. His eagerness to believe in something good—to see the best—defined my husband. I couldn't match his attitude, so responded in the only way I knew how.

"Come on." I dragged him to the bedroom, and this time, he followed. I stripped him down to the skin. He took over from there, until I took the lead again. We were living in the moment, a timeframe I could manage.

In the end, we were a collapsed tangle of arms and legs as we gasped for breath. But for those few minutes, pain had given way to pleasure right down to my toes, as I knew it would. Lovemaking allowed me to escape reality, recharge, and face the next day.

There would always be a next day—lots and lots of them—for however long I lived. And somehow, I'd have to get through each one of them.

#

"I should have waited to clean his room," I wailed, staring at Ian's gift to Maddy.

Propped on his pillow stood a hand-drawn graphic he'd called Girl Power. I wasn't ready for it. Wasn't ready to see Kayla and Maddy in their fantastical uniforms— including capes— guarding Heaven and Earth. Bold red and yellow for Maddy, perfect with her dark hair; bright green and yellow for Kayla, enriching her auburn shade. The girls flew, fingers almost touching. And surrounding them, scattered everywhere, were stars, flowers, balloons, kites, and the faces of children.

"Wow!" Jack stared in disbelief. "I knew he could draw, but...but this is terrific."

An understatement. But I, of course, couldn't take my eyes from Kayla's image. Swallowing hard, I brushed my fingers across her face. "Miss you, sweetheart, I love you so much. I'm so sorry."

Jack twirled toward me. "This isn't about Kayla or you," he said. "It's about Maddy. Can't you figure out what Ian's done?"

"Maddy'll take one look and start crying," I replied.

"No, no. This is a happy picture. Ian's giving her a message. Girl Power. Maddy has the power to do anything, including getting on with her own life. Naturally, her friendship with Kayla is part of her, but I think this picture will take the edge off her sadness. It'll give her permission to be happy again."

Peering at my husband, I said, "You have a habit of seeing only what you want to see. Only the bright side. I bet this picture can be interpreted a hundred different ways."

He started to speak, but I patted his hand. "This time, Jack, I hope you're right."

Not only for Maddy's sake but for mine. I couldn't bear adding the death of a child's spirit to my list of transgressions.

# CHAPTER TEN



*JACK*

*Sunday, one year after accident*

*September again.* A year could seem like forever, at least to me. Today the entire family was gathering at the cemetery for a memorial service and then lunching at our favorite Tex-Mex place. This commemoration was Claire's idea, and I went along with it. So now, I was dressed up in a black suit and tie—also Claire's idea—but the damn tie's choking me. Why in hell did I need a tie? Kayla wouldn't care. Before I could rip it off my neck, however, Claire was in front of me loosening it. One whiff of her familiar light fragrance and I pulled her close, realizing once again how waif-like she'd become.

"Look in the mirror, Claire. I'm glad we're going to Casa Olé later. You need those calories!" She was beyond slender now, heading toward skinny. Her cheekbones—both sets!—were sharp. When she sat on my lap, her bottom dug into my thighs.

"Oh, don't start that again. I eat all the time, just in little bits. Didn't you like the shrimp and veggies I made yesterday?"

"Loved them. But I wish you'd eat more."

"Trust me, Jack. I'm tasting while I cook. That's how I know I'm good."

She forced a smile, and I had to admit she was trying. Even at work, she and Barbara had become a team, and the design center was finally operating smoothly. She also went into her studio most evenings, leaving me in the house with the TV. I'd respect her choice more if she didn't fall into bed exhausted, but I wouldn't call her on it. Painting kept her busy, gave her less time to brood.

I kissed her and wanted to cry. Her blond hair was half gray again. She'd never gone back to her salon after the first visit. I'd see if Judy could book another appointment. Or I would. I'd insist. Claire was the artist. She knew the color wasn't flattering, and neither was the way she's pulled her hair into a rubber band.

What was she doing to herself? She brushed away my concerns as though they meant nothing. Clair was still beautiful in my eyes, but her indifference frightened me, and I was afraid to press her with more questions.

Sometimes I didn't think she was any further along than she was in the beginning. Maybe this one-year anniversary would be a new starting point. Maybe her grief would ease. Maybe mine would too. Maybe, maybe, maybe.

"Time to leave, honey," I said after glancing at my watch. "It's almost nine. Ian should be here any minute." I headed toward the kitchen just as the doorbell rang. Claire lagged a few steps behind me.

A moment later, I hugged my son and didn't want to let go. "Right on time, buddy. But you don't have to ring the bell. Use your key. This is still your home."

He shrugged. "So...how's it going? How's...Mom?" His voice cracked on the last syllable. He must not have noticed Claire yet. I stepped aside. "Ask her yourself."

Ian hadn't seen his mother all summer, not since he'd moved out. I'd met him for dinner a couple of times, but Claire had had five o'clock customer appointments on those days. She'd only spoken with him on the phone. But now, her eyes lit up when she saw her son.

"Your job must agree with you," she said before kissing his cheek. "You've filled out a bit. Looking good."

"Th-thanks."

He stared at his mother, and I could read his shock and concern before he shut down. "I brought flowers," he finally said. "They're in the truck. I'll get them." He dashed outside, and I followed him.

He was leaning against the beater, arms raised on the door frame, body shaking.

"Ian! What's the matter?"

He whirled toward me, tears evident. "Why didn't you tell me she was sick? Is she dying too?"

"No, no! Of course not. She's not dying. She just has a hard time enjoying food. Depression can do that. Besides, she's working hard at the company. Now that I think of it, I bet she forgets to eat. I'll tell Grandma to carve out a lunch hour."

"Good. Make her eat."

My son was scared, still just a kid in a world turned upside down, still needing both his parents. But now he was pretending to be a man, independent, beyond needing a mother or father. Of course, all swaggering eighteen-year-old boys pretended to be men. I went through the same rite-of-passage but didn't have to prove myself while mourning a sibling.

"She'll be okay, Ian. This depression won't last forever."

"Yes, it will. Kayla is forever. The accident is forever. Mom will never get over it."

Was he right? He spoke with such conviction that I remained quiet for a moment, gathering my thoughts. "I'm told the shock will recede. Grieving is a process we're all going through, including you. Aunt Judy once mentioned the idea of a support group. I've been thinking about joining one. Want to try it?"

Claire had dismissed the idea. She wasn't sharing her heartache with strangers. However, that didn't mean Ian would feel the same way. But he was shaking his head before I'd finished the question.

"No time. I can't get away too much. New job and all...."

Did the kid think I had time to spare? "And we want to hear everything." I dropped the painful subject and glanced at my watch again. "Damn, we've got to leave now or we'll be late."

As it turned out, we arrived at the cemetery before the others—I think. Although no one else appeared to be in the vicinity of Kayla's final resting place, a lovely wreath leaned against the headstone.

"Could your folks have come and gone already?" I asked Claire, pointing to the remembrance. My in-laws were strong people, all things considered, but perhaps they wanted to mark the occasion privately.

"They're pulling up now. And your parents are right behind them." She shrugged. "Maybe a friend stopped by. People visit here all the time. Some even bring their lunch and a book to read. It's a beautiful place, the green lawn easy on the eyes, restful and quiet. I've become a regular lately, and I'm rarely alone."

A regular? She'd never mentioned her visits to me, and I was too stunned to comment. Not in a million years would I have chosen to picnic in a graveyard.

As Claire and I turned to greet the family, Ian walked the other way with his flowers and laid them next to the wreath. He needn't have bothered. If I knew my wife, she'd be rearranging everyone's offerings until the ensemble was as beautiful a design as she could make it. Kayla deserved, and would receive, only her mom's best efforts.

My jaw tightened as I considered her search for perfection. What about Ian? What about me? We needed her best efforts too, now more than ever.

# CHAPTER ELEVEN

*IAN*

After I laid my flowers next to the wreath, I spotted the card attached to it and read: *I'll never forget what happened that day. You're in my prayers morning and evening. Rest in peace.*

No signature, but I knew who wrote it. Call it gut instinct. Call it intuition. But a clear image of Sarah, the driver, formed in my head. I tore the card off and stuck it in my pocket. I hadn't thought too much about the woman behind the wheel since a couple of weeks after the accident. I didn't want to think about her now. I didn't like thinking about that day at all. Especially the part when my mother yelled, *Ian, how could you have let this happen?* right before she jumped into the ambulance, just before the EMT slammed the door closed. Leaving me alone on the street.

Shit! I didn't need this. I didn't even want to be here. I wanted to get back to my new life. My new job. New people. Friendly, upbeat people like Colleen Murphy.

Pretty Colleen Murphy. It blew my mind how a distance of only fifty miles turned out to be a totally new world, a new future for me, uncluttered by family problems.

"Ian, Ian. It's so good to see you."

Grandma Barbara. Hugs and kisses followed her greeting, then Grandma Pearl had to join in. I towered over them both, but somehow they managed to get lipstick on my face. I felt their arms tighten around me and, unexpectedly, I didn't want to let go. A wave of comfort, of familiarity. A wave of love sucked me in, and I kissed them back.

"You should come around more often, sweetheart," said Grandma Pearl. "We miss you so much, and we don't even have your new phone number!"

"I can fix that," I said. "Got any paper?"

Of course they did because ladies' purses always contained a warehouse worth of stuff. I wrote down the number on two sheets, and my grandmas clasped them as though they were college diplomas with *summa cum laude* designations.

"Give me another copy for Aunt Judy," said Grandma Barbara, gesturing toward my mom's sister. "You'll be hearing from her after today. The phone's attached to her ear."

I grinned and scribbled. Then my mom walked over to us.

"Do you know who brought the wreath?" she asked, pointing to the floral assortment. "It must have been dropped off yesterday. I'd like to acknowledge it."

"Sorry. No clue." Instinct wasn't the same as a real clue, so I hadn't lied.

Mom shrugged. "Oh, well.... Come with me, Ian. The minister is going to start speaking. Let's stand with Dad as a family so Kayla will know we're fine." Was she kidding? "Mom? Are you really fine? You don't look so great. I almost didn't recognize you this morning. Kayla wouldn't either."

She shrugged and gazed over my shoulder. "You know I've been busy. Working, painting. I'm on the go all day, just like Daddy wanted. Now, please, let's stand together. For Kayla's sake."

*But not for mine.* My mother still blamed me for the accident. She parroted what she thought a mom ought to say, but I knew her true feelings. I was irresponsible and immature. Now, she couldn't even look me in the eye. I wanted to remind her about the hundred other times Kayla and I tossed a football in the front yard without a problem, but it wouldn't make a difference. It wouldn't bring Kayla back.

So maybe she was right. I may not have wanted to babysit, but I had been in charge that day. The accident happened on *my* watch. Now Mom wanted to pretend we were still a close family so Kayla wouldn't know the truth. Didn't she understand that her daughter wasn't here anymore?

I'd already said enough, however, and kept my mouth shut as I stood between my folks for the intimate service. I accommodated my mother, but not for Kayla's sake. It was for Grandma Barbara and Grandpa Mike, Grandma Pearl and Grandpa Dave, standing behind us, who loved my sister and me to infinity and back no matter what. Why should I heap more pain on my grandparents? My sister wouldn't like that. Wouldn't want that.

Kayla may not have walked the earth anymore, but if heaven existed, she was there now, and I knew she was smiling at me and nodding her head.

I bowed my own.

#

*Sunday night*

I was wiped out after dealing with my family at Kayla's memorial service. Trying to make the four grandparents laugh, support my dad, and be nice to my mom was more exhausting than playing a forty-eight-minute varsity basketball game. Living on my own was the best—the only—decision I could have made.

I returned to my improved but still sorry-looking apartment with a sense of relief and bags full of leftovers, each packed and labeled in a plastic container. My mother made sure of that. She never wasted leftovers, whether from a restaurant or her own kitchen. Danny used to say both our moms were afflicted with the "just in case" syndrome. Just in case an army invaded, they'd be ready to feed 'em. The overstocked Goldberg kitchen was a great alternative to ours. Last year, it was the only alternative.

Now Dan was a freshman at the University of Texas in Austin, and I was a pipefitter at Gulf Coast Oil. He was a happy Longhorn. I was a happy apprentice, thanks to acing the job interview, which wasn't too difficult with my Honors Chemistry, math, and plumbing background. It was all working out—not that I could have predicted it.

On my first day at the plant in the middle of June, I was chewing my lip. No nerves of steel then. I wasn't sure what I was doing or why I was there. I kept picturing my dad and wondering if I'd betrayed him. But that was three months ago, and I didn't worry about it anymore. Especially not since meeting Colleen.

Opening the fridge, I shoved the food inside, glad suppers would be taken care of for a couple of days, then powered up my computer. Emails first. Maybe Colleen had posted. We'd become pretty friendly, but I'd sure like to change that to very friendly.

I spotted her name right away. She'd logged on in the morning after I'd left the apartment.

*A group of us are going to the lake. Wanna come?*

I didn't know who the group was, but I would have joined them in a nanosecond just to be with Colleen—if today hadn't been Kayla's memorial service.

*Hi Colleen, Sorry to miss it, but thanks for asking. I had family stuff. How about next week? And I'll see you tomorrow.*

I couldn't wait for morning. Couldn't believe that three months ago, I'd walked into the Isomerization Unit wondering how I went from being the boss's son in a family business to a tiny cog in the huge wheel called Gulf Coast Oil. I was one of hundreds working to refine petroleum. As I'd looked at my new surroundings, all the changes I'd made in my life began to hit me. They'd been my choices, but now I was tense, feeling out of place. Then I'd seen Colleen Murphy, the unit clerk.

I'd taken one look at Colleen on that first day and tripped over my tongue, couldn't even produce a "good morning." She was so pretty, with bouncy reddish-brown hair like cinnamon, bright green eyes, and a friendly smile. She said hello as if she were really glad to see me. The truth? I was glad to see her. I was a stranger in a strange land, and I needed a friend. When Colleen said hello, my tension disappeared.

Next email, Danny.

*How bad was today? Sorry not to be there. How's the new girlfriend?*

Danny lived three hours away. No car freshman year, and I hadn't expected him to come home for the memorial. But I liked him thinking about me. Not everything had changed.

My reply: *I survived thanks to my grandparents. My mom's the same. As to the "girlfriend"—don't I wish!*

Nothing got Colleen down, and I loved that attitude. A year ago, she and her family left a hardscrabble life in east Texas and moved some ten miles from the plant. She drove an old Chevy in worse shape than my truck. Colleen knew troubles up close and personal but somehow didn't let them bother her. She had her goals too. And shared them that first week.

"C'mon, city boy. You're in for a surprise. Wednesday is open-mic night at the Roadhouse Café. And I'm taking you."

"Hey, slow down," I said. "I'm all for learning new things and meeting new people, but I can't carry a tune. I'm no singer."

She grinned up at me. "But I am."

By six o'clock, the place was crowded. We ordered a burger and fries first. I had a draft; she sipped water. By seven o'clock, you couldn't find a seat. When Colleen got ready to sing, I gave up the table and stood near the small stage, watching her reach for the microphone and smile at the crowd.

She hadn't been kidding. With her first note, I knew she was special. With her second, I was mesmerized. A moment more and she held the entire room under her spell. Somehow, her voice combined the emotion and clarity of Patsy Cline, my Grandma Pearl's favorite, with the contemporary feel of Carrie Underwood. I didn't recognize the song, "The Journey."

"A new one," whispered the guy next to me. "Colleen's been writin' again."

Then what the hell was she doing working in a refinery? It didn't take me any time at all to answer my own question: money. Like me, she'd just gotten out of high school, but I'd guess her pockets were emptier than mine. I'd been paid fairly for three summers and all holidays with my dad. I couldn't imagine Colleen earning the same.

She segued into a Taylor Swift number but changed it up a little. When she finished, my hands became sore from clapping, and my shout-outs and whistles split the air.

Colleen waved at the crowd and rejoined me, her eyes sparkling like emeralds. "Surprised?"

"Pole-axed! You are more than good. You're great." Impulsively, I hugged her.

"Thanks." She took my hand and looked at the next singer to take the stage. "One of these days," she said, "I'm gonna get to Nashville. One of these days..."

I believed her then, and I still did now.

After my tough day at the cemetery, I hit the sack, thinking about Colleen on stage with her knockout body and genuine smile. Since meeting her, I'd spent every Wednesday and Saturday evening at the Roadhouse Café with her and some new friends, and I'd gotten to know Colleen's smiles. Their warmth calmed me now, and I slept.

Reality surged with a bucket of ice water the next morning at work. Colleen showed up in huge dark glasses that couldn't hide the swollen cheek, the purple bruises.

"Wha...?"

She turned away before I could finish. "I'm too old to make up tall tales about walking into a door or falling down the stairs. Daddy got into one of his drunks last night. As mean as a wolverine, he was. There's no dealing with him when he's like that." Still avoiding my eyes, she added, "Go start your day, city boy, and don't forget to clock in."

But I couldn't focus on anything except her puffy face. I imagined big fists battering her and felt steam rising under my skin, my own hands clenched at my sides. I'd never met her old man, but if he'd been there, I would have busted his head open and worried about assault charges later.

"You can't go back home," I said.

She twirled to me. "What are you sayin'? I'm not spending one red cent on a motel. Besides, he'll sleep it off all day. I'll be fine tonight."

"What about tomorrow? And next week? It's no way to live, Colleen, not for anyone, but especially not for you." My thoughts were twirling faster than Colleen had just done, and my mouth began working overtime too. "You could stay at my place if you want. It's only one step better than a dump, but at least it's sort of clean, and you'd be safe. I'd take the old couch in the living room; you can have the bedroom."

She didn't seem to hear me. "What did you mean, *especially* not for me?"

Other employees were clocking in, chattering, milling about. Not a great time or place for this conversation, but what choice did I have? I stepped closer to her and squeezed her hand.

"I think you're great, Colleen. Special. You deserve a whole lot better than being black-and-blue. I-I never saw a woman with a beat up face before. I promise you'd be safe living at my place."

I meant every word, and she must have believed me because, with a quick nod, she said, "Thanks, Ian. I'll...I'll think about it."

On Tuesday, she drove to the refinery with a suitcase in her trunk and cartons on the back seat. Seemed I'd gotten myself a roommate. That's exactly what I told my dad when he called me that afternoon wanting to meet me for dinner. I had to turn him down and could tell he was real disappointed.

"Next week," I said. "Promise."

"Why did you take on a roommate? If you're short on cash, I can—"

Love that man. "Thanks for the offer, Dad, but I can pay the rent. No problem. Just helping someone out. A friend from work who needs a place to live."

"Well, he's lucky to have you in his corner."

I didn't correct his impression about my friend's gender. Didn't want him to read too much into it or get a hundred phone calls checking up on my "girlfriend." Especially when I didn't know how long Colleen would stay with me. But two weeks later, Colleen and I were living together in every sense of the word.

# CHAPTER TWELVE



*CLAIRE*

I took Monday and Tuesday off from work. I needed some alone time after Kayla's memorial, time to hold her close and understand that an entire year had gone by. I wanted privacy in order to browse the family photo albums at my own pace and work on art projects during daylight hours. Jack wasn't too happy about me being gone from the office and not because I'd fall behind with customers. I was challenging his notion that being busy was the best defense against crying.

I'd held my ground, however, and joined him for a quick breakfast while still in my pajamas and robe.

"You'd better not spend the day like that," he said, a line creasing his forehead. "Don't go back to bed."

"I won't." But I was tempted. The man knew me well. "I don't usually wear bed clothes in the studio."

"You're sure about that?"

"You'll have to trust me." *No, he shouldn't. I cost him his daughter. My daughter.*

Those blue eyes of his stared at me without wavering. "I trust you to try." Then his lips covered mine with a hunger that spoke more of concern than passion. As he left the kitchen, he turned in the doorway. "Why don't you get your hair done? That should pick up your spirits."

He must have read my "are you crazy" expression correctly. "Okay, okay," he added, "it would pick up *my* spirits."

"You'll be disappointed. The shop's closed on Mondays."

He shrugged. "Well, there's always tomorrow. I'll call you later." The door slammed behind him, leaving me with the quiet I'd wanted, the solitude I craved to peruse our photos. Jack would have told me to put the albums away.

First, I poured myself another cup of coffee and reached for the pile of untouched newspapers. Okay, so maybe I also needed a delaying tactic to psych myself up. I grabbed the Sunday edition, and by habit, I started with the Home and Garden section. The *For Sale* listings were interspersed with half-page ads by developers and builders. I nodded with satisfaction when I saw Barnes Construction represented in the various subdivisions with a couple of models pictured. Jack was being aggressive with his "it takes money to make money" approach.

Fifteen minutes later, as I was ready to fold the Community News section, my eye caught a display ad labeled *Volunteers Wanted.* Like I had time to volunteer for anything? But there it was, a listing for West Side Hospital:

*Pediatrics Department is looking for volunteers to visit young patients during the day. Play games, read stories, draw pictures. Weekly commitment. Call...*

West Side Hospital. Kayla's hospital. My heart pounded, and my breath caught in my throat as I tasted the idea. I could do it. I could help the kids. Hadn't I helped Maddy? Kayla had never left the ICU, so the pediatric floor wouldn't bring back memories. I paced and wrung my hands, my thoughts crashing into one another. Jack's reaction. My mom's and sister's too. The time element. But in the end, I thought Kayla would approve. Definitely. My daughter had a big heart. She'd hate knowing that sick children were alone all day lying in a hospital bed while their parents couldn't be with them. For Kayla. I'd do this for Kayla.

With shaking hands, I picked up the phone and made an appointment with Mrs. Elena Garcia, the director of volunteers. I wouldn't mention it to Jack until after my interview.

The family pictures would wait. An hour later, I was in the studio, sculpting again. The clay soothed me. I hadn't really painted all year, but I wasn't worrying about it. In the meantime, dozens of Kayla statues were keeping me company.

#

After saying goodbye to Jack the next morning, I refilled my coffee cup, took a deep breath, and opened the door of a bottom cabinet. I reached for my handy stash of photo albums as stealthily as an alcoholic with a hidden stash of bottles. With Jack not around, I had no fear of getting caught and suffering one of his rants. I sat at the kitchen table and opened a page at random. There was Kayla. Seven years old, arms wide, face tilted up and alight with joy—running toward me. So alive! Alive and well. I remembered taking that shot. I remembered taking hundreds of shots.

Sipping from my mug, I turned pages and stared at Ian, Kayla, Jack, and myself during that year. I saw my mom and dad, then Judy and Charles with their boys.

Everyone happy, everyone busy. When I closed that book, I opened the next and the next until finally, I held the last album. I studied every picture until my eyes burned, until I reached the final shots. Kayla at twelve. She would always be twelve, an unfinished story, always a girl with secrets.

The painting! I hadn't thought about it since I'd left school, but now it called to me. I wanted it. I wanted my *Girl with Secrets* here, at home with me. Now where had I put Colombo's contact card? I riffled through my purse, my wallet...found it. And punched in his office number.

"Clara! Wonderful, wonderful. How good to hear from you. You have caught your breath, no? And now you will return. To study. To paint. To do what you are meant to do."

As ebullient as ever. But clueless. I could never study with him again. So why did I feel like crying?

"I'm sorry, Professor. But no, I'm not coming back. I just want to pick up my work. You remember...it's that portrait o-of my daughter." I'd started out strong, but now I could hear my voice tremble, matching the tremble in my body. "So, when should I stop by?"

Silence. Then, "Clara, think again. Come back to class. Your easel is waiting. I am waiting to see more of you and how your work develops."

"You don't know how it is...I'm sorry. I just can't. So, about the painting. When can—"

He cut me off. "Then I'm sorry, too, Clara. It isn't here. It was a beautiful portrait, and it now has a new home. I knew it would sell. Others see what I see on the canvas."

My brain froze. Fortunately my tongue still worked. "Wait, wait. Let me understand. You sold it? You sold *Girl with Secrets?* But I never said you could. It can't be legal. Get it back!"

"I'm afraid that's not possible. It's paid for. I left it showcased in the *galleria* and last week, gone! Thirty-eight hundred dollars. You're an unknown artist, Clara. A sale should make you proud. Your commission is being mailed from the college, all but ten percent."

I tasted vomit. "You had no right. I don't care about the money. The portrait was mine!"

"Was. Was. Was. In the past tense, no? So you will paint another. Future tense, yes?"

I wasn't born yesterday. The guy was a conniver, a manipulator. "If this is some kind of joke...a scheme to get me..."

"Thirty-eight hundred dollars is not a joke." Click.

He'd hung up. On me! The man had gall. Nerve. I wanted to kill him. Jack—I had to tell Jack. He'd been annoyed at me this morning, but so what? I called him and exploded into the phone.

"Want me to get our lawyer in on this?" he asked.

"Definitely. A lawyer will scare them into retrieving the picture."

"Not if it's been sold on the up-and-up. University policy or something. And not unless the buyer is willing to return it."

"And do you know what else that man said to me at the end?"

"What?"

"'Paint another one.' As if I could just whip up a piece. Whip up another portrait of...of Kayla."

I heard him breathing, felt him thinking.

"You and I finally agree on something," said Jack. "It's a lousy idea. Don't do it."

I disconnected and slowly replaced the phone in its cradle. The photo albums remained arrayed on the table, the last one still open to shots of Kayla. My fingers brushed across the pages with reverence.

*Accept it, Claire. Keep her in your heart and find peace.* But when I finally closed the back cover, my hand lingered. *No goodbyes! I couldn't let her go. Not yet, not yet.* I grasped the book tightly then abruptly opened it again, this time scanning every photo of Kayla with a critical eye. I pulled the best pictures from their sleeves.

*Why must Kayla's story end? Why must she always be twelve? The hell with Colombo! The hell with Jack....*

I grabbed a pen, a bunch of colored pencils, and reached for a pad of paper. I didn't pause, think, or worry. My body tingled at the possibilities. Colombo thought I had talent, so who better to capture my young daughter as she matured? Police artists did it all the time. I could bring Kayla to life—for the second time.

Sketches. Sketches came first.

*Kayla at fourteen:* pierced earrings, baby fat all gone and cheekbones visible, hair in ponytail and out of the way...still playing soccer...some breast development...

*At fifteen:* Was she still playing soccer? Yes. A French braid would work. I turned the page and continued drawing....

*At sixteen:* eyelids half closed...ah, my girl had big secrets again...and multiple piercings. Spiked hair. A rebel? Oh, please no tats.... Would she still confide in me? My chest hurt.

*At seventeen:* hair longer, more flattering. Her brown eyes dark, mysterious. Maybe a boyfriend?

One drawing followed another, each one building upon the last. I added details and saw Kayla emerge as the young woman she might have become. I arranged the pictures neatly on the table, one next to the other, each one visible. The big wall clock hummed in the background as the final portrait appeared:

*Kayla at eighteen.* The lopsided grin with the tiny dimple alongside it just like Grandpa Dave's. Straight nose. Hair a bit darker and shorter, cropped behind the ears... My pencil kept gliding, filling in, a line here, a shading there....

Finally, my arm dropped to my side, the pencil hitting the floor as I stared at the final portrait. Stared until my eyes ached.

Ian. It was Ian who looked back at me.

My son. My beautiful boy. A prickling sensation traveled through my body all the way to my fingertips, and with my heart racing, I picked up the phone.

#

Jack arrived home at his usual time. I was anxious about the sketch, anxious about the call to Ian. My nerves were stretched not because I wanted Jack's approval but because I didn't understand what was happening to me. Jack would know. He always sensed the inside of a person. Colombo said I had a heart that sees, but he was wrong about that. I noted the outside details most of the time.

Jack's broad smile needed no words of explanation when he first saw the drawing. "Exactly right! Ian could step right off that page."

"Thanks, but...but I thought I was going to draw Kayla, and out came Ian. A-a bad feeling came over me, which I know sounds dumb, but I called Ian immediately. Just to make sure he was all right."

"What did he say?" Jack spoke quietly, holding his body still, his eyes boring into me—through me—as he waited for my reply. He made me more nervous than I already was.

"Why are you looking at me like that?"

"Because a call to Ian is rare. How many times have you called him since Kayla died?"

*How many?* "Well, I don't know....Who keeps count of phone calls?" I quickly backtracked in my memory and came up with half a dozen at most. I went on the attack. "You seem to be the conduit to him. You always beat me to the punch."

"Is that what you tell yourself? That it's my fault?"

"What are you talking about, Jack? I don't tell myself anything."

Disappointment etched his face. Sorrow. "Maybe that's worse." He sighed. "So, you called Ian. And what happened?"

"I had to leave a message."

Jack checked the time. "I'm sure you'll hear from him soon, but it'll be a quick conversation. He's out a lot in the evenings. Wednesdays and Saturdays are booked, but I don't know about Tuesdays."

I'd had no idea. "Overtime? Or a class? No, not a class, not on Saturday. Oh! Is he seeing someone?"

"Hopefully a hundred someones. He's too young, not to say confused right now."

As though Jack had been psychic, the phone rang, and Ian's voice came through to me, an anxious voice.

"Mom? What's wrong? Did something happen to Dad?"

"No, no, honey. We're fine. We're both fine."

I heard a huge breath of air escape from the other end. "That's good. I got scared."

I thought about what Jack had said to me a moment ago. "But why?"

"Mom? Are you serious? You've called me maybe three times this whole year and always for a reason, like don't be late for Kayla's memorial service. What should I think?"

"Oh, Ian. I'm sorry about that. But you were on my mind today."

"Yeah? In a good way or a bad way?"

"For goodness sake! More questions? Of course in a good way. I sketched your portrait. Dad says he'd recognize you a mile away, that you could walk right off the page. Of course, it's only a sketch...well, with details. But I was looking through our family albums—Kayla and you and all of us—and I suddenly started to draw. It was so strange because at first I thought I was sketching Kayla, but out you came instead. It's my first portrait in a long time, in fact, since your sister died. You were my inspiration."

A moment of silence. "Glad I could help. Congratulations." Then he was gone.

I looked at Jack. "He disconnected. What did I say? What did I do?"

Jack took out his mobile and called Ian's number.

No answer.

#

*IAN*

I heard the cell ring from way across the living room on the floor where I'd thrown it. The damn thing hadn't broken. For some reason, that made me laugh. Families broke easier than phones these days.

I returned my mom's call while Colleen unpacked her stuff in the bedroom. She didn't see or hear anything. Not that it would really matter, not with her family dysfunctional in their own way. I guess I wasn't used to my family being such a mess, and I wanted some privacy.

My mother was losing it. Totally. Sure, I'd been on her mind. She still held me responsible for Kayla dying. No matter what she said otherwise. Her apologies sucked. She thought I was a murderer or a negligent homicider, if that's a word.

At first, I'd hoped she called just to chat. To catch up. If she was short on topics, I could have supplied some—

How about our Houston weather? How's work? Do you like your job? What about those Astros? How's your life? Or I could have brought up the forbidden topic myself. "Do you want to talk about that horrible day?"

I had to accept that my mom didn't care about anyone but Kayla. And maybe a little about Dad. But he was still swallowing those antacid pills all the time, so she couldn't really be supporting him. Their anniversary was coming up. I wondered if they'd celebrate. Wasn't betting on it.

# CHAPTER THIRTEEN

*CLAIRE*

An hour after Jack left for the office on Saturday morning, Judy rapped at my kitchen door and walked in unannounced. I was about to start the dishwasher but forgot to press the button when I saw her. My petite sister stood straight and tall, reminding me of a fire-breathing Viking. I cocked my head, confused.

"What are you doing here? I thought your boys had soccer practice on Saturdays."

"Charlie can take them. You come first with me today," she replied. "You need an intervention, and I'm the one to do it. Get dressed. We've got an appointment with Juanita in an hour."

I touched my hair, glanced out the back window toward my studio, then looked at Judy. "Sorry, I'm working. I-I started something new yesterday. In clay."

"That can wait," she said. "The clay's not going anywhere, but you are, and I'm not kidding." Hands on her hips, she glared at me, but I glimpsed her pained expression before she could hide it. "I swear to God," she said, "I'll pull you into the shower if I have to. Now, get going."

Judy was normally a thoughtful, gentle girl, my friend as well as kid sister. Seemed she'd had a personality shift. "What's gotten into you?"

"I'm not going to let you drown yourself, Claire. Jack's afraid you're going backwards. Ian worries too. And Mom. You see her a couple of times a week. Haven't you noticed that she's lost weight just like you?"

"Oh." I hadn't noticed.

"Yeah. Oh," she parroted.

"But...but... I go to the office. I do my job. I make Jack happy." But inside, I scared myself. I was afraid, afraid to tell them that sometimes my chest hurt so bad I could hardly speak. "Kayla...." My voice broke.

Judy reached up and cupped my face. Her tears pooled. "I know, Claire. We all know. And we all miss her terribly." Stepping back, she wiped her eyes hard. "But I also know that you can't die too. I want my sister back."

"And I want my daughter." A third voice.

We both swiveled toward our mother. "Was that ten minutes?" complained Judy.

"Did you really think I'd wait that long?" Barbara Anderson, in full lioness mode, zoomed in on me. This was not the person who showed up at Barnes Construction twice a week. Definitely not."Get dressed and let's go."

But I didn't want to go. I didn't care about a stupid haircut. And I certainly didn't like them sweeping into my house with orders. My pulse rate soared. My skin burned. "Sorry for your wasted time," I said, crossing to the door and pulling it open. "I'll get my hair done when I'm ready, and that's not today. Just leave me alone."

Judy grabbed the door right out of my hand and slammed it shut. "No. Can. Do. You've not been doing your best, and we don't want you hiding away and feeling sorry for yourself."

Sorry for myself? How dare they! Had they walked in my shoes? I couldn't get the words out.

"You're coming with us." I turned toward my mother, whose no-nonsense voice echoed the sound of my girlhood memories. Barbara was still acting like my mom. I stared at the woman I knew so well and whom I resembled. I recognized her bravado, smelled her fear.

My neck swung around toward Judy, who continued to stare at me, chin up with challenge. Beyond her overt dare, however, I sensed a long-held breath waiting for release.

I couldn't fight them both. They loved me; they didn't blame me for what happened. How could they when I'd never told them why I was so late getting home, how Colombo had singled me out and how I'd reveled in his attention? I would have remained in the studio with him longer had I not seen the clock. I must have been developing a significant crush on the guy. The possibility made me wince and added to my sins.

If I'd left class on time that day, I would have changed history. That is a fact for which I will never forgive myself, but my family doesn't have to suffer more than necessary.

"You win, ladies. Let's see if Juanita can make miracles."

#

Juanita sat me down and muttered to herself as she hefted and stroked my hair. "*Hay caramba,* Ms. Claire! I can fix the color, but the shine is gone, the weight is going. What happened? It was better last time I saw you. So now you must eat protein. Salmon, fish, dark green vegetables, beans, nuts. *Comprende?* Yes? Eat protein, protein. Eggs are very good."

"Slow down," said Judy, "I'm taking notes. And she will eat the right foods if I have to spoon-feed her myself. She could also cut down on the caffeine. How many cups of coffee can one person drink?"

"Exactly," said Juanita, still mumbling about my lousy hair.

"Ahem. I'm right here," I said, waving my fingers. "And my ears still work. I can hear you." The entire scene suddenly struck me as absurd, and I felt my lips turn up. I almost laughed.

"She's making a joke! How about that?" said Mom.

"I'm writing that down too. It'll raise Jack's spirits."

I loved these women, these women who had my back when I could barely straighten my spine.

An hour later, I was a blonde again—with highlights. My hair was bobbing at its usual shoulder length, and I felt surprisingly good.

"Last Sunday, Ian thought Kayla wouldn't know me anymore," I said as we walked to Judy's car. "But now she will."

Judy halted her step, tipped her head back for the umpteenth time that day, and looked me square in the eye. "I know what he said about Kayla. He made the comment because she's all you think about. But what about us, Claire? What about the living? Don't we count anymore?"

They counted only if I didn't allow my guilt to swallow me whole. Oh, God, why had I lingered so often in my studio when Kayla wanted to gab about her friends? About which girl liked which boy in school? Mindless chatter I'd sometimes brushed aside as unimportant....

My mom started to cry. "Claire, Claire...my heart's broken too. Forever. Kayla was the sun and the moon and the stars to me. My only granddaughter. And now I worry that I'm losing you as well. You have to try to live again. You must live among the living."

Her words echoed. I'd heard something similar before. Leaning against the car, I whispered, "Jack said that once. He said he couldn't go on without both his girls."

Judy stared at me as though I were a child. "Of course he can't. You've always been his one and only. All these years. In fact, I can barely remember a time when he wasn't part of this family. Now, get into the car." She opened the front passenger door for me and said, "Let's pay Jack a visit. I definitely want to see his reaction to your makeover. And then we're going out for lunch."

"Right," said Mom, her finger pointing at my chest. "A relaxed lunch. You'll eat salmon and chicken and spinach. You heard Juanita. You need protein." The woman opened her door with vigor and got into the back seat. At seventy-one years young, my mother wouldn't—couldn't—be ignored.

The women in my life were acting like a couple of storm troopers, and I'd be overruled if I objected to lunching at a restaurant.

Once in the car, I pulled down my visor and grimaced in the mirror. I pulled the corners of my mouth up with my fingers.

"What the heck are you doing?" asked Judy, glancing at me.

I gave her a wolf grin. "Practicing how to smile. It's hard."

She burst out laughing. "Oh, my God, Claire. You can still be funny." Patting my arm, she said, "You'll be all right, sweetie. You're on your way now."

Being "all right" was the end game. I knew that. The hard part was getting from here to there. And I'd been hiding, hiding behind my mother. While she dealt with the customers, I went on site visits early or late in the day, checking paint colors, the placement of furniture and accent pieces right down to the coordinated bath towels. I studied blueprints and ordered items by phone. I didn't have to "put a smile on my face." She did. I just had to focus on the work.

Judy pulled up in front of Barnes Construction. "I'm always impressed by how beautiful the building is. A bit different from when you started out."

"Just like our house," I said. "Except at home, most of the improvements are on the inside."

We lived in the same family-friendly neighborhood we'd lived in since Ian was a baby. Jack had built the house, one of his first projects, and we'd been so happy there, we'd never considered moving. Until now. Until I'd brought it up because of Ian. But Jack hadn't mentioned it again now that Ian was really on his own.

Mom, Judy, and I walked up the steps and opened the door. In the reception area, Jack had used a variety of materials to educate visitors. Granite counters and tabletops caught the eye; large ceramic floor tiles installed on an angle added sophistication and the illusion of extra space. In the center of the lobby was a big display showcasing miniature home models. Large easels held visuals of subdivisions under construction, which featured Barnes homes.

"He could be anywhere," I said, taking out my cell phone.

A minute later, Jack danced into the lobby, looking like a kid on Christmas morning.

"What a treat! Wow."

He kissed each of us, stepped back a pace, and stared at me. "You're gorgeous, Claire-de-Lune." His shaky hand brushed my hair, lifting a section. Then he hugged me so tight I couldn't breathe. "My wife's back," he whispered.

"We're taking her out to lunch," said Judy. "Can you join us?"

From the corner of my eye, I saw my mother's brow rise as she gave Jack a look—one of those conspiratorial looks between people who've got a secret. And then I understood. He'd known about this. My husband had been part of this little *intervention*.

I could feel the fire growing inside me as I stared at my conniving family before pivoting toward Jack. If I'd been two years old, I'd have lain on the floor and kicked my heels. Instead, I had to rely on puny words.

"You sneaky…sneaky…how dare you? Don't you ever scheme behind my back again. Twenty-three years can be undone like that," I said, snapping my fingers. "I don't appreciate being manipulated by anyone, but especially not by you."

Jack's glare seared me, but before he could speak, my sister rushed in.

"Well, that's too damn bad," she said. "Because we're not giving up on you. You don't scare me, you don't scare Mom, and you don't scare Jack. It's tough-love time, big sister. And that's what you're going to keep getting from us.

"So, is it shrimp or salmon, Claire?"

I wanted to throw up.

# CHAPTER FOURTEEN

*JACK*

Conspiring with my in-laws had been a no-brainer. When Barbara and Judy came up with their intervention plan, I heartily endorsed it and wondered why I hadn't consulted with them much earlier. Tough love. I thought the concept was reserved for problematic children, but my sister-in-law didn't seem to have any qualms about adopting the method with Claire.

Some people might think we were being unreasonable, that a year was barely long enough to absorb the bitter truth about Kayla. With most people, they'd be right. But Claire was pushing us all away. I knew she was only going through the motions at work. She was getting it done, but there was no zip, no enthusiasm. She ignored the phone at home and would do the same at the office if she could. The only person she saw outside the family was her friend Anne with whom she jogged a couple of nights a week.

After her outburst, Claire sat next to me in the back seat of Judy's car. She stared out her side window, not speaking, her fingers turning white as they clutched the straps of her purse. She was sizzling because I "manipulated" her. I caressed her hand, putting mine over hers.

"Come on, Claire," I whispered. "Relax. You know we love you. Try to enjoy yourself. It's only a lunch, and you're with your favorite people."

With a quick movement, she freed her hand from mine. "I don't think so. Not anymore."

"Well, if you don't sweeten up, you won't be their favorite either."

"Stop talking to me like I'm a child. You betrayed me, and right now, I don't give a flying fig about any of you. In fact, I don't give a flying fuck. Especially about you."

Ow. I couldn't remember the last time I'd heard Claire use *the* ultimate of swear words. And never had she aimed it at me. I stifled a smile and refused to worry. Our nights were still going strong.

"A flying fig? Really, Claire? I don't believe that for a moment."

"Really, Jack?" she mimicked, swiveling to face me before shouting, "You act like you don't even miss her. Like you don't even know she's gone. The world's the same to you. You get up, go to work, and come home, talking about the business like it was important or something."

My brain got stuck on "not miss her." Not miss my sweet daughter?

"What the hell would you have me do?" I shouted. "Let the company go bankrupt? Someone has to turn it around. Someone has to keep promises made to customers and staff. I can't pretend it doesn't matter. It does matter to me. And it should matter to you."

Judy pulled the car to the curb. My mother-in-law began crying. But I wasn't finished yet.

"And don't you ever—*ever*—tell me how I feel about Kayla. Not miss her? Maybe you're losing your mind because only a woman not thinking straight could say something like that...about me!"

Breathing hurt. I dragged air into my lungs and heaved it out. More quietly, I added, "You think you own the corner on grief, Claire, but you don't. I just put on a better front—for your sake—so I won't drag you down further than you are. One of us has to function normally."

"My hero."

Sarcasm didn't become her. She looked me in the eye and added, "Don't martyr yourself for me." Then she stuck her chin out and spoke to her sister. "Either take me home or to the closest car rental place. I think there's one about a mile west of here."

I popped an antacid.

"This isn't the end of it," said Judy, game once more as she pulled into traffic and headed back to the office. "It's only the beginning. We may not be lunching, but the day hasn't been wasted. You got your hair done and...you and Jack...well, let's say you've communicated—in a new way. Sort of unpeeling the onion. I'm very satisfied with our progress so far."

Whatever the hell that meant. I ignored Judy's onion remark, but to be called a martyr? The word stuck in my craw. "I'll be home late tonight," I said to Claire as I exited the car. "Don't bother waiting up."

#

When I returned to my office, I shut the door, sat at the computer, and typed "support groups" into the search engine. In the time it took to sneeze, hundreds of listings

106

appeared. Who knew so many people depended on strangers for help? Yet here I was doing the same.

Trying to narrow the search, I added *Houston* and *death of a child* to my inquiry and studied the results. Interesting. I could choose to join an online group or an in-person group. I typed with only my two index fingers, so this was a no-brainer for me. Besides, as Claire had often said, I was a people-person.

Scanning the in-person list, my eyes halted like a spent bullet on one of them: The *Miss You Foundation*; a support group for Grieving Parents.

My throat closed, my eyes watered. *Miss you every day, baby.*

Without further thought, I clicked the link for the website, printed out the information I needed, and tucked the paper into my top desk drawer. I continued to sit there for a few minutes, catching my breath and enjoying the peace that settled inside me. I would have preferred Claire and Ian to attend at least one meeting with me, but I didn't need their permission to go alone. To help myself. Maybe learn how to help my family...before we disappeared.

The phone rang, and for the rest of the day, I wore my President-of-Barnes Construction hat. Saturdays were busier than weekdays sometimes, and I had plenty of work to catch up on. My watch said six when I looked at it again. Meeting Ian for dinner wasn't an option, not on Saturday nights. Making new friends required he be available to socialize. My stomach growled, but I wasn't ready to go home.

Claire had crossed the line today. My patience was gone, and I had no desire to handle more of her histrionics. Did I say handle? A joke. I tried. I did try. I was the guy who lived with her and loved her, but I was also struggling to survive myself. Something had to change. For the first time, I wondered if healing Claire was truly my job. A long time ago, she'd said not. But she was failing at it.

Tired, I leaned back in my chair and closed my eyes. Thinking about my wife required too much effort. My stomach rumbled again, and I suddenly realized I didn't have to go home to get a decent meal. Willie's Ice House was only a few blocks away. Picturing one of their thick, juicy burgers with a brewski on the side had me salivating.

I made the rounds of the building, shut off a couple of lights—another conservation reminder would go out in the morning—then returned to my office near the front entrance. Grabbing my car keys, I scanned the room and got ready to leave. Just as I reached the door, the phone on my desk rang. *We're closed, pal. I'm tired and hungry. Get a life.* If my name weren't on the building, I would've let it ring. Instead, I leaned over and picked up the receiver.

"Barnes speaking."

"Is this Jack Barnes?"

"That's me."

"Ahh, my name is Marc Levine. You might not recognize—"I cut him off. "I know who you are." And why the hell was he calling me? I had nothing to say to the man whose wife killed my daughter.

"I suppose you do," Levine said in a subdued tone. "I'm very sorry to bother you. I'm out walking the dog. Sarah doesn't know I'm calling. I took a chance you'd...I'm...I'm—oh, damn it. I thought I could put my words together, but..."

He sounded barely older than Ian. "What do you want? Just spit it out." And then I could get my burger and beer and pretend he hadn't called.

"Okay, okay. The bottom line is that my wife's having a-a nervous breakdown. The nightmares haven't gone away, the guilt is killing her and..."

I had my own problems. I didn't need his. "There are doctors who treat that."

"Yeah. I know. Except she's...she's not doing too well. She can't forgive herself. The psychiatrist suggested that Mrs. Barnes might be doing better than Sarah, and if Sarah knew that to be true, she might take heart. And then we could make a real beginning and...and have a future."

He paused, and I heard him breathing heavily into the phone. Maybe gasping. The guy was scared, almost too scared to talk to me.

"I know I have a lot of nerve calling, Mr. Barnes, but I don't know what else to do. Sarah left her teaching position, and she was the team leader for the third grade staff. Teaching was her career, and she loved it. She never went back after...afterwards. Doesn't trust herself to be around kids, not even ours."

For damn sure, I didn't want to know all this. "I'm sorry about your wife, but I can't help you."

"I'm begging you. Please. Just any bit of encouragement about Mrs. Barnes...?"

His desperation echoed in my head. I understood that feeling all too well myself, and I let my guard slip.

"You don't have to beg, Mr. Levine," I said quietly. "If I could help, I would." I sagged against the desk. "But I'm very sorry to admit that my wife's not much better off than yours. She's just going through the motions of living—at work and home—finding fault, not able to concentrate. She's not herself. I'm not sure what to do."

Silence on the other end. I guess he was processing another failed effort.

"Then I'm more than sorry to have bothered you," Levine said. I heard his sadness, resignation...and defeat. "It won't happen again."

I could feel the man's pain. It was my pain too.

"Don't give up!" How ironic for me to offer advice when I had no clue myself.

"I love my wife, Mr. Barnes. Giving up is not an option, but right now life is...is..."

"...difficult?" I completed.

"Amen. We get through one day at a time, which is the advice of the shrink, the rabbi, and the rest of our family."

The man had accomplished more than I had. At least Sarah Levine was seeing professionals who could take action. But Claire? Never.

"I'll save your number," I heard myself say. "I'll let you know if things get better."

I took my time with the burger then drove around for awhile, needing to unwind. When I pulled into our subdivision, I parked near the lake and walked twice around the water at a good pace. I could have done more. It was after eleven when I let myself into the house. I expected Claire to be asleep, and she was—on the family room sofa.

"I'm mad at you, Jack," she murmured when I gently woke her. "Very angry. I'm staying here."

"Suit yourself."

I could have told her about Marc Levine's phone call right then. She would have awakened fast enough, her anger deflected from me to the Levines, binding us closer against the common enemy. But talking about Sarah Levine would also reopen Claire's still-bleeding wounds, *our* wounds, and I had no heart for the drama to follow if I revealed my sympathy for the husband.

I made my way to the bedroom, relieved to be alone. For the first time in almost twenty-four years, I wanted my own space. This wasn't the kind of change I'd report to Marc Levine.

# CHAPTER FIFTEEN

*CLAIRE*

*October*

I pulled into the visitor's parking lot at West Side Hospital, relieved to be feeling strong and ready for my interview with Ms. Garcia. I'd had no flashbacks—at least not yet—and I took it as a good sign. I was ready for this, ready to give back. If all went well, I'd let Jack know about my new endeavor this evening.

Fifteen minutes later, I sat across from the volunteer director's desk, relaxed in her presence as we began to talk. It didn't take me long to figure out that behind her hospitality hid a very sharp woman.

"Our volunteer program enhances the services we offer here," she began after greeting me, "especially in the pediatric area, where we're dealing with both children and their families. So don't be fooled by the word 'volunteer.'

You are important! And I'm always happy to meet potential volunteers."

"It sounds like a well-run program."

"I like to think it is. We treat our unpaid staff as professionals. We run a background check and provide a full orientation to the hospital and department. We depend on our volunteers to take their work seriously."

"Wow. A background check? I hadn't thought about that, but it makes sense. We do the same thing when we hire staff."

She leaned toward me. "Good. So you understand. Now, Mrs. Barnes, can you tell me why you'd like to spend time with our young patients?"

*Because I failed Kayla. Because helping these kids might clear my conscience and make me feel better. Because maybe Kayla would be proud of me.* I am such an idiot. Why hadn't I prepared for some real questions? And this was so basic.

"Well, I think I have a lot to offer. Especially doing art projects. I can work with the children in any media. And...and I've got a lot of patience." *Used to have a lot of patience.* "I'd be able to stick with a hot Monopoly session for a long time."

"Sounds good," said Ms. Garcia with a smile. "I see from your application that you and your husband own a business. It's been my experience that owners work round-the-clock. Are you able to get away on a regular basis and not disappoint the children?"

I nodded before she'd finished asking the question. "I can usually rearrange my day without a problem. That's one of the perks of being an owner." I smiled back at her, confident I'd made a good rebuttal.

"Oh, that's excellent," the woman replied. "And what experience do you have with children?"

My throat closed. Pictures flashed through my mind. Kayla laughing. Studio. Clay. Kayla. Easel. Crayons.

Maddy. Paper. Laughing. Kayla. Dinner. Soccer. Running. Jack. Ian. Kayla. *Don't cry. Don't cry.*

"Mrs. Barnes? Are you all right?" The woman's voice seemed to come from afar.

"Fine. I'm fine. Just got caught up in the past for a moment."

Ms. Garcia tilted her head and waited. Patiently. Hands folded.

"I-I have a lot of experience with kids." My voice sounded like gravel hitting a cement pipe. "My son is eighteen. Thinks he's all grown up."

A quick smile, but she said nothing, just waited for me. I suppose she had the art of interviewing down pat. I could have walked away at this point and put an end to the whole experience. No one would know I'd failed again except me.

I didn't want to fail. "My daughter died last year. Here. At this hospital. A car accident. The staff was so good to her...and us."

Her warm hands wrapped themselves around my cold ones. Our fingers tightened on each other's.

"I'm very sorry, Mrs. Barnes. So very sorry. Let's take a moment to catch our breaths."

A good idea. Thirty seconds later, I sat back in my chair, in control once more.

"After such a loss, sometimes families make a donation or..."

I shook my head. "I want to be hands-on. I need to *do* something. And I know I can do this."

She tilted her head again in a way that was becoming familiar to me—her thinking position. "I tell you what, Mrs. Barnes. After next week's orientation, let's have a month's try-out. See how it goes for both of us."

Good enough. I chose Tuesdays from noon till two o'clock. Mom could cover the design center on those days, and Jack would have no cause to complain. Ms.

Garcia might have her doubts, but I was confident I'd "pass" the trial period and become part of the permanent volunteer staff.

#

Our twenty-fourth wedding anniversary came and went without much notice a few days after my interview at the hospital. We usually celebrated big, but Jack wasn't in the mood. Frankly, I wasn't either. We did, however, make love that night. Still enjoyable, but not the mind-blowing act it had been earlier on. My libido must have been on vacation. Jack didn't comment, and I fell asleep immediately afterwards.

"Who cares?" I pushed my thoughts of our lovemaking aside as I rinsed the breakfast dishes. It was Saturday, and Jack had gone to the office. I headed for my studio, eager to see what would happen using oils instead of clay. Since producing the sketches of Kayla and Ian last month, I now felt confident enough to try. What choice did I have? My portion of the *Girl with Secrets* sale money had arrived by FedEx exactly as Colombo had promised. He'd followed all the rules of the university, and now the picture wasn't mine anymore.

Okay. I understood that. But as for my daughter? The big-shot professor couldn't have her! Kayla would be mine until I drew my last breath and beyond. If I wanted to see her glowing with life again, I would simply make it happen—on canvas—regardless of Jack's advice to forget about another drawing.

A frisson of excitement ran through my veins as I gathered my materials. A new portrait of Kayla waited. Well...at least the blank canvas did. I positioned the easel to catch the natural mid-morning light of late fall. Natural light supplemented by electricity would suffice very well.

I'd already chosen a half dozen "best of the best" photos of Kayla to supplement my memories and taped them to the top of the easel. I'd also washed the entire canvas with the usual mix of turpentine and just a drop of yellow ochre oil paint and let it dry. Now I stared at the expanse of white, itching to begin yet hesitant. How to start? Where to start? So many choices. My arms didn't move. My fingers clung to my side. Trust, trust the process...breathe, breathe. I bit my bottom lip and eyed the door.

I walked outside and stared at the long swath of grassy yard. Like her dad, Kayla preferred the outdoors. She would have reveled in this clear day under blue skies and warm sun. Sun-kissed, that's what she was. I meandered across the lawn, picked up a pinecone, and admired the bower of yellow jasmine we'd planted long ago. A pretty backyard, pretty and perfect for kids. Kayla and her friends, Ian and his. I gently tossed the pinecone in the air and caught it several times, my thoughts drifting.

When I pictured Kayla, she was dancing—or running—down the hallway; walking was anathema. Or she was pitching a softball or kicking in a goal for her soccer team. Sometimes I saw her pounding clay, rolling and shaping it, totally focused on her work. I admit the athlete subsumed the artist, but I took comfort that she enjoyed her time in the studio with me. I squeezed the pinecone, wound up for a pitch, and let it sail. A direct hit against the tree trunk. "Your mom's not so bad, is she, baby?"

I had to be true to my girl, had to show her in action. Maybe a half-length portrait or even a full-length.... And at that moment, I knew exactly what to do. I ran into the house and down the hall to Kayla's bedroom.

Her middle school soccer team had retired her number in a solemn ceremony last spring. I'd barely hung onto my sanity watching the banner and her number being raised to the gym's rafters. Kayla's was the third banner up there, the first for the soccer team. I'd tried hard to keep my emotions under control, but when the young team captain presented me with her uniform and Madison Conroy began crying, I'd lost it. I'd hugged Maddy, the captain, and every girl on the team, as well as the coaches. Jack watched me with the girls, his eyes watering. At home, I'd hung Kayla's uniform under plastic, pressed, clean, just waiting for...I didn't know what, not back then.

Now I wasted no time bringing the green-and-white outfit to the studio. She'd been number one. So appropriate. I swallowed a sob. No more tears! At least, not today. I had work to do and Ian to thank for my breakthrough.

Maybe one day, he'd forgive me for being late and leaving him to cope with the cops, ambulance, the entire awfulness. Maybe one day, we'd figure it out.

I turned toward the canvas again. Kayla waited for me now.

# CHAPTER SIXTEEN

*COLLEEN MURPHY*

*November, Year Two*

Ian Barnes was just about the sweetest boy I'd ever known. When he said something, he meant it. A real promise keeper. He said he'd give me the bedroom, and he did. Then he refused my money toward rent. He said if I weren't there, he'd have to pay the whole thing anyway. But nothing was free in this life, so when I offered to do the shopping and cooking, his smile reached all the way from east Texas to El Paso and then some. After a week, his smile reached inside my heart. He tried so hard to be polite and honorable, but I could feel him staring at me special-like when he thought I didn't notice. When I looked back at him, his face would get as red as Texas clay.

Well, I had to admit we weren't any better than the birds and the bees, doing what came naturally, but I didn't mind at all. Ian was so different from the boys I grew up with, not better'n them, just...just different. Spoke different too.

"You must have had a lot of girlfriends in the city," I said one Saturday morning over breakfast, about a month after he'd left the couch for good.

"Why do you say that?" he asked, his cheeks coming up rosy again.

"Well, did you?"

He shrugged. "Some. But no one like you."

"Oh, shoot, Ian. There are plenty of girls like me. Just look all around the plant."

"Girl," he said, in a fair imitation of my twang, "the only female I see inside that refinery is you."

His eyes were shining, and my heart thumped like a big ol' bass drum. "Whoa there, cityboy. That's a real compliment, so thank you. But hold on now." I put my hand up like a cop. "What we've got going here is a...a playhouse or something. I'm heading to Nashville one day, and don't you forget that."

He grinned. "And I'm going to buy out every album you make," he said.

Beautiful words. Beautiful thought. That nice boy just about killed me sometimes.

But then my monthly was late, and I wanted to kill him.

God, I was so dumb. It didn't take but two months of being together for this to happen. I knew myself. I was a twenty-eight-day-to-the-minute girl. I didn't need a doctor or a test to know something was wrong, but just to make sure, I went to the big WalMart and bought a test kit at their pharmacy. Then I cried myself dry when the stick said yes.

#

I didn't say anything to Ian until the next day after work. It was a Wednesday, but we wouldn't be going to the Roadside Café that night.

"Don't rush your supper, Ian. We need to talk about a matter."

There must have been something in my voice, 'cause he looked up at me pretty quick, his deep blue eyes steady. "What's wrong, Colleen?" He took my hand, wrapped it in his, like he had the right to protect me. Sweet, but I hoped he could really be a man today. No fears, no tears.

"We've got a problem, Ian, but I already know what I want to do about it. And I can, ya know, 'cause it's my body."

His forehead creased, he leaned back in his chair, hands falling to his sides. "Wait a minute." He snapped his fingers. "You're already gorgeous. Perfect. I love the beauty mark on your cheek. You don't need any plastic surgery because of your singing career. Just be yourself."

I should've known. He was clueless. But boys were always dumb about the important things. I grabbed his hand and placed it on my stomach. "Here's the problem." I waited a heartbeat. "Now do you get it?"

It still took my cityboy a minute to figure it out. I saw exactly when his brow cleared. "A...a baby?" And his voice broke like he was no mor'n thirteen years old.

I looked at the wall. "No, sir. Right now it's a few cells stuck together in a little mess of blood that we're going to get rid of." I was breathless by the end of that little speech. Perspiration covered my entire body. No matter. I'd wanted to sing since I was a little girl, and nothing was getting in my way. Not even a blood clot.

Ian's hand still rested on my stomach, and I turned my head to see his reaction. He was paler than white; big drops of sweat plopped from his face to his shirt. His pupils looked black and were so large they almost filled the entire space in his eyes. Lickety split, I wet some paper towels and wiped him down. Yep, he'd been clueless. Now he was shocked and scared, too. Darn it.

"No more dead kids," he demanded quietly.

Jumping back, I stared at him, totally confused. "What did you say?"

"No more dead kids!"

He was yelling now. My sweet cityboy was yelling his head off and pacing, as nervous as a long-tailed cat in a room full of rocking chairs. He reached around to his back pocket and pulled out his wallet. Pulled out a picture of a young girl. Pretty and smiling and...

Dead.

I learned about Kayla then. About Ian and his sister playing football. I learned more than I wanted to know because afterwards, Ian sobbed. This tall, handsome, smart boy who treated me like a queen just sat on the floor, broke down, and cried his eyes out. I could see his suffering, I could feel it all the way to my bones, and then to my soul when he got to the part about his mother blaming him. Seemed she'd tried to backtrack, but Ian swore that, inside, she still found him guilty. Irresponsible. Holding him in my arms, I rocked him on that cracked linoleum floor. I soothed him and absorbed his pain into me, and cried with him. *That's what friends are for....*

The lyric echoed in my heart. Music was a way to tell the truth, and that included what I felt about Ian right now. My best friend. I hoped he understood that best friends had to be honest with each other.

"A new baby," I said, "wouldn't be Kayla even if it turned out to be a girl."

Ian's eyes brightened. "Of course not. But I'm not killing it. Him or her. Please, Colleen. I'll take care of you and the baby. I'll take overtime shifts. I promise. And we'll save for Nashville. We'll...we'll open a special account just for you. Or maybe we can all go."

Well, *that* would never happen—we'd need to win the lottery to have enough money. "A baby is a lot of work, cityboy." I could feel myself weakening. "And they cry a lot, disturbing everyone."

"Have you ever seen me run away from work?" he asked, gesturing at the apartment.

It was true he'd patched the walls better'n any landlord, and he'd painted every room. Even put in some new door sills and baseboards. It looked great to me. If he owned the place, he'd have repaired every single part of it. He wasn't lazy.

"I'll help you," he continued, "in every way. I'll change diapers. I'll make bottles. You'll still sing whenever you want." He paused a second. I could see him gathering more arguments. He pulled me into his arms and softly asked, "Are you afraid of your parents or what the neighbors will say?"

I'd written off my folks a long time ago. No support there, so my life was my own. "I don't care about the neighbors. As we say in east Texas, most people will simply think we planted a crop before building a fence." Shrugging, I added, "It happens all the time nowadays, and I suppose yesterday too." But God and I both knew I didn't want to build a fence. I wanted to be free. I *needed* to be free. What to do? What to do....

"So, Colleen?" I could hear the hope in Ian's soft voice. "Are we okay about this now?"

"You sure want to dot those i's and cross those t's, don't you?"

"Yes. Yes, I do."

I believed Ian would do his share, but...a baby? I really didn't want a baby. Not now. *So you should've been more careful! Selfish girl.* Now was a fine time for my conscience to holler its fool head off.

"Well...," I began, the words almost choking me, "at least I won't get calluses on my knees praying for forgiveness the rest of my life..."

I'd barely finished the sentence before cityboy jumped up from the floor, took me in his arms, and spun me around that kitchen.

"What about your folks?" I added when I caught my breath. "A grandbaby might make them happy again."

His frown came and went faster than heat lightning. "You said it before, Colleen. It won't be Kayla. So here's the deal. Your folks are out of the picture, and so are mine. We're on our own."

# CHAPTER SEVENTEEN

*CLAIRE*

"The Pedi Unit is impressive," I said to Anne as we jogged around the lake. "I had my orientation today, which included a tour. The children's floor is nothing like I imagined. It's colorful, playful. Large rooms. A teen lounge. There's a huge mural painted across the nurses' station, an outdoor scene of trains racing along their tracks beneath a perfectly blue sky and white clouds. You can dream about what lies beyond. The entire floor is the exact opposite from when I was a kid and had my appendix out."

"You mean a million years ago?" Anne teased.

Sometimes it seemed like a million years since Kayla died. Sometimes only a minute. She'd never "stepped down" from the ICU to the general pediatrics unit. But I just laughed with Anne and said, "At least a million."

"You didn't mention the kids. Meet any of them?"

"Not yet. Not one-on-one. No time today. But I start next week—for real."

Jack had done more than raise his eyebrows when I finally told him about my current endeavor. "Sick children?" he bellowed. "Are you crazy? That's a horrible idea. What are you trying to prove, or do you like being a martyr?"

"They need me...."

"I need you! And I need you to be healthy and strong. Remember your priorities, Claire. Work comes first. Before your art, before this volunteering business. We're not out of the woods yet. As long as the economy's down, people won't invest in a new home."

"My husband, of course, has a lot of reservations about my volunteering," I said to Anne.

"I can actually understand that," said Anne. "You're putting yourself in a place that could be hazardous to your mental health. I hope you'll go slow."

"Funny. I think just the opposite."

Anne stopped running and squeezed my arm. "I'll support anything you do, but please, don't go backwards. It's no crime if it doesn't work out."

But it had to work out. I had to make peace with Kayla.

I started jogging again, Anne at my side. Time to change the subject. "How's the book business these days?"

"How's any business these days?" Anne sighed. "As a part-timer, though, I think my job's secure. I've always wished I'd become a librarian. Maybe one day. Just like one day I'll remodel my kitchen. I want it to look like yours."

Granite. Cherry cabinets. Double wall ovens. Corner carousels. "My whole house is Jack's on-going experiment with products so he can talk to customers 'from experience.' Unfortunately, the kitchen is the most expensive room in the house to change."

"But the most important room, in my opinion," said Anne. "This neighborhood is twenty years old and so are most of the kitchens. Maybe Jack should take on remodeling jobs. I'd hire him in a heartbeat if I had the money. And I bet others would too."

Just what I didn't need. If Jack jumped on Anne's good suggestion, I'd be sucked under at work again.

#

When I arrived home, I heard Jack's voice joining the canned laughter of a TV sitcom and wondered how he could laugh at anything. I needed a shower and told him not to fall asleep.

A half hour later, I pitched Anne's idea—with a big caveat up front. "If you forge ahead with what I'm going to propose, then you should know you'll be hiring another person for the design staff. I will not-not-not take on more."

"I can't make a promise if I don't know what it's about."

"But I can. You know where I stand up front. So, here's the idea: Change *Barnes Construction* to *Barnes Construction and Remodeling. Motto: No job too big or small.* I think if you do the research, you'll find that remodeling is the way to go when money's tight. Folks think it's almost like living in a new house."

His eyes gleamed. "Check out Sunday's paper. We've got a display ad announcing the remodeling side. I would have told you, but you never seemed to be around."

"Of course I've been around."

He shrugged. "I guess we're those two ships in the night, except it's daytime. Neither of us is tied to a desk for eight straight hours. We could be anywhere."

Thank goodness. I needed some flex time. "So, are we in agreement about my role here?" I'd learned to get it in writing, at least verbally, when it came to Jack and his ideas for the company.

"Let's see how it goes," he temporized. "A boom or bust could get you off the hook completely."

What he didn't say was that most ideas had to take root and grow. And while it grew, I'd be stuck again.

Wasn't going to happen.

"By the way," said Jack, "tell Anne that if we can use their kitchen as a model for the people in our subdivision, I'll provide free labor and materials at my cost."

He wasn't kidding, and I knew Anne would snatch up the offer. But I was choking. Jack's generosity sounded like a bribe, a tacit understanding that one good turn deserved another. He wanted something from me.

"What you do for Anne and Tom is your business," I said. "It has nothing to do with me. I don't owe you for being good to them. They're your friends too."

"What you 'owe' me is some attention. This hospital work is a huge mistake. You'd be better off decorating homes and helping buyers. We'd both be better off, and I'm not talking only about the company now. I'm talking about us. You and I are not on the same page. That's what worries me."

I took a moment and replied in a calm tone. "But everyone's journey is different."

His eyes widened, brows lifted.

"I read it in a book."

"But where does the journey end?" he asked quietly.

For that, I had no answer.

#

*December*

A month after starting my volunteer work, I took Friday off from work and returned to my studio, hoping I'd finally make progress with Kayla's new portrait. Drawings of Kayla littered the place, but nothing appeared on the canvas yet. I'd begun this picture almost two months ago, revved up and ready to dive in—or so I'd thought. I didn't know then that I'd create dozens of small sketches first—charcoal, pencil, and pastel too. I'd had no idea I'd spend many evenings and weekends studying all the clay figures I'd produced of Kayla. More than a dozen of her, walking, running, sitting, kicking, pointing, laughing, laughing, laughing, oh, she loved to laugh.

No matter how I tried, however, neither the final sketches nor sculptures lived up to my memories of Kayla's sparkling eyes, the funny way she wrinkled her nose, and her body constantly in motion. Maybe creators—composers, writers, and artists—were never satisfied.

Or maybe they never tried to reproduce their own dead child.

Colombo haunted me, and once again I studied Michelangelo's magnificent sculptures—*David, the Pieta, Moses*. I worried that I was procrastinating the real work. I hadn't gone through this huge preparation in art class to produce my first portrait of Kayla, but I couldn't help myself now. I called it "the getting ready stage." I suppose I should have labeled it the "psyching myself up" stage. I needed time because I was plain scared.

I was afraid to fail. The mere possibility immobilized me. Failure was unthinkable.

I walked around the room, studying each piece, trying to be objective, finally admitting they weren't bad—Colombo would have called them good—and perhaps they'd provide the strong foundation for the final portrait. I took a deep breath. Preparation time was over.

"I'm ready, sweetheart, finally ready." I said. "And I've got lots to tell you about too."

Only then did I glance at Kayla's soccer uniform, still on the hanger beneath plastic. I slowly removed the protective cover and reached for a piece of charcoal. Across the top of the canvas, I printed *Kayla at Twelve*. Of course, she'd be twelve. Twelve was the child we all knew, loved, and would most remember. Any decent artist could capture her likeness, but only a mother could capture the inner essence of her child. My child.

I stared at the uniform again, remembering the dozens of times I sat in the bleachers cheering the team. The kids played fiercely—leg action, head action, running, running, running—but nothing beat the excitement of a win. The high. The unfettered joy. My mind's eye became clear. I knew exactly how I wanted to paint her, and for the first time in over a year, peace filled my soul.

"Here we go, baby." I took a breath and traded the charcoal for my palette. I used acrylics now—the oils would come later— and squeezed out a line of each color I'd need to create a variety of flesh tones. My breathing became regular as I got lost in the work, studying Kayla's photos then blocking out shapes of light and dark on the canvas.

"So, sweetheart, I've been volunteering at the hospital with lots of kids, some your age," I said. "I keep them entertained with books, games, art. One little boy had a broken arm. He was there for a few days, cracking a thousand jokes. I laughed at them all even though they were pretty bad. He said I was his best audience."

*Really?*

"Well, his mom was probably sick of them."

I wondered if I should tell her about the regulars. The chronically ill who stayed awhile, left, then reappeared when in crisis. My mom had gotten upset when I explained it to her earlier this week, after my third time at the hospital.

"The unit's like a home away from home for those kids," I'd said. "Like with Megan Sullivan, who I met yesterday. She's fifteen years old and has cystic fibrosis."

"CF? Oh, dear. Her poor lungs, digestive tract...that child has a tough road ahead." Mom bit her lip then startled me by squeezing my hands hard. "We know the nurses are wonderful, but Claire, please don't get too involved. Just visit for an hour and fly away...like...like a butterfly. Leave it behind you." Her eyes filled. "I'm...I'm afraid for you."

"Goodness! You and Anne both. But I'm stronger than you think and feel great helping out."

At that moment, I'd meant every word.

#

I left the studio and Kayla's painting just as the yellow school bus pulled up. Three o'clock on my wrist watch. Whoever coined the term "creature of habit" must have been thinking of me. I could have darted to the house, but like hundreds of times in the past, I watched the kids traipse from the bus. When I spotted Maddy, I waved, but she stared at the ground, putting one foot slowly in front of the other.

"Maddy," I called more loudly. She raised her head, searching the air as though my voice had come from a million miles away. Or perhaps she had been a million miles away in her own imagination.

"Hey, Miss Claire." Her fingers flexed in a tiny wave as she trudged toward me. No smile. No spark. A well-mannered child acknowledging an adult.

"Homework getting you down, honey?" I gestured toward the studio. "You're welcome to throw as much clay as you want." *Throwing* clay was a term for working with it; the girls used to giggle over the double meaning.

But Madison shook her head. "I'd only throw it at the wall, on the floor, at everybody." Her voice came in puffs, her little chest heaved, and then her tears came. I took her in my arms. Holding her...just holding her felt so natural. A child to embrace. But her sobs shook me.

"What's wrong, Maddy?" This girl was no actress. If she was crying, there was a reason.

She shook her head. "I-I can't tell you."

Uh-oh. "I can keep a secret. I know how to do that." And if her secret was serious, I'd figure out a way to deal with it.

But she pulled back, rubbed away her tears. "Mom said not to tell you or Mr. Barnes. She said you had enough to deal with. And I promised."

My stomach lurched. Something was terribly wrong in Madison's world. Anne and I hadn't jogged the lake in...let's see...at least two weeks, maybe three. Come to think of it, I hadn't spoken with her lately either. I wondered if Jack had started on their kitchen. What could have happened in a few weeks? And how stupid was that question? Plenty could happen in seconds.

"Is Mom home now?" I asked, not having kept track of Anne's part-time schedule at the bookstore.

Maddy's eyes widened and she nodded. "But...but I don't know if she wants...com-pan-y." Her words ended on a whisper. My fears rose, but I forced my voice to remain calm.

"Well, why don't we ask her?" Various ideas swirled in my brain, most of them dealing with illness or...or could it be marital troubles? Not my business if Anne didn't make it so. I'd soon find out.

Maddy unlocked her front door, stepped inside, and called for her mother. I heard Anne's light footsteps approach. But nothing prepared me for her colorful head scarf or her fragility. Had it only been a few weeks since I'd seen her? My friend looked pounds thinner than her usual trim self. She glanced at her daughter then at me and sighed. "I was hoping you wouldn't find out until after my treatments were over or at least for a while longer. Come on in."

Treatments. I didn't like the possibilities.

She put her arm around Maddy. "How was your day, honey?" A mother's voice, filled with love and tenderness...I stared at them, mother and daughter, and hunger rippled through me, a yearning that exceeded words.

"Good," said Maddy. "But Miss Claire was outside in the driveway, and she called me. I-I didn't tell. I didn't."

I jumped in. "That's the truth, Anne. I sort of forced myself on her when she looked so sad."

Anne's complexion reddened; she blinked rapidly. "A mom fighting cancer makes a child sad. But—" She hugged her daughter again. "Maddy knows I'll get better. It will take time, though, for all the treatments. Right?"

The child nodded quickly. "Right," she echoed, as though she'd been brainwashed into understanding.

"And I haven't felt any side effects yet, so I might be lucky."

My friend lied like a trouper. Of course she'd experienced side effects. Weight loss, hair loss...

She motioned Maddy away. "Miss Claire and I need some privacy in the living room. You grab a snack and do your homework. Some things haven't changed around here!"

Maddy grinned. Finally. A familiar expression, a touchstone to normalcy. Anne led me to her sofa then tapped her scarf and modeled for me, turning, inclining her head to the left, to the right.

"It's the latest in chemo gear. And I've got a lot more. Just wait till you see my wig. She's called Donna. When I wear it, Tom says he's on a double-date."

I burst into tears, and she sat down beside me.

"My goodness, Claire. I'm so sorry. That's why I didn't want you to know. You've had such a hard time, and I knew this would be too much to deal with...and everything happened so fast anyway. I got diagnosed right after we talked about kitchens. Mammogram, surgery a week later, and my first chemo this week. My hair hasn't really fallen out yet, but Tom and I were advised to shave it in advance, a week's difference. Who needs the added stress of waiting for it to fall in clumps?"

I took her in my arms. "I'm so sorry, Anne. About the cancer and because you didn't feel you could count on me. What a lousy friend I am." She was so damn tiny. And then I discovered something else.

"You've had a mastectomy?" I asked, leaning back.

She nodded. "I was lucky. Stage I, no lymph node involvement so I had a choice between a lumpectomy or mastectomy. It boiled down to a psychological choice, and I chose to—" She made a sharp gesture. "Take it all off. Tom was so scared, he wanted me to have a double." Rolling her eyes at the absent Tom, she added, "I had skin-saving surgery, and I'll do reconstruction later on— if I want to."

I tried to absorb all the information quickly, but in the end, only one idea stood out. "You're a strong person, Anne. A lot stronger than I am."

She rolled her eyes. "Nah. Not true. I think we're all as strong as we have to be." She nodded toward the kitchen where Madison was doing homework. "Maddy doesn't know how I fell apart when I got the news. Or how sick I really was three days after the infusion when the chemo was fully metabolized in my body. God, I dread that time."

"I'll stay with you," I offered. "I'm sure Tom has to go to work."

"Thanks, but my mother's coming when I need someone."

"Your mother? But doesn't she live in Atlanta?"

Anne nodded then shrugged. "It's hard, but she wants to be here. She thinks if *she* cooks for me, I'll eat." Anne's nose reddened as she started to cry. "My mom just...just wants to help."

I pushed back my own tears. "Of course she does. She's your mother. But you can tell her to take a break whenever she wants. Tell her that your friend Claire will be coming around as often as needed. "My thoughts raced. "What foods can you manage to keep down?"

She stared as if I'd sprouted another head. "Just soup," she whispered. "My word, Claire. This has not been a good time for either of us or our families."

Of course, she was right, but at that moment, I felt stronger than I'd been in a very long time.

"Whatever you do," I said, leaning closer to my friend, "don't get into a conversation with the self-righteous bitch around the corner. She'll tell you it's all God's will, and you'll have to slap her."

We stared at each other with one of those tacit understandings between women that lead straight to laughter. Uncontrollable laughter. On and on we giggled like two little girls. I'd try to stop, then Anne would try, and we'd both start up all over again. But the release felt darn good; in fact, it felt as wonderful as the grin on Maddy's face when she ran into the living room to investigate our shenanigans.

"Wow!" she said. "I'm glad you came home with me, Miss Claire. I've got so much to tell Kayla tonight."

From laughter to tears in an instant. Luckily, Maddy ran away before she could see me cry. Hearing Kayla's name unexpectedly could still set me off. I guess I wasn't as strong as I'd thought a few minutes ago.

I turned toward Anne and gulped, "So, what kind of soup would you like?"

"If you're sure...?"

Sure? I wasn't sure about anything, but I nodded. "Jack loves my chicken soup, but I also make a wicked lentil..."

A smile slowly crossed Anne's face. "Broth, please. No meat."

Broth? No wonder she'd become a rail. But I knew a trick with cooked root vegetables and a food processor. Anne's chicken broth would have strength in it. She'd like it and never know the difference. I kissed her goodbye, waved at Maddy, and with new energy flowing through me, made my way home. By the time I got there, I'd figured out my shopping list. I'd go to the supermarket after dinner then start cooking first thing in the morning. An efficient plan with a purpose satisfied me.

#

Two hours later, I returned from Kroger's loaded with groceries. Jack met me at the kitchen door, silently took the bags I held out to him, and retrieved the rest from the car while I unpacked. Helpful as always, but...I knew the signs. Tight mouth, narrowed eyes. No small talk.

"I called Tom Conroy while you were out," he finally said when I'd finished storing the food. "And you know what he did? He *thanked* me for calling about Anne. *Thanked* me as though we were mere acquaintances and I'd done him a favor. His wife's dealing with goddamned breast cancer, and he thinks he has to thank me for a lousy phone call?

"He told me that's why they postponed the new kitchen. I said we'd use ours in the meanwhile. Tell me, Claire, how many years have we lived on the same street with the Conroys? How many times did he and Anne visit us after Kayla died? They were here, Claire. They cried with us. They held our hands. And yet, they didn't call us when they needed friends.

"Is that fair? I sure as hell don't think so. And it's your fault."

"I've already apologized to Anne for that. So lay off."

He gathered all the plastic bags together, shoved them inside the pantry, and pounded his fist against his thigh. "But you've been avoiding all our friends. We don't see them. You don't return phone calls. You hide away in your damn studio or at the hospital. And your mother's doing more and more work, instead of you. That's not fair."

My husband's anger rolled off me. I wasn't going to make his issues my issues. I responded in a controlled voice.

"You're the one not being fair, Jack. Every morning I go to the new home sites, creating and checking displays and layouts. I visit with the building crews and sales agents. How can I be hiding when I'm placing phone orders for custom products or searching samples in our own decorating studio? I'm out there. I'm working hard, just like you."

He held my gaze when I would have looked away. "Not quite true. So don't lie to me about visiting with the staff. You don't chat with them. My sources say you wave, do the work, and leave. I hardly see you at the office. Are you holing up in the studio in the afternoons? I'm sorry I ever built the damn thing!"

The ensuing silence roared louder than a Category Five hurricane churning up from the Gulf. I thought of Kayla's new portrait and all the time I'd spent figuring out what I wanted to do before starting the piece.

My control vanished as I poked him in the chest. "You stay away from *my* studio," I ordered. "I don't care how sorry you may be, but now it's mine. Keep out." I flung open the kitchen door. "I'm going for a walk."

I let the door slam behind me and headed for the lake. By the time I arrived, my walk had become a jog, which became a run as I began my first loop around the water. I soon found my rhythm and, a few minutes later, could feel the tension drain away. Jack and I used to complement each other like two pieces in a private puzzle. JackandClaire. ClaireandJack. Our names were linked as though they were one word. *Drifting apart* seemed too mild a phrase to describe us today. The thought made me ache, but we seemed like two different people now. Maybe we were. I couldn't remember when I'd last called him my CrackerJack.

Maybe I'd sleep in Kayla's room tonight. And I'd talk to my mother tomorrow. I started my second loop, focused on the running, and slowly got into the zone. Bolstered by endorphins, I could have run forever. I sure as hell wanted to.

# CHAPTER EIGHTTEEN

*IAN*

*February, Year Two*

I pulled into The House of Wong's parking lot and saw my dad's pickup with both parents inside. *Dang!* as Colleen would say. The restaurant, midway between my old home and my new one, had become the usual place for a father-son dinner a couple of nights a month. Occasionally, my mom showed up as well, but I think she tagged along just to make herself look good in my dad's eyes, to show she was doing her "mother" thing. I enjoyed myself more when it was just the guys.

"So, how's the best apprentice Gulf Coast Oil's ever had?" Dad's bear hug almost lifted me from the ground. Almost. As though he read my mind, he added, "I think you've gained a pound or two, boy-o. Looking good."

"I second that," said Mom. "Handsome and healthy. So, how are you?"

"Starved."

They both laughed, and I joined in. They had no idea their starving son was going to be a dad this summer. *Not such a boy anymore.*

Once at our table, Dad glanced at me and ordered dinner for four. "Gotta fill you up and then some." No argument. There'd be leftovers for Colleen, which she'd inhale. She wasn't nauseous anymore, and Chinese was her favorite.

Next came conversation. Q and A was more like it with Mom around. To distract her, I plunged in first with a safe topic. "So, how's your painting coming?"

Her smile disappeared before she pasted it back on. "It's just fine, Ian. Coming along."

Whooee! Something's going on there. First time at bat and I'd hit a nerve. Even Dad stared at her as though she'd spoken Mandarin. She must have picked up on our silence because she added, "But you know I never show anything until it's done. We *creative types* are funny that way." She exaggerated her words, rolled her eyes, and I gave her points for the save. "Nothing's changed about that."

It's true that she always hid her ongoing projects behind a screen or cloth. Kayla and I were trained to ignore those pieces in the studio. So were our friends. When we invaded her space, she always helped us with our pieces. For a moment, I wondered what she'd be hiding now.

"Speaking of art," I said, "do you happen to have any cheap prints I could use to cover the barracks' walls?"

"Barracks? Good grief. Is it still bad? I thought you cleaned it up."

"I did, structurally. But it needs...something. I'm refinishing some furniture—cheaper that way—but we figure pictures would help."

"We?"

Shoot! I had to watch myself. Be cool, be cool. "Yeah. I've made some friends, and the girls say I live in an igloo. Every wall is white." Of course, it was Colleen who said that, and I would have repainted the walls in any color she wanted, but paint fumes wouldn't be good right now.

Dad was grinning like that old Cheshire cat. "Girls, huh? Anyone special, son?"

And dang if I didn't feel my neck get hot. Real cool, idiot. "Nope! No one special. Can't a guy have buddies of both sexes? In fact, we're all watching the SuperBowl this Sunday at my place. That's why I mentioned the pictures."

"Nice. Very nice," said Mom. "So I guess your new life is working out. The new job...and new friends...a whole new beginning where you can...can for—" She heaved a deep breath. "Oh, forget it."

She was fishing for more, and I knew why. She thought I'd put the accident behind me. My own mother— and she didn't know squat. But she'd given me an opening, and I'd seize it. My heart began to pound, my palms felt damp. Maybe we could talk about some important stuff now.

"New job, new friends, and Kayla's picture always in my wallet. Are you thinking I've forgotten about her, that I've forgotten about that day?"

"Ian!" Dad's voice in warning.

"No!"Mom's knuckles whitened as she grabbed the table's edge. "I never said...never thought..."

"Then why do you try to make me feel guilty for moving out? Moving on?"

"You're imagining things, Ian. I just said how glad I am that life's good for you here. That you're happy." She took my hand in hers and kissed it.

Too weird. I pulled away. "Mom?"

"I want you to be happy, Ian. For God's sake, I'm your mother!"

"You're Kayla's mother too." I forced myself to look her in the eye. "You know it was an accident, don't you?"

She rose, leaned over the table toward me. "Of course I know."

"And that it was random chance and nobody's fault," I added, still not sure she understood my point. *I had not been careless.*

But that's when her gaze shifted over my shoulder to the windows beyond. And that's when my hopes fizzled again. No matter what I said or did or how I explained, she'd always blame me.

"Nobody's fault that Kayla died? That's not true," she whispered.

Her voice sounded odd, a sad note...almost frightening. But a spark of hope rekindled inside me one more damn time. Was it remotely possible she was referring to someone else?

Dad twisted in his seat. "What are you talking about, Claire? Accidents are accidents."

"Have you ever checked the dictionary?" she asked, pouncing on him like a cat with a ball of string. The woman had attitude to spare. She was looking for a fight.

Dad shook his head. I said nothing.

"An accident is 'an unfortunate event resulting especially from carelessness or ignorance.' So an earthquake is a random event beyond human control. With Kayla, someone was careless. Someone was ignorant—"

"For God's sake, Claire! Accidents just happen. Don't blame Ian. And don't blame yourself. I doubt we can even blame the woman behind the wheel. A bright, blazing sun could blind anyone. It wasn't intentional, and God knows she's suffering."

How did he know that? Dad glanced at me then at Mom. He shook his head and squeezed my shoulder. I got the message and agreed. Mom made no sense, but her words still had the power to hurt.

#

*JACK*

The meal arrived, and I turned toward Ian. "You've given so much attention to the barracks," I said, "I'm thinking you might want to buy the place and fix it up right."

My son grinned an honest down-home grin. "Have you ever heard of a money pit? Trust me, Dad. Not worth it. The dump is good enough only for now."

An idea ignited, an idea that excited me. "I agree about money pits, but since you're getting to know this area, you might keep an eye out for some real estate. I'm not adverse to developing or managing some property, especially if you're a part of it." I'd manage a whole city to entice my son back to Barnes Construction.

For an instant, a gleam appeared in his eye, and happiness surged through me. My boy's roots were all Barnes. All construction. I knew it!

But a moment later, his expression changed. "Sorry, Dad. I won't have time. Ben Parker's beginning to count on me. He's a great guy. Said I was the best rookie he's ever had."

"I'm not surprised, not at all surprised."

"Of course," Ian continued, "he could be full of bull, but I can read a set of blueprints like no other beginner." A satisfied grunt followed his words, and my stomach began to burn. I needed an antacid but continued chewing my House Special Lo Mein.

"What kind of blueprints?" Claire asked, her voice sounding suspicious. In Claire's world, blueprints meant houses. Nice to know she was on my side—for once.

"Pipelines, Mom. Pipelines. I need to know the kind of pipe and tools to use when I replace corroded sections."

"He's a pipefitter, Claire," I added, "or more exactly, training to be one. Ain't that sweet?" I couldn't contain the trace of bitterness in my voice and actually winced when I heard it.

Ian pushed his plate away. "Thanks for the meal. Sorry you're disappointed, Dad, but that's the way it's got to be."

Spoken like a man, but I didn't want to listen. Didn't want to hear it. I signed for the check, watched the waiter box the leftovers, then signaled Claire.

"Before we all leave," Claire said to Ian, "we have to tell you about Anne Conway."

Ian froze. "What happened? More bad news?"

Claire explained about the cancer, and Ian's hands turned into fists on the table. "Poor Maddy. What a crappy year for her. First, she loses her best friend, and now she's afraid of losing her mom." Shaking his head, he mumbled, "I can sure relate. I'll call her later."

Pride mixed with pain as I watched him walk away. He found time to do the right thing with everyone except his old man.

# CHAPTER NINETEEN

*CLAIRE*

*March, Year Two*
*18 months after accident*

Late again. I pushed open Macy's big plate-glass door, took a sharp left, and headed for the Human Resources office. Ever since the first "intervention," Mom had urged us to lunch together on a regular basis. Judy backed her up immediately and suggested meeting at her office each month on one of her working Saturdays where we could select from a variety of restaurants. Mom was thrilled at the idea.

"What could be better than sharing a meal and shopping with my daughters?" she'd ask.

*How about shopping with a granddaughter?*

I found it difficult to thwart my stubborn lifeguards, however, who insisted on keeping me afloat. Maybe I needed them more than I'd wanted to admit.

My sister had always been an entertaining raconteur, and she usually kept Mom and me chuckling with stories about her job, her sons, and their antics. But it was the large department store, with its detailed selections of clothes and accessories, that returned me to periods of before-the-accident normalcy. Shopping offered me a comfort zone. I was used to being surrounded by fabric and styles, to making choices, whether dressing homes or people. Even now, as I walked toward Judy's office, colorful displays nabbed my attention—the cut of a dress, the ruffle of a blouse, an asymmetrical hemline on a skirt. For a moment, my heart trembled as I pictured Mom, Kayla, and me poring through the racks together—three generations on the hunt.

I plowed forward. Nowadays, Mom and I focused on Judy, whose interest in clothes was limited to business suits or jeans. "Jackets and skirts match," she said, "and I don't have to think about it." I was convinced Judy was dropped on our doorstep. However, she was smart enough not to complain about having personal shoppers.

"Woo-hoo, my second handmaiden has arrived! What more could I want?"

I hugged Mom and smiled at my sister. "That's easy. You'd prefer us to do the dirty work without you." I shook my head with mock sympathy. "Not going to happen, baby. Let's go."

Thirty minutes later, Judy slumped on the dressing room bench, handed me an unwanted blouse, and begged, "Can't we have lunch now? I'm *starv*-ing."

After glancing at the sportswear arrayed on our "taking" hook, I winked at my mom. "Has she been punished enough?"

"Her! What about us?" Mom wiped her brow.

"Point taken." I grabbed the merchandise along with Judy's credit card and headed toward the register. And that's where I spotted the driver. Sarah Levine. She stood behind the counter—wavy, brown hair, brown eyes, slim, in her thirties.

Half the garments slipped from my hands. As I bent down to retrieve them, I kept my eye on her. At least, I thought it was her. If not, then my photographic memory had deserted me. On the surface, the sales associate could have been a replica of the woman sitting on the curb the day of the accident. I'd tried not to think about the driver too much. After all, Kayla's death had been an *accident.* Everyone said so, including the cops. So she couldn't be blamed. I stepped forward and put the clothes on the counter.

The clerk looked at me, her eyes widening. "Are you all right, ma'am?"

All right? I'd never be all right.

"Do you need a glass of water?"

"I'm fine. I'm fine." I breathed deeply, quickly absorbing the creased brow and worried expression of a woman doing her job. Thousands of women had brown, wavy hair and brown eyes. I had to be mistaken. Maybe I was starting to hallucinate. Maybe I did need to see a shrink after all. "Here you go," I said, handing her Judy's card.

She smiled and got to work. I watched her, knowing I'd never say anything about this to my sister. Goodness, if a woman named Sarah Levine worked for Macy's, Judy would have known. And if a woman who was a doppelganger for the driver who hit Kayla worked for Macy's, Judy would have known that too. And she would have told me. For crying out loud, as director of Human Resources, Judy knew everyone in the store.

I heard my family closing in behind me and stepped aside. Judy approached. "Hi, Sarah," she said. "Sportswear today, huh? How's it going?"

Sarah? My sister had called the clerk Sarah. Colors blended into a hazy rainbow behind my eyelids. Garments and shoppers floated around me, and only by sheer force of will did I make it back to Judy's office where she wanted to leave her purchases before going to lunch. The thought of eating made my stomach heave.

I swallowed hard, kicked the door closed, and stepped toward my sister. Nothing could stop my verbal assault.

"That's her, isn't it? Sarah Levine? The one behind the counter. And you never mentioned it? How could you? She's been working here all this time...with you?" My voice hit a high note that only a violin could replicate.

"No!" Judy turned toward our mother. "Never a dull moment, is there?"

"Then let's get to the bottom of this." Barbara Anderson was attempting her mother role, but her voice quivered, and she grabbed my hand.

"Mom...i-it's her. I know it." I fell into a chair. "I just need a minute, and I'm going back out there."

"Oh, no you're not," said Judy, squatting next to me. "Because you're wrong." She stood again. "Come look and see. I'm going to show you something that will shut you up but can also cost me my job."

I held up my hand. "Then don't do it."

My sister stood quietly, so unlike her normal self that the stillness stretched into every corner of the room. "That's my choice." She sat down at her computer, punched some keys, and an alphabetical roster of employees appeared on the screen.

"Look through the L's," Judy said. "There are no Levine's here at all."

I browsed slowly and nodded but couldn't believe it. "What about that sales associate out there?"

"I've got three Sarah's in the store," Judy said as she scrolled the list. "A popular name, and she's simply one of them. Hmm. Let's see. Sarah Cohen's in sportswear today. Great attendance; in fact, her first anniversary with the company is coming up. Looks like she's a floater."

"What's that?"

"She's not assigned to any one department, but floats among all of them. Most associates prefer a permanent home where they get to know the regular customers and merchandise. They also befriend their co-workers. But some employees like changing around and feel comfortable anywhere."

That characteristic bespoke of a confident person. Constant change. Comfortable anywhere. Probably not someone who'd run down a child with a car.

"Ooh. I hadn't noticed this before," said Judy softly.

"What?"

"Sarah Cohen floats to every department except Children's. She's made a specific request not to be assigned there."

Judy's gaze met mine. I knew we were on the same wavelength now and said, "Strange that a personable woman doesn't want to be around kids. Can you still state with certainty that this woman is not Sarah Levine?"

"I can only say she's not using that name here, and I have no proof she's anyone other than Sarah Cohen." Judy took my hand and squeezed it. "You may have your suspicions, but please don't go out there and make a scene. You could be wrong. I could lose my job. And what good will it do? I know you don't agree, Clarabelle, and I can't say I blame you, but Sarah is really not a murderer."

My head swam. I struggled to breathe. "Technical details. I-I just want her to know...to know what she's done. To feel what I feel just for one lousy minute..."

"Will it help you move on?" asked Mom. "Will it ease your grief?"

"Let's find out!" I stepped toward the door.

"But you're not sure it will, are you?" Another challenge from Mom.

I froze. Our individual breaths reverberated in the silent room. My mother was right. The answer should have been an easy yes. Enacting one of my revenge daydreams should have been sweet. Satisfying. But I was living in the real world now and couldn't count on that outcome. A zero end game. The thought frightened me.

"I won't make a scene out there, but I'm leaving now. I couldn't eat anyway." I slipped through the doorway before they could respond, unwilling to verbalize the maelstrom of emotions and the confusion running through me. Could I do anything to ease the grief? The guilt? Oh, God, the guilt had me doubling over sometimes, piercing me as sharply as glass shards cutting flesh. How many miles around the lake would it take to expunge it? How many homes would provide enough decorating challenges? How much art would it take to bring Kayla back to us? Well, as close as I could get her. As for my hospital work? The kids responded to me, and I felt useful there. Maybe I'd put in more hours. Maybe volunteering would fix everything. I had no answers, but I had to keep trying.

I got into my car and headed toward Barnes Construction and Jack.

#

My husband could have been anywhere in the building, but I found him talking to a cross-section of employees, waving his arms, excitement in his voice. He was in the middle of a brainstorm. I stood on the threshold, watching and listening.

"Active seniors," he said. "A new type of subdivision for retiring baby boomers. Let's get ahead of the curve. I'm thinking one-story, wide doorways and halls, walk-in showers, levers instead of doorknobs. Why should retirees think of going to Florida or the Texas Hill Country when we can offer the same amenities right here—a large clubhouse, pools, and most importantly, a lifestyle. A full-time activities director. An exercise club. Crafts. Tennis. Softball. Card games, billiards, shows. On-site dining—a bistro."

Jack was at it again, words rolling from his tongue but barely keeping up with the ideas in his head. He was fully engaged. His timing was right, the ideas fit. And he was looking toward the future with eagerness and imagination, leaving Kayla behind. I figured a clear conscience helped.

Jack usually managed to pull out a win no matter the circumstances. He certainly didn't need my intrusion into his grand schemes and employee meeting. I turned away.

"Claire!"

I felt ten pairs of curious eyes on me.

"Hey y'all." I finger-waved. "Sorry to interrupt. I'll see you later, Jack."

"No, wait. Did you hear any of this? Whadduyathink?"

An echo of the old days. Brainstorming new ideas, next steps, building a business. The question was a no brainer. "Find the land. Get the permits. Houston can use a day camp for adults."

"A day camp?" His eyes lit, their corners crinkling. "Bingo!" And suddenly, I was in his arms, being twirled and danced around in front of everyone.

"A new assignment for you, Claire-de-Lune. Go research some practical conveniences for active seniors. Think day camp. Not God's waiting room."

I looked at the group of happy employees, everyone joining the conversation, rejuvenated by one idea. A good idea. The business was Jack's salvation. He knew how to survive anything.

"I just came from Macy's," I said. "We need to talk."

"Bought a mink coat or something?"

"Or something. A big something."

Jack turned to his assembled group. "Think about this new project, but keep it to yourself. We want to be first. Bring me your ideas. You know my door is always open." He scanned the room, making eye contact with each employee. "Any questions?"

Five minutes later, Jack and I were alone. I shut the door, took a breath, and blurted, "I saw the driver in Macy's. I'm sure it's Sarah Levine regardless of her alias. I know it's her."

He jumped back as though I'd burned him, swear words softly rolling from his tongue.

"And what if it is?" he finally asked, his moderate tone a burr under my skin. "She's got to earn a living somehow."

"Does she? Why? Why should she go on smiling at customers like nothing's changed? Like she didn't kill our daughter!"

His face scrunched up until his eyes almost disappeared. I saw his Adam's apple bob a few times as I waited.

"The woman's not my favorite person, but she's not a murderer either." His chest heaved as his words came and, for some reason, the movement satisfied me. My husband wasn't as sanguine as he pretended. He was hurting, still hurting, just like I was.

"It wasn't premeditated," Jack continued. "And if it makes you feel any better, Levine's suffering too. She gave up her teaching career, which she loved. Doesn't trust herself with children anymore. So I'm guessing she took a job that was meaningless to her, where she could go through the motions and only pretend to care." His breathing morphed into a wheeze as he spoke. "Kayla ran into the street, Claire, her eyes on the football instead of traffic. And life has to go on."

"No, it—"

"Yes! Not only for us but even for the Levines and their two kids. Can't you understand? The woman's seeing a shrink and a rabbi; she's taking medication." His gaze met mine. "But maybe she's not the only one who needs a psychologist."

I jumped backward as though he'd struck me. "Dr. Freud, I presume?" Pausing only for a second, I asked, "How the hell do you know all this, and for how long have you known it?"

Jack emitted a huge sigh, but his eyes continued to look into mine. "Her husband called me about six months ago, about the time of the memorial service, and almost cried on my shoulder."

"Six...months...ago? And you didn't say a word about it? How could you not tell me?"

"Easy. You slept on the couch that night—too angry about a lousy haircut and too busy sending out your own message to hear anyone else's. And despite your working again, not much has changed inside you. You're still deaf to everything but your own ideas."

I ignored the personal comment. "What else did the husband say? Was he looking for sympathy? Calling you took a barrel full of nerve."

Jack blinked. His shoulders slumped, and he turned away, collapsing into a chair. "The man was looking for a spark of hope," he murmured, "and wondered how you were coping."

"Hope? Then he's either stupid or naïve. Doesn't he know that hope died with Kayla? No joy in Mudville anymore...You'd better have told him the truth."

"Oh, yeah. I apologized for disappointing him. No encouragement to be found at the Barnes's house."

He expected too much. "That woman...Sh-she still has it all. She still has her two children...her precious children...

"But do they have her?" he asked softly. "We weren't the only ones devastated by the accident. Marc Levine was desperate when he called, at his wits' end."

I shrugged. "That's tough but not my problem."

"Nothing's your problem anymore. You walk away from everyone who wants to help. Your family, your friends, and even me."

"That's not true. I helped Anne. I have lunch with Judy and Mom. And as for you?" This was tricky. "You're a good man, Jack, and I love you, but we're bumping heads all the time. Or maybe hearts. We're not...not in agreement about anything. Maybe we need some space." Maybe I'd sleep on the sofa again.

# CHAPTER TWENTY

*JACK*

I watched Claire leave my office, knowing my marriage had gone from a roller-coaster ride of hope and despair to a steep downhill spiral. I didn't know how much longer Claire and I could go on this way. Maybe we needed a break.

*Kayla*. My sweet, wisecracking, little girl. I could sense her presence as if she were cuddled against me, like a solid memory. She was with me every day and night whatever I was doing. When I mowed the lawn, I brought her up to date on what was happening. Then I told her how much we loved her and always would. No one could take her place. No one. Not ever.

I fumbled in my desk drawer for my antacids then reached for my cell with Marc Levine's phone number. I'd hoped never to call him unless I could provide good news. But I wasn't sure what Claire would do next. She wasn't herself, and I didn't know if I'd ever again recognize the girl I married.

I connected to Levine's number, and he picked up on the first ring.

"Mr. Levine, this is Jack Barnes." My voice was low, hoarse.

"Hello! I'm glad to hear from you...I think."

"Well, forewarned is forearmed, so I'm doing what I can for you."

"That doesn't sound good, but I'm listening."

"Claire recognized Sarah in Macy's today, and only my sister-in-law prevented a confrontation. I'm afraid Claire won't let this rest. Maybe your wife should transfer to another store or something."

Silence reigned at the other end of the phone. Then he spoke softly. "It's so ironic.... She used her maiden name for this job search to avoid being recognized, at least on paper. The newspaper accounts scared her. She thought she was under a microscope. But I guess you can't hide forever. The real problem is that if she goes backward one more time, I don't know what we'll do. Maybe my in-laws are right. Maybe we should move in with them. At least they'd provide more security for the kids."

Was he looking for affirmation? Or just thinking out loud, struggling to make decisions? "Grandparents could be a great idea."

"You know why Sarah was on your street that day, Mr. Barnes? She was checking out a house for sale a few blocks over. We thought it was time for a new place, larger than this condo, and with my oldest starting school and everything... And now we'll probably share with my in-laws." I heard him sigh then say, "But...if it will help Sarah, we'll do it."

I felt myself step back. Housing was my business but not with the Levines. Some boundaries couldn't be crossed.



I felt myself step back. Housing was my business but not with the Levines. Some boundaries couldn't be crossed.

155

# CHAPTER TWENTY ONE

*CLAIRE*

As weeks passed, I got to know my regulars at the hospital. The chronics: Megan Sullivan, Aisha Brown, and Colin McCarthy with their cystic fibrosis treatments. Neil Schulman with his kidney dialysis and a half dozen other children with a variety of conditions from gastro-intestinal to neurological.

I also saw the staff in action, not only the nurses but the allied health professionals: respiratory therapists clapping chests to loosen phlegm, physical therapists with their exercises to strengthen muscles and balance, and occupational therapists with their games and tasks to reinforce patients' skills.

I started to feel like part of the team when they took an interest in the kids' art projects and started chatting with me about particular patients. Their questions and comments, however, also made me nervous. The staff was always searching for clues about their patients and thought I could share some new insights. It seemed my devotion to the volunteer schedule had caught their notice. The youngsters had come through with a variety of projects, giving the staff new areas to explore.

"My goal is for the kids to have fun," I said one afternoon as I was packing up. "That's why I bring a lot of different media to work with. I can't read their minds, and I'm not here to give them therapy." I wasn't qualified, had never considered the medical field, and wanted no responsibility for guaranteeing results. Or improvements. Or whatever they were looking for.

Rose Taylor, the head nurse, patted me on the shoulder. "You're the whipped cream on the cake. Just keep doing what you're doing. We've had other volunteers before you, but we've never seen the pride or, frankly, the hidden talent that's coming through. Look at Neil's cartoons! Who knew? He's only ten years old."

"Neil?" I chuckled. "You can't measure all the kids by Neil. He's the exception. He's got real talent. Reminds me of my son." Which was probably the reason I liked him so much.

Rose smiled. "Well, he's never shown off his talent before. It's made Dr. Henderson very happy too."

"His nephrologist?"

"His shrink. According to Henderson, Neil's cartoons show he's feeling good about himself. That's half the battle, maybe more, when you're dealing with life-threatening illnesses."

That's the part I didn't want to consider. The complex medical issues. I planned the art, brought materials, and worked with the kids in groups or individually, but I tried never to think about their futures. Although these kids did have a fighting chance, something would go wrong someday. Hopefully, a far-off someday. I couldn't help Kayla when she most needed me, so maybe I could help these children have fun whenever they could. And I reminded myself that medical miracles were being made all the time.

"Art should be for healing," I said, surprising myself. "I know that psychologists use play therapy—dolls, puppets, drawing—when kids won't talk, but that's when they're trying to discover the problems. I'd argue that art could be used at the other end, the healing end, to gain confidence and...and open up the world once more." Maddy Conroy was proof.

A slow smile grew across Rose's face. She patted my shoulder. "And I'd argue that the kids have found a gem in you. Not only with art but with everything you do with them—games, stories, and essays too."

Maddy again. "I can't take credit for that. Combining drawing and writing worked with a young friend of mine. She went through two terrible experiences, but now she's doing well. Really well."

"That's wonderful," said Rose. "Thanks for being here."

If Rose was happy with me, Jack was furious. I was late for an appointment with new buyers. My mother had gone home, and the couple almost walked out. My apologies spilled over, and once the buyers were involved in their selection, their frustration vanished. But it was a close call.

Jack stomped into the design center as soon as the couple had left.

"You have no slack time now, Claire. How can I make you understand? We're going full bore with remodeling jobs, new homes, and more décor selections than ever. How can you be late? Every sale counts."

"I'm sorry. I got caught up with the staff."

"The staff?" He glanced toward my door, his forehead wrinkled with confusion.

"At the hospital," I explained.

"Geez, Claire. Haven't you had enough? Take a break. I need your full attention on the business. Last week you fell asleep at your desk before an appointment. Mary had to run back here to check on you."

Right. I'd worked late the night before in my studio. I supposed Jack wasn't wrong from his point of view. But his viewpoint wasn't mine.

"This isn't working," I said.

A moment of silence preceded his, "Be more specific."

"Hire someone else. My heart's not in customer service and high-toned decorating. That's for sure." Not when I could be in my studio with Kayla, at the hospital with the kids, or at Macy's, just watching *her*. Surreptitiously, of course.

"Tough. I'm putting in fourteen-hour days," said Jack. "My heart's not in all the extras we're doing either, but it's our job to save the company. And we will. In fact, we're beginning to." He rubbed the back of his neck, his eyes closed. I couldn't tell whether he was merely easing a headache or wanted to shut me out.

"When our cash flow improves," Jack continued, "do whatever the hell you want. Do you think I like having you around these days? Your attitude weighs me down."

He'd surprised me. "How can it? We don't see much of each other while we're here."

"But you're my wife, Claire, as well as an officer of this company, and in this critical time, you haven't come through for us." He paused, stared at me, "You haven't come through for me." His voice cracked. "Why shouldn't I feel let down?"

Silence echoed in the room. It slammed against my ears and my heart. "I'm sorry, Jack. I just can't help the way I'm feeling either."

But he wasn't listening anymore, at least not to me. Just to himself. "First Kayla, then Ian, and now you.

Everyone's disappearing." He walked toward the door, leaving me with my mouth agape and my stomach twisted in knots.

When he reached the threshold, he turned his head. "I'm calling the support group I mentioned. Want to go? Maybe we can figure stuff out."

Group talk was not on my itinerary, but Jack...? Jack needed help.

"I'll get back to you on that. But you should make the appointment."

His condescending smile was coupled with a mock salute. He knew as well as I did that he'd be attending that group alone.

# CHAPTER TWENTY TWO


*IAN*

*August, Year Two*

A girl. Small but perfect. That's what the nurse said as I stared at the baby for the first time through the nursery window. Beautiful too. But I couldn't get past small. Five pounds, six ounces was supposedly normal. I glanced at my hands. Good for palming a basketball or swinging a hammer, but a baby?

I was covered in sweat; a vise gripped my stomach, and a million doubts raced through me quicker than sperm racing toward an egg. I'd been so sure about this decision, but maybe Colleen and I had made a mistake. No, no, not Colleen. Me. *I'd* made the decision. *I'd* talked her into keeping the baby. Because I couldn't handle another death, another girl or boy gone to nowhere, not even one as tiny as a seed. I kept staring at...my daughter? She was here. Real. And as the reality set in, I began to smile. Grin, really. A silly, goofy grin remained on my face as a wave of pride suffused my body all the way to my fingertips. My doubts receded like the ocean at low tide.

"Hey, little girl," I whispered. "Your daddy's here. And he'll take care of you and love you, and you're going to be just fine." Irresponsible, Mom? I think not. No regrets about this.

"Hey, new daddy." A friendly nurse winked at me as she headed toward the secured door and pushed a series of buttons. "How'd you like to see her fingers and toes?" she asked. "She'll need a diaper change, so just give me a minute to get inside."

I watched her unwrap the blanket, and my little papoose became a squalling infant waving skinny arms and stick-like legs, her complexion changing from pink to rosy red. I heard her lung power through the glass.

*You go, girl!* She sure sounded healthy. Maybe the nurse was right, and all babies started out this small. I glanced at the other cribs. Yup. Those kids seemed the size of a football too. So, okay. I was ready to handle this. I earned a steady paycheck and could provide a home—if I could hold my make-believe family together. My mouth tightened. A family sounded like a dad's job. But even my dad hadn't managed to get us back to normal again.

After the nurse wrapped up the baby, I went to Colleen's room, a semi-private, covered by insurance for a one-night stay. I walked to her bed and watched her doze, her long hair like a crimson cape around her. Restless, she kicked the sheets and moaned. I reached for her hand.

"Still hurting?"

"Hi, Bonehead. Men have no idea," she whispered. "Even I had no idea."

"You'll feel better tomorrow."

"Couldn't feel worse. I shouldn't have gone through with it."

"Don't say that. She's beautiful, Colleen. Just like her mother."

"You've seen her?"

I nodded. Colleen had wanted to be knocked out, didn't want anything to do with natural childbirth and pain. So I'd seen the baby first while Colleen slept.

A brief knock on the door preceded the entrance of our assigned nurse. "Hey, you two. Time for Mama to meet her baby girl."

Colleen groaned as she pushed herself higher on the bed. I tried to help adjust her pillows and turned to the nurse. "Do all women feel like Colleen after they've given birth?"

"Everyone's different, but Ms. Murphy is doing just fine. She's had stitches."

Embarrassed, I knew my face mimicked the same rosy hue on my daughter's face a few minutes ago. From now on, I'd keep my mouth shut about Colleen's recovery. I'd been heading for engineering, architecture or business after high school. Medicine had never been in my playbook.

The nurse placed the baby in Colleen's arms and studied the two together. I watched also, happy to see how carefully Colleen held her daughter and how hard she stared at her, as hard as I had earlier.

"You were right, Ian. She's a pretty one, for sure," the new mama finally said. And then she began to sing a lullaby in the soft, clear voice of an angel. *Hush, little baby, don't say a word...*

The nurse's mouth dropped open. I knew the feeling. Of course, I'd heard Colleen sing many times, but each time she did, she managed to grab me by the gut.

"That was church-bell beautiful," said the nurse when Colleen had finished. "I'll leave you guys alone now, but you can expect a social worker to come around soon with some paperwork. So, do we have a name for this baby yet?"

"We sure do," Colleen replied. "This little gal's name is Martina Faith Barnes, after Martina McBride and Faith Hill, two of my favorites. I love Shania and Taylor too...but how many names can one baby have?"

I didn't care about names as long as we didn't name her Kayla. That would be too painful. "Let's call her Tina for short," I said. "But maybe we should have named her Dolly. She looks..."

"I know, I know," Colleen interrupted with a shake of her head. "And I love Dolly Parton, but I've made up my mind. It's Martina Faith."

I didn't see the nurse leave after that. I just focused on my daughter. Little Tina resembled a baby doll Kayla used to play with. One of those dolls that said Ma-ma when the string was pulled. Ma-ma. Ma-ma. Claire Barnes. Damn! *Don't go there.*

I studied Colleen and Baby Tina. I had a new life now. A better life. I started singing a song just for myself—quietly, of course. *Let freedom ring...* I could almost hear the white dove singing his heart out because man, oh man, talk about a day of reckoning.

Colleen joined me and bestowed a quick smile. "See? You like Martina too! Not a bad job, but for the fact you got the message turned around." Her brow wrinkled and shadows darkened her eyes as she looked from me to the baby. "Today's not *Independence Day* for us at all. We've got a kid now. Cute as pie too, but we've lost our freedom, city boy."

Her tears seemed about to fall, and I felt sick again. "I said I'd help you with everything. I promised fifty-fifty and more."

"And I'm gonna hold you to it. But..." Her lids closed, and she sighed on such a mournful note that I saw a shudder run from her head to her feet. This time, I knew her pain had nothing to do with childbirth.

"Ah, Ian," she whispered. "You just don't know what it takes to care for a baby. And you don't know what it takes to build a singing career. Ever watch *American Idol*? Even that's a full-time gig for the contestants. And remember, I'm heading to Nashville one day soon— before I'm too old."

My chin dropped to my chest. She'd always been truthful about that, but couldn't her career wait awhile until we figured out how to be Tina's parents?

# CHAPTER TWENTY THREE




*CLAIRE*

*September, Year Two*
*Second anniversary of Kayla's death*

Another year gone. Another year loomed. As the two-year mark drew closer, tears, tension, and zombie periods ebbed and flowed. I lost track of time. Of where I was supposed to be. Pain enveloped me again, as deep as when we first lost her. No matter what I'd heard about other people's grief, time wasn't healing mine.

I expected the family to show up at the cemetery today, but not together. First, it was mid-week. And second, although I hated to admit it and I was ashamed, Judy was barely speaking to me and had banned me from Macy's.

After identifying that Levine woman six months ago in the store, I couldn't stay away. Every other week or so, I'd find some excuse to stop in. A scarf. A cosmetic sale.

I'd buy anything at all to soothe my conscience for spying. Cohen? Levine? No matter what name she used, she was the one.

Last month, I finally introduced myself to the slender brunette. I simply walked over and said, "Sarah? Sarah *Levine*?"

She caught my emphasis and grasped the countertop, the tips of her fingers turning white. She stared, eyes narrowing as she tried to identify me. "Y-yes. Can I help you?" Her customer service training shone through. I knew I had the advantage, and it wouldn't be a fair fight, but Kayla hadn't had a fair chance either.

"My name is Claire Barnes," I said slowly. "Mother of Kayla Barnes."

I heard her gasp, and her overall skin tone quickly matched her pale fingers. So ghostly white, I could almost see through her. She peered over my shoulders then turned in a circle. "Am I under arrest?" she whispered when she faced me again. "Are the cops incognito?"

Obviously, the shrink hadn't helped her. Or maybe her husband had fed Jack a bunch of baloney about a doc and a rabbi. Not my concern.

"No cops...today. I just wanted to see you up close. To see the woman who killed my daughter." I stared at her hard and gave her credit for not flinching. When a customer interrupted, Levine's hands shook as she rang the sale.

"I'll be back," I said when she was done.

"Come as often as you want," she said. "I won't be here."

And with that, she bent down, took her purse, and headed to Human Resources. Judy's office. And that's when the dirt hit the fan and where Sarah Levine managed to touch a corner of my heart.

The woman faced me in Judy's office, her dark eyes shadowed, cheeks caved, her stricken expression for all to see. "I know you hate me," she said. "I don't blame you. I hate myself too. In my tradition, to save one life is the same as saving the world. So what does it mean to take one life? That I've destroyed the world?"

First she looked at Judy, then at me, and answered her own question. "Yes. Of course it does. I've destroyed the world. I can never forgive myself because I-I can't fix it. Forgiveness for this tragedy is beyond any human being."

At which point, Judy interrupted. "But I can fix this particular situation," she said, pointing at me. "You, Claire, are no longer welcome in this store. Sarah is an excellent employee, and I will not tolerate your behavior toward her."

Now I was the one taken aback. "You're kidding," I finally said to Judy. "I'm your sister and a loyal customer. I've been shopping here for years."

She reached for the phone. "I hate to do it, Claire, but I can't overlook this. I'm calling Security."

"See, it's true!" cried Sarah. "I am destroying the world!" With a jerk of her arm, she ripped the name tag from her shirt and threw it on Judy's desk. "I don't belong here. I don't belong anywhere. There's no place for people like me. I quit. Now you two can be friends again. Good-bye."

Light on her feet and moving faster than a hummingbird's wings, Sarah Levine disappeared. But her voice still rang in my head, her words a portrait of despair.

Judy offered to rehire her, begged her to return, but in the end was unsuccessful. Sarah's departure didn't affect my status, however. I was a nonentity at Macy's— all locations.

On the second anniversary, I forced a smile at Jack and reached for the colorful wreath I'd bring to Kayla today. "Ready?" I asked, stepping toward the back door.

"Always ready to visit with my daughter."

"Always?" We didn't go to the cemetery together during the year. "Do you visit her sometimes on your own?" If so, he'd never mentioned it.

Jack popped one of his pills and said, "The gravesite? No."

"It works for me. You could come."

But he shook his head. "I don't need a stone marker to remind me she's gone."

"Well, that's true enough." I reached for his hand. "It's the heart that doesn't forget, isn't it?"

His Adam's apple worked hard before he managed to grunt something affirmative.

We entered the car in silence and belted ourselves in. "You know what, Jack?"

"What?"

"We finally agreed on something."

#

*IAN*

Long rays of sunlight stretched across the park-like grounds when I finally arrived to visit Kayla. I'd knocked off work an hour early—my boss had no problem with that because he liked how I took on projects. "I'm countin' on you, college boy," he'd say at least once or twice a week. So far, I'd never let him down, and today he repaid the favor.

I figured that early evening was the best time to show up. My folks would be gone by now, so there'd be no emotional scenes between us. I needed a break from ongoing scenes. The baby's first month at home had been tough. Colleen had the post-partum blues. Anyway, that's what she said, so I looked it up online, and she was probably right. She had no spark, no joy, and cried for no reason. She was just going through the motions of being Tina's mother.

My own mom could teach her a thing or two. In the old days, she was our biggest cheerleader, Kayla's and mine, no matter the activity, no matter how important or small our role. She used to attend every school game we were in. When I was driving at the fifty-yard line, I could hear her from the bleachers.

Suddenly I was rubbing away tears. *Damn memories. Don't go there, Ian. You're dealing with enough right now, and you're doing fine.*

I approached Kayla's flower-strewn resting spot, the large stone engraved with two angels and inscribed with Kayla's name, dates of birth and death, Beloved Daughter-Sister-Granddaughter, Rest in Peace. It was beautiful, and I had to give my mom credit.

Lost in my thoughts, it took me awhile to notice the other two visitors camouflaged by the evening's shadows. A woman sat cross-legged on the ground maybe ten feet away, her lips moving. Was she talking to Kayla? A man stood a short distance from her, his back toward the woman. He was gazing out at the horizon. They hadn't noticed me yet either, and I kept still because the woman looked familiar. With my second glance, I knew who she was.

"Hello," I said softly.

She jumped to her feet, panicked, eyes wide and wild.

I put my palm up and stepped back. "It's okay, Mrs. Levine," I crooned. "Don't be afraid. I thought you might come round again. Last year, you brought a wreath and wrote a nice card, didn't you?"

She tugged at her clothes, looking like she didn't understand a word I said, looking anywhere but at me. Then she spoke.

"I have a better plan this time." Her hands fluttered this way and that, her fingers raking her hair. "Today's my last visit. I won't bother you anymore." She tiptoed closer to me and whispered, "I'm going to see Kayla soon. I'll take care of her."

"What!" Now I was the one panicking. The woman was talking crazy, and what could I do? I hoped to God the guy standing there was her husband. I opened my mouth to call him, but the woman spoke first, this time at a normal volume.

"If I take care of Kayla, then everyone will feel better," she continued, "not only me but your mama too."

The man approached quickly then, his distress palpable, his face a network of sorrowful lines. He put his hands on the woman's shoulders. "No, Sarah. No. That's not going to happen. Come on, sweetheart. Let's go... "

"But ma'am, you already took care of Kayla," I interrupted, my frightened thoughts chasing each other faster than cars at the Indy 500. "You did a great job. When the accident happened, you told me to call the police, you told me to get a blanket, you told me not to move her. *I* didn't know what to do, but *you* did. And we did it. And when you spoke with the cops, you gave them the whole story. You left nothing out."

Breathless now, I waited and watched. Her eyes were bigger than hubcaps, so she must have been listening. Her husband's painful expression had changed too. He looked interested, eager.

"Did I really do all that?" she asked. "I don't remember much more than shaking hard and throwing up."

"But that was afterwards," I said. "After you did everything right."

She stared at me. "Everything right?" she whispered.

I nodded so fast my head almost snapped from my neck.

"Are you sure?"

"Yes, ma'am. I had a brain freeze. I was glad you were there."

And then she cried. Her husband held her, but she couldn't stop the tears. "But we knew all this, Sarah," said the man. "The officers said so." He looked at me. "You spoke with the police too?"

I nodded, remembering.

"Sarah, Sarah," he said, holding her, his hand slowly rubbing her back, "no one could have done more than you."

"So, I'm not a bad, bad person?" She appealed to her husband, then to me, her voice high and childlike.

"No! Never," said Mr. Levine. "You're the sweetest, best, most loving person in the...in the..." And then he lost it.

"But am I forgiven?" She was looking at me now, and I wanted to howl. *I'm just a kid!* What do I know about these big questions? Where was my dad? Where was *the man*? I glanced around quickly, hoping for a miracle, but got none.

I took a deep breath and figured there was only one answer to give a woman who lived on the edge of sanity. "I forgive you, Sarah. You didn't mean to hurt Kayla. You weren't drunk. You weren't speeding. It was a god-awful, terrible accident. You're not evil. So, yes, I forgive you."

Desperation mingled with hope, all illuminated on her face, a search for salvation. Once more, I couldn't stop my own tears from falling.

"But your father? Your mother?" she asked. "Oh, your mother hates me, how she hates me—but I'd go to her anyway. I'd go to them both—this week, in fact, before *Yom Kippur*, the Day of Atonement—to ask pardon for this awful, awful thing I did. Do you think they'd open their door?"

The question caught me off guard. I looked at her husband then back at Sarah. Regardless of her great need, I had to tell the truth. "I don't know. Maybe my dad. My mom...? I don't think she's forgiven me yet, so I wouldn't hold your breath."

"I-I don't understand. Forgive you for what? You didn't do anything wrong."

*But I'm alive while Kayla is not.* "I threw the ball. I was in charge. She says we should have been doing homework."

Mr. Levine kept his arms around his wife but addressed me. "I'm sorry, very sorry for the grief you've endured, but thank you for talking with us. I think it's made a difference. Right, Sarah? Now you'll have something new to tell Dr. Lipton. And maybe one day, someday, you'll be able to forgive yourself, heal, and start to live again."

"I can never forget about this, Marc."

"I didn't say forget. I said forgive."

Mr. Levine turned to me. "Your parents have a remarkable son. When the time is right, you can tell them that. Thank you again."

I watched them walk away, a young couple, moving as cautiously as my grandparents sometimes did. I felt the weight they carried because it sat on my shoulders as well. When they were out of sight, I finally hunkered down near my sister.

"I've got something good to tell you, Kayla," I began. "You've got a brand-new niece. Her name's Tina and she's...she's th-the cutest little ba..."

My throat closed mid-sentence. With the impact of a sledgehammer, I realized that Kayla would never, ever get to know Tina, and Tina would never know her aunt. No kisses and hugs. No laughter. No shopping trips and girl stuff together. Not in this life anyway. The reality check drove a sudden chill through me, a chill that traveled deep into my soul, making me shiver and shake. As I looked ahead to an uncertain future, I wondered if I'd ever feel warm again.

# CHAPTER TWENTY FOUR

*IAN*

*Early October, Year Two*

"Hey, Barnes. Catch!"

I pivoted, reached, and caught the set of blueprints Ben Parker threw.

"That's just one section," my supervisor said. "The unit's shutting down for two weeks. We gotta do a complete maintenance overhaul. You'll be checking the pipes inch-by-inch, looking out for corrosion. And verifying the online monitoring that's been done. Then you'll fabricate new pipes and fittings to replace the worn ones. I'll be around, but you'll be working on your own, kid."

Whoa. On my own? A lot of responsibility for an apprentice, even a second-year apprentice. I must have looked a little scared because Mr. Parker started to laugh.

"Nothing to worry about, boy. There's a meeting at ten o'clock. Everybody in the unit. Be there."

"Yes sir."

"And another thing," the man said, more slowly this time, his big body pausing along with his words.

I inclined my head, ready to listen.

"I know Colleen's fixin' ta be back here the same time as the shutdown..." The question lingered.

"Yes sir. She'll be here."

"Good. I don't need you going missing to babysit." Parker walked closer to me, his lined face relaxing. "You're the best apprentice I've ever had, Barnes. And I proved it to you, didn't I?"

"You sure did," I replied, thinking about my nice raise. "And I appreciate it."

"So don't let me down. One day, with your brains, you could be my boss and run this place."

I couldn't stop myself from grinning. The man was good for my ego. "Well, an engineering degree isn't in my future, but I appreciate your faith in me. Thanks."

I watched him walk away. A confident man who loved his work, just like my dad loved his. I quickly focused on the blueprints. Mr. Parker wasn't wrong. I could do this job. Whatever I hadn't known about crude oil at the beginning, I'd learned during the past year. I now understood the distillation process and how petroleum's hydrocarbons were separated to produce gasoline, diesel fuel, and dozens of other end products. Being an apprentice here was more than learning a trade. It was learning a new industry, a new world. But I'd slipped into it as though born to it—thanks to math, science, and Barnes Construction.

I needed this raise, needed to do well and support my little family like a responsible man. Right now, that included assuring daycare for Tina. Colleen was supposed to be in charge of finding one. So far, no luck. She'd said the closest ones were full and had no room for one more baby. Worry niggled at me. Colleen had been so half-hearted about everything, I wondered if she'd really checked them all out. Or would I have to take over that project too?

#

*COLLEEN*

Free-dom. Free-dom. Free-dom. My steps matched the rhythm of the word echoing in my head as I pushed Tina in her stroller. Free-dom. I should've been happy. My baby girl was a healthy, beautiful infant, almost two months old, a true mix of Ian and me. Right now, she was asleep, so innocent, so at peace, and my heart filled with my love for her. But who the heck wanted a baby right now?

Ian. This whole mess was his fault. Although our neighbors minded their own business, they probably thought Ian and I were aiming for the altar. But we knew the truth. It wasn't about getting married. Neither of us had ever mentioned the M word but once or twice. It was all about the baby. It always came back to Martina Faith Barnes.

I should've stuck to my guns in the beginning. I should've taken care of it as soon as I missed my period. I probably shouldn't have told Ian. He was the sensitive type, filled with kindness. If I'd known about his sister, I definitely wouldn't have said a word.

Well, I couldn't undo it, and I couldn't fault Ian for breaking promises. He'd kept them, taking care of us as best he could. But now we needed a daycare 'cause in a couple of weeks I'd have to go back to the refinery. The thought made me want to puke. Not that I hated the job so much, but sometimes, just sometimes, I worried that I'd never escape.

My legs felt heavy. My heart felt heavy. They were keeping slow time with each other as I trudged down the street. God Almighty, I couldn't remember ever being so depressed! I had to think about something happy...like singing at the Roadside Café. Today was—I checked my watch—Wednesday. All right! Open mic time this evening. Amazingly, my feet barely touched the ground as I headed to the last daycare center on my list.

#

*IAN*

"Ben Parker asked about you today," I said to Colleen that evening. I'd just washed up after getting home and stood on the threshold of the small living room, watching Colleen feed the baby. "He wants to be sure he can count on you to return to work on schedule, what with the daycare and everything."

"Here you go, Daddy," she said, rising from the sofa. "You can finish giving her the bottle. I've got to get ready." She shoved Tina at me and raced toward the bedroom.

"Ready for what?" I called.

"Singing."

I nuzzled the baby just as my stomach began to growl. "I'm just saying...about Ben. So, what's for dinner?"

"How about fixing yourself a hotdog?"

Hotdogs? I snacked on hotdogs. I was running on empty and wanted a real meal. Roast chicken, turkey, my mom's sweet potato pie... My salivary glands started a ruckus, and loud rumbles came from my midsection.

"How come you didn't make anything? I'm starving."

"Look at me." Colleen strode into the room, patting her stomach. "I can get back into this skirt again." Her eyes sparkled. The denim hugged her hips and thighs and ended mid-calf. Sitting on the bed, she pulled on high leather boots.

"Great," I said. "I'm happy for you, I really am, but a hotdog's not dinner."

"I didn't have time to cook."

"No time?" I couldn't believe it. "The baby sleeps at least half the day."

"Maybe in fits and starts, and that's no help. Our sweet little thing keeps me busier than a hound in flea season. She may be a cutie pie, but she's more work than you know, so don't start preachin' at me."

She slipped on a red, silky shirt and began to close the buttons. Twirling toward me, she posed. "Should I leave the top two open...or maybe three?"

Another hunger grew, and I forgot about food. Colleen was one sexy woman, a woman who didn't care about my opinion regarding buttons or anything else. I could see her drifting into her own world now, her mind tuned to the karaoke session ahead. She probably used every spare daytime minute to write new songs.

"You look...nice." I lifted Tina for a burp, and without missing a beat, she performed.

"'Atta girl! Whee. You did it." Then I laid her back on my arm and headed for the kitchen. "Let's see if your daddy can rustle up something as good as your bottle."

At that very moment, Tina opened her blue eyes and smiled directly at me. Holy Toledo! Could she actually know her daddy? I grinned back at her, a wave of love washing through me unlike anything I'd known before. My little girl blinked and kept looking up at me.

"Hey, Colleen? Tina smiled at me."

"Probably just gas," she replied, walking toward the door.

"But she's already burped. I think she knows who I am."

Colleen paused, caught my eye. "Well, sir. Whether she knows you or not, she can sure make you smile a lot better'n I can these days."

I became hyper-alert. "What's that supposed to mean?"

She grabbed her guitar and slammed the door behind her.

What was she so mad about? I'd catered to her during the pregnancy with back rubs, foot rubs, making her rest. I even brought flowers to the hospital. But I had to admit, Colleen had been right about one thing. One big thing. Little babies demanded a lot of attention. They caused lots of hard work and worry. Not to mention a way of interrupting any romantic inclinations between parents.

I'd bought Colleen candy and more flowers when she came home to show her it wasn't only about the baby. Besides, wasn't that what grown men did, buy women stuff like that? But sometimes—and I hated to admit it— I didn't feel like a grown man at all, especially with money being so tight.

I was trying to be more like my dad, who not only talked the talk but walked the walk. Everyone looked up to him. Even after...after Kayla died, he got back to work as busy as ever with his phones ringing and Realtors coming in and out and different shifts working on the sites. He took responsibility, always building something to be proud of. Jack Barnes loved the business. And I'd loved it too. Or had I just loved trailing after him?

"Can't worry about the past, can we, Tina?" I whispered, laying her in the crib. "That's for losers. We need to think about the future and...oh, dammit!"

Oops. "Sorry about the language, sweetie."

Daycare. I'd gotten distracted earlier and forgotten to follow up with Colleen about daycare. If we were lucky, she'd found a place. But wouldn't she have mentioned it? Damn, dang, damn. I needed a backup plan. Maybe I could work a double shift and Colleen could stay home. Or maybe I'd work nights and Colleen work days....

I knew I'd figure out something. When my back was to the wall, I always managed to come up with ideas. Of course, according to my dad, not all of my ideas were great, just inventive. I chuckled at the memory. If Colleen returned to the plant, her income would make life easier, could provide the occasional pot roast or steak. The thought had me salivating again as I opened the freezer door and reached for the hotdogs.

More important than steak, however, I couldn't let Ben Parker down, not when he was counting on me. Especially not after that generous raise he'd worked into his budget.

# CHAPTER TWENTY FIVE



*CLAIRE*

*Late October*

I put my brush down. The finished portrait stood against the wall of my studio. An oversized canvas. A full-length rendering with a new title: *Girl Exhalted*. In her green soccer uniform, Kayla jumped high, knees bent, with her arms up in victory. Winning goal scored by number one. Joy radiated from every part of her. *We did it!* she seemed to shout.

"You sure did," I whispered. "And I did too."

I enjoyed a moment of inner peace. The same calmness I'd felt when I'd finally started this portrait, the same calmness I'd managed to recapture from time to time as I lost myself in the work. It had taken much longer to finish than I'd anticipated, but pain had given way to pleasure as I saw Kayla come to life under my direction.

This canvas had become my driving force, my primal energy. Soccer action was classic Kayla, and my daughter in motion was exactly what I'd needed to paint. Jack hadn't seen it yet—I was planning to surprise him—and I hoped he'd love it as much as I did.

We'd be celebrating our twenty-fifth anniversary this Saturday at Casa Olé. The party had been my idea, and Jack had gone along with it, although I must admit he'd seemed surprised at first.

"Are you really willing to celebrate? As in, have a good time?" he'd asked.

I took a moment. "We're still here, aren't we...after twenty-five years?"

A lovely smile appeared. "I guess so, Claire. I hope so."

My plan was to wait until after dinner and then unveil the portrait for all the guests to see. Everyone would be there—family, friends, and key people in the business. And, of course, Ian. Oh, I hoped he'd like it. Afterward, we'd display it in the family room where Kayla could be present in our everyday life. She'd be with us again, just in a different way. I'd never worked as hard on any project as I had painting this portrait, and I've rarely been this happy about what I produced. Professor Columbo used to say: *you don't see what I see. Your work is good, more than good. It's magnifique!* His unconscious drifting from one language to another always amused me, but when I studied *Girl Exalted*, I agreed with him.

Most importantly, maybe after the party, after sharing the portrait with family and friends, I'd be able to laugh again. Maybe I'd be able to maintain peace within myself and make peace with everyone I loved.

#

I showed up at work smiling. I ate lunch with an appetite. Jack noticed. Mom noticed.

"You've got something up your sleeve," said Mom before biting into her sandwich. Her eyes shone, the corners crinkled. "Whatever it is, I love it!"

Hopefully, she'd love the picture when she saw it at the party.

On Tuesday, I whistled as I entered the hospital and made my way to Pediatrics. After seven months, the staff counted on me showing up with my overflowing tote bag and ideas for the kids. Today we'd work in the lounge where tables and easels were available. I'd brought a pumpkin and a witch's hat to set the mood for Halloween, but the children might have other ideas entirely. It didn't matter. All that mattered was that they had a chance to enjoy themselves just like anyone else.

Within five minutes of arriving in the unit, I knew something was wrong. The nurses' smiles were forced as they greeted me, and a short time later, Rose Taylor showed up in the lounge. I was setting up a finger-painting area for the younger kids or anyone who wanted to jump in but stepped away when Rose motioned me over.

"Come see me before you leave," she said.

My stomach tightened. Bad news was etched all over her. "What happened? Who?" I asked the questions but wanted to hide from the answers.

Rose nodded at the children waiting to make art. "You've got to pay attention to them right now. Talk to you later."

To my amazement, the hour flew by. The little ones needed constant help, and a handful of parents assisted. So maybe Jack was half right. Time went quickly when you stayed busy. But I thought "busy" wasn't enough. You had to be doing something you liked, something meaningful.

None of my regulars showed up. I hoped they were home and healthy this week.

Rose was waiting for me at the nurses' station. I followed her into a private office.

"There's no way to break it gently, Claire, so I'll just say it. We lost Neil Schulman yesterday. His kidneys just gave out before a good match could be found for transplant."

"Neil! Oh, poor boy." I blinked hard, but not hard enough.

"I know he was special to you."

"Every child is special, Rose." And that was the problem. Neil was my cartoon-drawing young artist. "How awful not to find a match."

"Yeah. A parent can often be a donor, but Neil was adopted. The family genetics were random and didn't work out."

It made sense. "After I first meet the kids, I never think about them dying," I whispered. "They get such great care, and everyone is always so positive. Maybe I believe there's magic here." Or maybe I was in denial.

"I wish it were easier. We have to be upbeat or we wouldn't survive. Sometimes, however, our humor can verge on the macabre. But it gets us through."

"Neil was a fighter," I said. "His poor parents..." I flashed back to the weeks after Kayla died. How Jack and I had died too. Zombies. Without warning, I doubled over, arms wrapped around myself, a familiar pain piercing my stomach. Would Megan be next? Cystic Fibrosis wasn't curable.

I'd been delusional, pretending to be strong and making art with the children as I'd done with Kayla. Sure, I was trying to provide some happiness for the patients and an hour of diversion. But what was the true reason I'd taken this challenge on? To show Kayla I was...was...what? A good mommy after all? To earn her forgiveness?

I couldn't continue to fool myself. Despite the fabulous staff and medical miracles, every chronically ill youngster would not go on indefinitely when the shadow of death lingered. Jack and Anne had been right. I'd taken on more than I could handle.

I grasped Rose's hand. "I might need some time off."

"You've made a difference, Claire. Don't forget that. And isn't that the goal? To help the living?"

"My husband agrees with you. But I think about my daughter all the time."

She patted my arm and leaned toward me. "One day you won't. She'll be nestled somewhere else inside you, and you'll move on. You're just not there yet. But with a little more time, you will be."

Maybe. Maybe not. I didn't respond, but Rose didn't seem to expect me to. She reached for an envelope instead.

"These are some of Neil's drawings that hung on the walls around here. I think you should have them. A remembrance of the good work you've done."

"He hardly needed me. I just gave him a few pointers."

"Well, you must have made an impression. He talked about you all the time. 'Miss Claire is a real artist,' he'd say."

*A real artist.*

"Sounds like a professor I once knew—in another lifetime." I took the envelope, promised to return to the unit at some point, and went home. I'd give the pictures to Neil's family. I had Kayla's, and his work belonged to his parents.

# CHAPTER TWENTY SIX


*CLAIRE*

*Saturday night*

A cheerful place, Casa Olé was dressed in funky, garish décor. Red, yellow, and green plastic chili peppers were strung everywhere, and exotic orange and blue murals covered the walls. Not my usual taste but great for a party. I'd even asked for a large parrot piñata to hang from the ceiling because a celebration should have games to keep it lively—not that the margaritas couldn't do it by themselves. The aromas wafting across the room promised a fine meal, but I knew I'd barely nibble. My mind was on the main event—Kayla's portrait.

Guests had started to arrive, and I noticed Jack standing near the door, handsome and trim. Forty-eight looked good on him. I watched him shake hands, smile, do a little back slapping. I recognized the gestures and knew he'd say all the right words. A successful businessman had to be good with words. And tonight, Jack seemed happy, happy enough to be in his Cracker Jack frame of mind. His good humor gave me hope that all would go as planned, and I felt a smile emerge and morph into a wide grin.

Maybe we were still perfectly matched. Maybe we would come out of this crisis. I thought *Girl Exalted* would not only help but would be the key to a new beginning. Of course, Jack had thought the same about passing the first anniversary of Kayla's death. Did anyone have the right answers?

Approaching me at a fast clip, Jack said, "Love that smile. Keep it up." He kissed me on the mouth before walking to another table of friends. Then the restaurant door opened, and it was my turn to greet the visitors. Judy and Charles entered.

"I'm glad you came," I said.

"We're still sisters. And always will be. Besides, a twenty-fifth is something to celebrate. I wouldn't have missed it for anything."

I kissed her and Charles, pushing away all thoughts of Sarah Levine. The woman had nothing to do with tonight, or with my expectations of renewal.

Judy spotted our folks, and I followed her to their table.

"Claire, honey," said my dad. "I want to know where my grandson is. Haven't seen him in too long."

And suddenly six pairs of eyes rested on me, waiting for a response. Oh, God. I couldn't remember what Ian had told me. Was I supposed to call him back? Had I remembered to call him at all? My good spirits vanished.

"I'll ask Jack," I said, pointing at the man two tables away.

Moments later, I reached for his hand but addressed his companions. "Mind if I borrow him for a moment?"

"Do you still want him after twenty-five years?" That voice came from my cousin, Marilyn, always a gentle teaser. "Go, go, mingle," she said with a quick gesture of her hands.

I dragged Jack outside. "Ian. Did you speak with Ian? I can't remember if I did, if I called him." My last words hit high notes that startled me.

"Sure, I spoke with him, but you know how he's been with us lately."

Us? I'd thought it was just with me. "What do you mean?"

"For God's sake, Claire. Wake up. He's drawn a sharp line in the sand concerning us. He didn't promise to come." He started pacing. "I don't know what he's up to any more than you do. Maybe if you'd speak with him more regularly, pay him some more attention...?"

I tuned him out and scanned the street in both directions. Nothing. "Call him now, Jack, on your cell. He might be on his way."

Cars doors slammed, and I went to greet our latest guests, leaving Jack to his assignment.

#

*JACK*

"Sorry, Dad. I thought I told you I'd be tied up tonight. But give my love to the grands...and to Mom."

"I don't remember that." But I wasn't surprised. Simply disappointed. "Your grandparents feel abandoned. This is important, Ian. Can't you postpone whatever you're doing?" Fat chance. My good-looking kid was probably with a girl, probably anticipating a roll in the hay, and nothing was more important at nineteen than getting laid. "Look, if you've got a date, just bring her along. There's plenty of food and beer."

"I'm really sorry, Dad. I can't get away tonight. Can you just tell the folks I'm working overtime and the money's good? The plant operates around the clock. Tell them and they'll understand."

But I didn't. The plant, the plant, the plant. Had Ian's job become the most important part of his life? A pipefitter instead of a college student? I wanted him at the university with his friends. I wanted him learning the business and finance end from the get-go, not like me who attended night school while working full-time in the trades, struggling with the debit and credit side later. If Ian studied finance, he could talk to bankers in their own language as soon as he took over the business.

Instead of college or Barnes Construction, he'd chosen the refinery. It wasn't about the money. His disappearance from the family stemmed back to the accident. Was he really working overtime tonight, or was he simply continuing to avoid us?

"Don't be surprised if Mom calls you back," I said.

The silence on the other end of the line preceded the quiet click, and Ian was gone. Disconnected. I stared at my cell. Disconnected—a perfect description. We'd each disconnected from one another. Mentally, emotionally, physically. I knew it. Claire knew it too. And Ian had made his choice clear. Sometimes, when I let my guard down, when I allowed myself to think about what happened to my family, I wanted to howl. Instead, I popped an antacid.

Despite my disappointments, however, I still had hope. I'd been called a cockeyed optimist many times in my life. With Claire in such a good mood tonight, we had a chance to reconnect, to communicate, and rekindle the flame after twenty-five years. Of course, I had to deliver the bad news about Ian's no-show, but my heart was light as I entered the restaurant.

# CHAPTER TWENTY SEVEN

*IAN*

*Same night*

After I hung up on my dad, I shoved the phone in my pocket and just stared into space. I saw nothing but heard Dad's words. He'd said to bring a date. That was almost funny enough to make me laugh. I knew he wanted me back, but I couldn't do it. No matter how many times I went over it in my head, I always came back to the same conclusion: I'd had to strike out on my own in order to survive. Kayla had died. I'd thrown the ball. Ergo, my fault. According to my mother. Not that she quite said it like that....

Whatever.

I ambled to the bedroom doorway and glanced at my sleeping daughter. Two months old. It seemed like two years. Colleen had been right about a few things. I really hadn't known anything about babies. The crying, feeding, and checking on every minute. Thank God I hadn't dropped her. In the beginning, I'd practiced holding her while sitting on the bed. Then I made Colleen walk next to me around the apartment while I carried Tina in my arms.

I bought one of those disposable cameras, and now a picture of Tina was in my wallet, along with the one of Kayla, the only family picture I'd brought from Bluebonnet Drive.

Yawning wide several times, I couldn't believe how tired I was. I still didn't understand how one little baby could cause so much work. She took short naps rather than long sleeps. Which meant I napped more than I slept even though Colleen had night duty, or was supposed to. Colleen slept deep. I slept light. She reminded me often that *she* was the one who'd been pregnant forever and given birth and had a right to be tired. Well, maybe so, but for how long? The best answer would be for Tina to sleep through the night. But when would that happen?

But she was so darn cute, so perfect, and I loved her so much! I walked closer to the crib, wanting to kiss her soft, rounded cheek, but checked myself against waking her. I back-stepped, returned to the living room, and reached for the baby-care book I'd picked up at the used bookstore. I dropped onto the couch, stretched until my feet dangled over the opposite arm, and started to read about sleep patterns. My own eyes closed within minutes, and I thought about Colleen at the local karaoke club and the fight we had before she left.

She'd written a couple of new country songs and wanted to try them out. "There's nothing like performing for real, live folks to see what works and what doesn't."

"I understand that, you know I do. But why tonight? I'm tired. I may fall asleep and not hear her."

"Then don't lie down. How will I ever get to Nashville if I don't sing my new songs?"

She could be damn stubborn when she had something at stake. "It's not happening tomorrow, Colleen. Be reasonable."

"I am reasonable. Tina's got two of us, and tonight she's got you. It's your turn, Daddy."

"And does she have a daycare next week?"

"No!" She grabbed her guitar and left the house.

Crap. Colleen was expected back at work on Monday. So now what? Finding a daycare was falling on me too. Did I have to manage everything around here?

And then it hit me. Maybe I did. Maybe I'd have to be the adult because Colleen, despite her career ambitions—or because of them—was still a girl. I was still crazy about her, but...well, if that's the way it was, then I'd have to do whatever it took.

Tomorrow was Sunday. Maybe I could scout around and ask a neighbor to babysit. And pay her, of course. Or maybe Colleen should quit her job, and I'd take double shifts.

And Dad wanted me to bring a date to the anniversary party. If he could see me with my Saturday night "date," he'd laugh. If I weren't so tired, I'd laugh too.

#

*COLLEEN*

I held the last note of my second number almost to infinity, and when I finally took a breath and smiled, the awesome silence in the Roadhouse Café turned into raise-the-roof applause. And a standing ovation. What a rush! Nothing could compare to the high of performing one of my own songs for a crowd who got it. Nothing was better than this, not Ian, not even the baby, although she was a close second.

The shout-outs were sending goosebumps up my arms. I smiled and waved. I could have sung for an hour, but I turned the mic over to the next person on the program. On Saturday, the open mic was by invitation only, and I couldn't hog it up, no matter how much I wanted to. I'd missed performing after Tina was born; I missed it as deeply as I'd miss the sun if night took over the world. Writing songs and singing them was what I was meant to do.

"This one's on the house, little lady. "Behind the bar, Ted Willis slid a longneck at me. "You're singing better than ever. Maybe the baby's a good influence, or maybe it's the baby's daddy." The old-timer waggled his bristly eyebrows, and I chuckled, even though his words shot a familiar pang of guilt through me.

Ian was the best. A great guy. Loving. Sweet. And he'd offered me a home when I'd needed it. I owed him. *But...*Such a big word for three little letters. *But.* It had the power to make my tongue freeze, and what I couldn't say in real life, I guess I put into my songs.

I chose to linger at the bar, nursing my beer, postponing Ian, postponing Tina and the small apartment where the shiniest piece of furniture was the crib. My dreams far outreached the pokey East Texas town I'd come from. They outreached the helpless baby who needed me every minute of the day and night, and certainly outreached the day-in, day-out routine of the refinery where I had to return, if I could stand it.

I wanted a whole bushel more than I had now. The Grand Old Opry. *American Idol.* I knew I had the talent and drive. I was as good as Kellie Pickler. Even better. And now Pickler had released albums and earned a whole lot of money. Best of all, the young country star didn't have to depend on daddies or boyfriends or anyone but herself to make it in this world. That's just what I wanted too. Was that so awful? Too bad Ian wasn't a musician. Then both of us could just take a bus to Tennessee.

"Hey, Colleen," called Ted. "Here's someone who wants to meet you."

I woke from my thoughts and saw a man slip up next to me but not too close. He handed me a card: Roger Smiley, Talent Scout. From a music producer based in Nashville.

"I liked what I heard, Ms. Murphy," he said. "You've got promise in those pipes. And Ted, here, says you often sing your own stuff, and they're as good as the one you sang tonight."

Taken by surprise, I could only nod my head and whisper, "Yes. Yes. I write a lot of songs and sing them here. To try them out. And if you don't believe me, I've got notebooks to prove it." He smiled like he thought I was a dumb country bunny. And I had to admit I sounded like one.

"I believe you, Ms. Murphy. Ever make a demo?"

I shook my head. "Never had the funds, but I always had it in my mind to do it."

"Well, it's probably cheaper to do it in the heart of country music. In fact, my company will back a demo if I recommend it."

He looked at me straight on, like he wanted this dumb bunny to understand. "I don't often make those recommendations," he said, "but there are exceptions. You'd be one of them. So, when and if you get to Nashville, look me up. Or if you cut a demo here, send it to me first. You've got something going on." He slipped his card into my hand. "Remember, me first."

"Oh, I will, Mr. Smiley. I surely will. And I'll get there. You'll see."

The man stayed with me until the next singer finished then met my eye and gently shook his head. "That one misses long and wide."

I agreed with him. I really tried to be as objective as I could when listening to other singers, but in this case, I had to say he was right. "I'll keep your card safe, Mr. Smiley. Count on it."

"That's just what I wanted to hear." He got up, lifted his broad-brimmed felt hat, and said, "Till the next time."

I watched him walk away and felt Ted staring at me. The bartender kept up with everything going on.

"What ya make of him, Colleen?"

"You tell first."

"I'm thinking he's got a bit of snake oil on him to ease the way, but he's serious about discovering a diamond in the rough. He's a legit scout in the business. I looked him up on the computer while he was talkin' to you. Him and his company."

"Why, Ted Willis. You're watching out for me." I felt good about that. He acted like a real dad would.

"You bet I am. I discovered you first!"

Floating high on praise and promise, I got into my old car, while reality started sinking in. Once again, I wondered how I wound up doing everything backwards.

# CHAPTER TWENTY EIGHT




*CLAIRE*

*Same night*
*At Casa Olé*

I knew it was a great party when I started to relax. The noise level, laughter, dancing, as well as the eating and drinking, were echoes from a former life. It had been a long time between parties. A long time since our friends gathered with us in celebration of anything. Only Ian's absence dampened the mood for me.

Of all our guests that evening, however, Anne Conroy's smile was the widest. Simply put, she not only looked amazing but pulled her hubby onto the dance floor time and again.

"Credit to my chicken soup?" I joked as they stopped to chat on the way back to their table.

"Absolutely." Anne beamed at me then squeezed my arm. "I'm a survivor!" she said. "I went through hell and came out the other side. So far, I've made it." Now she hugged me with a strength that impressed. "And so will you," she continued. "Just look at yourself tonight. Gorgeous in that beautiful silk dress. Those shades of green are perfect—totally you. You and Jack...I think the two of you are more than surviving. You're coming back; the real Barneses are coming back to us."

Were we? I would have liked to agree, but I knew some of my excitement came from the surprise I had waiting: Kayla's portrait. I'd wrapped it in a king-size sheet then in a large woven blanket and brought it over in Jack's truck early in the day. It now leaned against the restaurant manager's office wall. But it could wait awhile. Jack looked ready to dance.

"You remind me of someone," he murmured, taking me in his arms.

"I do?"

"Yes—the girl I married twenty-five years ago. And not looking a day older."

"Nice hogwash."

"You're more beautiful than ever and still fit right here." He pulled me closer, and I knew he was right. My head fit perfectly against his shoulder. We moved to the music in step with one another, as though dancing was part of our daily routine.

"Fred and Ginger?"

"Better," he said with a grin. "Jack and Claire."

"I guess we're muddling through okay."

"Tonight is better than a muddle. If all you needed was a big party, I would have thrown you one months ago. Any excuse would have been fine with me."

As if to prove it, he whirled me faster as the lyrics urged us to "Celebrate good times, come on."

"Are the good times coming back, Claire-de-Lune?"

"I-I hope so." I pressed his shoulder and slowed our steps. "I've got a surprise for you tonight. For everyone. Later on."

I waited for the perfect moment, the pause between dinner and dessert, before the anniversary cake would be cut and served. I waved to the DJ, and he allowed the music to fade out.

"What are you up to?" asked Jack.

Instead of answering him, I made my way to the manager's office, and as previously arranged, he helped me carry *Girl Exalted* to the front of the room and onto a chair. I stood tall, hands raised, and slowly the noise level diminished as our friends and relatives became aware of me waiting and perhaps noticed the large package still under wraps.

Jack stared from me to the covered picture, his brow creasing as his eyes focused from one to the other and back again. I caught the exact moment when he became uneasy, the moment he turned to me in silent question. I smiled, urged him to join me, but with a deliberate pivot, he mingled among the guests before alighting at our parents' table. He was normally one who embraced and conquered the unexpected. Tonight, however, I wondered if he might need support himself or might need to provide it. His distrust after our lovely time together disappointed me.

"Thank you for sharing the evening with us," I began, "and stick around. There's more to come with dessert and coffee and another set of music—if your feet can handle it."

I paused for their reaction—laughter and groans. After watching Jack give dozens of talks over the years, always inserting humor and measuring his delivery, I'd learned a little something about timing. But now, my heart raced. My palms felt damp. To speak out loud of the children...of Kayla...made my throat close. And what if my work disappointed? What if no one else saw her as I did? The room seemed eerily quiet.

"We would have wanted our kids to be here too, of course, for this special celebration. But Ian is out doubling his money tonight with OT and asked me to say hello to y'all for him. So, I guess he's here in spirit."

I'd actually hoped Ian would show, and I hadn't prepared this speech. But somehow, the words formed and flowed.

"And as for Kayla, she'll always be with us in spirit, in love and memory, and as real as I could make her."

With a quick movement, I let the covering drop to the floor. And there stood my daughter in her full glory of victory. In her full glory of life.

Seconds passed. A silent freeze-frame. The kind of awed silence that follows a show-stopping moment. From a distance, I heard the gasps. The murmurs. The "Oh, my God's." "Look at her." "It's Kayla!" "Amazing." "Claire's work?"

Someone called my name. Someone else joined in. Claire! Claire! Claire! Soon a chorus of "Claire" filled the room.

Relief turned my legs to Jell-O. My arms quivered, eyes watered. The spontaneous remarks rang true, and the shout-outs...? The room swam, everyone a blur. I guess I'd done it. I had done Kayla justice. *There's my daughter*, I thought, *"...looking as if she were alive...."* The line from Browning's poem sprang suddenly to mind. And it was true. Kayla sparkled with life, and I was so grateful. Grateful and happy.

Happy? Me? Were the trembling corners of my mouth arcing upward?

People came forward, surrounded me. Surrounded the portrait. But I wanted Jack. I wanted us together, finally sharing a deeply joyful moment. After all, it was our anniversary. And our daughter was here...at least in spirit.

#

But Jack wasn't in the restaurant, and when I finally stepped outside, a quick glance told me the car was gone. Once again, I was lost in silence. Jack gone? Without a word? He must have hated the portrait. Or the surprise of it. Or...or what? Maybe he hated me. I leaned against the wall of the restaurant, my energy flagging along with my hopes.

"Claire?"

Mom's voice.

"Right here."

"People are looking for you. The party's breaking up, and they want to say goodnight. Your phone rang, and I brought it."

I glanced at the missed call. And there he was. I connected.

"Where are you, Jack? Folks are leaving."

"I'm getting the truck. Tell everyone to go home. I'll speak to them soon." He hung up.

Getting the truck? A dozen pickups waited for their owners in the parking lot. I could have gotten a ride with the Conroys, for goodness' sake, right in our own neighborhood.

When Jack finally reappeared, I was wiped out from maintaining my smile and making excuses for his absence. The few remaining guests surrounded him now, eager with a new round of congratulations. He laughed but, with a short gesture, cut them off.

"Need to take care of a certain bill inside," he said, "or we all stay and wash dishes."

It was a poor joke from a guy almost good enough for an improv gig. No doubt, he just wanted to get away from everyone, including me.

Five minutes later, Kayla's portrait was wrapped and ready to go, but I needed help getting it to the truck. Just as I approached the manager's office, Luis appeared and walked toward me.

"Your husband had some gifts to carry. It is my pleasure to help you once more."

"Thanks, Luis. *Muchas gracias*. I told everyone not to bring presents. Even had it on the invitations."

The man chuckled, and together we carefully hoisted the canvas into the truck bed while Jack sat behind the wheel, the engine idling. After thanking Luis again, I climbed into the front seat. Jack pulled out of the lot without a word and kept his silence for a long minute or two. An awkward silence and I wasn't having it.

"What's wrong—"

"Congratulations, Claire—"

I settled back into my seat.

"It's your best work ever. I could have—" He cleared his throat. "—reached out and hugged her."

He seemed to be sincere, but his voice was flat, as though he resented paying the compliment.

"Well, thank you. I think." Peering up at him, I added, "You don't sound very...let's say, enthusiastic. I'm sorry if I shocked you."

He shrugged. "I guess I'm not that teacher you were always yapping about from the college. The one who thought you could do no wrong. Maybe you should go back to school."

Jack was changing subjects as quickly as my sister changed clothes in a dressing room.

"Why are you talking about Colombo? I've barely thought about him or my classes since I left. Especially not since he sold my painting without telling me."

"Well, you should think about them now. They'll keep you busy."

My nerve endings jingled as the conversation became too bizarre for my liking. "I've got enough to do, Jack. Now what's really on your mind? A-and maybe you should pull over...?"

He continued driving too fast, heading toward home. "I'm talking about us. You and I. It's not working out for me. Not anymore."

He gestured over his shoulder. I turned my head and, for the first time, saw the bulging suitcase resting on the floor behind us.

Another nightmare. One that shouldn't happen, not after all this time. And definitely not tonight.

"I've got a room at the Marriott Suites," he continued calmly, as though he hadn't just strewn my path with landmines. He pulled into our driveway and hopped outside before I could speak.

My insides trembled. By the time I managed to unlock my door and make my way to the ground, Jack had retrieved the picture and leaned it against the wooden gate that led to the house.

I knew Jack hated to see me cry, but I couldn't stop tears from rolling down my face. I couldn't let him leave. He was still my CrackerJack, still my best friend. Beyond the rush of tears, I stood in front of him, my hands grasping his.

"But why, Jack? Why? I thought tonight would be a new beginning, that it was time for one. I was so happy a-and I wanted you to be happy, and you were, Jack, you know you were happy when we were dancing...and...and..." Babble, babble. I was never as articulate as I should be.

"An illusion doesn't last." His mouth tightened. He pulled his hands from mine and pointed at the canvas. "That's what made you happy. That was the purpose of the whole shindig. You had to show everyone. 'See? My daughter is still here. Don't forget her.' So, what's next, Claire? A watercolor? A statue? A copper relief? It'll never be enough for you. You're so wrapped up in Kayla, there's no room for anyone else."

His voice had risen with every sentence. He was shouting now, and I wanted to cover my ears.

"Well, I'm tired of waiting for my turn," he continued. "I'm tired of waiting for you to pay attention, for us to resume a normal life together. A real life. Not make-believe. I'm done here. I've had enough. I. Am. Done." His hard gaze and tone left no room for doubt.

I was in the fight of my life now, fighting for a way to keep going, for my very existence. So how could I give up?

"You say *you're* done, but *I'm* not done. You're wrong about me this time, Jack. You think you know everything, but you don't. We can't have the old normal life anymore. We have to find a new normal. That's what people like us do, and I'm ready for it. I'm ready to try, a-and besides, it's our anniversary."

My voice cracked, my soul ached. Frightened didn't come close to how I felt because I wondered if he could be right. Instead of tonight being a turning point, maybe the picture had only been a therapeutic exercise for me, and I'd need more of it.

"I don't believe you," said Jack. "A new normal? Does it include keeping secrets from me? Ignoring our son? And as for our so-called anniversary? Well, a celebration is for couples who are truly devoted, who share with each other what's in their hearts and minds, who think about each other first. We don't do that anymore. Haven't in a long, long time. These days, we go through the motions, but we don't have a marriage."

He climbed back into the truck and rolled down the window. "I'll be in touch."

I could barely comprehend the whole of it. Was Jack actually leaving me, or were we acting out a scene where I hadn't been given the right lines? I felt myself floating, drifting away to another world. Someplace else. What was real? What was not? I began to tremble, full head-to-toe tremors. Goosebumps covered me, and my stomach began a tarantella. A new world without Jack? My arms, legs...so light. I heard someone moan. From far away, someone howled.

A miasma of haze surrounded me. Maybe I'd float on a cloud. Up. Up. Oh...yes...Just as I'd imagined, floating was lovely, painless. And the moon...only on the far side did the moon shine bright, and the stars were large, as unique as snowflakes. Everything below looked wee small. Was that a tree or a hunk of grass? Talk about perspective. And right over there, that's...that's my daughter! I just spotted Kayla—my Kayla—leaning on the fence.

Wait, wait for me. Don't leave, sweetheart. I'm coming, I'm coming. Blindly, I reached, my arms outstretched and ready to hug. I locked onto her! She felt real-world solid. Feet-on-the-ground solid. Kisses, kisses, kisses—butterfly kisses in the air.

My breathing slowed, and with eyes opened now, I saw myself lying on the ground, my arms wrapped around my waist. The air seemed heavy again and hazy. My lids drifted down, and I just breathed. Maybe I'd been in shock. Or maybe that flight-or-fight reaction had kicked in. I didn't know, didn't care. Inhale. Exhale. In. Out. Once. Twice. I opened my eyes again. The house, the garage—everything came into focus. Too real. Much too real.

I sat up, disappointed, and reached toward Kayla's picture. I stroked the frame. "Not your fault, sweetheart, not your fault. *Mea culpa.*"

Slowing rising, I grabbed the top of the fence for balance and watched Jack back out of our long driveway and onto the street.

I guess my long flight took only a few seconds. *Jack! Wait. Tonight was supposed to be our new beginning....*Soon the truck's headlights illuminated Bluebonnet Drive while the truth illuminated my senses: I'd been too late to save my family again. Once more, I was too late. All my good intentions gone awry, not only here but at the hospital too. Why did I have such poor judgment that I'd failed everywhere?

Kayla was gone. Ian had left, and now Jack. I was alone, the only family member still at home.

What a laugh. How could our house be a home if no one wanted to live there? My husband had just walked out drenched in anger and disappointment; my son didn't trust me. My family was disintegrating before my eyes. Was it all my fault? Jack said he was done. Done with us. But I knew he loved me, at least I think he did. And I loved him. Why wasn't that enough?

What to do, what to do...I had no idea how to fix us, and God knows we needed fixing. I didn't want to believe our life together was over. I wanted to make love to Jack again and help Ian through whatever he was going through, and I wanted to continue painting—maybe a portrait of Anne and Maddy. Tom would love that. And Jack needed me in the business. Unless he hired a replacement now.

I gazed at the empty house. If I was the underlying cause of all our problems, then I'd better figure out how to resolve them. Was there a superglue for families, or would that be too easy? All I knew was that as long as Jack, Ian, and I continued to walk on God's green earth, I couldn't give up.

# PART II

Children are the anchors

That hold a mother to life.

—Sophocles, *Phaedra*

# CHAPTER TWENTY NINE


*CLAIRE*

*Sunday morning*

Too much thinking kept me up last night. The sofa had seemed more cramped than usual, but I'd chosen it over the bedroom. Facing a half-empty closet had been beyond my capabilities. I'd tossed and turned, haunted by a kaleidoscope of scenes from the party and the horrible after-party where my high hopes for a new beginning with Jack had burst in my face like an overfilled balloon. His disappearance from the restaurant was my first clue to his distress. His silence going home was the second. Even without the kudos from our friends about the portrait, I knew he wasn't ashamed of my work. He'd said something about Kayla being so real he could have hugged her. But then he'd driven home too fast, his mouth clenched, his words coming through lips that barely moved. Angry barely described him.

But why? Analyzing behavior had never been my strong suit, and as the hours crept by, I wondered where I'd gone wrong. Or had it been Jack who'd screwed up? He'd said I didn't care about him. But hadn't I just given him the most wonderful present I could imagine giving anyone? I'd put in the work—untold hours—on something I thought he'd cherish. Why was all the blame mine?

Oh, Lord, did assigning blame really matter at this point?

I'd known enough couples who'd separated and divorced to understand there was usually plenty of blame to go around. The he-said-she-said arguments accomplished nothing. A marriage at the breaking point required a lot of untangling between two people. A lot of talking.

*Whoa, Claire. Breaking point?* How could that be? Jack and I...we...We were the grounded, steady couple. Everyone said so. We'd said so. We'd always had the epitome of a great marriage. I groaned. How could I ever make sense of this? Jack was the people-person. He could figure out somebody's *modus operandi* after one conversation. Me? I went to my studio and worked alone. I used to tease him about a picture being worth a thousand words. I guess I really proved it last night.

At noon, I sat at the kitchen table with my second cup of coffee. When the phone rang, I grabbed it, thinking it was Jack...maybe to apologize? Wrong. Cousin Marilyn's cheerful voice thanking us for a wonderful party, wishing us well one more time on our special anniversary, and praising Kayla's portrait with heartfelt enthusiasm. I thanked her, of course. And that's all I said. I wasn't broadcasting the problems my talent had wrought. Nothing was official. And besides, maybe those problems would be resolved quickly.

Hers was the first call of the day. After chatting with a few other guests and pretending everything was fine, I began checking Caller ID before picking up. I deserved an Academy Award for my performances so far. Man, I was good at pretending, but then again, I had secrets to keep.

"We had a great time too," I'd say. "Thanks for coming."

"No, I'm so sorry. Jack just stepped out. I'll tell him you called."

"Thank you. The spitting image? Glad you liked it. Yeah. I didn't know I had it in me either."

The happy messages threatened to send me bawling, and by late afternoon, I was exhausted from keeping up pretenses. I thought about escaping to my studio, even walked to the kitchen door, but turned back before I opened it. A visceral reaction with a bitter flavor.

Not once was I tempted to tell the truth to anyone. After all, what could I possibly say? That Jack had hated Kayla's portrait so much he'd walked out on me? Too intimate. Too personal. Too bizarre. My friends wouldn't understand.

When I saw my mom's name on the Caller ID, I almost didn't answer. Almost. But I knew her well enough to know she'd keep trying until someone picked up the receiver. My hand hovered above the phone as, once more, I braced myself for the role of hostess.

"Hey, Mom."

"Hey, yourself, and happy anniversary again. I waited to call in case you and Jack wanted a quiet, lazy day alone. Alone, together." She laughed as she spoke. "Oh, you know what I mean."

I sure did, and I wished it were so. I wished I could laugh with my mother, whose spontaneous good humor had been lacking in recent years. She didn't deserve another blow. Neither did my loyal dad.

"Yeah...I...we...ah... Mom?" My voice squeaked, and my Oscar disappeared.

"What's wrong, Claire? Oh, good heavens. Never mind. We'll be right over."

"No, no. I'm fine."

"Something's wrong. I know my daughter, and you're not fine."

The next sound I heard was the dial tone.

Fifteen minutes later, my folks were at the door. My dad embraced me then peeked over my shoulder.

"Where's Jack? What's going on now?"

It was the "now" that got me. My parents had had a brief respite from my troubles last night. They'd gone to bed happy and hopeful, enjoying a lovely celebration, and had awakened to a new disappointment.

"Jack's not here," I said, leading the way into the family room where my portrait of Kayla stood against the near wall. My voice quivered, but I got the words out. "Jack is...he's checked into the Marriott." The last part ended in a rush.

Confusion. Shock. And then, "He's done what?"

Daddy turned on his heel. "Then that's where I'm heading."

"Oh, no you're not." Mom at work. She glommed onto his arm and pulled him back. "Listen to Claire. We don't even know what happened."

With an airy gesture, I pointed at the picture. "That's what happened."

Both my parents turned and gazed at Kayla. The silence this time had a softer, poignant quality.

"I'm admitting," said Daddy, "that I got all choked up last night when I saw this here picture. And as for your mother...

"It almost killed me. I had goose bumps everywhere." My mom cupped my face in her palms. "Not only because I wasn't expecting to see Kayla but because I actually saw her. You are *that* good." She turned from me to look at her lost granddaughter again. "I guess I haven't seen your studio work in a long time. You are beyond being a hobbyist. You are exceptional."

"I don't know about that," I whispered. "It might seem so because it's...it's Kayla. And...and Jack couldn't stand it."

"He'll be back, sweetheart," said my mother. "He loves you, adores you. We saw it last night every time he looked at you, and when he danced with you? It was almost like...Well, let's just say that nothing's changed there."

"Your mother's right. You two kids have been together for so long, Jack wouldn't even know how to go a week by himself."

Kids? I hugged them. Hard. "Have I mentioned recently how much I love you? I'm wondering why a grown woman still needs to hang onto her parents."

"That's an easy one," said Dad. "When times are tough, we all feel like children again, scared and wanting our parents."

"Amen." Mom walked to the picture then scanned the walls of the room. "This is quite large, Claire. Where do you want it? Daddy and I can help you hang it right now."

I hesitated. Not about the placement, but whether I should display the portrait at all. Jack hated it, or what he thought it represented. In either case, he couldn't look at the work.

"Thanks," I said. "But let's just leave it where it is. I might even store it in Kayla's room for awhile."

Jack had accused me of wrapping myself up in Kayla to the exclusion of anyone else. I loved that child. I'd always love her and miss her, but I didn't want to choose between my daughter and my husband.

#

*JACK*

*Sunday*

When I woke up this morning, I wondered if I'd slept on a bed of rocks. Every muscle ached, including the ones in my jaw. I couldn't blame the suite. In fact, it contained everything a guy could want—fridge, sink, a loaded bar. I couldn't blame the bed, although I could have done with something smaller. Glancing at the partly messed-up covers, I put two and two together. It seemed I'd kept to "my half" of the king-size mattress. Just proved that old habits were hard to break.

I soon discovered the suite's excellent shower and hot water supply, and when I emerged from the bathroom, I finally felt, if not totally human, at least almost there. Almost ready to face the day on my own without my wife.

The thought perked me up, imbued me with a sense of freedom I hadn't known I'd needed until now. Freedom from Claire and her never-ending focus on Kayla. That picture last night? Well, I was sucker-punched when I saw it. Shocked to bits. God knows, I didn't need any more surprises. I'd been trying with Claire, trying to get us up and running again, and I was failing. One step forward and three steps backward type failing.

But here I was at the Marriott, trying to coax this stupid, tiny-sized coffee filter into its basket. If my hands would stop clenching the thing, I could do it. But shoot! I forgot to fill the canister with water. So much for facing the day in a good mood...good enough anyway, considering.

In the end, I suppose, it came down to survival. Every last one of us—man and woman—fought to survive, and we were all selfish. Claire had to do her thing, and I had to do mine. If Claire continued what she'd been doing, would her grief ever ease? And where would I fit in? If we didn't overlap anymore, well then...so be it. We'd become a divorce statistic in the column labeled: after death of child. I'd tried hard to support her, to support us. At least, I think I'd tried. And I was very tired. Sometimes, I sat and stared out the window, saw nothing, and felt too fatigued to get up. Grief, worry, and stress. What a friggin' life.

None of that mattered now. I had the whole day ahead of me, free to do what I wanted. I had no to-do lists, no obligations, no work. I could swim laps in the pool, do miles on the treadmill, or join a group for a round of golf at the local course.

An hour later, I was at the office immersed in the Active Seniors project. Every ten minutes, however, I wanted to call out to someone on my staff and had to remind myself that it was Sunday. A day off for most people. I jogged to the drafting room to examine blueprints then jogged to Claire's office for her files on architectural accommodations for seniors. I couldn't find them. But I wasn't calling her, not today.

*Note to Self: Tell Claire to give me a duplicate file.*

I began reviewing the art team's rendition of the acreage we'd develop—the clubhouse with its arts and crafts rooms, gym and aerobics center, library, game room, bistro, and auditorium for shows and events. Outside were the pool, tennis courts, shuffleboard court, even a dog park. All good work. I focused on the home sites next and the nine models we'd created. Did the layouts make sense? Did we have enough variety? Should the architectural accommodations be a choice for the individual buyer or a constant in every home? Raised dishwashers? A shallow ramp from the garage into the house? Immersion in my work was nothing new. I was damn lucky to be part of such a creative business. Damn lucky my own dad had led the way. If only Ian were here. If only...

Dusk had fallen when I finally glanced through my window. Evening already? I stood, stretched out the kinks, and listened to my stomach rumble. Shadows filled the corners of my office, too; a single light over the desk couldn't alleviate them. I looked at my open door. Beyond the perimeter of this efficient, comfortable second home, I knew the entire building was dark. No lights, no people, no noise. Just me and my work. In the past, I'd never considered that a bad thing, but suddenly I wasn't sure. A full Sunday at the office was not the same as dashing in for an hour or so as I'd been in the habit of doing for years. Even that one hour had normally been broken up by a phone call from Claire or the kids.

Was this all I had now? Was this what I wanted?

No. I wanted more. Claire and I could not go on as we were, yet I didn't know how to fix us. Me! The guy who could fix anything. The guy with the overflowing toolbox. No job impossible. Except this one.

I began pacing, began mumbling. *Focus on what really matters. Figure it out. You're clever and creative. Fix it! Or get help.*

In a flash, I pulled open my desk drawer and reached in the back for that special printout I'd hidden: The *Miss You Foundation* website. Attending support group meetings had always been in the back of my mind, but I'd hoped Claire and Ian would join me. I'd never forced the issue and never gotten the buy-in from them. Their cooperation didn't matter anymore. In fact, I might be better off on my own. I was a dad who'd lost his daughter. The support group would be for me. I picked up the phone and made the call.

# CHAPTER THIRTY

*COLLEEN*

*Monday, noon*

"I've got it all figured out, baby girl." I picked Tina up and snuggled her neck, inhaling her sweet, powdery scent. Delicious. Adorable. And I'd miss her terribly. For a moment, I thought about taking her with me. Or not going at all. Torn between two loves, I was truly in that spot between a rock and a hard place. Talking helped.

"You're going to have a fine life, little girl. Your daddy thinks you're a miracle child. You'll live like a princess in a big house, and he'll take very, very good care of you." I carefully deposited Tina into her car seat, the one Ian had taken an hour to pick out with all the questions he'd asked. Then I grabbed the tote bag that I'd stuffed with lots of salves, diapers and formula as well as a few clean one-piece outfits. I placed it on the seat next to the baby, and we were ready to go.

I drove across town, the address and directions on a piece of paper on the seat beside me. My spirit lightened because I was doing the right thing. Right for everyone, even Ian. Anyway, that's what I told myself. Maybe he'd mend fences with his folks. The thought made any last doubts fly away. Surely, the Barneses were good people to have raised a great guy like Ian. Maybe I was nuts to leave him, as kind as he was and a hard worker too. He never got drunk. Never raised a hand. Tina really was lucky to have him for a daddy. I shouldn't have to feel guilty. I'd never lied to him. Never made long-term promises.

I started to hum a new tune then began floating a few words around the notes:

> *My Texas knight in city armor*
> *Gave me a home when I had no other*
> *Saved the life of our unborn daughter,*
> *I waved goodbye in late October...*
> *I couldn't stay—*
> *Had to be on my way,*
> *But for them I'll pray...forever.*

My fingers itched to write more verses, but I had to concentrate on the unfamiliar exits. Not to worry. I had a good memory and a long bus ride ahead with plenty of time to write down lots of melodies and ideas.

# CHAPTER THIRTY ONE

*CLAIRE*

*Monday, noon*

I slammed the phone back in its cradle, disgust and disappointment flooding me after speaking with Jack. I'd been staring at a picture Anne had emailed, one of Jack and me dancing at the party. I remembered the strength of his arms around me, his spicy fragrance of aftershave and tequila, and thought we simply had to speak to each other again—and soon—but not at the office.

I'd taken the first step and called him, suggesting we meet for lunch. My husband, however, seemed to have other ideas and had made himself perfectly clear.

"There's nothing to resolve right now," he'd said. "And last weekend proved we need a break from each other. Fortunately, the business has started to turn around, so we've got options. In the meantime, your mother said she's available all week, so let's you and I stick to email for awhile and see how it goes. I've already left you a message." Then he'd disconnected.

Yet he was the one who'd talked about the importance of communication? Hypocrite. But I logged onto my computer, scanned my Barnes Construction inbox, and sure enough, among the posts from our home goods suppliers and construction foremen, there was Jack's note. It was a list of on-going projects and their deadlines—as if I didn't know them—and a demand for a duplicate file on the active seniors project. Not one personal word. Not one. After twenty-five years...and after I worked so hard to make the party a success...

I couldn't force him to have a meaningful conversation, not until he was ready. What a concept. The idea lingered a moment. Was it a concept that applied to me as well? I had to admit there'd been plenty of times when I wasn't ready either. I recalled all those instances when I'd disappeared into the studio because...because...the pain! The grief. Jack had begged me to talk, but speaking about Kayla...so many words, words, words. And words wouldn't bring her back. Jack and I weren't in synch then, and time was slipping away from us now. If we lived separate lives and never spoke, we'd be doomed. A few tears escaped, but I forced the rest back. He'd been gone only a day and a half. I couldn't allow myself to break down so soon.

And my poor mom. She hadn't signed on for a full-time position, but I knew she'd push herself to help us. To help me. So unfair. I glared at the phone. *You know what, Jack? You can take your email and shove it. I'll be back to work in the morning.*

I heard the doorbell ring but didn't feel like investigating. Who'd be visiting in the middle of the day anyway? Everyone I knew was working. Except...maybe Anne. Part-time Anne who'd barely missed a day through her treatments, and whose schedule I never remembered.

Maybe she figured I'd be home today after the big party. Good. A power-walk was exactly what I needed, and a friend was exactly who I needed. The thought energized me, and I ran to the hallway, eager to see Anne and get into my running shoes.

I felt my smile disappear when I saw the pretty girl in front of me. Nothing personal, just disappointment. Her car idled noisily at the curb.

"Car trouble? Or are you lost?" I asked, noting the paper she held and aware how easily a first-time visitor to the subdivision could get confused with all the cul-de-sacs and winding streets.

She read from the paper. "Ma'am, if this is 3225 Bluebonnet Drive like it says on the mailbox, and if you're Claire Barnes, then I'm exactly where I should be."

Her country-flavored speech fell pleasantly on my ear until her impatience came through as she repeated, "So, are you Claire Barnes?"

Nervy. She must have seen the suspicion on my face.

"Please, ma'am, it's very important." She reached forward, beseeching me, her brow wrinkled and her bright green eyes darkening to olive. Whatever this was about was important—at least to her.

"What's your name?" I asked.

"Colleen Murphy."

I mentally rummaged through our contact list of friends and relatives and came up empty.

"I-I work with Ian."

My stomach tightened, and my mouth went dry. "Ian? Is something wrong? At the plant? Was there an—"

"No, no. Not that kind of accident anyway. But now I know you're really Ian's mama. Wait right there."

Hot pokers couldn't get me to leave.

She scampered to the car, opened the back door, and lifted out a big—I didn't know what—by the handle. I stared until I identified what she carried. An infant seat. She reached into the vehicle again and came out with a tote bag.

Good Lord, was the girl in trouble? Had Ian said his mother could help her? Maybe she had no mother? A dozen possibilities scurried through my head as I watched her come closer and then gently place the "packages" on the ground.

"Gosh, now that I'm here, my tongue is all tied up," the girl said. "Maybe the best thing is to come right out and introduce you to each other." She took a deep breath, deep enough so I could see her chest rise. "This is Martina Faith Barnes. She's Ian's daughter and mine. S-so she's your granddaughter. We call her Tina. She's healthy. I brought most of her stuff because I can't take care of her anymore. And I even brought her birth certificate. She's a good baby. I've tried not to love her too much because I never promised Ian I would stay forever, and he knew that. I've got other plans, big plans, far away from here."

She spoke fast, without pause, and I had to listen hard. And then she walked backwards toward the car.

"Wait a minute, Colleen," I said, panicked. "Don't run away. Tell me what happened. I'll help. We can talk....I bet you're a good mother. Maybe you're just scared, maybe you've got some postpartum depression. I can help you learn.... " If this baby were truly my granddaughter, I'd help her every single day. *Mamas don't give away babies like they're cupcakes.*

"I left Ian a note. He'll understand."

"But you're her mother...."

She slammed the back door, turned toward me, and said, "It wasn't my idea." I watched her scurry around to the driver's side.

Oh, dag nab it! This girl—this Colleen Murphy—was really going to leave, disappear. I glanced at the innocent baby sleeping on the ground in her car seat. My granddaughter? Somebody's granddaughter? She needed care. "What kind of formula?" I called out, thinking about how I'd sterilized bottles.

"In the tote bag, and besides, Ian knows everything."

With those last words, she got into the car, pulled away from the curb, and headed out of the neighborhood with a fine sense of direction.

I, on the other hand, was not so fine.

#

"Just get yourself home, Jack. We have an emergency that requires both of us to handle, and I'm not kidding."

"Is the house on fire?"

"No."

"Then all else can wait. I'm busy."

"Don't you dare speak down to me like that. After what went on between us this weekend and your attitude earlier this morning, do you think I'd call you without a good reason? This involves Ian."

"Ian? Why didn't you say so? Tell me what's going on, and I'll take care of it."

Just like a man. Tackle and stomp a problem. "Absolutely not. This...this situation requires a mother and a father. You've got to trust me and see for yourself." I slipped the receiver into the cradle. Knowing Jack as long as I had and knowing the distance between home and office, I figured he'd be here in fifteen minutes.

It took him twelve. He stormed into the kitchen after a preemptive knock. I was surprised but gratified he'd bothered with that much, a subtle acknowledgement that I was entitled to privacy. Or a subtle reinforcement of our new marital status.

"So, where's Ian?" he blurted.

"Ian's not here. I didn't say he was."

"Then what's going on? What are you up to now? And it had better be good."

*You have no idea.* "Actually, Jack, *I'm* not up to anything. It's Ian who seems to have been busy, but you'll have to judge for yourself. Come into the family room. There's someone you need to meet."

I'd placed the car seat on the floor, removed the light blanket, and had simply stared at the little peanut while she slept and I waited for Jack. I couldn't detect any family resemblance, and I couldn't believe Ian had a child. A child! But she certainly was beautiful. I put the thought on hold. *All babies were beautiful.* An envelope had lain right inside the tote, and I'd taken it out. The birth certificate. I probably should have examined the rest of the bag's contents, but I was afraid to get distracted. What if the peanut moved? Cried? Opened her eyes? I didn't know her habits, so my job was to be alert.

Jack was scanning the family room at the six-foot level. "I don't see anyone. Where? Who? What?"

The baby cooed.

Jack jumped.

I pointed. "Over there. Lower your gaze."

He did. His lids opened wide, the only part of him that moved, until he slowly turned his head to stare at me. "Whose baby is that?" he asked in a harsh whisper. "What the hell is going on around here? And I want a straight answer! I'm gone for one blasted day and the sky falls down?"

"I'm just as much in the dark as you are," I said, "except for this." I offered the birth certificate, and he grabbed it like a lifeline.

"Martina Faith Barnes? Barnes?" He looked at me, eyes narrowed, complexion starting to pale. Again, he focused on the paper in his hand. "Mother: Colleen Murphy of Houston, TX. Who the hell is she? Father: Ian Barnes of Houston, TX. Ian Barnes? Our Ian?"

Could a man's deep voice actually squeak? "That's what the girl, Colleen, said when she dropped the baby off. Our Ian. She had our address."

"Date of birth: August 15, 20...why, Claire, that's only two months ago!"

"Ergo—this giant." I was tempted to laugh despite the seriousness of the situation. My husband wasn't usually put off-balance about anything. Then again, a possible grandchild was not just an anything.

Jack started pacing. "Our Ian?" he asked again. "Our straight-A Ian? Well, I don't believe it. Maybe it's a blackmail scheme. Maybe this Colleen knows we have a business, a good business, and is using the baby to get to us. Or maybe it's a phony birth certificate. I'm not ruling anything out. Ian's never said one word about a girlfriend or...or..." Now his complexion went from pale to alabaster.

"Jack, what is it? What are you thinking?"

"You don't want to know. I don't want to say it. But is there a chance, any chance at all, that Ian's gotten married?"

That idea hadn't crossed my mind. I took a moment to respond, reviewing the brief conversation I'd had with Colleen and the impression she'd made on me. She was a woman on a mission that had nothing to do with a baby or a husband.

"Possible," I finally said, "but not probable. A real long shot."

Jack's sigh of relief was interrupted by the sudden cries of a wide-awake baby. Cries that turned into piercing shrieks of hunger even empty nesters could recognize.

"Good grief." I ran to the car seat and tried to unlock the straps. "How the heck does this work? Push, pull. Ow!"

"Let me try. Go make a bottle or something."

Or something. I dug into the tote bag and came up with a can of powder, plastic liners, and nursers. "I'm going to the kitchen for some filtered water."

"Okay, the straps are unlocked. I'll just pick her...Geez, Claire, she's soaked," said Jack. "Everything. You change her, and I'll make the bottle."

"Whatever." I spread her blanket on the carpet and held out my arms. "Remember to support her head and neck," Jack said, safely transferring the tiny cargo.

"Thank you, Dr. Spock. Like I haven't done this before?"

"Not recently." He took the bottle fixings and headed out of the room.

I turned my full attention to the unhappy baby, who quieted briefly before taking a deep breath and letting loose with another shriek. Murmuring as I worked, I tried to calm her down with my voice and my touch, but every item of clothing had to be removed. And the baby girl wasn't happy.

"Some lotion to clean you, a bit of salve, a nice dry diaper, and you're going to be just fine," I said softly, before maneuvering the diaper in place. Peanut had skinny legs and arms and a little pot belly. A milk belly. I found a clean outfit and began to dress her, fastening the snaps all the way up from her feet to her neck. Pretty in pink.

"Okay, sweetheart. Let's see where that bottle is." I carefully stood up, the baby in my arms, and began to walk. That's when she finally quieted down. That's when she opened her blue eyes, looked right into mine, and smiled a crooked smile. With a dimple on the side. And that's when I knew she was ours.

I stared at Ian's daughter. My granddaughter. And fell in love. My heart, my spirit, my body overflowed with a cataclysm of joy. I had trouble catching my breath. I never thought I'd feel these emotions again in my life. The wonder of it...

Waltzing into the kitchen, I savored my discovery yet couldn't wait to share it.

"She's our granddaughter, Jack. No doubt about it." I told him what I'd seen.

"It could have been gas," he argued, handing me the milk.

"So what? Her lopsided smile is all Ian, and a matching dimple is unique. I've sketched that combination a million times. I know what I see." I touched the nipple to the baby's mouth, and she latched on as greedily as her father digging into a Chinese dinner. Or any dinner, for that matter.

"Or maybe you see only what you want to see." Jack's forehead creased as he took out his cell phone. "Babies can be irresistible, especially after...well, you know. After what we've gone through. So now I can't trust your judgment."

His words hurt. I tried to borrow the cop's face, the one who gave me the ticket, and changed the subject.

"Are you calling Ian?"

"Don't you think it's time?"

"Yes, but..." I bit my lip and gazed into the distance. "The baby's adorable, but where's he going with his life? I wish he'd gone to UT with Danny Goldstein and their friends."

Jack stared at me, his mouth agape, his eyes popping. "Then where the hell were you when it mattered? When he was making these unilateral decisions? When I needed you to back me up?"

Had he forgotten what that year was like? "You know the answer. I was lost the year Kayla died. In an unknown world." Day and night had rolled into one another, a continuous misting of time. "And I'm still trying to deal with it and...and all the repercussions.

Maybe I didn't say the right things. Maybe Ian needed more from me than I was able to give. Maybe I wasn't a fit person, never mind a fit mother. I don't know. And you know what I think?"

"I know you're going to tell me," Jack replied.

I shifted the baby to my shoulder for a burp. She performed magnificently, but the quick smiles it brought from her grandparents couldn't negate the topic under discussion: Tina's father. "I think Ian's situation is as much our fault as it is his."

"Our fault? As in yours and mine? Oh, boy. Let's postpone this conversation, Claire. We've got more immediate issues to focus on now."

"All right," I said, watching him punch in Ian's number. But I knew that sometime in the near future, a blame game would commence. And I had a bad feeling I'd lose.


#


*IAN*


I checked my cell for messages immediately after work, wondering why Colleen hadn't returned my calls. She knew what was on the line now that she'd missed her first day back at the plant because of the daycare situation. She'd been put on notice until Friday, and then she could be fired for abandoning her job. Ben Parker was so disappointed at Colleen's no-show today, I couldn't look him in the eye. Hopefully, Colleen would have connected with a daycare by now.

But there was no message from Colleen, just one from my dad. I listened to him say he had an important package at the house for me, special delivery, but I shrugged it off. Colleen and the baby came first. I got behind the wheel and headed home.

Looking from the outside, the apartment seemed dark. No light shone through the living room window, and I wondered if Colleen and Tina had both fallen asleep. It had happened before, and I grinned at the memory. The girls had looked so cute, napping together.

Whistling as I opened the door, I felt the emptiness before I confirmed it. No light. No life. I went from room to room in thirty seconds, finally spotting a note taped to the fridge:

*Dear Ian – I'm so sorry but I couldn't go back to the job. I'd be a flower begging for water in that garden. I sold my old heap and headed to Nashville today. I didn't touch your money, only my own little bit. Tina is all yours. I'll sign any legal paper you want me to. I'd just like to visit from time to time.*

*God Bless. You are a good person, better'n most and better'n me.*

*Colleen*

*P.S. I left Tina and her birth certificate with your mom.*

I ripped the note from the fridge, ready to pull the whole damn door off. She'd really gone and done it. I grabbed my cell and called her.

An electronic voice told me the number was not in service; the message was louder than any verbal one from Colleen. Coward! She was a stinking coward, sneaking away without a word. What kind of mother does that? Mine would never have...

Damn. Now I had to deal with my parents. Dad answered after the first ring.

"I'll be there ASAP," I said and hung up. Couldn't handle any long conversations now. Walking through the apartment, I began to notice the empty spaces. No formula and bottles on the counter, no blankets in the living room, no diapers in the handy basket we'd set up. I opened the bedroom closet, and Colleen's empty side hit me like falling timber. Not even a belt remained.

I dropped onto the edge of the bed and stared at the floor. She'd disappeared as though she'd never been here, following her damn dream that could have waited. Messing up our family.

*C'mon, Ian. You knew it was pretend. You knew all along it was make-believe.*

God damn it! The baby wasn't make-believe. Neither was my job. I had real responsibilities, and I was screwing up again. Just like with Kayla.

I started crying, crying like a girl. I couldn't help it and didn't care. I was just glad to be alone.

# CHAPTER THIRTY TWO

*CLAIRE*

*That evening*

The baby was stirring, waking up after a catnap. Jack stepped into the hall bathroom, once more washing his hands before picking her up, a total of three wash-ups for three pick-ups since he'd arrived. I stifled a grin.

"You're sure taking grandpa-hood seriously."

"That's the point. I'm trying to see a resemblance. I barely remember the kids at this age." He held Tina cradled in his arms and began making baby noises at her. I hadn't realized what a silly picture we, adults, made with our funny faces and vocalizations, and how strong our instinct was to communicate with our offspring.

"Claire!"

I rushed over.

"The dimple. I just saw the dimple, the cockeyed smile, just like our son's. You were right. She really is Ian's daughter."

Was that all? I almost collapsed in relief. There was no blood, no fever, no serious problem, but my nerves were frayed. "Nice of you to believe me after twenty-five years. Should I celebrate?"

"Hey, calm down. What's wrong with wanting to be sure?"

Hadn't I seen Ian reflected in the baby? Hadn't I shared that news with Jack? Hadn't I brought him to his knees over Kayla's portrait? "Hells bells, Jack. If it makes you happy not to trust my eye for detail, then confirm for yourself."

"I certainly will. In fact, I have to. Your vision's blurred. I don't know what's going on inside your head, and I can't cope with it now."

I gulped but thrust my chin out. "I think you made that perfectly clear the other night, and it's time to change the topic. We need to handle this situation with our son." I'd think about Jack later, when I was alone. Now my thoughts raced to the future. Ian. Tina. Jack and I. "Hmm...So what do you think the next step is with peanut and her dad?"

"Isn't that up to Ian?"

"But he's still a child, and we're still his parents. We still have some influence."

Jack emitted a long, low whistle and stared at me as though my nose had grown a foot. "And I'd say you're living in a dream. He purposely left us. It wasn't a spur-of-the-moment decision. Since then, he's had a serious relationship—and obviously a serious breakup—and is now a daddy. Most importantly, he chose to keep us in the dark. So, where in that story is the part about him still being a child? Where?"

"I'll tell you where. Rerun the ending. That very last line about keeping us in the dark. That's not the decision of an adult. He wasn't grown up enough to share his life."

"Because he didn't want to, Claire, because he couldn't connect with you."

So the blame game had begun. If I'd had the strength, I would have thrown the piano at him. "Ian has two parents, Jack, and I accept my half of the responsibility. I don't accept a hundred percent."

The baby started to cry, and I speared Jack with a look. "She can pick up on the tension, so be quiet."

"Hey, everybody! Where are y'all?"

Never had Ian's voice filled me with such gladness. I ran toward the kitchen. "Right in here, sweetie. Dad's holding your gorgeous daughter."

My son didn't look well. Pale, fidgety, and with red-rimmed eyes. "I suppose you had a shock today," I said softly. "Your girlfriend...?"

He nodded and made a beeline for the baby. "I'll take her, Dad." He scooped Tina up, nuzzled, and murmured comfort words—

"Daddy's here. How's my girl?"—similar to what Jack and I had done. Peanut curled into Ian, a little arm thrusting up. She recognized her daddy's touch, voice, face, and was happy.

"Another little athlete in the family," I said.

Ian eyed me without blinking and managed to cuddle the baby at the same time. "What family?" he asked. "Our family doesn't exist anymore."

Jack broke the silence that followed. "It's true that we've taken a big hit." He spoke slowly, with deliberation, as though Ian were a stranger to us.

Ian nodded. "Yup. But people rebuild after hurricanes and tornadoes wipe them out. We didn't."

The my-dad-is-the-greatest son had changed into someone else.

"On the ride over here," continued Ian, "I thought about...about the best thing to do, the best thing for Tina because I want her to be part of a strong family." He looked away, stared at a wall of pictures, but I was sure he saw nothing.

"Her mother won't be coming back. Not permanently. She's giving me legal rights." His voice broke. I stepped toward him, but he waved me off. "And even though it'll kill me, I'm calling an adoption agency. I bet there are plenty of couples who would give anything to have such a terrific baby. My daughter deserves better than you and me. Tina deserves more than what we've got to give her."

I heard nothing but the sound of my own heartbeat. Saw nothing but black spots and knew I'd be in trouble if I didn't keep my wits about me. Breathe! Breathe. I reached for the nearby club chair and fell into it. Jack stepped toward me, gave me a once-over, then changed direction.

"Tina is your child!" Jack said, his arms wide open, exhorting Ian to listen. "She's your flesh and blood. You can't just throw her away like unwanted trash. Especially when she already has a family with built-in grandparents, great-grandparents, cousins, aunts, and uncles. I'm surprised at you for even thinking about this. Never thought you were a-a fraidy cat."

I thought Jack was doing well. Except for that last line, he'd made the same arguments I would have if I'd had the strength and presence of mind. We did have a great family. Tina Faith would be surrounded with love from every tree, branch, and twig.

Ian placed the baby in the carrier and loosely adjusted the straps. Then he straightened, standing tall between Jack and me, and glared at us both.

"Talk about unwanted trash! Tina's my child, but I'm yours. You haven't given a rat's ass about me since

Kayla died, so why would you care about my baby? A kid dies, and the family goes to hell. Who needs it?"

He was wrong, but that didn't matter. He'd nailed *his* truth and shared it, without even knowing about Jack moving out.

#

*IAN*

I let the words rip and felt darn good. Even great. I'd never spoken to my folks like that before. Never needed a "gotcha" moment. But two years was a long time to keep big stuff bottled up.

"Not give a rat's...? How can you say that? You're our son! We love you."

"Jack. Jack. Calm down."

They were like that. A tag team. Always supporting each other. Even as a kid, I could never play one against the other. I kneeled down to pack up the baby. Time to get out of Dodge.

"Did you know, Ian, that it took us two years to finally get pregnant with you?"

I glanced at my mom. "Nope." And I didn't want to know. Tina's dirty clothes were in a plastic bag. "Thanks for taking care of her."

"Two long years." She kept talking. As usual, she never even heard me. She was in another world; her eyes were sort of glassed over like she was dreaming up a painting scene.

"We went through every fertility test known to science until we lucked out. And when you were born...it was like a miracle. Heck, it *was* a miracle. Being a mom was more awesome than I'd dreamed. Sweet, sweet Ian. You turned a couple into a family. We were so happy that, a few years later, we tried for another child. When Kayla was born, your dad and I...well, we truly 'had it all,' as the saying goes."

*Kayla.* The room got so quiet I could hear the clock ticking. And the air...suddenly the air grew heavy with thoughts no one dared to say out loud. Except me.

"So I guess you don't have it all anymore." And I wasn't apologizing for saying it. "But you still have each other."

I picked up Tina's carrier. "Gotta go. Ben Parker doesn't know about Colleen yet, and I've got to call him. I'll have to miss work tomorrow."

"No, you don't." Mom jumped right in. "Stay here tonight, and I'll watch the baby."

It would be such an easy fix, but it would cost me later, and the price was too high. I shook my head. "I'll handle it."

Dad approached. "We want to help, son. Don't be so stubborn. The baby's supplies are here, so there's no problem." He extended his arm as if to take Tina's carrier from me.

"Sorry, Dad. I've got to take care of my own business, and I know how to take care of Tina." For crying out loud, they looked awful, like the end of the world was happening again. "You know," I continued, "kids in regular families move out. They don't stay home forever, and the parents are a couple again, just like you two. Not so bad, is it?" And why the hell did I have to be the cheerleader? I'd had a lousy day myself with Colleen taking off. Maybe she was sick of an ordinary life, but I still couldn't wrap my mind around her really leaving the baby.

"Ian?" Mom was coming over. She leaned down and kissed Tina then kissed me. "Don't make any rash decisions you might regret later. Dad and I are here for you. We'll help in every way."

They were here for me? If I weren't so worn out, I'd laugh. Of course, all their concern was about the baby. "I'm sure Tina appreciates your offer." Even I heard the edge in my voice, and Dad rounded on me.

"That wasn't warranted," he said. "I understand you're angry with us, so let's talk."

"Too tired. I'm done here tonight." Turning toward the doorway of the family room, I said, "It's been a long... Oh, sweet Jesus!" I stopped cold, slowly letting Tina's car seat slip to the floor, and stared at my sister in her soccer uniform, my sister leaping with joy. I had to swallow a couple of times.

In a moment, the two years disappeared, and once again I was on the front lawn throwing, running, feeling the hot sun on my head. I planted my feet, palmed the football, and raised my arm. "Catch!" I yelled, releasing the ball. My arm remained extended as I watched the newsreel in my mind. As I relived the moment.

"Kayla...sh-she waited for the pass then ran for it. And that's exactly how she looked...excited...happy.... She jumped high to intercept, and I saw the car come around, and I yelled and screamed, and I ran straight to her...." My arm dropped. I whirled on my parents. "What the hell do you do here all day? Torture yourselves?"

I grabbed Tina's carrier, rushed out, and didn't look back.

#

*JACK*

The kitchen door didn't have a chance to slam before I was there, right behind my son. While Ian installed Tina's car seat, I made my pitch.

"If you think I'm giving you up without a fight, you'd better think twice. I love you, and I miss you every day. And it has nothing to do with Tina. I didn't even know about her until tonight."

Ian finished adjusting the baby's straps and stood erect, glanced swiftly at the house then back at me. "It had to be that way."

Claire. He was blaming Claire. I didn't know exactly what Ian was thinking, but I couldn't defend Claire anyway because she and I were at odds too. But if there was the slightest possibility, a Vegas long shot, that our family could once more be happy and together, I'd take it.

"Give us a chance, Ian. I know we're still struggling, but if we try hard, we'll get there. I'm actually going to that support group I once talked about. My first meeting is tomorrow night and every Tuesday afterwards. And that portrait you saw? Mom saved it for the anniversary party. On purpose. From the moment she unveiled it...man, oh, man, it was the topic of conversation."

"That's a no-brainer. I can just imagine it. Grandma Barb and Grandma Pearl must have cried. Mom's...she's really losing it, isn't she?"

"That's what I thought too. But she volunteers at the hospital with the kids, and she works in her studio every day. She says this painting has given her a new beginning." Not that I'd believed it either two nights ago. But it was all I had.

Ian stared at me wide-eyed. "Are you kidding? That's not a new beginning. She's living for Kayla. Living in the past."

"I'm not a shrink. Are you? I have to believe anything's possible." Well, maybe....

Ian looked at the house again. "If you need a break, Dad, you can visit me. Colleen's gone now, so it doesn't matter." He walked around the car and got in. "I've got to get Tina home and down for the night. If I'm lucky." The last words were muttered, and I barely heard them.

"Please, Ian. Like Mom said, don't do anything rash. We love you. We love Tina. We can work it out."

"You just met Tina. How can you love her?"

He didn't understand at all. Well, what could I expect? He may have fathered a child, but Claire was right. Ian was still a kid.

"We love Tina because she's part of you."

With a quizzical glance, he drove off. It didn't take a genius to know that he didn't believe me.

#

Claire met me at the door. "Did you say anything to him about moving to the Marriott?"

"No ma'am. I did not. He's got enough on his mind, and besides, didn't you hear him earlier? He still thinks we've 'got each other.'"

"Yes, I heard that. He missed the mark by a couple of days, didn't he?" She invited me in and stared at the floor. "I didn't hang the picture, Jack. I was going to put it away in Kayla's bedroom so you wouldn't have to see it."

"You mind looking at me when you say that?"

She tilted her head back.

"Even though I'd already packed a suitcase and lit out?"

She nodded. "You didn't understand. Or didn't want to understand. Sometimes, I don't know what drives me myself. My instincts said I had to paint her again. I had to. And it made me feel good. Like I was saying, 'Hi, Kayla. There you are...almost the spitting image of yourself. I've done a good job.'"

A modest statement. "Claire, it was a great job. I've never seen better from you."

"But it's not making you happy. And now...?" She shrugged. "So where are we, Jack? And where are we going?"

Excellent questions. And I didn't have the answers. Not yet anyway. "Where do you want to be?"

Her eyes shone, she looked thoughtful, then a blush stained her face. "Truthfully?"

I nodded.

"Back with the tomatoes and broccoli at Kroger's."

Memories stirred. In an instant, they flooded my brain. Claire and I, the vegetable aisle, and the crash of shopping carts. That's how we met, although Claire always said that our carts "kissed" among the fruits and veggies. We were a couple of busy college students, juggling jobs with homework—and shopping for groceries on a Sunday afternoon. The carts had definitely crashed head-on. I'd taken one look at Claire and didn't see anything or anyone else. I hadn't thought about that first meet in a long time. Seemed my wife still had the ability to land a punch.

"I haven't forgotten."

"I know. You have an excellent memory, and besides, we've told that story at least a million times."

She was beautiful. Laughing, sparkling. For this moment, carefree. Other memories bloomed. Happy ones. Exciting times. Buying this house and turning it into a home. Making love together.

She must have read my expression, probably that of a lovesick calf.

"Jack..." she whispered. "Do you really want to walk away fr-from...us?"

Sucker punched again. But warning bells chimed in my head. "From which 'us'? The couple we were before Kayla died or the couple we are now? Because the status quo won't do. I want some joy again. I want more. Believe me, Kayla wouldn't resent us having a laugh or two."

"I'm trying, Jack. I was trying to start over, but..."

"If you're serious," I interrupted, "then you'll come with me tomorrow night to meet some other grieving parents at a club no one wanted to join. We're not the only ones who've lost a child."

"Are you really going to a support group?"

"I am. And frankly, Claire, I expect you to go as well. That's the cost of tomatoes and broccoli these days."

# CHAPTER THIRTY THREE




*Next evening*

Hush little baby, don't cry tonight, I've got to call your grandma, and I'm feeling uptight."

I rocked Tina in my arms while singing in my horrible voice. My sweet little girl closed her eyes. Maybe she had a tin ear too. I felt her body relax as she drifted into sleep and cautiously laid her in the crib. She'd had a hard day. As my friend, Danny, would say, I'd *schlepped* her around to a half dozen daycare centers until finally, we lucked out. Sort of. The good news was that I'd found a really nice place. The bad news was that Tina couldn't start for two more weeks when one of the current infants would graduate into the toddler group. They adhered to strict teacher-child ratios, which I suppose was a good thing. But two weeks put me in a tough spot. I promised Ben Parker I'd be back at work tomorrow.

I would have asked either set of grands to watch her—or all four of them together—but I didn't know if my mom and dad had told them about Tina yet. Cursing under my breath, I auto-dialed my folks' house, hoping my dad would answer.

Two rings and my mom picked up. Suddenly, I was a tongue-tied idiot kid.

"Ian! I'm glad to hear from you. You ran out of here so fast..."

"I need a babysitter tomorrow and maybe Thursday and Friday. By six in the morning. Can you do it?"

"Me? With Tina? Yes, yes, of course I'll do it. I'd love to take care of her."

"But don't get too...too attached."

"Oh, Ian...it's much too late for warnings. We love her already."

Colleen was lucky to be a thousand miles away. Smashing her guitar would only begin the payback for leaving me alone in this mess. "I haven't decided what to do yet."

"Oh, yes, you have."

In an instant, she sounded like my mother from the old days when she used to laugh and tease us. When she used to say, "I have eyes in the back of my head, so don't even try it," whatever *it* was at the time. I almost believed her back then. I was tempted to believe her now.

"How do you know what I'm going to do?"

"Because I know my son."

"You knew a high school kid, Mom. You don't know me anymore. Just like with Kayla, you're living on memories, and that sure doesn't work for me."

She was silent for a minute. "I get it, Ian. I do. Now what's your address?"

The question would have almost been funny if it weren't so sad. My mother had never been to my place since I'd moved out of hers.

#

*CLAIRE*

Jack knocked and walked in just as I hung up the phone. His eyes lit up when he saw me dressed and ready to go to the support group.

"Looking good, Claire."

I'd made an effort with a red-ribbed jersey, black slacks, and a chunky black-and-silver necklace. Jack was used to seeing me in fun accessories because I enjoyed using them, mixing and matching, trying things out. It's amazing how an eight-dollar bauble could finish off an outfit and garner compliments. Besides, I needed to wear my own armor for this event.

"Thanks. I guess Kayla would say I'm in my 'girly-girl' mood, but never mind that. Guess who called to ask me to babysit for the rest of the week?"

Jack's brows hitched to his forehead; his mouth made a perfect circle. "You're kidding?"

"Nope."

"Want some company?"

Now I was the one open-mouthed. "That would be fun, but you're committed to this meeting tonight, and I have to be at Ian's by six at the latest so I'll aim for five-thirty...."

Now his brows lowered as he studied me. "Whoa! Wait a minute. Are you standing me up? After you promised?"

"But I'll need some sleep. I can't take a chance of being late."

"So set your alarm clock."

Sometimes his irises could transform from a merry blue to a thundercloud gray. I saw a storm rising and held up my hand. *Think, Claire, think.*

"All right," I finally said. "Short-term pain for long-term gain. But if we're late getting to Ian's, I'll blame you."

"I'll take my chances. Let's go."

At the last minute, I stuck a pad and a bunch of pencils in my purse. Always a comfort to have them close, like I was a kid with a security blanket. If I needed a distraction from the support group conversation? Voilà. I'd have one.

#

We found the conference room at Texas Children's Hospital without much trouble, but I was so tense by the time we arrived, I moved like a mannequin. So much for fashion plate armor or womanly grace. I clutched my purse.

Jack had spoken with the facilitator on the phone, and I watched as they shook hands like old friends. Bill Thompson looked older than us, but I'd already learned that grief could age a person. He might have been older...or ten years younger. When Bill turned toward me, I looked into his face and saw only kindness.

My mouth started trembling, and I bit down on my bottom lip. Well, that didn't take long...and geez, how I disliked public displays of private emotions.

"Claire, isn't it?" he asked. "Hope you don't mind wearing a name tag. We always wear them 'cause it makes it easier for first-timers."

I pasted it on and glanced at the others. About eight or nine people, softly chatting, smiling at me now and then, each with special memories. I could barely handle my own pain, so how was I supposed to "support" them? Oh, boy, coming here was a big mistake.

Everyone pulled a chair away from the conference table to arrange more informally at the side of the room.

Not exactly a circle, but we could see each other well, and there was more floor space. I made a silent bet that by the time the night was over, Jack would be pacing—and he'd know everyone's name without needing a prompt. I remained at the table but turned my chair to face the group.

Bill introduced us. I nodded, said a quick hey y'all, and glanced at Jack. *The spotlight's all yours, buddy.*

"Hello. Like Bill said, I'm Jack Barnes and that's my wife, Claire. This is our first time talking with other parents." He paused. I could see him take a deep breath before he could go on. "We lost our daughter, Kayla, two years and one month ago. She was twelve years old, beautiful, full of life, full of joy. God knows, she was my joy."

No one spoke, as though everyone waited for his permission. But Jack added more. "To tell the truth, I can't believe it's over two years. Sometimes, it feels like yesterday. And sometimes, it feels like a million years ago since she died."

Beads of sweat gathered on his forehead; one dripped from his temple down the side of his face. He wanted this, I thought, but he's suffering.

"We've all felt that way," said Bill. "Time is elastic, like a rubber band, with all its stretching and compressing. It's a relative thing."

"The emotions always seem fresh..."

"And just when you think you've got them under control, then boom! You get hijacked by a memory."

Others were joining the conversation. Not I.

"You know what I hate?" asked one woman. "When people say they understand. But they don't."

"They can't."

"And when they think you should be over it using *their* timetable. Especially after the first anniversary."

My ears perked up. My chin perked up.

Bill noticed. "Does that bother you, too, Claire?"

I nodded and glanced at Jack. But I wasn't putting our marriage front and center with a group of strangers, nice as they were. I kept quiet.

"Getting over it is just not possible," a woman said. "The family has changed forever. For always.... So how can you completely recover?" Her name tag said Laura, and she walked over and patted my hand. "You'll see though. In awhile, the good memories, the warm ones, will replace those intense, painful ones."

Jack interrupted. "Right now, it's not about 'getting over' it; it's about 'getting on' with it. With daily life."

"That's true," said Laura. "The days and weeks keep rolling around. Holidays, birthdays...You can't stop the solar system."

"Luke's birthday is this Friday," said one of the men. "He would have been sixteen, so we're bringing him a set of car keys when we visit." Luke's dad put on a game face, but his eyes...oh, his eyes!

My palm started to itch.

"Great choice," said Bill. "Every kid counts down the days to the car keys. Birthdays are tough." Again, he looked my way.

"Every day is tough," I managed.

"So, what did you do on Kayla's last birthday?"

My throat closed; I waved him away. He turned to Jack.

"I-I went to work as usual. For lunch, though, I ate a peanut butter and jelly sandwich. Kayla's favorite."

"Favorite foods are a good idea," said someone else. "We always go to Travis's favorite restaurant or try one we think he would have liked. The important thing is the whole family's there, talking about Travis and remembering him. It makes us feel like he's somehow...closer."

I could only imagine what the guy meant. Jack and I didn't "celebrate" Kayla's birthday together.

"Claire?" Bill sounded far away.

"Hmm?"

But it was Jack who walked over. "Claire! What are you doing?"

Startled, I jerked in my chair. And then I saw what he'd meant. I'd sketched Luke's dad—with emphasis on his shadowed brown eyes—so sad, so sad. I pushed it toward the man. "For you." Then I turned to Jack.

"So, you want to know what I did on Kayla's birthday?" I asked, yanking a clean sheet of paper. With three bold strokes, I produced Kayla's grave. A dervish of swirls showed the flowers I'd planted, then came the soccer ball. Of course.

I grabbed another sheet and, with lightning speed, drew a cartoon Claire sitting on a bench, a sandwich in her hand.

"Mine was a PBJ too." I looked up at Jack. "You should've been there."

"Well, bless my soul," said Bill. "She doesn't say much, but she sure packs a wallop when she draws."

"I'm getting used to it," Jack replied before turning away.

#

*JACK*

Personal man-woman stuff between Claire and me wasn't meant for the group, at least not to my way of thinking. This wasn't a marriage counseling session, nor did I want it to be. So I waited until we were back in the truck before spitting out what was gnawing at my insides.

"Why didn't you tell me about your plans for Kayla's birthday? Or are you giving up speaking in favor of pencil drawings?"

"Would you have come with me if I'd invited you?"

Answering a question with a question. When had she learned to play defense?

"Probably."

"That's bullshit, Jack. You would have made excuses and gone to work. You bail out on everything I do for Kayla. You didn't even want Reverend Carroll to be with us for the first anniversary."

She was right. "Who else does what we did, asking a minister to conduct another service a year later—and at the cemetery to boot? The answer is, nobody. But I went along with it, didn't I? I did it for you."

"Well, thank you very much," she replied. "Want a pat on the back? There's no law prohibiting what we did. And there are no rules we have to follow about remembering our daughter. Marking the anniversary just made sense to me," she said more quietly. "I thought gathering the family together there would keep her closer to all of us."

"Well, it didn't work. You know what we should have done? Balloons! Like what the folks in the group suggested after seeing your drawing. We should have gone to the soccer field and let balloons go for her—with messages inside. Something fun and meaningful. Something Kayla."

She was listening, her head cocked toward me, but she remained silent. Still, I was encouraged to push on.

"Our daughter is always with me, Claire. And I know she's with you too. In our hearts. In our thoughts. Don't you find it ironic—sadly ironic—how, in her absence, Kayla's the one who remains close while everyone else has drifted apart?"

I watched her wipe her eyes from time to time, but I wasn't going to be the comforter. My brain was filled with everything I'd heard that evening, with some hard truths I had to accept. I was having my own issues. I started the truck and made our way down the ramps of the garage. Once outside, I lowered the windows.

"Fresh air all right with you?"

"Perfect. Maybe it'll clear my head."

Hers wasn't the only one that needed clearing, but for awhile, I concentrated on finding my way out of the unfamiliar medical center area and back to the interstate.

"The meeting was a lot tougher than I thought it would be," I admitted.

"Really? I found comfort. In fact, I intend to be a regular now. I liked that the people weren't preachy. I'm so glad you talked me into going."

More irony. I guess I should be used to these roller-coaster days, where nothing went as planned. "What a switcheroo—you rushing back while I'm not sure I want to give it another shot."

"Why not? The group really understands what we've been through. More than my mother and your mother do. More than my sister does. When I cried tonight, no one told me to get over it."

"Don't exaggerate about our families. No one says that."

"Maybe not always with words, but with their expressions. I can read their nuances, so don't tell me otherwise."

"Fine. If you're happy, then I'm happy. The group's working for you, and that's the whole point of the exercise."

I guess I came here tonight looking for some 'atta boys.' But it didn't turn out that way. No one I'd met tonight seemed to understand that however hard I'd tried to pull the family together, I'd failed. I'd lost everyone—

not only Kayla. But then I wondered if maybe I hadn't explained it well enough. Maybe I hadn't *communicated.* Now, there's a word that came up a lot.

"Did you say something?"

I shook my head. "Not important." Her quizzical look fell on me just as I exited the freeway and headed toward our neighborhood.

"Well, if you don't want to talk, I will," she said, turning my way. "I was just thinking that we were the only couple there who...who weren't a couple anymore. Who live apart."

The sound of her drumming fingernails echoed in the vehicle, but before she could continue, I cut her off.

"That's true. We have issues that these people don't. These couples are focused only on their child and remembrances. Warm memories. Each couple is a team on the same wavelength. But you and I? Hell, we're in two different worlds." I could feel my stomach start its familiar burn. "Can you reach into the glove box and grab my antacids?"

By the time she managed to find the roll, I was pulling into our driveway. I let the motor idle as I popped a pill. "Jack?"

Her fingers curled around mine. By the dome light, I could see how compressed her mouth was, how tense she looked. "Different worlds?" she whispered. "If you think there's no road back, then we might as well call it quits."

*No!* I reached across the wheel and turned the key to the off position with my left hand. Silence settled around us, except for the sound of cicadas in the grass.

"Never mind about Ian and the baby," she said, "because this is about Claire and Jack Barnes. About how you and I fell apart in the face of every parent's nightmare. In the end, our problems are not about Kayla. They're about us."

Her hands clutched mine now, their strength matching the passion in her voice, the passion of a valid argument. I recognized this wife of mine, this familiar version. Intelligent, caring, brave. I hadn't seen her in a very long time.

"When did you get so smart again, Claire?" I sounded hoarse. My throat hurt forming the words.

"I don't know what you mean, but..." She gestured widely with her arm toward the house then back to us. "Do you really want to walk away? Give up on us? Give up on making a life together?"

We'd need a new foundation for that life, but I was starting to believe I couldn't pour the cement by myself.

"The truth is, Claire, that I'd rather continue at the motel than come home to...to what we've had recently. What kind of relationship is it, with you in the studio painting secret pictures and me at the office until after dark? That's not how we used to be. That's not a real marriage."

"I agree," she replied quickly. "But you heard what they said tonight. Our family isn't what it used to be either, and if you think we'll ever recover completely from losing Kayla, you're deluding yourself. Nothing will ever be the same."

"Please. Give me some credit."

"Point taken. Sorry." She sighed and glanced at the home we'd built together. "You know, the house wasn't so big when the kids and their friends were around. But lately, man, has it grown!"

We both laughed; we needed the comic relief, dark though it was, and whatever tension remained between us dissipated into the soft night air. "Not to worry, Claire-de-Lune. It's a sturdy house. Just needs a bit of remodeling." I looked into her eyes. "A bit of work."

"Yes. It's something to think about."

I wanted to kiss her. Hell, I wanted to make all-out love to her. I wanted to remove every piece of clothing she wore, one by one by one, until silky skin was all I saw and touched. But love making was a trap. It would be too easy to fall back into old, comfortable habits.

Comfortable? I swallowed a laugh. With a single sultry look, Claire could make my heart pound, pulse race, and manhood stand at attention, as it was threatening to do right now. But the future was too important to ruin with an impetuous evening's delight.

"Go inside and lock up. I'll be back at five."

I watched until the kitchen light went out and wondered if I was just a damn fool.

# CHAPTER THIRTY FOUR


*CLAIRE*

*Wednesday morning*

Ian lived in a second floor unit of an eight-plex of apartments. My first glance took in window shutters hanging askew, missing sills, and neglected landscaping. The clapboard siding, surely pristine white in earlier years, was now faded to gray. All in all, a sad greeting to visitors.

"There should be a large protest sign on the roof saying, 'Paint Me,'" said Jack.

"You read my mind."

He drove around back to the assigned parking areas for each cluster of buildings as if he'd done it a dozen times. I, on the other hand, would have needed a GPS system to find the place.

"I'm impressed."

He cocked a brow and grinned. "You should be. I've been here only once."

"I hope Ian's apartment looks better on the inside than the buildings do on the outside. Maybe I should have brought rubber gloves and detergent." I took a sip of my to-go coffee and started opening the door.

"Claire?"

"Yes?"

"Take a hard look around. Can you guess which apartment is Ian's?"

I felt my forehead contract. The entire complex was a mess. How would I pick out Ian's unit? Jack continued to stare at me, a gleam in his eye, and I began examining the exterior of the building.

It took less than the minute Jack gave me to figure it out. I pointed above and to the right. "Second floor at the end. Of course that's his," I whispered. Two pairs of windows sported gleaming white shutters, hung straight and square, with sills to match. Jack's smile stretched across his face.

"The Barnes genes are still thriving, so you can forget about rubber gloves and detergent. But he needs us, Claire. He doesn't even know how much. We're here to help, not criticize him."

"I don't need a lecture from you."

He put up his hands. "Okay, okay. Everyone is so damn sensitive, I feel like I'm walking on hot coals."

I waited until he exited the truck, then stood before him, tilting my head back to see him eye-to-eye. "I'm willing to walk on hot coals for the sake of our son and granddaughter. Thinking about that little peanut makes me happier. Whatever we do and say today affects how Ian sees us and his future."

"So we tread carefully. The boy has pride. He's been through a lot, not only with the baby but with a girl he must have loved."

"I know, I know." Sighing, I touched his wrist. "This isn't the way I thought we'd become grandparents. Having grandbabies wasn't even a blip on my radar with our kids being so young. First, I thought we'd have watched them fall in love...."

Jack's fingers threaded through mine as we started walking toward the entrance. "We would have planned a wedding or two."

"But that's not going to happen now," I said quietly.

He stopped cold. "Congratulations. That's the first comment you've made since Kayla died that's grounded in reality. You're finally seeing straight."

"Damn it, Jack, stop judging me! Didn't you hear what they said at the group last night? What I've tried to tell you a thousand times, but you never believed me? Married or not, we're different individuals. So we grieve at different speeds and in different ways. Our own ways. There's no right and wrong."

We pushed the entrance door open and searched for Ian's mailbox and bell.

"Seems to me, we weren't so different after Kayla died. We both cried so hard we couldn't breathe without pain. Off-the-chart kind of pain," Jack said. "We were in unison then, weren't we, Claire?"

He had a point, but I was trying to let go of the past and look ahead. "As the saying goes, that was then, and this is now."

"Oh, for Pete's sake. I don't believe a word of that. Especially coming out of your mouth. Sure, it's time to forget the old dreams we had for our kids—the graduations, the falling-in-love, the marriages, and all the frippery. But after we push those disappointments away, we've still got two children in the apartment upstairs who need us. And our son needs to dream again. He...he deserves to dream again."

The heart of the matter. I smiled up at him and stroked his cheek. "This is finally something we can agree on." After pressing Ian's bell in the downstairs lobby, I waited for his voice over the intercom and the electric buzz to let us in.

They didn't come. "This is ridiculous. The system's probably broken. I'll need a set of keys if I'm to be a regular sitter."

Jack reached for his mobile. "We'll need two sets."

My good mood faded. I guess he liked motel living more than he let on.

#

*JACK*

Ian showed up in thirty seconds cradling the baby in one arm like a football.

"Dad! I didn't expect you. What about work? Come on up."

His surprise at seeing me was comical. Claire and I followed him up the stairs and into the apartment. "The office can wait till tomorrow while I visit with my son and granddaughter for a bit."

"A bit is all you'll get of me." He looked at his watch. "I've got exactly ten minutes."

"Still loving it, huh?"

"It's a great job, Dad. Pays well enough to handle most expenses. Colleen never chipped in for rent anyway." His tone went from upbeat to hurting in a single breath.

The girl had had a good deal—and a good eye. My son was fighting through his disappointment. A man in the making.

"So, who wants Tina first?"

He offered up the baby like a prize, and Claire reached for her with the speed of light.

Next he grabbed for his keys and wallet.

"Whoa, Ian," I said. "We'll need a few items such as house keys, car seat, formula, some directions for her. Where are the diapers and salves?"

My son stared at me as if I'd landed from Mars, and I chuckled. "Don't you think I know how to diaper a baby? Your mother didn't change every single one of yours."

"Well, I guess it runs in the family then. Tina's stuff is in the bedroom, and I'm outta here." He waved and closed the door behind him, then popped back in, kissed Tina, and left again.

I looked at Claire. She looked at me.

"Three times," she said.

"Huh?"

"You changed his diaper exactly three times."

"Well," I said, grinning, "those were three less times you had to do it."

Forty-seven and still so cute. Especially when she rolled her eyes. And when she cast them on Martina Faith Barnes, my wife was absolutely beautiful.

"Born to be a mother," I said.

Instantly, tears emerged. "Don't go there, Jack. Not today." She lifted her chin. "I'm a woman of many talents...as you well know."

Oh, I knew all right. And I always appreciated a couple of those talents very much. She, on the other hand, was probably thinking about different skills—painting, decorating, mothering. Now she was a grandma...and it was time to put my mind on other things.

"How shall we spend the day with our gorgeous grandbaby?" I watched Claire nuzzle the infant, face buried in the tiny neck, inhaling the aroma of innocence and new beginnings. The sight jogged my memory. I saw

Claire holding Kayla again, and my chest hurt. I'd wanted to be the Hulk, strong enough to protect the people I loved from any and all danger. I knew better now. My sweet Kayla. I hadn't been able to save her. No one had saved her.

My fingers trembled, and I stared down at hands usually so strong and capable, just like dads were supposed to be. Like I was supposed to be. Perhaps in my former life...not so much now.

"What are we doing, Claire?" My voice rasped, and Claire spun toward me.

"What do you mean?"

"Another child."

"Another chance to love."

"Or face more heartbreak somewhere down the line."

She didn't reply immediately, and I remained silent too. Then she said, "We're marching toward fifty, Jack. How many people get that far without heartache?"

A pulse throbbed in my forehead, and I automatically pressed hard on the bridge of my nose. Of course, she was right, but after two years of traumatic grief, Claire seemed easily reconciled now. Too glib with her philosophy.

"That baby you're holding is *not* Kayla," I said, my tone hard.

Her body jerked, and her dark eyes flashed. "I know exactly who this baby is."

"Really?"

"Of course. And she needs grandparents."

"She's *Ian's* daughter, not yours and mine. She needs *him*, and he needs us. So how are you going to handle that?"

If I'd thought I could trip her up or make her pause long enough to think about the big picture, I was wrong. She had an answer to any question I could throw at her.

"I'll handle it by being practical and taking each day as it comes. I'm helping out with Tina for the next few days and maybe the entire two weeks until that daycare can take her. I'll be waking up before the birds to get here on time. But it's an opportunity. We'll have to tell our folks, especially my mom. Maybe I can take the baby to work."

"Better if you can get Ian and the baby to come home to us. That should be your goal."

She leaned toward me. "Home?" she challenged. "What are we offering him? More trauma and confusion? Or are you planning to return to Bluebonnet Drive as well?"

She had me there. I guess I'd been picturing myself at the house already, an assumption that had no basis in fact, and did, indeed, make an ass out of me. So I said the only thing that could possibly bring me redemption.

"I'm sure our granddaughter could use a few things. Let's go shopping."

#

*CLAIRE*

I accepted the olive branch before we actually investigated the state of Tina's supplies. We found lots of formula, disposable diapers, and toiletries stored in closets and in the bedroom. I'd never seen such a large collection of skin care products, thermometers, infant fever reducers, cotton balls. Half the items were still sealed in their packages. I noticed a few soft baby books. Had Ian been reading to his tiny daughter? A lovely thought.

"The toiletries far outnumber the clothing," I murmured, opening and closing drawers. Jack held the baby as I riffled through the short pile of onesies and receiving blankets. Then I searched the closet, remembering how I'd used miniature hangers for the bounty of gifts we'd received when the kids were born. Now Ian's man-sized shirts and pants greeted my eyes with the exception of one tiny pink sweater, tag still attached.

"Our winters might be milder than elsewhere in the country, but this is ridiculous," I said.

"Is that all the baby has?" asked Jack, peering in.

"Unless there's a laundry hiding somewhere."

There wasn't.

"It looks like Ian spent most of his money on formula and bath supplies. Tina doesn't have enough clothes."

"Then we'll have to buy more, especially since she keeps soaking through everything she wears."

What grandma needed a practical reason to shop? But if it made Jack happy...great. We used Jack's laptop to go online and find a nearby mall. By mid-afternoon, Tina Faith Barnes owned an array of size nine and twelve-month adorable outfits, several blanket-sleepers, tights, booties, and a knit hat with a pom-pom. Grandma and Grandpa owned a roomy travel bag.

It was Jack's idea to stop at the supermarket for dinner ingredients. "Something simple and tasty, like a meatloaf and baked potatoes—if you're not too tired."

"I'm not too tired to feed my son a home-cooked meal every night I'm here."

We shopped until the cart was full. I'd be able to prepare a variety of dinners in the days ahead. Maybe Ian and I would share meals and talk. Back at the apartment, we put Tina down for a nap while we stocked the fridge and small pantry closet.

"This is great," Jack said. "If your cooking doesn't get him to come home, nothing will."

"Don't count on it. He called me to babysit only because he was desperate."

Jack fell silent for a moment. The truth didn't warrant contradiction. "He's angry. And let's face it, he's angry with you more than me. The other night at the house, he said you were still living in the past. His expression said a lot more."

I had to agree. "He relived the accident in front of us. His memories are horrible, and I know he blames me. He can't forget—how could he?—and I can't undo it." But how I wished I could. I wished I hadn't stayed late with Colombo. I wished I hadn't enjoyed his compliments so much, I wished I hadn't wanted more of them. Shame seared my body. My cheeks felt hot with embarrassment and guilt. And I deserved a lifetime dose of all three.

"Talk to him, Claire. Communicate."

"Like you and I have communicated?"

Silence followed, a deep, dark absence of sound. I wondered exactly how long two people could stare at each other in such an atmosphere. My answer came when our glances fell quickly, each of us refusing to admit our failings. Or our desires.

Nothing, however, interfered with preparing the meal. When Ian walked through the door that evening, he halted on the threshold, inhaling deeply, glancing toward me then Jack, before finally scooping up his daughter from my arms.

"Smells good in here for a change, doesn't it, baby girl?"

The infant gurgled her assent as Ian kissed her and handed her back to me. "Gotta get washed up before I really play with her. Is whatever you're cooking almost ready?"

"Five minutes. Hope you don't mind me meddling through the kitchen."

"Are you kidding?"

I laughed. That was the kid I knew, and when he left the room, a seed of hope blossomed inside me. Our brief conversation had been so wonderfully ordinary. Unless, of course, he'd say anything for a decent meal. I supposed that was normal, too, for a growing boy. Boy? He was not yet twenty-one, but could he already be a man?

This glimpse of a familiar life, an ordinary life...I yearned for more of it. How extraordinary the ordinary could be! What was in Ian's mind? Heart? We couldn't keep drifting away from each other as we'd been doing. Maybe Tina was the wake-up call I'd needed for reclaiming my loving relationship with her father. Whatever the cost of the knowing, I had to face the truth.

"I'm hoping Ian and I can talk over dinner each night. I'll keep cooking, we'll both keep eating, and hopefully we'll 'communicate.' I'll try to figure out where his head is." I sighed. "That's the best I can come up with at the moment."

"Sounds good," said Jack. "Keep me in the loop, will you?"

If I wanted to rebuild my relationship with Ian, I couldn't make promises to Jack. "I'll use my judgment. You and I have our own issues, and I'm not going to use Ian to deflect them."

# CHAPTER THIRTY FIVE

*IAN*

*November*

After one week of Mom babysitting, I could have been fooled into thinking I was back on Bluebonnet Drive. Those dinners she prepared every night? Wow. Just call me a Pavlov dog, salivating the moment I caught a whiff of them as I neared the apartment door. If Tina weren't so cute and now old enough to recognize me, I'd head directly to that kitchen table without saying hello.

But of course, I gravitated first to my daughter, who now greeted me with a toothless smile, a scorcher that made me feel like the world's Number One Daddy. I took her from her grandma, kissed her all over, and then blew gentle raspberries on her belly. Her giggles almost did me in—she was so cute. In those moments of homecoming, when the place felt safe and secure, exactly what I wanted for my daughter and what I had known growing up, I wondered how I could have thought of giving her up. I wondered how Colleen could have lit out.

Tina had a grandma, daddy, clean bed, plenty of bottles, and a mess of new clothes. And sometimes Grandpa was around too. But a mama should have headed the list. Wondering about Colleen always brought my good moods to an end. She hadn't called in the two weeks she'd been gone, and I tried not to think too much about that. Maybe when she got a job, she'd have enough money to buy minutes for her cell phone. Or maybe she didn't want to talk to me. Maybe she wanted to start a new life and forget the old. I couldn't guess what was in her mind, so maybe I didn't know her very well after all. A lot of maybes.

"Had a good day, Ian?" Mom was smiling and eager to please.

"Always do. Good team, no slackers. We get things done."

"Oh."

I swallowed my chuckle as I read her expression as easily as I read one of Tina's baby books. She was hoping I was so miserable at work and being on my own that I'd return to Barnes Construction and get back into the family fold. But that wasn't going to happen without a miracle. And I wasn't expecting any of those.

I put Tina in her swing and turned my attention to the turkey breast and mashed potatoes Mom was dishing out. A minute later, I was wolfing them down.

"This is great, Mom. Super. I'd like to freeze half of it for next week when Tina starts at the daycare center."

"I'm glad you brought that up," she said, laying down her own fork. "I've been thinking.... Do you really want the baby with a bunch of strangers every day? She's so little. I could either take her to work with me or Dad said he'd hire someone to replace me as long as necessary. So I'd be happy to continue coming over."

"Fifty miles? Before the birds are up? Come on. You can't do that indefinitely, and I'll lose my place on the waiting list at the daycare."

She stared at me with such determination and strength she was a picture of how she used to be. "You can count on me, Ian. I'll be here every morning by six, you'll get to your job on time, and the baby will have loving, undivided attention. It's a perfect solution for everybody."

Except for me. But she didn't understand that. "Thanks, but no thanks. I'm happy with the temp arrangement we have."

She rose and gripped her chair so tightly, her knuckles turning white. "But why not? I love that baby. No daycare can replace a grandma."

Mom was trying too hard. Whenever I had these suspicions, the cause always came back to that day we didn't talk about. Something was up for sure, and I wished to God for a complex pipeline assembly problem instead of a mother problem. I always had to struggle to figure her out. Dang, I hated psychology. But I was Tina's daddy, and she was my daughter, so I'd do what I had to do. Nowadays, I was the man.

"We had a temporary deal," I said sharply, also rising but towering over her, "because I have to protect my daughter. You just said that a daycare can't replace a grandma, so now chew on this." I pointed first at Tina and then punched the air with each word I spoke. "She. Isn't. Kayla. Get it?"

Mom backed up in surprise, but then her chin rose and her eyes bored into mine strong and steady. "You and your father! Listen to me, Ian. I know exactly who that baby is."

I didn't believe her. "Kayla's dead, Mom, and Tina's not her replacement. And I don't ever want her to feel she is." I stepped closer. "Why do you want to take care of her so much?"

"Why? Because she's yours, and you're my son. I love you both. What's so difficult to understand about that?"

What the hell was she talking about?

"Love?" My voice cracked. "Let's get this straight. You don't love me anymore. You blamed me for Kayla's death. You said we should have been doing homework and that I was 'irresponsible.' And you still think I am. But I'm not! I'm taking care of business, aren't I? Taking care of Tina. Earning a living."

Her face turned as white as one of her blank canvases. She grabbed me by the shoulders. "Oh, God, Ian. A messy bedroom is not the same thing as causing a death. You weren't driving the car that hit her, and I knew that. So how could you possibly think I blamed you?"

I loosened her hold on me, rolled back on my heels, and took my time. Her words on that day had haunted me for over two years. I remembered every single one of them.

"Well, Mom, maybe I had that impression because the last thing you yelled at me before disappearing with Kayla was: *'How could you let this happen? You were in charge. You should have been doing homework.'* And that's a quote. And maybe because I was the one who threw the ball? And then you told Dad to let me go...."

I watched as she paled further to a chalk white. Her hands fluttered, and her eyes started to roll. I caught her before she hit the floor.

#

*CLAIRE*

I heard a baby crying. Short cries followed by a long cry. On and on, non-stop. *I'm coming, I'm coming.* But my limbs wouldn't cooperate, and I fell back against the cushions. Ian's lumpy sofa. That's where I was. On Ian's sofa with him in front of me holding an overturned glass, water trickling from it drop-by-drop to the floor. That's when I realized my face and hair were soaking wet. "What the...?"

"You fainted."

"And you tried to drown me?"

"No!" He shrugged and looked away. "I saw it on television once. It worked."

"Okay then, thank you...I think." I swung my legs to the floor and sat up, only slightly dizzy. "The baby's crying. Pick her up."

"You're welcome," Ian said, ignoring my instructions. "Uh, should I call Dad?"

I hadn't fainted in quite a while. Couldn't blame an empty stomach this time. Probably too much emotion. Too much deeply felt emotion. And now, the last thing I needed was Jack's interference just as Ian and I had started talking.

"No need to call Dad. I'm fine. I'm fine. But you and I? We're not so fine."

Water trailed down my neck while the baby's cries stretched my nerves. "Tina needs you, Ian, and I need a towel." Fortunately, I was steady on my feet after leaving the couch and made my way to the bathroom without further trouble. The minute of privacy was welcome.

Ian had sounded so sure of himself, so very sure in his accusation, that I took time to search my memory of that never-to-be-forgotten day. I recalled Anne running toward me, I remembered the crowd on the street, Ian among them; I could see Sarah Levine sitting on the curb and could almost feel Kayla's hand in mine when I'd held it in the ambulance. I remembered the hospital in a blurry way, the five days melting into one another as she faded.

But recalling the moment I entered the ambulance was impossible. I played the tape over and over in my mind—and came up with nothing. I leaned against the sink, needing its support. My heart lay as heavily in my chest as it had during the darkest of times. Ian wasn't lying. He'd thrown those words at me as though he'd been savoring them for years. But how could I have said them? No wonder he hated me. I wished I could remember.

I took a shaky breath, squared my shoulders, and re-entered the kitchen in time to see him toss his phone on the counter while holding Tina in his other arm.

"Dad's coming over," he said. "So you won't have to drive home by yourself."

So he'd ignored my wishes. "I'm perfectly cap—"

"It's great that he joined a gym. When did that happen?"

I had no idea. "Hmm...a little while ago."

"Yeah. He wasn't at the house or the office. So I wound up calling his mobile. Should have done that to begin with."

Nervous chatter. While talking to me, however, he continued to smile and coo at his daughter as naturally as he tossed a basketball.

"You're really terrific with her. I don't imagine many young guys could handle a baby as well."

"It's not like I had a choice. Colleen...she did her best, she knew how to handle babies, but she wasn't the type to cuddle Tina all day."

Picking up Ian's phone, I auto-dialed Jack. "Forget what Ian told you. I'm fine. I don't need any help."

After listening to how "fainting has become my style and do something about it," I hung up and smiled brilliantly at my son. "The cavalry's not coming this time. It's just you and me. And I'm sorry about Colleen."

His mouth tightened, and he said nothing further about the girl. Instead, he kissed the baby's cheek. "It's you, me, and her."

"Tina's a bonus. A sweet gift. Innocent."

"Kayla was innocent," he snapped. "But Tina's not Kayla."

He simply didn't trust me to know the difference between my daughter and granddaughter. "I get it, Ian. I understand. Now, look at me. Listen to me. Kayla's gone, and I don't blame you at all!"

"But that's not what you said then."

"Oh, sweetheart, I can't recall what I said. I don't remember what you remember. None of it. I know I raced into the ambulance and the doors slammed closed. That's all."

"You're lying."

I shook my head. "I'm not—"

"Yes. You have to be because you've got that photographic memory. You remember everything."

But where was that memory when I needed it? Or did I not want to remember, just like...? "I don't remember Kayla's funeral either," I whispered. "And I'm not lying."

He paused for a moment, and inside me, a seed of hope cracked open its shell. "But that makes sense," he said, "because you fainted. You didn't black out when you got into the ambulance."

It seemed Ian was the one with the excellent memory, not me.

"And then," Ian went on, "when we all ate at the House of Wong, you said something about an accident not being just an accident, and that 'someone was careless.' And you meant me, didn't you? You always think I'm careless or irresponsible."

Not in the ways that count. I had to clear the slate between Ian and me at all costs, even if there was a drop of truth to his accusations. Two years ago, I was blaming everyone, with the lion's share divided between Sarah Levine and myself.

"Sarah Levine," I whispered. "How could she not have sunglasses? In Houston? Kayla died because of the sun and a sneeze? I couldn't accept it."

A statue would have reacted more, so I plunged ahead. "But more importantly...you know what I've been thinking all this time? The reason you've avoided me? That you hated me for coming home late, and that Kayla wouldn't have died if I'd been on time. And then you wouldn't have had to cope by yourself. You wouldn't have had to live with those memories. Hear me, Ian? That's what I've believed all this time about you."

His eyes shone, but not with hope. "That's so lame," he whispered. "You've apologized a hundred times for being late. Traffic's not the problem. We've got four and a half million people in the area, and folks are always running late.

"Face the truth, Mom. You were always nagging me about something. You never trusted me with anything important, but I was all you had as a babysitter. And when the accident happened, of course you blamed me. But guess what? I didn't blame myself. Kayla and I threw football passes loads of times in the past and nothing bad ever happened. I wish I could undo it, but I can't, and I'm tired of feeling like a murderer."

He pivoted like a soldier doing an about-face and left the room. Left me alone with his resentment, anger, and possibly hate, although I didn't want to believe that. I did know, however, that we were still hurting each other. I'd been told to communicate, and I'd tried. Now, I was exhausted and disappointed. Nothing had changed. Nothing had been accomplished. But if he thought I'd give up on our relationship, he'd have to think again.

I reached for a pad and pencil. "Back at six a.m."

I signed off with a quick sketch of a sad me. If I was lucky, he'd believe that communiqué.

# CHAPTER THIRTY SIX

*CLAIRE*

My two weeks with Tina flew by, and suddenly I was back at the office, regaling my mom with stories of her great-granddaughter. I also insisted my hard-working mom take a week off from work. I assured her we'd have a family gathering when Ian was ready to introduce Tina to the rest of the crew.

"I will take a week's vacation," Mom said. "Frankly, I need one. And your dad suggested we relax on a little cruise as soon as you returned. We've already booked it— one of those inexpensive last-minute deals. It'll be good for both of us."

"You surely deserve it. I don't even know how to begin to thank you for all your help."

"You don't have to thank me. I love helping buyers choose their options, and besides," she whispered, "I'm getting paid."

I grinned at her and shooed her out of the office, strangely energized and ready to return to work but not ready to return to my volunteer job at the hospital. I called Rose, however, and got Neil Schulman's phone number. His mother seemed glad to hear from me and expected me for a visit the next day. I'd offered to mail Neil's pictures, but she definitely wanted to meet me.

It had only been three weeks since Neil's death. At that point with Kayla, I'd been hiding in the house. Maybe Mrs. Schulman was doing the same.

When she opened her door, I greeted her with condolences. She greeted me with a smile and a hug. She didn't act like a zombie, just seemed strained and sad.

"I'm so glad to finally meet Miss Claire," she said, inviting me in. "Neil talked about you nonstop. He said you made his art better." Her lips trembled, but her voice never faltered. She looked away for a second then met my gaze again. "I can never thank you enough for making his time at the hospital so much happier."

I wanted to bawl but tried to take my cue from this woman who seemed so much stronger than I had been.

"I loved knowing Neil and making art with him, Mrs. Schulman. He had real talent."

Family pictures were displayed wherever I looked, Neil and a little girl clearly the focus of the lens most of the time.

"Let me show you something." Neil's mom led me to a hallway in the bedroom area of the small house. I came to a full stop as I saw a gallery of the boy's work, each drawing in a simple frame. A sign of respect.

"Your son was quite remarkable," I said, slowing down to look at each one. "And I've got two more for you."

She nodded. "H-he was a remarkable boy. He was a gift."

She led me toward the kitchen and, before I could stop her, put a kettle of water up for tea.

"If you have a minute, I need your help. Neil's dad and I want to donate art supplies to the pediatrics unit. We want to put a gold plaque up that says 'Neil's Art Closet' and make sure the shelves are always filled. It would make us feel good knowing other children could spend happier hours in the hospital."

She had such plans, such energy. Was she not even mourning Neil's loss? Or maybe she was keeping busy enough not to feel it, sort of like Jack?

"How do you do it?" I asked, my thoughts not on the art closet.

Mrs. Schulman looked confused. "Do what? I was asking you about..."

"No, no. Not that." I leaned forward. "I lost my daughter more than two years ago. A car hit her while I was away from home. I hid in the house for months. Never thought about "doing something" for others. You're as remarkable as Neil."

And now, tears came to the woman's eyes. "Oh, dear. I'm so sorry. All I can say is that Frank and I have been living with the possibility of losing Neil for a long, long time. Years. We always knew the worst could occur. It doesn't make it easier, but in the end, we have to accept that death is part of life."

A phrase that comforted so many. I wasn't there yet. "With an illness, you can blame genetics. With an accident, there's human error. I blame myself."

She took my hand and looked at me with such compassion I could have cried. "Blame is a mind game. Until you let it go, you'll never find peace. Imagine how the person who actually hit your daughter feels."

A video of my last encounter with Sarah Levine ran through my mind. "I've met her. I know how she feels." *As if she'd destroyed the world.*

"And you pity her."

I startled. Hadn't Sarah Levine been my nemesis all this time? I'd never acknowledged her feelings.

"Why are you so surprised at yourself?" Neil's mom asked. "You're a compassionate woman, and even through your own grief, you know life has to be hell for the driver. He or she can never forget."

She wasn't the first one to tell me that. Judy had said it. Jack too. And I'd brushed them aside. But I believed Neil's mother. Either she had a way a speaking or I was ready to listen.

"You're as good or better than the support group I've started going to. And of course, I'll help you stock the art closet. Let's talk to Rose about it."

"Thank you so much. I really know nothing about art supplies except for what Neil used. Let's make an inventory list."

I guess I'd be going back to my volunteer job.

# CHAPTER THIRTY SEVEN

*IAN*

*Saturday, mid-November*

My cell phone rang just as Tina and I were finally ready to leave for the welcome-to-the-family party at my parents' house. That's how Mom put it a couple of days ago when she suggested it was time for my grandparents to meet their great-granddaughter. I considered myself a single dad now and figured the more family Tina had, the better. So I agreed to the party, and I imagined Mom and Dad told the immediate world about their granddaughter.

Mom and I had become...hmm...I guess awkward would be a good way to describe it. Awkward with each other since the night of our confrontation, but I still trusted her to be a good grandma.

Annoyed at being delayed by the ringing cell, I picked it up and barked a hello to Ted Willis from the

Roadside Café. We'd spoken once or twice about Colleen, of course, and the baby, so I wasn't shocked to see his name on the ID. The shock came when he told me Colleen had gotten in touch with him.

"Nice of her," I said. "She finally remembered your number after a month?"

"She asked about you, boy-o. But I gotta warn ya, seems like things are working out for our girl. They liked the demo, and she's got an agent. She thought I'd want to know because of the karaoke at my place. Anyway, she said to tell you to expect a call...unless you don't want to hear from her."

*Tell her not to bother*. That's what I almost said, but frankly, I had a lot to unload on that girl.

"What's her number?"

"Her number? I don't know. I didn't ask."

"Check your readout."

"She was calling from someone's office at a studio. That's what she said."

Ted was covering for her, but there was no use asking more questions. Colleen's actions spoke for themselves.

"So when you magically communicate with her, you can tell her to call me."

"Aw shucks, Ian. She didn't do right by you, but maybe it will all work out in the end."

I let it go, took Tina, and went to the truck. Made sure my cell was on. I drove on autopilot, and the miles to my old house sped by. I guess Ted's message had me thinking hard. As I turned onto Bluebonnet Drive, however, and glanced in the rearview mirror at my sleeping daughter, I forgot the past and focused on what lay ahead. My stomach tensed. Tina would be the star of this rodeo, so why was I so nervous?

*Maybe because you haven't kept in touch with the grands the way you promised? Maybe because you've let them down?* I didn't even want to imagine Aunt Judy's greeting. My cousins were old enough to understand but young enough not to understand. Dang, I liked my privacy.

The driveway was packed with familiar vehicles. Seemed my relatives couldn't wait to meet Tina. I parked in front of the house then glanced at the dashboard clock. I was five minutes late because of Ted's phone call. Mom was probably pacing right now. Getting out of the truck, I took a moment to look around in daylight. Familiar, yet strange. The mature live oaks, Bartlett pear trees standing sentry along the street and property lines, the landscaped bushes and flower beds filled with pansies and petunias forming clouds of blue, white, and pink.

But my eyes rested on the open lawn of our corner lot. Extra room to play, my dad always said. True enough, but now I turned away. My new place may not be the greatest, but I'd choose it over this one. And I guess I did. When I thought about that last year of high school...I still shook my head. If it weren't for Danny and the rest of the guys, I never would have made it. Email was the biggest connector now. Danny would meet my daughter when he came home for the holidays next month.

I unlocked the baby's car seat and murmured, "Might as well get the whole shebang over with."

Tina kept on sleeping, which is what she did best. I chuckled, wishing her good luck with her nap while being surrounded by assorted grandparents and a host of close relatives.

Mom met us at the door, arms open, hugging me. "You're late. I was worried."

"Afraid we wouldn't show?"

She staggered backwards, like I'd slapped her in the face. Maybe she wanted to slap mine. "Sorry."

"Please, Ian. I know you hate me at the moment, but please sweeten up for everyone else. They're as innocent as our sweet Martina Faith Barnes." Then she leaned over and kissed my daughter on the cheek.

Just saying the baby's name the way she did showed me she was laying claim to her. Maybe it should have hardened my heart some more, but I felt it soften instead. Barnes. Tina was a Barnes. We all were her family. "It's a deal."

"Good, good. Come on in. Everyone's waiting."

And they were. In five seconds, I was surrounded by an assortment of family as well as a few friends, including Anne and Tom Conroy and Maddy. I wondered if she still wrote to Kayla. The house was decked out in pink bows and baby decorations, like a birthday party. The table was decked out in platters of deli sandwiches.

"It's a shower," said Grandma Barbara. "A shower of gifts and hugs for the new baby and you! Oh, Ian. She's just beautiful. May I hold her?" Grandma Pearl stood beside her. "Me too?"

Their smiling faces and deference erased any concern I had about being judged and having to answer a hundred questions about my "girlfriend." My grandfathers slapped me on the back and started talking about opening a savings account for their great-granddaughter. One after the other, they surrounded me with oohs and ahs and kisses.

Aunt Judy was the one who came closest to acknowledging the truth behind the scene when she said, "You must have gone through quite a time, Ian, but in the end, you made a good decision. Welcome home to both of you."

So this party wasn't only about Tina after all, which I guess was all right now. I horsed around with my grandpas, asked Maddy how she was doing, and kept an eye on the baby, reaching for her whenever I thought she needed the comfort of her daddy. The afternoon continued with everything going great until my cell phone rang. I didn't recognize the number, but my gut said to answer it. Sure enough, I heard a familiar female voice.

"Hey, Ian! It's Colleen. Did Ted tell you what's been happening? About the demo and my agent. The producers liked my music, and it's just like I dreamed. I'm gonna make a record and then an album. I knew it! I just knew I could do it. I bet your mama's happy now with her arms full of baby. And you? Are you in college now?"

"Hang on," I said when I could get a word in. "Mom, could you take charge of the baby?" She saw me on the phone and scooped Tina into her arms. I walked into my old bedroom and closed the door.

"What the hell are you talking about, Colleen? I work at the plant. Tina's in daycare. Where'd you come up with those fairytales, or is that how you make yourself feel better about walking out on us? Well, let me tell you, girl, I'm glad you showed your true colors early. I sure am."

I was on a roll now and shouting, but I couldn't help it. "Tina is my daughter. Mine. Not my mother's. And it hasn't been easy, but we're doing okay."

"Ooh, Ian, honey. You're so upset. But why? You got what you wanted, and so did I. But I have an idea. Why don't you come down here so there'll be two of us—
"

"Two of us? You've got to be joking. The last time I looked, there was only one of us, and that was me. When the going got tough, you ran. You may be pretty and talented and the future star of country music, but you're not family material. You're not the kind of person I want to share my life with."

"Oh, Sweet Jesus, you hate me. But I don't want you to hate me. I don't hate you, even though you made me have the baby. I did it for you, Ian. You know that. So please don't yell at me. Please."

Maybe that was true. Or maybe I was a convenient excuse to ease her conscience. Did it really matter now? Tina was the only person who mattered.

I took a breath. A deep one. "I don't hate you, Colleen. I can't hate Tina's mother. I'm just disappointed. Maybe I was in my own dreamland." First, I had to calm her down and then remind her of her promise. "So, congratulations on the contract. I hope you're a big hit."

"Thanks, Ian. Thanks a lot. You know I've wanted this my whole life."

"I guess I did know. Are you planning to live in Nashville now?"

"Yup. As long as my career is here, I am."

"Well, that makes a lot of sense, you know, to live near where you work. That's what I did."

"That's how we met."

True enough. "So, Colleen, we need to talk about one more thing...that letter you were going to write giving me custody of Tina. You working on it?"

"Working on it? Why, I wrote it the first day I left. On the bus. Oh, heavens. Maybe I never mailed it...."

Figured. "So send it today. And I'll tell you what. You and I—we really don't know the legal stuff. I'm going to ask my dad's lawyer to draw up an agreement. I'll make sure everything is just like we talked about with you able to visit Tina."

"That sounds good. Especially someday when I'm on tour. I trust you, Ian, but I'll want to read it first. I didn't understand a thing about these contracts down here. My agent helped me."

I'd had some limited experience with legal documents because of building contracts. I knew enough to understand how long and involved they could be.

"Not a problem. You'll have time to read and ask questions." I remembered to get her address and phone number and told her I'd keep in touch. I suppose I should have told her to get her own lawyer for those record contracts. That'd wait for another time. After she signed our agreement.

I hung up and collapsed on my bed with relief. My shirt was soaked with sweat. All I could think about now was my daughter. Suddenly, I was glad to be with my family. Glad that Tina would be surrounded by their love and support.

As for me? I'd given Colleen her freedom. I'd promised visitation. I owed her nothing. It was time to move on.

#

*JACK*

Amazing how one thing could lead to another as quickly as it takes a snake to strike. Amazing how Claire talked Ian into sleeping over in his old room, the baby safely in something called a Pack'n Play she'd bought, hoping for these occasions. With Ian in the house, I wound up sleeping in Kayla's room because I'd developed a 'snoring' problem that kept Claire up all night. Seemed my son bought into it hook, line and sinker, but I suppose he had others things on his mind.

In Kayla's room, however, sat Claire's portrait of our daughter, which was the most amazing thing of all. My wife had truly done a magnificent job. So good that my chest constricted every time I looked at it. So good that I expected Kayla to step into the room at any moment and give me a hug. So good that I needed a glass of water at midnight, at one, and two. I had to face it. I couldn't bear looking at the picture too often. She was so real, and yet, she wasn't there. Maybe I'd bring this up at the next support group meeting. With that decision, I relaxed, turned over, and closed my eyes.

Then I heard Ian get up with the baby. Oh, yeah. I remembered those middle-of-the-night feedings when the rest of the world slumbered on. Hmm...This could be the perfect time for an intimate visit, and after today's family reunion, the perfect time for a job offer.

*Slow down, Jack, slow down. Wait till he's ready.*

I got out of bed anyway and made my way to the kitchen, where I watched my boy be a daddy to his little one. I listened to his soft, deep voice making silly noises at her. I'd had no idea that my kid could be so gentle. His young man's body was still filling out—he was still so young. I marveled at his self-reliance.

"You're incredible, son." Maybe even more incredible than Kayla's portrait.

"Hey, Dad. Sorry to wake you."

I waved his apology away and watched my granddaughter suck hard on her bottle. "Won't be long before she'll put on some baby fat, and you'll toss her around like a football."

"She's already gained five pounds," announced the proud father. "You should've seen her in the beginning. Teeny tiny. I was scared to hold her. But the nurse showed me how."

He was right about one thing: I should have seen her in the beginning. I let that go. "Glad you were a quick study."

"Me too. Although Colleen actually did all right in that department."

"How'd you meet her?"

He looked thoughtful, a smile came, and for the next ten minutes, I listened to how the girl had made Ian feel welcome at his job and after hours too. How he was blown away the first time he'd heard her sing. How pretty she was. I started to wonder and worry if she'd left town with a piece of his heart.

"So how are you feeling about her now?" I dared to ask.

"That is a complicated question, Dad. And I'm basically a simple guy."

Simple? I disagreed but once again kept my mouth shut. Claire insisted I had great intuition about people, but all I ever really did was listen.

"Colleen thinks, and maybe it's true, that she's the next big discovery, the next Taylor Swift. They don't sound alike—Colleen's got more country twang—but she's really, really good."

I emitted a low whistle.

He cocked his head. "Yeah. She's aiming for the stars."

"And what are you aiming for?"

"Me? What are you talking about? I'm aiming to take care of Tina Faith. It's a full-time job, and I'm the dad."

"Single dads can often use some help. It's nothing to be ashamed of."

"I've already gotten some help from you and Mom. Thanks for watching her. And...and for making this party. I'm glad the grands and all the relatives know about my daughter now. I want Tina to have family around her."

"And the family wants you and Tina around them too. Nearer."

His face closed up tighter than a knotted shoelace. "I'm doing fine where I am. I-I can't even drive up to this house without starting to shake. You don't know. You weren't there."

But I was with him now just as I'd been with him in the early days. I knew the story and what he'd gone through, but it seemed my son suffered flashbacks especially here. "So tell me about it, Ian. Just take your time and tell me what it was like."

I listened to his memories and wondered if we could ever get together in the future without discussing the day of Kayla's death. Would we ever simply enjoy watching a game, grilling a burger? What would it take for the wounds to scab over?

"...And then Mom showed up. She ran to the ambulance, the doors slammed in my face, and they took off. Someone led me to the sidewalk. The cops were there. And Sarah—Mrs. Levine. I felt sorry for her."

I did too, after speaking with her husband. But Ian didn't know about that. "You felt sorry for her? That's interesting, considering she'd been driving the car."

"She'd thrown up and couldn't even stand. Sitting on the curb, she kept praying for Kayla, sometimes in Hebrew." His face lit up for a moment. "Remember way back, Danny begged me to listen to him practice for his bar mitzvah? I didn't understand a word, but he needed an audience, so I did it. That's why I recognized the language."

I hugged the two of them, son and granddaughter. "You've got some big heart, Ian. I love you. I'm proud of you. Never forget that."

He squeezed my arm and turned away, but not before I saw the pain etched on his face. That girlfriend of his was happily chasing dreams while my son was running from nightmares.

# CHAPTER THIRTY EIGHT

*CLAIRE*

The holidays came quickly, and I didn't dread them quite as much this year. Judy hosted Thanksgiving, which helped. I wouldn't have minded preparing the feast, but in Judy's house, Kayla's empty seat wasn't as prominent as it was in mine.

Ian seemed to enjoy himself, teasing his grandmothers, joking with his younger cousins, discussing sports with his granddads. His sweet demeanor had returned. He was relaxed with everyone except me.

The baby provided a loving distraction for us. I, for one, was thankful for that distraction which took some attention away from my situation with Jack, who still lived at the Marriott. We pre-arranged to arrive at Judy's in one car. No point in rubbing salt on that unhealed wound at holiday time. I could feel my mom's eyes on us. Watching. Evaluating. Hoping for the best. I kept a smile on my face and tried to appreciate the blessings I had instead of what I had lost.

I especially wanted to reassure Ian that he'd made the right decision in keeping the baby and that I truly understood she was not a substitute for Kayla. Tina had her own unique personality, voice, and behavior. I adored her for herself and had a hard time sharing her with the rest of the family. Now that she was in daycare, I didn't get to see her as much as I would have liked. Ian, however, wouldn't be budged, and I backed off.

I handled Thanksgiving, but navigating Christmas and New Year's in an empty house made me cringe. I'd tried to make the place cheerful—wreaths, tree, candles, and whimsical Santa figures—for the sake of Ian and Tina's visits. And of course, gifts! Piles and piles of presents for Tina and Ian grew under the tree. I should have remembered that a baby's greatest pleasure came from tearing up all the wrapping paper! My camera never paused; I had wonderful entries for the new album I'd started the day of the baby shower.

Christmas cards and letters began to arrive, sometimes filling the mailbox so tightly I had a hard time retrieving them all. And that was why I almost overlooked the large square envelope sporting the university's return address, but definitely not from the registrar's office. I slit the envelope open and pulled out a beautiful invitation to a champagne reception honoring Dr. Cristoforo Colombo. I'd lost track of his status, but it seemed his three-year stint as Visiting Professor of Fine Arts was ending.

*In appreciation for his dynamic leadership...increased prestige of the department in the greater community...*

Yada, yada, yada...

Without a pause, I reached for the phone. Mom would love an event like this. Any talent I had came through her genes. And Judy? She'd want to tag along. As for me...Well, I guess I needed to thank the man for his encouragement. My work was now so damn good my husband lived at a hotel. I would have laughed if I hadn't wanted to cry. Jack and I weren't enemies, but we weren't best friends anymore either. I guess he didn't trust me, and without trust...well, forget about rebuilding a solid relationship.

I blinked hard at the invitation, an old flush of guilt racing through my body. Still there, still haunting me. Yes, I wanted to see Colombo again. The real reason? To test my own reaction to the powerhouse. Had I been the one sending out signals? Or had I reacted to his? I felt secure knowing I'd be safely ensconced in the crowd.

#

"Holy smokes, this place is packed," said Judy as we entered the overflowing *galleria.* "It's a good thing you made me dress up."

"It's a good thing we took you shopping is what you really mean," I said, eyeing my sister's simple but elegant attire. A sequined, rose silk top over a classic knee-length black silk skirt, dark hose, high heels, the ensemble was perfect for her petite frame.

"Now we fit in with all the lovely butterflies in the garden." I noted the women in their cocktail dresses and evening gowns, the men in tuxedos. "The press is here too," I said, nodding toward a guy with a camera. "The event is for the art patrons and supporters."

"I guess the arts are thriving in Houston."

Judy was right. The city boasted a wonderful theater district, symphony orchestra, opera and ballet companies. But I was interested in the art scene, and I was in the right place.

"I recognize some of my old classmates." As we made our way through the room, I waved, said hello, but didn't stop to chat, thereby avoiding another round of condolences. "Let's keep walking."

"You go ahead," said my mom. "I want to browse the exhibits. Maybe I'll buy something. After all, that's what this shindig is all about...besides honoring the professor, of course."

"Enjoy yourself. We'll catch up later." I'm sure Mom barely heard me as she'd already stopped to study a contemporary piece. "She's in her own world," I said to my sister. "That didn't take long."

"You should talk! You're exactly like her."

I chuckled. "Maybe a bit."

Judy and I continued to stroll, viewing the exhibit and accepting an hors d'oeuvre from a passing waiter. "I think your professor has created a real buzz," Judy said. "I can feel the vibe in the room. I bet the school is sorry he's leaving."

I shrugged. "He...he did make an impression on me. I'll admit that, but...maybe the university will attract someone else of his caliber next year." Next year. What would I be doing then?

"Clara! Clara, is that really you?"

I'd drifted away for a moment, and he'd caught me by surprise. With one glance, however, I knew Colombo hadn't changed a bit. Still full of energy and charisma, still more handsome than a man had a right to be.

"Clara. So good to see you. And of course, your beautiful companion."

"Clara?" muttered Judy into my ear. "And you must be the professor." She raised her decibel level and offered her hand. "I'm *Clara's* sister."

"Excellent! So you will convince her to return to the university. You have the power to do that."

He looked at me again, his eyes assessing what normal mortals didn't see. "You are finally where you belong, Clara. You have come back to life. Delicate, but strong, no? So...it is time to make art again."

"Don't worry about that," said Judy with airy grace. "She knocked us out some weeks ago with her art."

"So I was right! Again, I was right."

The man actually raised his arms in victory. I almost laughed at the picture he made. And he wasn't finished.

"Clara, Clara, with the eyes and the heart and the talent. Special, special talent. You must paint. You must create. You have no choice."

Someone called his name, and with a cheerful "*Ciao*, enjoy, enjoy," he spun on his heel and was gone.

"Whew!" said Judy. "He's the president of your fan club. To him, you are an *artiste* personified."

She had it right. Colombo brought drama in his wake, but he was a sensitive and passionate man—who believed in me. I could see now that he'd been driven only by my work and potential. To the professor, I was merely a talented student who he'd wanted to encourage. But I'd eaten up his praise like a teenager with a crush and convinced myself his interest was as personal as professional. Which had made me late getting home that day. Seemed he was cleared on the flirting indictment, but I was guilty as charged on the lateness one. Lord help me, I was such a fool. A simpleton who should have known better. And whose daughter had paid the price.

#

"Time to find Mom," said Judy. "It's getting late."

"I think she's found us," I replied as my mother approached.

"Have you seen what these students have produced?" she began. "Watercolors, oils, hand-built ceramics, wheel-built ceramics, life drawings, weaving—can you believe weaving?" She paused for breath. "I'm having such a grand time I may take a course myself. It's been too long between canvasses."

"You go, girl!" I said. Mom's brown eyes sparkled like Kayla's used to whenever her enthusiasm rang true. I blinked and looked aside. "You go too, girl." This time I whispered.

"And you'll come with me."

"No promises, Mom. We'll see, we'll see."

"At least that's not a no," Judy said.

"I'm counting on a yes. But now I'm going to the portrait exhibit. Right there on the left," said Mom. "Let's all go." She set out, and we watched her disappear without waiting for us.

Judy and I looked at each other. "What's gotten into her?" my sister asked.

"Maybe she and Dad should get out of the house more often." Or maybe Mom was too tired after working at Barnes Construction. Seventy years young was still seventy years.

"Frankly, I think she's happy out and working with you. The cruise was great. Did you see them all lovey-dovey—"

Our mother's scream interrupted us, a primal cry ringing through the large hall. "That's my granddaughter! Ooh, oh. Claire, Judy...."

We ran. Totally clueless. Mom pointed, and I looked up and saw what she saw. I looked up and saw...Kayla. *Girl with Secrets*. It hung on the wall as though it had a right to be there, with a small "not for sale" sign taped beneath.

*Don't faint. Be strong. Be strong.* But oh, my God, words of comfort for my mom were beyond me as I stared at Kayla. My precious Kayla, standing before me exactly as I'd remembered painting her. Beautiful to me, of course, but there was something else as well, something beneath the depiction that made it glow with heart, soul, and truth. I could see—finally— what Colombo had seen: the ephemeral quality of an adolescent girl's coming-of-age. The wonderment within.

I heard my sister speak, loud words, soft words. I couldn't understand much. Something about the not-for-sale sign....

"Forget the stupid sign, I'm buying it!" My mom's declaration. "No one else would dare. Now, where is that crazy professor? What is going on here?"

A lioness. I turned my head and snapped a mental picture. *The Grandma Roars*. Later...later, maybe I'd sketch her.

"It's good, isn't it?" I whispered, looking at Kayla once again.

"Oh, you idiot," said Judy. "It's fantastic."

Electrical charges continued to zap me, the initial jolt at seeing the portrait giving way to shock waves. I wondered if Jack had felt the same undertow when he saw the soccer portrait at our anniversary party. Had he been overwhelmed and breathless like I was at this moment?

"The two of you need to sit down," said Judy. "And recuperate."

"I'm fine, but Mom has a point. We just can't help ourselves to the picture."

My sister's mouth tightened. "Hang on, and I'll drag the honoree back here by his fancy lapel if I have to."

"Way to go." Sometimes Judy's terrier qualities served a good purpose.

Mom couldn't take her eyes from Kayla. Neither could I. "This one's coming home with me," she said. "Daddy will love it too. And no arguments."

"You'll get none, Mom. The big portrait's still in Kayla's bedroom, leaning against the wall. After Jack's reaction, then Ian's..." I exhaled. "I seem to make things worse, not better."

Her hugs were just what I needed. "It'll be okay, sweetheart. Jack's a good man—even though I want to shake him hard right now. You and Jack...I think you're sort of slip-sliding around each other, not dancing to the same beat. You're each walking your own paths in your own time."

*Alone.* Her observation was painful to hear. It reinforced what I'd already figured out. Instead of sticking together, we'd gone our own ways. I'd shut Jack and Ian out in order to lessen my own pain. My own guilt. They may have abandoned me, but I was the one who'd been so critical and stubborn I'd forced them out, putting us all in a position of trying to survive alone.

"I-I think Jack and I—and Ian too—had better work it out together and quickly, or...or it won't matter anymore."

"Oh, sweetheart, I'm sure you're wrong."

"He's been at the hotel for eight weeks, Mom. With no indication of coming home."

"So join him there. Show him what he's missing."

I patted her arm. Sex games weren't the answer. "He wants me to be the woman I was before Kayla died. But that's impossible. Inside, I'm not the same."

On the other hand, some of the real me had to be around. I certainly wasn't still hiding in the house. I worked, painted, volunteered, jogged, cooked, loved. But it wasn't enough. I wanted my family back! Jack and Ian and little Tina. And Kayla, in our hearts. Her joyous spirit cheering us on.

I'd messed us all up, so I had to fix us. I had to take the lead in healing my family. In healing myself. In getting rid of the guilt and pain. I wanted to be whole again.

"More later, darling. Here comes your outrageous professor."

"Good grief. He's got an entourage with him."

"Clara, Clara, Clara. You have found me out. Discovered my secret, no?" The guy beamed like a little boy who'd discovered the last cookie in the jar. He turned to the group and thrust his arm toward *Girl with Secrets*.

"Magnificent, yes? And this is the artist, Signora Clara Barnes, from this very city. The best student of all. But then tragedy strikes, and Clara disappears. Not another class did she take. But this...this beautiful work I kept for her, hoping for her return."

An artist and a storyteller. "I think we should set the record straight, Professor. In real life, I'm a hands-on decorator. I furnish homes, design window treatments—"

"And is that not art, Clara? You select the color...just so, just right, and the proportions for each piece, and most important, the light! The sun. You must know where it rises and sets. Where is it each hour? All the elements must be considered because, Clara, every room is a canvas. Do you not see that? You have been an artist all your life, and now, you are branching out. *Brava, brava!*"

Yes, he had an audience, a cadre of followers, but I didn't care. I kissed him. And watched him blush. A unique happening. "*Grazie, Signor.* I needed to hear that."

"Well, your plot worked in the end, Professor," said Judy, stepping forward. "She wanted to attend your send-off tonight. But I'm telling you right now that the picture up there is going home with us. So, how much?"

I interrupted. "Thirty-eight hundred, wasn't it?"

He turned toward my mother. "Mama Mia! These two daughters of yours...? It's a miracle you survived!"

Mom's eyes glowed hot. The lioness had returned. "Didn't need a miracle, Professor. My girls are perfect just the way they are."

"But of course, of course. I would not say no."

Mom smiled. "In fact, you'd say yes. I'm glad you recognized Claire's talent, Professor, and the woman behind it. Thank you for saving the picture. You took a financial risk, and I'm happy to repay you. You did the right thing." She thrust her check into his hands.

His skin turned from olive to ruddy to red; he'd been embarrassed twice in one night. My mother could still shake things up.

"I'll be ready to try again soon." To spare him from further discomfort, I hesitated giving him a quick hug. But he had no compunction about his good-byes, and I found myself being kissed first on one cheek and then on the other.

"There's only one thing left to do," said my mother.

"And what's that, Signora?"

"Put a SOLD sign on it."

A perfect ending to the evening. *Girl with Secrets* would have a loving home, but it wouldn't be mine. I wanted to see Jack. More than want, I needed to see him. But I couldn't and wouldn't jolt him with any more surprises.

#

At midnight, I moved the soccer painting out of Kayla's bedroom and into the studio. I'd dropped Mom and Judy off at their homes, watched my dad tear up when he saw *Girl with Secrets*, and then made my way back to Bluebonnet Drive. Despite the emotional evening, I wasn't tired. My thoughts were spinning. If I wanted my family back, I had to come clean with them, but first, I had to come clean with myself. And that meant talking to Kayla—which was not a problem.

I'd kept her alive in my mind, heart, and on canvas. I'd kept my dreams alive of watching her grow up and share her life. But I knew now that my dreams for Kayla had come at a price. Not only the loss of Jack and Ian but the guilt that rode on my shoulders, the constant irritant that wouldn't let me heal. If I gave up my guilt, it would be easier to let Kayla go. And I couldn't do that.

But was I truly responsible for Kayla's death?

No.

I removed the drape from the canvas and looked again at my daughter exulting in victory. No false modesty if I said I'd done well. And I did say it, finally. I pulled over a chair and sat in front of my daughter.

"In my heart, in my thoughts, you are so full of life, Kayla, and yet you'll never grow up to be the woman you should have become. By now, we would have argued about texting. Or tweeting. But we would have been laughing, too. I miss you dreadfully. But I can't go on this way.

"It wasn't your fault that you ran into the street; it wasn't your brother's fault that he played ball with you; it wasn't the driver's fault that she happened to be there; and it wasn't even my fault. Not really. Had I arrived home five minutes sooner, you and Ian might have still thrown a ball while I went inside the house for a moment. Who knows? Ian was right about randomness. But oh, how I hate that it happened. So unfair to you.

"All I know, darling, is that I can't bring you back, and I can't ruin Dad's and Ian's lives anymore. The only direction for me to go is forward, Kayla. And I'm so very, very sorry."

And that's when I broke down. That's when the tears wouldn't stop flowing. And that's when I heard Jack's voice calling my name from outside. No hallucination. He stood in the doorway, focused on me.

"Your mother phoned and demanded I come over. Since I don't mess around with Barbara, here I am. What are you doing?"

I looked up at him, smiling through my tears, mascara probably all over my face. "I'm making peace with our daughter. I'm searching for hope."

He glanced at the painting, his love and longing as clearly written as a poem. I heard his deep exhalation before he met my eyes. "And?"

I stood and approached him. "And you're next on my list. Right here. Right now."

"Peace? Hope? You must have had quite an evening at the big shot's party." He sounded suspicious.

"You can judge for yourself." I took his hands and pulled him toward a chair. "Sit, please."

My heart beat like a bass drum. I wanted that new beginning with Jack, the one I'd gone after the night of the anniversary party. I was ready to open up to him. To talk! And I hoped Jack would listen and believe me. I refused to consider the alternative.

I plunged in. "Judy and Mom went with me to the champagne reception for Professor Colombo earlier tonight. That big shot you just mentioned." I described the scene, the people, the gallery exhibition, and my mom's excitement at being part of it.

"Do you remember me calling you in tears a couple of months after Kayla died with the news that Colombo sold my painting without permission?"

He nodded slowly. "I was willing to get our lawyer involved."

"Good, you do remember. Here's the point. Tonight, we were browsing the displays at the *galleria* when Mom decided to go off on her own." The memory of what happened next had me perspiring and made my legs feel weak. I pulled a chair over and sat down across from Jack.

"Suddenly, Judy and I heard her scream." I leaned toward Jack and grabbed his hand. "In the middle of this fancy gala reception, we heard my mother shouting, 'That's my granddaughter.' And her voice echoed throughout the entire place. Everybody heard. Everybody looked."

My fingers ached from gripping him so hard. "I ran to her, and when I got there, I understood everything. As if a wave of light passed through me, the secrets of the world. I saw what she saw, and I screamed too. Looking at Kayla, at *Girl with Secrets,* I wanted to howl. My world tilted and went awry. What was real and what wasn't?

"Jack, Jack...This is one of the things I need to tell you. I now understand how you felt that night of our anniversary party. I really get it. Back then, I was only thinking about myself and how the painting made me feel better. I'd assumed the same for you. I was wrong, Jack, and I'm so sorry. So very sorry."

Silence. I watched his Adam's apple move up and down a couple of times. My grip loosened, but I continued holding his hand. He coughed, a clearing-the-throat type of cough.

"Thank you for that."

"You're welcome." I took a deep breath. "But I'm not finished yet."

"It's enough for me. Validation is everything."

I stood, held up my hand. "Wait. There's more. Tonight I'm putting everything on the line. I know I'm taking a chance, but it's better than being in limbo. I don't want us to be the only couple in the support group whose husband and wife don't support each other."

Jack leaned forward in his chair, head cocked, eyelids slightly closed. "What do you want?" he asked softly.

"Everything. I want everything, but I can't have *anything* until I confess all my *mea culpas.*"

"Oh, please, Claire."

When he seemed about to stand up, I placed my hand on his shoulder and pressed. Like trying to move a boulder. "No, sit and listen for a minute, like you used to." I'm sure he complied out of courtesy rather than curiosity. It was good enough for me. I took a breath.

"I've been blaming everybody else for Kayla's death. Certainly Sarah Levine, and the cop who stopped me, then poor Ian. But all the time, I really believed the accident was my fault. You didn't think it made sense to blame myself when I wasn't even on the scene, but you didn't know everything that happened beforehand."

I started to pace then stopped myself. Jack deserved to see me straight on, eye-to-eye. Nothing to hide.

"With Colombo on that day in class...I felt like a teenager. He loved my work—his compliments overflowed—and I thought maybe it was more. The other students gathered round also; their awe of my work kind of surprised me. But Colombo held my attention, and I stayed late, not because I was actually painting, but because we were having a-a repartee. A flirtation. And I was flattered at his interest. I ate it up like I was a starving child.

"But I saw the truth last night when he bragged about me to a roomful of art patrons and art lovers. I understood that, in class, he'd been talking only about the feelings between the artist and her art. He'd fallen in love all right, but only with my blossoming talent, with what he saw on my canvas.

"But the big question is, how could I have gotten so carried away when I love you so much?"

I collapsed into the chair again, but before he could speak, I gripped both his hands. "I believed Kayla died because...because I was basking in his compliments. And I wa-wanted to know him better. That's the reason I was l-late. In the end, I believed she died because of me-e-e.... That I destroyed everything I treasured. You and Ian. Us. Our family."

I'd used up my last drop of courage and was sobbing now. To my surprise, tears streamed down Jack's face too.

"But you don't blame yourself anymore?"

I shook my head. "I have to let it go. If I don't, there's no hope for a future." I stared at the man I'd loved for more than twenty-five years, tried to get myself under control. "Do you want a future...with me? Can you forgive me?"

"For what? A marriage involves two people, Claire. I pace the floor at night wondering where I went wrong with you. Maybe I buried myself at the office too much. Maybe I should have taken your art more seriously. Maybe I wasn't strong enough for you to lean on. If I'd been a better listener, maybe you wouldn't have been compelled to paint that exquisite portrait in the first place. So I'm not guilt-free either. *Mea culpa.*"

If he was trying to make me feel better, I wasn't having it. "You were the sane one. I was the crazy one. I closed myself off from you and Ian. But you? You've been there for me and for our son. For God's sake, you even conspired for an intervention. How many people do that?"

"Hmm. I guess the desperate ones do. And I was desperate to have you back with me before it became too late. I wanted the real Claire."

My breath hitched. "Do you still feel that way?"

He stood, opened his arms, and I stepped inside. "You've always been the one for me. In sickness and health. And everything in between. A new beginning will be our salvation, Claire. Yours, mine, Ian's...everyone's."

Wrapping myself around him, I said, "So, come home, Jack. Please come home."

His arms tightened around me. I felt his kiss on my cheek. "Aren't we there right now?"

Yes. Yes, we were. *ClaireAndJack. JackAndClaire.* As long as we flourished, anywhere was home.

I'd married a very smart man.

# CHAPTER THIRTY NINE

*IAN*

*January*

Thankfully, the holidays were over. In my opinion, Tina's first Christmas was just too much. Too much fuss, too much running from one house to the other. Grandma Barbara's on Christmas Eve, Grandma Pearl's the next day. The baby and I actually slept at Grandma Barbara's. Funny that Mom didn't host, but it was good to know my grands hadn't slowed down. As for the presents...well, just too darn many. I wondered if the doting grandparents believed I couldn't provide enough for Tina.

I was happy to return to normal routines. Yesterday, Ben Parker called me into his office. After a year and a half with the company, I'd gotten a raise and continued to do my work well—at least, I thought so—and couldn't imagine what Mr. Parker wanted. He'd had a gleam in his eye as soon as he saw me, and I didn't have to wait long to find out why.

"Full tuition paid by the company," my boss said. "Just like a scholarship. Now you'll be a real college boy. Take as many courses as you want each term at night or even Saturdays. Can't beat that, can ya? Told you I'd pull out all stops."

The man looked as proud as a new dad, eager for his "boy" to jump up and down with excitement. And all I felt was overwhelmed and exhausted. How could I work full-time days, attend school at night, and be a good daddy to Tina? But I tried not to let my doubts show. One thing I'd learned from my own dad was never to burn any bridges.

"Wow, Mr. Parker. Thanks. Thanks a lot for recommending me. It's a great opportunity...and it's a lot to think about right now."

"Figure it out, Ian. And don't take too long. You're a young man. You've got the energy. Think about your future and where you want to be in five years."

This time I couldn't hide the grin. "Five years? I'm lucky if I can see ahead five minutes at a time."

He waved away my lame joke. "Hire a babysitter. It'll be worth the investment. Later on, you'll be able to support that daughter of yours without a worry in the world. The industry offers real opportunities for a smart guy like you. With the right education, the sky's the limit. You're a science guy, aren't you? Geology, earth sciences, chemistry.... Heck, boy, I never had those kinds of chances. Grab it while you can."

Parker's sincerity rang true. The schooling sounded good. Tempting. But I wasn't ready to sign any paperwork for the Human Resources Department or apply to the university yet. I needed time to think. Being responsible for Tina had me thinking two and three times about every decision I made. Truth was, I didn't dream about my own future too often. I was buried in schedules and chores and trying to get through one day at a time. Which seemed like a reasonable goal to me.

When I left Mr. Parker's office, however, his enthusiasm grabbed hold. I found myself hoping that my tomorrows held more than changing diapers and sleeping whenever I could.

I wished Ben Parker didn't remind me so much of my dad.

#

"Hey, Barnes. We're going out for drinks and some fun. Wanna come?"

In the locker room the next day, I looked up at the new guy offering the invite.

"Sorry, Pete. Can't make it tonight. Maybe another time."

"Ian can't make it any night," chimed in one of my teammates. "Now that Colleen's gone, he's on the mommy track."

I couldn't take too much offense. What he said was true. I hadn't gone out with the guys after work since Tina's arrival, but still, the words stung.

"I'd call it the daddy track. Next time give me some advance warning, and I'll arrange extra daycare. But last-minute is out."

Leaving the plant, I thought about how I'd never connected with Danny in person during the holidays after all. He may have been on vacation, but I wasn't. A telephone call was all we'd managed. The daddy track had won out again. But Tina was my responsibility, and I couldn't take a risk of something terrible happening to her like with Kayla.

I drove directly to Tina's daycare center. Despite my mother's concerns, I thought the place was terrific. Finding it had been a major victory, one that I'd managed without anyone's help. Most importantly, my daughter seemed happy there. The moment she spotted me today, her arms started waving, and her verbalizing got louder.

"Hey, little girl," I said, scooping her up. My heart pumped bucketfuls of love every time she cuddled in that sweet spot under my neck. "Ready to go home?"

Legally, she was now one hundred percent mine, and having sole custody scared me, so I pushed those thoughts aside. Dad's lawyers prepared the paperwork. Dad said he and Mom had walked on eggshells until they saw the final documents. They simply couldn't imagine a young woman giving up custodial rights to her child. Well, they'd never known Colleen, never heard her sing or heard about her plans. If Mom ever looked in the mirror, she might see some of Colleen there. Babies might be more helpless and cuter, but I was still a kid in high school when she gave me up.

Once at home, I tossed the mail on the counter except for the small, flat package postmarked Nashville, TN. I put that one aside. Anytime Colleen got in touch, whether with a rare phone call or a letter, I needed quiet time to give her my full attention. As Dad had explained to me over our occasional dinners, Colleen and I would always be connected to each other because of Tina, regardless of legalities. A happy, successful, and independent Colleen could only be good for all of us, including her.

Tina came first. Before my supper, before Colleen's package, before cleaning the kitchen. All the books on divorce said the child needed stability and routines. I could provide that better than Colleen. Even Ted Willis didn't dispute that fact when he found out about the arrangement. "It's best for little Tina," he'd said while giving the baby a kiss on the forehead.

Between facing Kayla's death and Tina's birth, there was no going back to being a boy again. My childhood was long over; my teenage years were over too.

Sometimes I thought I'd skipped them altogether and that I'd never been a happy-go-lucky kid. I'd graduated to adulthood as soon as I became Tina's daddy.

After I got Tina down, hopefully for the night, I took Colleen's slim package into the living room. When I slit the cardboard, a jewel case with a CD fell onto the couch. The enclosed note said:

*Dear Ian,*

*The final version of the song on this CD will be released next Tuesday as a single. (Every new song in the music industry is released on a Tuesday). If anyone finds out I've sent this, I could get into trouble. I thought you deserved a heads-up because the song's about us. I hope you like it and aren't embarrassed. It will be part of my first album, which I think will come out next Christmas. Woo-hoo! Can you tell I'm excited?*

*Colleen*

*P.S. I've got my own computer now. Here's my email address.*

*Please write and tell me what you think of "Late October."*

Embarrassed? That's the word I was stuck on. What the hell had she written? I liked my privacy, but if she'd used my name in the song, I'd be hearing from everyone I ever knew. Dang, dang, dang. I looked at the jewel case as if it were Pandora's Box. Yup. That's what it was, but I had no choice except to open it. Tuesday would come, and I'd need to be prepared. Heck, my whole family listened to country music as well as rock and everything in between. I'd have to prepare them too.

I slipped the disk into the player and held my breath. First, Colleen announced: The following song, "Late October," was written and is being performed by Colleen Murphy.

LATE OCTOBER

FAMILY INTERRUPTED

*Chorus:*

My Texas knight in city armor
Gave me a home when I had no other
Saved the life of our unborn daughter,
I waved goodbye in late October...
I just couldn't stay—
Had to be on my way,
But for them I'll pray...forever.

*Verse A:*

My true-blue Texas knight
Knew what was wrong and what was right,
Came with a heart in need of mending
From a loss not of his making—
An innocent,
Taking consequence,
A true-blue Texas knight.

*Verse B:*

When the daddy saw his girl,
The love he kept inside unfurled,
And the heart in need of mending,
Had found a new beginning,
Time to say so long,
Time to write my songs,
Of a true-blue Texas knight.

*Chorus:*

My Texas knight in city armor
Gave me a home when I had no other

Saved the life of our unborn daughter,
I waved goodbye in late October...
I just couldn't stay—
Had to be on my way,
But for them I'll pray...forever.

Long after she'd released the ballad's final note, I remained sitting quietly, lost in a state of wonder. I hadn't given her enough credit. Whether it was the song itself or the way she sang it that moved me so much, I couldn't tell. It might have been the memories she'd rekindled. Colleen had always said that a good song must be based on truth. In my opinion, she'd nailed it with this one. "Late October" was a piece of honest storytelling. Without regrets, resentment, or hate. Just the truth.

Colleen understood what my dad had explained and what I didn't totally get until now. I would never forget her, but she would never forget me either. Like Kayla, Colleen would always be a part of me.

#

Colleen was not on my mind the next morning when I brought Tina to daycare and found parents milling around in the dark, some on their cell phones, and the teachers apologizing for the electric system malfunction. Without electricity, they couldn't open for business and didn't know how long it would take to fix. Half the parents worked at the plant. The ones on their phones had backup plans; the others viewed the situation as an unexpected day off.

Once again, I hated asking for favors, but I pulled out my cell and auto-dialed my folks. No vacation day for me. After the tuition offer from Ben Parker yesterday, showing up late was bad enough, but I couldn't be absent because of stupid child care issues. Besides, my projects at work couldn't wait. Mr. Parker counted on me.

# CHAPTER FORTY

*CLAIRE*

"Are you thinking what I'm thinking?" asked Jack.

I yawned, peeped at my husband from under half-closed lids, glad not to be the one driving to Ian's this morning.

"If you're thinking we both need extra bold roast caffeinated coffee, then yeah, I'm thinking what you're thinking," I replied with another yawn.

Ever since Jack had checked out of the hotel and come home, we'd been making up for lost time, communicating in every way possible too far into the night for super-early mornings to be welcomed. Jack said we had triumphed over our trial by fire and called it a rebirth of our marriage. We would live with an ache in our hearts for the rest of our lives but were basically a very recognizable Claire and Jack Barnes.

We were not, however, a recognizable Barnes family. The trial by fire would continue for me as long as my son's resentment burned. And burn it did. He still thought I blamed him for Kayla's death, regardless of our recent conversations about new beginnings. I'd rejected him, and now he didn't trust me. He thought I'd say anything, even lie, in order to be near Tina. I worried that his feelings were so bruised and sore he didn't want to figure out a way back.

My one comfort: he trusted me with his precious daughter.

"Strong coffee is only part one and easily accomplished," Jack continued, pulling alongside the McDonald's drive-up window. "Part two is bigger than that. Driving fifty miles or more whenever Ian needs a babysitter is ludicrous. Look at this traffic, and the day's barely begun."

"That's nothing new." Was traffic not my "lame" excuse, according to Ian, for being late the day Kayla was killed?

"We've got to talk him into coming home," said Jack, "where he'd get all the support he needs, but we can't guilt him into it. We can't use Tina as the excuse. So I've been thinking—thinking hard—and I have an idea."

He always had ideas. I stroked his cheek, feeling his pain. My Cracker Jack longed for his son. Longed for the old rapport between him and Ian. Longed for Barnes Construction to sport another generation. Who could have foreseen he'd ever be jealous of a belching oil refinery?

"How would you feel," said Jack, "about putting the house on the market and building elsewhere?"

I needed a moment. It wasn't the first time I'd considered the idea and knew it wasn't a gotcha remark on Jack's part. I allowed the words to wash over me and sink in. Jack barely blinked as he waited for my reply.

"Leave Bluebonnet Drive?" I murmured. "Leave twenty years of our history there?" A kaleidoscope of family memories filled my mind. I heard the faint echo of Kayla's footsteps in the halls. Clearing my throat once wasn't enough. Finally, I could speak.

"Like you always say, Kayla goes everywhere with us—right here." I tapped my chest. "I-I think she'd approve, if the rest of us could be a family again."

Jack reached for my hand. "That's exactly the point. I'm pretty sure the house is an obstacle to Ian. He once told me that he relives the accident every time he pulls onto the street. A new place might tempt him to move back with us, and the promise of a full fridge might seal the deal. If he's concerned about privacy, we could plan a separate suite for him and the baby. What do you think?"

I didn't have to think. "I want my son at any price. And besides, I bet you've already started a design."

"I'm not taking your bet," he replied with a laugh. "I love you, Claire. Thank you." His kiss occupied us until the server coughed discreetly and thrust the coffee our way.

Jack paid, and we drove off in silence, each of us now lost in our own thoughts. Mine included the location of a new place.

"Jack?" I began almost hesitantly. "Have you considered the huge commute Ian would have if we stayed in this part of town?" Near Barnes Construction is what I meant. If Jack thought he could use those long miles to get Ian back in the family business, Ian would resent it.

"Let's take one step at a time. At this point, he's against living with us, and we don't know if he'd consider coming home under any circumstances."

His advice was perfect. One step at a time. Nowhere in our conversation, however, had Jack and I discussed the one obstacle Ian could not overlook: his mother. Knowing how he felt about me, I couldn't picture him falling in with our great plans...and yet...and yet...I was excited by the tiny spark of hope Jack had kindled. I loved the whole idea, didn't care about the location. Surely, the two of us as a team could make this happen.

#

"You're babysitting too, Dad?" Ian asked while handing Tina over to me. My granddaughter grinned and chortled, and I fell more deeply in love with her, as I did with every visit. Five months was a perfect baby age, or maybe being a grandma fit me like a comfortable sweater.

"Not only babysitting but I've got some business not too far away," Jack said. "Some parcels I'm looking at."

Ian's eyes widened, but he didn't say much except good luck and thanks for coming especially because of his conversation with Mr. Parker yesterday. Then he rushed out the door.

"What conversation?" asked Jack.

I shrugged.

"Probably wants to make him president of the damn place. An offer he can't refuse."

"He's not even twenty-one, Jack. I think you can relax. And by the way, what parcels of land are you talking about?"

He chuckled. "I have no idea yet. I'm just planting seeds of possibility—backed up by research. I brought my laptop."

"Good. Let Tina help you type while I investigate other parcels—the ones in the fridge and freezer." And scrub down the kitchen and gather up a laundry. There always seemed to be a wash that needed doing.

It took me less than ten minutes to complete my chores and plan a grocery run. In the living room, I saw Jack lying on the floor with Tina climbing up, down, and over his chest, both of them having a grand old time. The laptop sat unopened next to them.

"I'll just mash up a banana..." I began when I felt the ground rumble and grabbed onto the doorposts. Jack wrapped the baby in his arms and rolled sideways, covering her with his body.

"What the hell?"

*BOOM. BOOM.*

Thunder in the apartment?

"Look, Claire! Look out the window."

Plumes of smoke filled the sky. Flames shot upward. And dread settled in the pit of my stomach.

"Call Ian! Call him right now." I took the baby and held my breath while Jack searched his pocket. His hand shook when he removed his mobile and connected with Ian's. Weirdly, I heard a constant ringing in the apartment and followed the sound to the dresser in the bedroom.

"Oh, my God. He forgot his phone. What with being late and leaving in a rush, and now it's here and ringing and he can't reach us either, and what are we going to do?" I paced up and down then in circles. The baby began to cry. I cuddled her. "Shush, sweetheart. You're fine. You're fine."

Comfort words came automatically until I heard the sirens wailing, and those wonderful possibilities for new beginnings Jack had spoken of earlier faded away, faded away like Kayla had faded. Darkness threatened. Blindly, I reached out a hand. "Jack?"

And he was there, one arm strong around my waist, the other now holding Tina.

"Breathe, Claire. In. Out. In. Out. Sit on the bed, head down."

I followed orders. My vision cleared. "Thank you. Now, let's go."

"We can't get near the refinery," Jack said, practical as ever. "I'm turning the TV on."

The news was just breaking on all local channels. No details available yet except for area residents to remain indoors until further notice in case toxic chemicals had been released into the air.

"So, we wait," said Jack. "We're not taking any chances with Tina's lungs—or our own."

He glanced at his watch, paced the floor, a restrained racehorse, chomping at the bit, wanting to run, run to his boy. Thirty long minutes later, we were free to go.

"We'll head to the closest hospital. If anything happened, that's where they'd take the injured."

I'd already packed a bag with baby supplies— diapers, jarred food, bottles of milk and apple juice. Who knew when or where I'd be able to refill? We left the apartment and headed to the car. Other people were already gathering in the street.

"Not good, not good," mumbled a man who'd seen younger days. "A surprise with all the safety measures."

"What do you know?" Jack asked.

"Probably the same as whenever this happens," was the reply. "Usually during a start-up, after a unit's been down for maintenance. That's when they need to take extra care."

"Do you know which unit?" I asked, trying to remember the strange name Ian used—something starting with an *I*.

"Ian's was down last month," Jack said. "It's not his. It *can't* be his."

The old man looked weary. "Good luck then. Sorry not to know more. We're all waiting for information. But sometimes it don't much matter. Depends on how bad. How many workers on site."

Half sentences, sighs, head shakes. The old timer had seen it all.

"My boy's in there," said Jack sharply. "Where's the hospital they'd take him to if he were hurt?"

While Jack conversed, I tucked the baby into her car seat, even managed to lock the belts correctly. And I chatted to her nonstop. Tina liked my nonsense, but frankly, talking kept me sane—by a thread.

"Good job, honey," said Jack, as he started the car.

"Yeah." But I'd run out of both baby and grown-up talk. My thoughts traveled back to other trips. To a hospital. Similar trips filled with similar dread.

Jack glanced over at me. "You're too pale again, Claire. Don't go there. Not there! Don't get lost. Talk to me, damnit! Stay focused right here and now."

He knew me well, but I knew him too. He'd flashed back to Kayla just as I had. "Are you a mind reader or something?" I tried to joke while taking deep breaths.

"Or something. Only with you."

"We've gone down this path before," I whispered. "Turn on the radio. Maybe we'll get some new information."

"There's only one thing I want you to get. So listen up."

I looked at him.

"We're not shutting each other out no matter what happens. No separate worlds, Claire. We're in this together. We communicate. Otherwise, what's the point?"

He was right. Of course, he was right. "I love you, Jack."

"That's my girl." He reached for my hand, brought it to his mouth, and kissed every finger. "I love you right back, my Claire-de-Lune."

I loved Ian too. My son. My first born. The boy who could make me laugh. The boy who made me proud. The boy Kayla had adored and trailed after whenever he allowed her. A wonderful big brother, Ian was now trying hard to be a great dad. Maybe he'd gotten some training time in with his sister—a practice round.

Too much thinking. Not enough doing. We weren't the only ones driving to the ER, and our slow progress had me wringing my hands. The police had begun to set up barriers and direct traffic, leaving lanes open for ambulances and other emergency vehicles. My legs started to jiggle, my stomach rock-and-rolled as I felt my stress mounting. *Ian. Ian. Ian.* Two kids lost just wouldn't be fair. Not fair at all. Please, please, please...no fatal injuries. Mercy, mercy for my son. Strength for us all. I sent up a prayer for every worker in the plant.

"We're almost there, sweetheart."

"You're in charge of the baby," I said. "I'm going after our son."

# CHAPTER FORTY ONE



Someone was yelling, high and loud, and I wished she'd stop. My head pounded. I couldn't see beyond the curtain and didn't want to. Just wanted to sleep and sleep. I closed my eyes, started drifting, and heard that voice again. This time, it sounded familiar.

"Where is my son? Ian Barnes? They said he was here. Now where is my son?"

Geez, Mom could wake the dead. If she didn't quiet down, she'd be thrown out. Maybe I should answer her. Maybe Dad was here too. And the baby. I moved my lips.

"Mama?" Barely a whisper before I zoned out, dreaming crazy dreams about falling metal. Fire. Smoke. Then came a movie, a happy one where Kayla and I kicked a soccer ball in the backyard. No holds barred, we got a good workout; both of us dripped with sweat. A good time, a very good time. I felt myself smile.... I wanted to smile, but I needed to sleep.

When I opened my eyes again, I saw Mom right away. Sitting close, talking to me.

"He's up! He's up. Thank God, he's up."

Her smile was Jack-o-lantern wide. And her eyes were awfully shiny. "Are you laughing or crying?" My throat hurt, and I rubbed it.

"Both." She turned toward Dad. "Did you hear that? His brain works."

"Best brain in the family," Dad said.

But there was only one thing on my feeble brain at the moment, headache or no headache. One thing that had been haunting me for the past two years. And if I were dying now, I had to get it off my chest. Again.

"I didn't kill Kayla. It wasn't my fault."

Mom's eyes got bigger than hubcaps. Her mouth quivered, and she took my hand. "Of course you didn't. It was an accident. It really, truly was an accident," she said. "Ian, Ian. I'm so sorry about what I said in the ambulance. I love you so much. Please, sweetheart, believe me." She leaned over and kissed me gently on both cheeks.

"You do?" Ouch, my throat.

She looked like I'd punched her in the stomach. I thought she'd faint again. "Oh, my God, of course I love you. And I'll love you forever and ever. Until...infinity!" She started to cry, and I had to blink away my own tears.

"Mom?"

"What, sweetheart?"

"I love you, too."

Her smile was kind of shaky now, but it was real. Very real.

A nurse walked in just then, a nurse with energy and sharp eyes. I whispered, "If my brain is working, how come my head hurts and my throat?"

In an instant, everyone got quiet, and the questions started via the nurse, who held out water in a plastic cup with a straw. I drank.

"Do you know where you are?"

Duh. Where else but a hospital were there so many white jackets?

"Do you remember what happened before you arrived here?"

A trick question. I had to think hard. Very hard. And then I had it, the horror show. "The building shook. Vibrations like a thousand locomotives. An explosion. Everything blowing up." I'd gotten to work late, so I was still checking in, wasn't in the worst part. I turned on the hard bed, searching for my father.

"Dad! Dad! Where's Ben Parker? You gotta find him. He was in the unit with the full shift. A fire. I saw the flames roaring up and up. A prototype...for hell."

I could envision it again, and I was afraid. Chunks of metal blasted from their moorings, flying everywhere, even where I was checking in. And I'd stood there, a frozen target in death's path, except for the words that had come quickly in that moment of moments. Words that mattered although no one could hear them but me: *Mama, I forgive you....*

"Mama, I forgive you. I forgive you. And you have to forgive Sarah. She didn't mean it. She's a nice lady. She took care of Kayla...." My eyes closed, but the sound of my mom's sobbing kept me from dozing off again. The touch of her hand holding mine comforted me, and I finally relaxed.

"How did you get so smart, son?" Dad whispered.

"Gen-e-tics?" I offered before falling asleep.

#

*JACK*

I handed the baby to Claire. "Ian won't rest easy until he knows what happened to his boss. God forbid it's bad news. I'm going to find out."

The emergency room was overrun with the injured, their families, friends, and co-workers. Groans, tears, and screams of pain made me wince. Triage areas had been organized; every medic was busy. How in the world was I supposed to find Ben Parker, a guy I'd never laid eyes on?

In the end, it was no problem. He found me.

A big man with soot and blisters on his face, he looked as if he'd seen better days. He was calling names from a clipboard and making notes. I watched and listened, soon realizing he was going down the roster of the Isomerization Unit. Ian's unit.

"Barnes. Ian Barnes. Where the hell's my college boy?"

*His* college boy?

I walked over, extended my hand, then noticed his was blistered.

"Another time, then. I'm Jack Barnes, Ian's dad. He'll be fine. A mild concussion, but they're watching him."

His eyes bulged. "Ian's dad? Well, waddyaknow? I thought with Colleen gone the kid was alone in the world—except for the baby." He scribbled a note on the clipboard.

Pain sliced through me, a pain which had little to do with Ben Parker and everything to do with Ian, Claire, and me. Our son had truly written us off. He felt close to Parker, talked about him with us, yet hadn't mentioned us to him. Ian had become an expert on keeping secrets recently. But...that was before this accident, before he and his mother talked. Hope bloomed again. We'd tell him about the plans for a new house, and we'd all reconnect.

We'd become strong. As Claire would say, I was ever the cockeyed optimist.

"Those hands of yours can get infected," I said, a voice of experience. "Better get some antibiotic ointment on them. Want some help with that?" I nodded at the clipboard.

"To hell with my hands. I need to find my crew. That's all that counts. If you never ran a department, you wouldn't know what that responsibility feels like. Tell your boy I'll catch up with him." He called two more names and walked away.

Ran a department? How about a company? I shoved my feelings aside. The man was worried, totally engrossed in doing what he had to do and wanted to do. This was no time for games. I returned to Ian's cubicle, where he was surrounded by nurses.

"Easy does it." They helped him sit up and monitored his vital signs every five minutes. I liked that. Claire and I had more experience with head injuries than a couple should have, and we weren't going to complain about any exam, test, or treatment Ian needed.

"Your Mr. Parker doesn't look pretty, Ian, but he's running around out there keeping track of everyone. He'll be fine."

My kid grinned. Just the reaction I'd wanted.

"Hey, Dad?"

"Yo."

"In case I die too, then you and Mom need to adopt Tina."

I heard Claire gasp, but my attention stayed focused on Ian, who'd evidently dismissed his concerns about Mr. Parker and was now thinking about his sister.

"What put that stupid idea into your head? You're not going to die. Heck, Ian, football players suffer worse injuries than you've got."

And damn if his eyes didn't light up. I took Tina from Claire and held her close enough to receive kisses from her daddy. "Your daughter needs you, Ian, so your job—your only job—is to get better."

"She doesn't have a mom, so I guess she needs me a lot."

A fine time to bring up this sensitive topic. We'd never really discussed his deep relationship with Colleen Murphy and how heartbroken he'd truly been. I knew little about her other than her commitment to her career. So far, the only fact about Colleen that mattered to me was that she'd given Ian custody of the baby. His daughter. Our granddaughter. Colleen got high marks for that in my book. But we all knew Tina would have questions later on.

"Maybe one day, Martina Faith will have a full-time mom," Claire said. "But let's put first things first. Don't you think it's time we were a family again?"

"Hey, y'all. How's my college boy?"

Ian grinned. "Mr. Parker! My dad said you're okay?"

"Sure, I'm okay. He also said I should take care of my blisters."

Ian's eyes darted toward Parker's hands, then his face again. "My dad knows his stuff. I think he's right."

"Hmm."

Parker was making small talk, buying time with Ian, studying his employee, assessing him with his own yardstick.

"It wasn't our fault, was it, Mr. Parker? I mean, we shut down when Colleen left, and we started back up just fine.... I-I did everything right, didn't I?"

For how many years, I wondered, would Ian view life's events in terms of fault? His fault? Someone else's fault? I remained quiet. This conversation was between Ian and his boss.

"College boy," said Parker, his voice gruff, "your work was great. You'd done everything right. The accident didn't start in our unit, but two of my men were critically injured. Wrong place, wrong time. You know how that goes." His eyes scanned the room, not resting. Anxious.

"It's been twenty years between incidents," Parker continued. "Safety measures have improved a thousand percent since the old days. You can almost forget the past...and then, boom! Something happens, and you remember."

He sighed a big sigh. "Check out of this hotel as soon as you can, Ian, and don't come back to work until you're called."

"Uh, Mr. Parker?"

"Yup?"

"I've been thinking about our last conversation, thinking about it a lot, and I have to turn down that offer of tuition."

My son had commanded everyone's attention.

"Sure about that?" Parker asked.

"I can't accept a gift under false pretenses. And that's what it would be. The baby needs her grandparents. And I-I miss my family, Mr. Parker. We got off track for awhile, but it's okay now. We're going to try again."

Parker turned to me. "I've worked with your boy for two years and know him better than he thinks. I have no sons, Mr. Barnes. But the truth is that if I could pick one, it would be yours. You folks did a great job raising him, but don't discount luck. Sometimes, kids don't turn out right. No matter what."

I wasn't sure if he spoke from personal experience or from years of living and observing those around him, but I did understand why Ian liked him. He cared about people, and my son lapped up the attention. As for the luck part? Well, the man didn't know about Kayla and how unlucky the Barnes family had been. He didn't need to know. I'd gotten what I'd wanted.

"I won't shake your hand," I said, "but I will say thanks. I'm glad Ian had you when he needed a...a mentor in his life."

The man nodded then looked at Ian. "The door will always be open to you, college boy. But I hope I don't see you again until you have that diploma. Take care of yourself, ya hear?"

"I hear. You too."

We watched him leave, a man who wouldn't rest until his entire roster was accounted for and double-checked. "I liked him, Ian."

"Yeah. I knew right from the beginning that I was in a good place. Want to know why?"

"Sure."

"Mr. Parker reminded me of you."

With that confession, he closed his eyes, lay back, and fell asleep again.

"We've got quite a son," said Claire. "On the outside, you and Parker don't resemble each other at all, but on the inside? A different story. And that's what attracted Ian. He saw two honorable men."

I took out my mobile. "First we phone the grands. And then...?" The question in my voice caught her attention. "It might be hard for you, Claire, but we have another important call that must come from both of us."

Her brow contracted for a moment then relaxed. Her eyes showed an understanding, a new maturity in a woman who'd barely lived through her worst nightmare. "I know," she said. "The Levines. Sarah and Marc. They're still suffering, and we can relieve some of that...I think."

I had no words for this wonderful woman, so I kissed her as though I'd never let go—which wasn't easy with Tina in between. "Thank you."

Hopefully, a good start, but I kissed her again before dialing Levine's number. "Marc? Jack Barnes here. Got a minute?....Good. Good. Claire and I didn't want to wait any longer to call. To let you know that life is getting better. A whole lot better....Yes, I'm sure....That's right, it's the truth. And Claire is hoping she can speak with Sarah."

I gave her the phone.

#

*CLAIRE*

A minute later, I heard Sarah's quiet hello. Soft, yes, but with a note of hope. I pictured her as I'd last seen her, distraught, scared, running from Judy's office filled with self-blame, self-hate. The poor girl. I spoke softly, too, and slowly, trying not to scare her.

"Hi, Sarah. It's Claire Barnes, but please don't be alarmed. I have good news...Yes, really. First of all, my sister and I are friends again. Bet you thought that would never happen. But it did....That's right. I promise it's for real. And there's more good news. My son is coming home. It took awhile, but the Barnes family is back together. So now you know that the world you thought you'd destroyed is being repaired piece by piece."

She mumbled something about being happy for me.

I tried again. "There's one more thing I want to say...about the accident...about Kayla...? So please listen—it's important for both our sakes.

"You need to know that I forgive you, Sarah. And that Jack forgives you, too. So now you must forgive yourself and become strong again. Your children need a strong mother. Your husband needs a strong wife."

Silence on the other end. I had to try harder.

"Kayla's death was an accident, a true accident. It was bad luck and nobody's fault—not yours, not Ian's, not mine. Love wins, Sarah. It's stronger than hate. It's stronger than revenge. I finally understand that now myself. And you must, too."

As I listened to my own words, a weight lifted from my heart and disappeared. I had set myself free.

The end

Dear Reader:

Thank you for choosing to read *Family Interrupted*. I hope it kept you turning the pages. If you enjoyed the story, please help others find it so they can share the reading experience and perhaps discover a new author.

You have choices! One or more of the following--it's all up to you:

- Post a review on Amazon, Barnes and Noble, GoodReads or any of your favorite book sites.
- Check out my website www.linda-barrett.com for upcoming books and current happenings in my writing world.
- Join me on Facebook at: www.facebook.com/linda.barrett.353
- Tell your friends! The best book recommendations are from friends because we trust them.

I truly appreciate your help in getting the word out about *Family Interrupted* and my other novels.

Whether you most enjoy romance, family drama or are curious about my memoir of surviving two bouts of breast cancer, you can find all titles on my website. They are available both as ebooks and in print.

Many thanks and happy reading!


Linda Barrett

FAMILY INTERRUPTED
QUESTIONS AND TOPICS FOR
DISCUSSION

1. Do many contemporary women "seize their moment" like Claire and Colleen did in order to follow a dream?

2. Do you think the extent of Claire's flirtation with her professor is more real than imagined or more imagined than real? Does it matter?

3. If the Barneses are a loving family, why do Jack, Claire and Ian go on separate emotional journeys after the accident?

4. Claire's family treats her to some tough love after a year of grieving. If everyone grieves at his or her own pace, is a year long enough?

5. If Ian had gone to college, he would have been away from the house anyway. Why do you think he moves out and takes a job instead of attending school?

6. Do you think it odd that Jack can feel sorry for Marc Levine?

7. How does Ian show his maturity? In what ways is he still a teenager? How does he wind up at the end?

8. Claire's journey is filled with the blame game, including blaming herself. Why is it so hard to accept that bad things happen to good people through no fault of their own? Why do we search for logical explanations?

9. We can follow Sarah Levine's emotional journey through various scenes in the book. Is her reaction to the accident very different from Claire's?

10. In drawing Kayla again and again, do Claire's skills as an artist serve her well or not?

11. Claire is not a saint but some might say she acted like one in the end. Why? Can you imagine forgiving someone who's fatally hurt your child?

12. What do you think happens next? Where does the Barnes family live? Does Ian go back to school? What does the future hold for him and Colleen, if anything?

# MEET LINDA

Linda grew up in Queens, NY and earned her B.A. and M.S. at Hunter College. She's also lived in Massachusetts, Texas and currently resides with her husband in the greater Tampa, FL area. "Enjoying different areas of our country has been a wonderful experience, and I've made life-long friends everywhere."

Linda's written fifteen contemporary romances, three books of general fiction focusing on families in crisis, and a memoir about surviving breast cancer twice.  She's won industry awards such as the Holt Medallion, the Award of Excellence, and the Write Touch Reader's Award through Romance Writers of America.  To learn more, please visit her website: www.linda-barrett.com

# READ AN EXCERPT FROM
# THE BROKEN CIRCLE

## Chapter 1

*January 2009*
*Boston*

A knock at her grad school apartment door pulled Lisa Delaney away from Commonwealth of Massachusetts vs. Torcelli Construction. Eyes burning, she rubbed her lids while, from her iPod, she heard Bryan Adams insist that everything he did, he did for her. Old song. Easy words. If the man really wanted to impress, he could take her contracts exam in the morning.

She pushed away from her desk, covered in law books and case briefs, and rose from her chair, stretching, bending and groaning. Her knees creaked like an arthritic old lady's. Shaking her head, she emitted a long sigh and promised herself a gym visit the next day—after the exam.

A second knock echoed, this time more impatiently.

"I'm coming. Hang on." Nimble again, she rushed across the room and opened the door.

Her eyes widened, her stomach began to roil as she looked at two uniformed state troopers, snow melting on their jackets, cop faces in place. Her thoughts raced with possibilities. Classmates? Mike? Oh, please, not Mike.

"Are you Lisa Delaney?"

She stared at bad news and froze. All of her. Nothing worked. Not her mind, tongue, or breath. Perhaps her heart had stopped, too. One man coughed. The other repeated the question.

"I-I'm Lisa."

"Are your parents' names Robert and Grace Delaney?"

Oh, God, yes! Her heart raced at Mach speed, but she couldn't feel her legs at all. "What happened?"

"May we come in, Ms. Delaney?" Taller cop.

She nodded and pulled the door wider, but the knob slipped through her sweaty hands and she lost her balance.

"You might want to sit down."

As though moving underwater, she struggled into the closest chair.

"I'm afraid there's been an accident on the turnpike," began the quiet-till-now officer. "A fatal accident."

"Not…not my…my parents?" She barely got the words out before the officers' sympathetic silence answered her question.

"But that's impossible! I just spoke to my dad…"

"When was that, ma'am?"

When? When? "I think…maybe…last…last night…." Her voice drifted. Daddy had been checking up on his eldest, his numero uno child, joking with her about an apple a day. Staying healthy. A convenient excuse to call. To keep in touch with the one who'd left home. She'd understood his M.O. a month after arriving at school. Sweet, loving man. A man with a phone.

"Wh-what…?" Her throat closed.

The cops seemed to understand her intent. "The official investigation is ongoing, but according to preliminary reports, the other driver lost control of his vehicle and did a one-eighty."

"Drunk? But…but it's the middle of the week." As if that fact could change things.

"The driver's blood alcohol was normal."

"Then what…? The road…?"

"Icy conditions contributed. The temperature drops at night, and your folks were approaching at just the wrong moment. There were no survivors. I'm very sorry."

She nodded. *No survivors? Mom and Dad?* She wanted to cover her ears.

The other officer looked at his notes and said, "The Woodhaven police are with your brothers and sisters."

*Oh, God, the kids… She had to get back to Woodhaven!*

Standing quickly, she was hit by a wave of nausea and fell back into her chair. She doubled over, hand on her stomach. The phone rang, startling her further. She stared at the instrument, half-buried by textbooks, reached forward, and slowly lifted the receiver. "Hello?" she whispered.

"Lisa! Lisa! The police are here. Mom and Dad were in an accident. You have to come home! Now! I'm scared."

Jennifer. Her social butterfly teenage sister whose life revolved around boyfriends, best friends, and having fun. Except, not tonight. In the background, she heard the cacophony of younger voices crying and talking at the same time. She heard little Emily's high-pitched wail. "When is Lisa coming?"

"Hang on, Jen." She took a breath and looked at the officers. "There are four of them. Emily's only seven. My twin brothers are nine. Jen's sixteen. I've got to get there—a hundred miles—and I don't own a car." She couldn't afford one and didn't need one in a city with mass transit.

The troopers nodded, and she spoke into the phone again.

"I'll be there soon, Jen. As soon as I can. Maybe William and Irene can stay with you meanwhile." Her fiancé's parents lived across the street.

"They're not home. They went to Miami to see Mike play. Didn't you watch the game yesterday?"

"Of course I watched, but I didn't know his folks flew down." Mike had subbed for the starting quarterback and played an entire quarter. It was only his first year, but now the Riders were in the play-offs.

"So, Jen, you need to be in charge now until I get there. You and the kids sit tight and wait for me." She glanced toward the window, where falling snow was reflected by the light of the streetlamps.

"It might take a little while," she added. "It's a big trip, and the roads are bad…" What was she saying? Her parents had just been killed on those roads. "Jen, honey, let me talk to one of the officers there."

Her hand shook as she gave the receiver to the state cop. "Ask if they told the kids the truth."

In seconds, he shook his head. "Not yet. They're getting a social worker in on it."

She raised her eyes to his. "Please tell them not to do or say anything until I get there. Okay?"

Perspiration trickled from every pore. She shivered and sweated until finally her stomach lurched. Running into the bathroom, she vomited until nothing remained. Then she brushed her teeth, packed her suitcase to the brim, and snapped it shut. The sound focused her, and she inhaled a deep breath. *Be strong, be strong...*

One of the troopers held the door open. Her gaze skimmed the small apartment. She'd been happy there and ecstatic at being accepted into the program. She glanced at her textbooks before locking on to her college graduation photo. Her parents stood on either side of her, their smiles wide.

"Oh-h… One second." Her own future was now uncertain. Dropping her suitcase, she darted to the wall, took down the picture, and tucked it under her arm. Their dreams and her dreams might have to wait awhile.

#

Michael Brennan needed three days to get home to Woodhaven and to Lisa. It seemed like three years.

He tossed his luggage in his parents' front hall, turned around, and headed directly across the street. The Delaneys lived in a two-story wood-framed house with a front porch similar to his and to all the other homes on Hawthorne Street. He'd grown up there, but Lisa and her family had moved in over four years ago in June, right after her high school graduation. He'd graduated from a neighboring high school that same year. Their paths hadn't crossed until the evening his mother baked a cake and insisted their family welcome the new neighbors. Moaning and groaning, he'd given in, and the Brennans had gone to visit the Delaneys.

When Lisa opened the door and walked outside, he'd almost tripped up the front steps. One glance and he couldn't speak. His brain froze, too, as if a lightning bolt had slammed him head to toe. Big violet eyes, long, dark wavy hair, and a killer smile. A friendly smile. *Who wouldn't have fallen in love with her?* But he'd been the lucky one, the lucky guy who'd relished every single day since Lisa Delaney had first appeared at that front door.

Now her sidewalk needed shoveling. The streets had been plowed since the storm a few days ago, the walkways, too, but snow had fallen again yesterday, and surfaces had turned icy. He flexed his shoulders and entered the house. He'd take care of the snow after he wrapped his arms around her…if he could find her.

The Delaney house was packed. He recognized Lisa's aunts and uncles from out of -town, and all the neighbors, of course.  Lisa's closest friends, Sandy and Gail, were there, too. Either they'd stayed all day or had just come from work. He waved and searched for his mom.

"Where's Lisa?"

"I'm glad you're here, Michael," she said, giving him a quick kiss, "but don't expect too much from Lisa. She's overwhelmed as…as we all are." Irene Brennan gazed up at the ceiling, indicating the second floor. "She's got the kids with her. The funeral's tomorrow, and she wants time alone with them."

"Alone doesn't include me."

He took the stairs two at a time, sensing the glances, the sympathy of the visitors as he made his way up. He appreciated their support, but they didn't have to worry. Surely, he could handle whatever he found. Surely, he and Lisa could handle it together.

He paused in the hallway at the top of the stairs. Each of the four bedroom doors stood ajar, but he could hear nothing. He started to push the first door open when, from the end of the corridor, he heard Lisa singing quietly, "Too-ra Loo-ra Loo-ra, Too-ra loo-ra lie…"

Was she trying to put the kids to sleep at five o'clock in the afternoon? He slowed his pace and walked the last few steps before knocking softly and entering the master bedroom. Lisa sat on her parents' bed, leaning against the headboard, the twins dozing on either side of her, little Emily sleeping on her lap. Jennifer lay across the foot of the bed, also sound asleep. He took it all in and understood that day and night had no meaning to them.

"Lisa…" A whispered prayer.

Her red-rimmed eyes brightened, her arms opened, and he was there. Kissing her and gently shifting one little brother lower on the mattress. She began to cry, her tears mingling with his as he rained kisses, and his tension melted simply by holding her in his arms. Tears flowed as he continued to embrace her and grieve while remembering Grace and Robert Delaney.

They'd been wonderful neighbors, wonderful parents, and good friends with his folks. The Delaneys had worked so hard to finally become "owners" instead of "renters," and celebrated their move to Hawthorne Street each time they'd made a mortgage payment. Lisa had told him how her dad would brandish the check and twirl Grace around the kitchen every single month. With their growing family, it had taken them fifteen years to afford their own home.

"How long can you stay?" Lisa whispered.

"He can't," mumbled nine-year-old Andy, rousing slightly. "He has to go to the conference championship game. And maybe to the Super Bowl."

"But not yet," Mike said, rubbing the boy's head with affection, but focusing his gaze on Lisa. "I'll be here for the funeral tomorrow. You won't be alone. Then

I'll be back in a week. One short week." Which might feel like an eternity to Lisa.

"I'm glad, but-but everything has changed," she said, pulling a tissue from the nearby box and blotting her face. "We need to rethink our plans."

"The basics haven't changed," he replied quickly. "I love you, Lisa Delaney. And don't you forget it."

Her eyes shone. She pressed his hand, her fingers narrow and delicate around his broader ones. "I love you, too, but-but…." She sighed and glanced at the assorted children. "I'm not sure what's going to happen next," she said quietly.

"I am," he said. "I'm going to kiss you again."

And he did. When she kissed him back, when she lingered and leaned against him, he almost collapsed with relief. She was *the one* for him. No matter what. Her needs, the kids' needs….

"We'll sort it out when the time comes," he said. "I'll support you in every way I can." The logistics would no doubt be complicated, but he had faith that he and Lisa could do anything as long as they did it together.

She offered a wan smile. "I know you'll do your best, but you have commitments to the team. You're so talented! We all know you're being groomed as a starting quarterback, maybe even next year. So I think, for both our sakes, I need to handle this-this family situation by myself."

No, she didn't, but her brave effort tore a corner of his heart. "I think you're right about my place in the team," he said slowly, "but that's in our favor. The money's good." He'd worked hard with his coaches, and his natural talents had been recognized. His dream career loomed just over the horizon.

"I must be weird," said Lisa. "I never think about your salary. Even your first year minimum is like make-believe Monopoly money to me. It doesn't matter. I'm just so…so proud of you."

Men cry. Even big football players. But once that afternoon was enough. His throat ached as he swallowed to stem more tears. Lisa needed him to be strong.

"Have I ever told you about my conversation with your dad at the end of the summer you moved to Hawthorne Street?" he asked. "It was right before I went off to Ohio State on my scholarship."

"All Daddy told me was that you were too big for your britches, but he was laughing."

A surge of love and a wave of sadness—both raced through Mike. The words sounded exactly like something Rob Delaney would say. And the laughter– well, laughter was the norm in Lisa's family. Her dad loved to tell a good story and could imitate the comedy greats and their jokes. Rob had been a natural "on stage," and no one had a bigger heart.

"Before I left for college," Mike continued, "I told him I was going to marry you someday."

"You've got to be kidding! We were only eighteen. We'd just met that very summer." For a moment, her expression lightened. She tipped her head back, and her eyes met his. "And what did he say?"

"He said that I'd better treat you like gold—always. And I promised I would."

"O-o-h…." Despair once again etched her face. "Our lives… everything..."—she waved her arm— "has changed. I can't-I *won't* hold you to any promise."

"You have no vote." He kissed her again, vowing to keep that promise. Loving Lisa was the easy part. Building a solid future together…well, that goal might be more difficult to reach now. Lisa was in no condition to make any decisions. Their next steps would be decided by him.

His gaze rested on each of the youngsters, one at a time. Four sweet, innocent children. Without warning, his heart started to race, and his palms became covered in sweat. Fear. Like Lisa, he was almost twenty-three, and deep down, he was scared, too. He had no experience with kids, not even a younger brother or sister. But he wouldn't give himself away, wouldn't let Lisa know. A quarterback led with confidence on the field. Now he had to do the same at home.

# READ AN EXCERPT FROM
# THE HOUSE ON THE BEACH

## PILGRIM COVE SERIES, BOOK ONE

### Chapter 1

"I'm sorry, Ali, but I'm not ready to make such a big decision." Laura McCloud sat at the kitchen table across from her sister the morning after their mother's funeral sipping coffee and nibbling a piece of dry toast. Her Boston home had overflowed with visitors the evening before, but she and Ali were alone now. The house was almost back in order. Leftovers filled the refrigerator shelves--not that she had much of an appetite.

"But you know how much we'd love for you to join us in Atlanta," continued Alison. "Charles especially wants you to know that the invitation comes from him, too. And the kids would adore having their Aunt Laura close by."

"I do know it, and I love you all for it, but...

"And we have fabulous medical centers, too," interrupted Alison. "As good as here. Not that you have anything to worry about anymore," she added quickly.

Right. Nothing except the knowledge that there were no guarantees. "I'm not concerned about finding medical care. It's just that I have another idea."

"You do? What?"

"Remember Pilgrim Cove? Remember the beautiful beach?" Laura watched her sister's eyes widen and a grin light up her face.

"Do I remember? Of course I remember. What great summers we had. So, what's your idea? A summer vacation at the beach?"

"Not exactly," replied Laura. "I'm not going to wait that long."

"You're going to the beach in the middle of winter?" Alison asked in disbelief as she hugged herself. "Brr. Not me."

Laura laughed at her sister's antics. They'd always gotten along well, and Laura had really missed Alison when she'd left Boston. Suddenly, Laura had to blink back tears. Alison was now her only family.

"I'll think about what you said regarding Atlanta, but I've got a career here and...I need some time. Time for myself."

Alison's hand reached for hers. "I'll support any decision you make, sis, but are you sure you really want to be alone?"

"With the sand and the ocean and my work...don't worry, Ali. I'll be very busy."

"Yeah, yeah. The sand will blow in your eyes, the ocean will crash against the seawall and the ferry won't run. So much for winter at the beach!"

Laura smiled. "I'll wait until next month. March should be somewhat better. I wonder what Pilgrim Cove is like during the off-season. At least the rent should be cheaper."

"Wait a minute. Why are you concerned about rent? A few dollars one way or another for a week's vacation shouldn't make a difference."

"I'm thinking about more than a week," Laura said in a slow, deliberate tone. "I'm thinking about a three month lease, maybe through Memorial Day. A small house might not be too expensive, not too hard to keep up, but I'd want it right on the beach."

She stood as the image crystallized in her mind. "I need a change, a complete change of scene. And I need it now. Fighting with the weather will be much easier than fighting for mom's life and my own."

She reached up and tousled her short blonde curls. "Look at me, Alison. Look at these ringlets. I'm delighted to have hair again, but I don't recognize myself when I pass a mirror. Where's the sleek blunt cut that was so easy to manage?"

"You're adorable in those curls! In fact, you look wonderful, Laura, just wonderful." Laura could hear the passion in her sister's voice.

"Donald didn't think so," she responded.

"Donald Crawford was a jerk!"

Laura shook her head. "No, Alison. Don wasn't a jerk. He was just human. He had a girlfriend with a huge responsibility to an ill mother--and he handled that--but my getting sick was just too much. He wasn't prepared for all the emotional turmoil. Who can blame him?"

"I can," replied Alison.

"Be fair," said Laura. "We weren't engaged. He didn't owe me anything."

"He wasn't worthy of you!" Alison insisted. "You're the most outstanding person, the most beautiful, wonderful woman...

"You're hardly objective," laughed Laura. "But can you really blame Don for wanting a normal life? What man wouldn't have second thoughts when he heard the words 'breast cancer?'"

"A man who loves you," came the quick reply.

"Well, I'm not going to count on that happening," said Laura in an even tone. "So I'll have lots of time and energy to rebuild my interrupted career." She leaned across the table. "I'm thirty-three. It's now or never. And you heard my agent last night. 'Work is therapy, Laura,' she mimicked Norman Cohen's low voice. She relaxed in her chair. "Norman is a dear friend as well as a business man. And he's got some radio ads lined up for me."

Alison would have protested again, but Laura held up her hand. "I'm not discussing men anymore, Ali. I'm not sure there's a man in the world who could look past this. Anyway, it's too soon. All I can do is take one day at a time. *Capice?*"

"Sure," replied Alison. "I understand, but I don't have to like it. I love you, and I want you to have..."

"I know," Laura said in a hoarse voice. "You want me to have everything you have...loving husband, healthy children...but that's probably not going to happen for me. What is going to happen, however, is a nice long stay in Pilgrim Cove."

Alison remained quiet for a long moment. "I recognize that expression and that tone," she finally said. "You've made up your mind. But my invitation remains open--will always remain open."

Laura looked at her sister's face, at the sincerity clearly written there. "Thanks, Ali, thanks a lot. But I've got to figure it out my own way."

She reached for the phone. "I'm calling Bartholomew Quinn, the man who arranged the summer rentals when we were kids. I remember going with

Daddy to Mr. Quinn's real estate office. And I remember him. A head of thick white hair."

"White? And that was how many years ago? Sixteen? Seventeen? He might be dead by now!"

"Nope. He has a website."

#

Bartholomew Quinn stood at the large front window of his Main Street office in Pilgrim Cove, his hand cupping the bowl of the empty pipe in his mouth. A comfortable habit he hadn't bothered to break even though he'd given up the pleasure of filling the beauty with fine tobacco.

Promises. He'd made promises. A promise to his daughters and to his beloved granddaughter and to her precious daughter. Four generations of Quinns, three of whom had said, "No more smoking, Dad, Granddad, Papa Bart!" He shook his head remembering how they'd ganged up on him. Foolish girls to worry so much. He was as strong as ever and as sharp as ever, and maybe just as hard-headed, too. He sighed. Except these days he chomped an empty pipe.

His eyes focused on the late model blue Honda Accord pulling into a visitor's spot in front of his building, then he glanced at his watch. If this was Laura McCloud, she was right on time. He'd been astonished to hear from her last week. Astonished that she remembered him. But then again, he grinned to himself, he was a pretty memorable guy. Just ask his kids. Or anyone in Pilgrim Cove. Everyone knew Bartholomew Quinn!

The car door opened and a woman emerged, golden hair tossing in the wind. Bart tsked. She should have worn a hat. Wasn't she aware that February was the worst of the winter months in New England? He straightened his silk bow tie and adjusted the comfortable woolen cardigan he wore. Bart Quinn knew how to adapt to weather and to life. After seventy-five years on the planet, he'd had plenty of practice.

He watched the young woman check the sign-- Quinn Real Estate and Property Management--and walk to the front door. He went to greet her.

"Well, as I live and breathe," he said, shaking Laura's hand. "The young McCloud girl. All grown up."

She had a delightful laugh, but it didn't quite hide the sadness in her dark blue eyes. Strain showed in the too-thin face.

"Come in and have a hot cup of Earl Grey." He ushered her to a small round table. After calling to an assistant for the tea, he took a seat opposite Laura.

"You've had a hard time of it, haven't you?" Bart began. "A fine woman was Bridget McCloud, and your dad, too. I remember Connor well. Two good people, and now their daughter's come to see me." He sat back in his chair and waited.

Laura nodded. "Yes, I've come to you, Mr. Quinn, with a request." She moved her chair a fraction closer. "My question is, can you help me find a house to rent immediately? A house right on the beach. I want to be able to open my eyes and see the ocean."

Her voice had the clarity of a bell. A musical quality, Bart thought. She was so lovely despite her distress. He cocked his head as he listened.

"I-I need to get away for awhile," Laura continued. "I need to be here, near the water. Can't wait for summer. I need to...to..."

"Lick your wounds? Heal a little?" suggested Bart.

Her eyes widened. "That's part of it. Mom's illness...she was in remission for so long, and then three years ago, the nightmare began again. Her nerve cells deteriorated. In the end, she couldn't walk, couldn't talk... I need some time to recover and to adjust." She paused in thought. "Long walks on the beach, fresh air, time to read, and to cook simple meals. And with some basic recording equipment, I can work here as well as in Boston."

"And what exactly does Laura McCloud do to earn her keep?"

A dimple appeared as she shot him a small grin. "Laura McCloud earns her keep on the radio and telly with her commercial announcements."

Her language and Irish lilt matched his, and he roared with laughter. "Oh, you've got it down, girl." Bart was pure American, but his parents had emigrated from County Cork at the turn of the last century and a bit of their flavorful speech had taken hold in him.

She nodded. "I've always been good at languages. I seem to have the ear and the voice. In college, I majored in Speech and Theater and found my work in narration and voice-overs. But," she turned away from him then and stared through the window, "my career has fallen apart in the last few years. I've been...distracted. And now I've got to rebuild."

Her eyes glowed as she turned to him again, and Bart saw the strength behind them. This girl would make it somehow, with or without his help. But he wanted very much to help her. He thought about a property he managed--a unique beachfront property--with a sliding scale rental fee for people in difficult circumstances. His gut told him Laura qualified, and his gut was rarely wrong. He nodded his head. "Sea View House."

"Excuse me?"

"You'll be wanting Sea View House." Bart stood up and walked to his big old-fashioned roll-top desk, selected a key from among many on his ring, and opened a small drawer. He reached for one set of duplicate keys and relocked the drawer. Picking up the phone, he pressed the intercom. "Lila, come in and meet a special friend of mine." He winked at Laura and opened his office door just as Lila rushed through.

Bart chuckled. Lila never walked.

"Laura McCloud," he said, "I'd like you to meet my partner, Lila Quinn Sullivan, who also happens to be my granddaughter.

#

Bart's granddaughter was lovely, thought Laura, as she extended her hand. Twenty-something. Bright blue eyes, with an intelligence behind them.

"I'm looking for a place to rent," Laura said. "Your grandfather suggested Sea View House."

The girl looked startled before a wistful expression replaced her surprise. "Sea View House." Her soft-spoken words were followed by a sweet smile. "It's a special place."

"Yes," Bart confirmed. "And Laura's a special guest. Used to spend summers here as a child." He looked at Laura. "About ten consecutive years, was it?"

She nodded. "What's so special about this particular house on the beach?" She needed a quiet routine, nothing out of the ordinary.

Lila stared over Laura's shoulder, her eyes unfocused and dreamy. "Sea View House has this reputation," she began. "Good things happen to everyone who stays there..." She paused, then shook her head, a flash of pain visible for barely a second. "Well, no. I guess not everyone...but, I know *you'll* be happy there, with the ocean right at your door. Welcome back to Pilgrim Cove."

And she was gone.

"Moves at the speed of light, my Lila does," said Bart, as he led Laura to his car. "She's the joy of my life, she and her little Katie. But...well, there's a sorrow on her heart, too." He sighed. "Everybody's got troubles, but I can't think of a better place to be than Sea View House while you figure them out."

Laura murmured noncommittally. She scanned the town as they drove, excitement mounting as she recognized some of the businesses. From Bart's office on Main Street, they passed a bank, then a barber shop called The Cove Clippers. She'd gone there with her dad each year for his "summer cut." And there was The Diner on the Dunes! Happy times and delicious meals with her family.

"There's Parker Plumbing and Hardware," Bart pointed out. "They carry everything. I'll call Matt to turn your water on. My friend, Sam Parker, started the business, but now his son, Matthew, runs it. Good family. Not without their share of heartaches, too. But they carry on."

Laura sighed. If Bart thought he was giving her a lesson in life, he was wasting his time. She was already an expert. But she didn't interrupt him, instead continued to look at the town, trying to recognize landmarks from her childhood.

"Is Neptune's Park still here?" she asked.

Bart grinned around his pipe. "Sure it is. Can't imagine Pilgrim Cove without it, but it's only open in the summertime, mind you."

She nodded. Carousels and Ferris wheels were the stuff of sunshine and warm nights. Too bad she wouldn't be in town long enough to enjoy them. She refocused on the route Bart was taking and memorized it. He made a left from Main onto Outlook Drive.

"The whole peninsula is six miles long and less than two miles across, so we'll be at Sea View House in just a couple of minutes. Main Street divides the town.

We have a beach side and a bay side. There's always a breeze when you're a finger in the ocean."

"That's why you have so many summer people every year," Laura said. "The news is out. Pilgrim Cove is the place to be during the season."

"For me, it's the place to be every season," said Bart. "Look ahead now. You'll see the front and side of the house.

Laura complied and felt herself grinning. Sea View House. Weathered wood, a big sloping roof, two stories with a third window above--maybe an attic--and a big brick chimney in the center. A white picket fence surrounded the front yard on Beach Street.

"Wow! What a wonderful house. And only a vague memory to me. I didn't know anyone living here when I was a kid."

Bart pulled the car into the driveway. "It's a Saltbox, the kind built in the 1700's. John Adams, our second president, was born in a Saltbox. And William Adams, a shirt-tail cousin of John, founded our town in 1690. A hundred years later his great-great grandchild, also named William, built this house. Of course, it's been remodeled several times, and now it's been converted to two apartments. There's a lot of history here, but for a later time."

Laura nodded and got out of the car. "Let's walk around the house first," she said.

"You go. I'll open her up," replied Bart. "The sun is bright enough, but that ocean breeze is whipping big today."

True, but Laura reveled in it as she followed the paved driveway to the back of the property, past a deep covered porch leading to a backyard bordered by a low cement wall at the sand line. Inserted into the cement wall were tall boards standing upright. Laura studied the strange arrangement and saw loose sand blowing against the boards. Sand that would otherwise be hitting the house. She smiled, appreciating the simplicity of some solutions.

And then she was on the beach, the powerful Atlantic in front of her, surging and ebbing as far as her eye could see. The heels of her boots hardly dented the hard packed sand as she walked closer to the water. She could have stood for hours mesmerized by the rhythmic motion of the waves. She turned, eventually, to look back at Sea View House.

For the first time in too long, a frisson of excitement flowed through her. A sense of anticipation. Suddenly she knew exactly what she was going to do.

She hurried to the front door, ran down the center hallway and found Bart Quinn in the kitchen. "Where do I sign?"

# LINDA BARRETT BOOKS

NOVELS—ROMANCE

**Starting Over Series** (coming in 2018)

*True-Blue Texan* (Bk 1)
*A Man of Honor* (Bk. 2)
*Love, Money and Amanda Shaw* (Bk.3)
*The Inn at Oak Creek* (Bk.4)

**Flying Solo Series**

*Summer at the Lake* (Bk. 1) — Free!
*Houseful of Strangers* (Bk. 2)
*Quarterback Daddy* (Bk. 3)
*The Apple Orchard* (Bk. 4)

**Pilgrim Cove Series**

*The House on the Beach* (Bk. 1) — Free!
*No Ordinary Summer* (Bk. 2)
*Reluctant Housemates* (Bk. 3)
*The Daughter He Never Knew* (Bk. 4)

**Sea View House Series**

*Her Long Walk Home* (Bk. 1) — Free!
*Her Picture-Perfect Family* (Bk. 2)
*Her Second-Chance Hero* (Bk. 3)

NOVELS—WOMEN'S FICTION

*The Broken Circle*
*The Soldier and the Rose*
*Family Interrupted*
*For Better or Worse* – A boxed set of all three WF
novels at a discounted price

MEMOIR

*HOPEFULLY EVER AFTER: Breast Cancer, Life and
Me* (true story about surviving breast cancer twice)